HURRICANE HOTEL

2008

J. K.
LAWSON

HURRICANE HOTEL

A BOOK OF VOICES

A NOVEL

Foreword by ANDRE DUBUS III

Order this book online at www.trafford.com/07-1131
or email orders@trafford.com

Most Trafford titles are also available at major online book retailers.

Cover Design by: Sebastian Lawson
Foreword by: Andre Dubus III

This is a work of fiction. Names, characters, places and incidents either are the product of the author's imagination or are used fictitiously. Any resemblance to any actual persons, living or dead, events or locales is entirely coincidental.

Note for Librarians: A cataloguing record for this book is available from Library and Archives Canada at www.collectionscanada.ca/amicus/index-e.html

Printed in Victoria, BC, Canada.

ISBN: 978-1-4251-3096-1

We at Trafford believe that it is the responsibility of us all, as both individuals and corporations, to make choices that are environmentally and socially sound. You, in turn, are supporting this responsible conduct each time you purchase a Trafford book, or make use of our publishing services. To find out how you are helping, please visit www.trafford.com/responsiblepublishing.html

Our mission is to efficiently provide the world's finest, most comprehensive book publishing service, enabling every author to experience success. To find out how to publish your book, your way, and have it available worldwide, visit us online at www.trafford.com/10510

www.trafford.com

North America & international
toll-free: 1 888 232 4444 (USA & Canada)
phone: 250 383 6864 • fax: 250 383 6804
email: info@trafford.com

The United Kingdom & Europe
phone: +44 (0)1865 722 113 • local rate: 0845 230 9601
facsimile: +44 (0)1865 722 868 • email: info.uk@trafford.com

10 9 8 7 6 5 4 3 2

ACKNOWLEDGEMENTS

For permission to reprint copyright material the following acknowledgements are made:

DEATH IS NOT THE END. BOB DYLAN. Copyright © 1988 Special Rider Music. All rights reserved. International copyright secured. Reprinted by permission.

RIGHT PLACE WRONG TIME. MALCOLM J.REBENNACK. Copyright © 1973 (Renewed) Walden Music, Inc. and Cauldron Music. All rights administered by WB Music Corp. All Rights Reserved. Used by Permission of Alfred Publishing Co., Inc.

ST. JAMES INFIRMARY. Traditional, Arranged by IRVING MILLS (published under the pseudonym Joe Primrose). Copyright © 1929 (Renewed) EMI Mills Music, Inc. Worldwide print Rights Administered by Alfred Publishing Co., Inc. All Rights Reserved. Used by Permission of Alfred Publishing Co., Inc.

LAZY RIVER. HOAGY CARMICHAEL & SIDNEY ARODIN. Copyright © 1931 by Peermusic III, Ltd. Copyright Renewed. International Copyright Secured. Used by Permission. All Rights Reserved.

Thanks to Terri F. Baker for making the impossible possible, my editor Amanda Metcalf, Gordon W. Bailey for believing in the beads, DNA's sanctuary, WWOZ, and the LaPlace House, where the Spirit of Jelly Roll is alive and kicking.

FOREWARD

It was August of 2005, and we knew nothing of what was to come. We did not know of the tropical depression forming over the Bahamas, that it would grow and roll over south Florida, uprooting trees and smashing homes, that it would kill eleven people before it left land and found the warm waters of the Gulf like a junkie finding her fix, that it would rise up and bear down on the coasts of Mississippi and Louisiana and that by then the southern parishes of Louisiana would be evacuated; Plaquemines and St. Bernard, St. Charles, La Fourche, Terrebonne, and St. Tammany, that the mayor of New Orleans – that haunted and blessed mother of jazz and voodoo, of Creole and blues and all that is free - would issue the first mandatory evacuation order of the city's history, and my cousin John Lawson and I would stand together in my library in my house in the woods north of Boston and watch this on my color T.V., a helicopter shot of the slow crawl of loaded cars and pick ups and mini-vans on the 24 mile lake Pontchartrian Causeway.

And just days before, John and his wife, my first cousin Aimee, had finished renovating their house in the Broadmoor neighborhood of New Orleans, a sunken bowl of ground south of Lake Pontchartrian. They then drove their three-year old son Sebastian up here for some late summer rest and high times. They'd spent a few days with us, and now they were headed farther north to Maine, to friends on an island overlooking cold waters.

Standing there in my library, John looked concerned but unafraid.

I said, "The mayor's evacuating the whole city."

"We see a lot of hurricanes, Cuz."

I nodded, my eyes on the screen, on those hundreds and hundreds of cars taking up so many miles of the causeway. Then there were the hugs goodbye, a plan to see John and Aimee and Sebastian on their way back from Maine. They told us how much they loved it up there, how good their friends were, how there was no T.V.

So they didn't know anything until later, that the eye of Katrina passed just east of

New Orleans, her battering winds a Category 2 but her tidal surge a Category 3. For a day it looked like the worst had come and gone; this had been a bad hurricane but also another New Orleans had survived. But by the last day of August, the levees began to crack and give, first the smaller drainage canal levees, then the big navigationals, those designed and built by the Army Corps of Engineers – the 17th Street Canal Levee, the Industrial Canal Levee, and the London Avenue Canal floodwall. And it was as if the maternal waters of Lake Pontchartrain had gotten drunk and rolled over in her sleep, crushing the baby she had always slept beside, and now nearly all of New Orleans was underwater, including John and Aimee's one-story home in Broadmoor.

But, those first days after Katrina, they didn't yet know this. Because their friends in Maine had no T.V., John climbed into their dingy, rowed to the mainland, and read in the New York Times about the flooding. He'd lived through two down there before, though, and he assumed it was like countless other times the Big Easy didn't have it so easy.

It wasn't until they were back at our place in the woods did they see a T.V. for the first time, did they see all the live footage of people stranded on rooftops they'd chopped through, those who were fortunate enough to remember Hugo and had stowed a hatchet or chainsaw in their attics. Some of those that didn't drowned in their homes. Others climbed into passing boats, or swam to waist-deep water, then waded to higher ground and joined thousands of others heading for the Superdome.

John saw all this and knew then that their house had to be underwater. He knew it in his head anyway. But late that night, my wife and kids asleep, Aimee and Sebastian too, John stayed up and watched Geraldo standing in front of the Convention Center pleading for help that would not come, and that's when John's heart and body knew his house was gone and everything in it.

He was right; it was under nine feet of water and stayed that way for six weeks. Their sofas and chairs floated. Art on the walls crumbled with the walls. The books and albums they'd collected over twenty-five years were lost. So were precious photos, letters, and family documents, as well as Aimee's production notes from years of her work in theater. All of John's handmade films.

All gone.

But then another feeling came. The blessed knowledge that *they* weren't gone. His family. They had *survived*. His lovely wife and their miraculous son, they were upstairs in this very house fast asleep. That night, his mouth went dry, his heart began to pound, and the Muse sat up inside him: he flicked off the T.V., found his notebook and pen, and began writing Part II of *Hurricane Hotel*, a novel that had been coming to him for a long while now, a novel that rose up out of his own years living in New Orleans as a younger man and artist. Lean years of squatting at the C Note, stepping over drunks to get to his room. Years living at the Audubon Hotel, the guy upstairs who earned his keep doing his bead work for the owners, though it was far more than that.

It came to him as visions do – complete and pristine – millions and millions of Mardi Gras beads lying in the streets and on the sidewalks, scattered in darkened doorways and hanging over black iron fences and gnarled tree roots, the purple and red and green and gold refuse of revelers come and gone, this material that John would spend days gathering up into plastic trash bags, then months and years fashioning into art.

He was writing, too, and it's all here: from Ruth's gentle touch to the joyful rituals of the hell-bound Chemical Sisters, from the drunk and redeemed Arlen to sexy Sophia and trigger-happy Treme, from mad Martha, Mona and Moose to predestined Zane and long suffering Emma Jane, wise-cracking Jake and Molly and the paternal Guy Upstairs, all blind to the rising muddy waters of the Mississippi, the wind-blown salt of the Gulf, the heavy waters of Lake Pontchartrain, spilling over, then rising, rising, rising, taking everything and nearly everyone.

Hurricane Hotel is a love letter to the drowned city that gave birth not only to it but also to the Muse of J.K. Lawson, my cousin, who serves us here a final image of redemption that rises from the very center of his own psyche: children taking shards of stained glass from a ruined church and fixing them to the mud of an entombed car.

And who else to deliver this letter back to New Orleans but the Spirit of Jelly Roll that John so passionately evokes here? Who else but a ghost of a rambler and gambler and pool shark, of a pimp and vaudeville comedian and master of the ebony and ivory keys? Who else but a man who died of an evil voodoo spell but left behind so much goodness?

For, as J.K. Lawson shows us again and yet again: from devastation, truth. From devastation, beauty.

Andre Dubus III

"Of course everybody in New Orleans was organizationally minded. Which, I guess, the world knows. And a dead man always belonged to several organizations, such as clubs, and er, we'll say, secret order and those ... so forth and so on. And every time one died, why, nine out of ten, there was always a big band turned out, when the day that he was supposed to be buried ... never at night, always in the day. And, of course, a lot of times right in the heart of the city, the burial would take place..."

Jelly Roll Morton

HURRICANE HOTEL

Jump I say! Jump back into the skin!

And here we are all here again, the start and the finish. The Yin and the Yang, all meshed into one. Wearing a pair of Air Walk shoes with stretched out soles and neon stripes, torn by glass shards from kicking in a window of the Hurricane Hotel. That's soggy confetti you can see sticking to my ribs. Ha! Ha! As I stumble in the middle of the old dance floor, littered with the debris of a Grande Finale, armed with a craving for just one more. Knowing I'm trapped inside a condemned leaking building, breathing in the stains of a familiar bar room, loaded with spirits I'm destined to un cork, there's someone I have to call but I can't think who because the angst of these surroundings compels me to mention the water is rising and the levee gone broke!

So don't pester me now if my thoughts seem despicably scattered as I wobble on tipsy toes unable to stay dry. Chances are they are! Never the less and straight off the bat, from topless bar to bottomless dance floor, in the moments of movement licking up the last dregs, I make no apologies for I am merely the messenger. A grubby soul, who has swallowed mouthfuls of vows and taken an oath, with what's left of my word, to say a few words for all the guts that were spilled and all the brains dislodged in the sleaziest hotel on the prettiest avenue....At least, that's what the locals often called her! And for several years she called me home, along with a cacophony of like minded fiends and fragile specimens whose splintered circumstances cannibalized us into the deserted and drunk, the spat out and stuck, the shell shocked and homeless, slipping and sliding, in through the cracks of twenty four seven. Every one of us kings for a day and queens for a night! All of us dysfunctional certifiably angelically demonic, trying to escape from an impenetrable heaven by wasting away in rented wombs with personalized graffiti and hand made tattoos, sprayed on the walls and inked in our skin, hoping to evolve from a mess of aliases spun off the charts into something we were never really quite sure of!

Sure, everything wasn't the perfect everything all of most of the time. But can you tell me in whispers what is? Someone's body part was always ending up in someone else's lost hole. Or waking up next to another spat out life time with just enough psycho drama to forget the world's stopped spinning and plenty of madness to keep you begging for more as you lay cocooned in the banality of your own rented asylum with mouthfuls of remorse echoing through your skull or cupped in the hands of full blown hard on…Our ever present companion, who blankly stared at a lover's heel grinding hot ash into your sweating palms.

Do you still want to follow me now into this daze of lost time and in no time at all where the disco ball above me spins out of control before tearing from the ceiling and rapidly sinking into a quagmire of questionable answers and unanswerable lies. Displacing the shadows and filling up the bar with talk drink laughter, cry smoke sigh, shout shoot dance, all at once if you want to!

Take a look around, why don't you? It's the same old scene! It's like we never left! It's like the building is full up again with the same busted voices, diving in a little deeper, swirling and gliding, seeping up through the cracks by the revolving door with its broken lock and AWOL locksmith…A keyless character if ever I saw one. Ha! Ha! Decked out in his schemes and constantly plotting a debauchery of glorious oops-a-daises!

Excuse me a sec…I gotta go pee. Before my mind slips back into a sticky wet substance, covered in a mosaic of Mardi Gras beads. A mural of sorts, stretching over a 50ft bar top that ruinously doubled up as a trashed out runway for the 4am hookers, offering a much needed sanctuary to a thousand crooked pairs of blood shot eyes. 'The Garden of Unearthly Delights', the local Press did call it. With its cartooned portraits of the denizens who crawled in here, sporting perfumed wigs in Telly Tubby costumes, with blow up lips sacrilegiously stuffed onto day glow dildos and cruise control strapons. A multi denominational malady of ram shackled posers and cracked out mirrors, mimicking loose facts and bottled up screams! Castaways who had lost their island as they snorted away a million dime bags filled with life long dreams. Merrily boozing on anything that fell off the shelf with a cloister of sighs unable to exhale the vacant prayers of blank disbelief!

Who cared if self-absorption was a mandatory fee, we were way too busy perfecting a cure for remaining in pain! Shuffling our concoctions from hand to mouth then back again. Every one of us a doctor, doubling the dosage until the script was refilled or flushed in paranoia down the blocked up bowels of busted up commodes. This formula of self medication allowed us to demographically agree we were 100% proof there wasn't one amongst us who should ever be trusted! Leaving us to deal from a deck of misplaced hearts, randomly peeling on cardboard grimaces and ready to expose your cute little secrets we so fondly unzipped in public bathrooms with oblivious banter…After all, pimping ourselves meant steady employment and the chance to escape from the lurking shadows of Time!

I wish I could tell you how long this all lasted but there wasn't one amongst us who ever owned a watch. Perhaps it was our way of pampering immortally as we fully submerged into a parade of glittering mannequins, sexually vandalized by any form of normality and banned from sleeping until unmentionable demons had been sufficiently fondled or crudely discharged down the back of each other's throats. But I can tell you this, that was then, and this is now, and like it or not, I have signed a contract, and taken the oath, knowing full well the dice have been rigged and the plug's been pulled, to leave this barstool and search of a familiar flight of stairs, leading me to the raised tombs of my absent friends—soul mates in skullduggery, who patiently wait to replay a lifetime of scratching at the need for just one more So be my guest!… I must insist! … Go right on in and jump my friend! … Jump! Back into the skin!

PART I

Back Then

RUTH

Lighting twelve votive candles that were on the faux-marble mantelpiece, Ruth ran her fingers over the waking flames as the sharp splinters of uncertainty, buried beneath her skin, started to itch again. She watched the candles' nymph-like shadows dance within themselves, their delicate presence reminding her how little time there was for worrying, emotions clinging to her like sultry humid air.

Ruth made a point of staying on top of everything—her medications, the time of day, even the occasional lover. Thankfully, her work kept her focused, kept all the nagging doubts under the surface, some place almost invisible. She just hoped her brother was all right. That's all, really. He was having a rough time of it at home, and boy, did she know how that goes. Bunkie City is no longer a place for a boy once the fascination of the outdoors has worn off, and Zane was never the type to sit still in a classroom, either. "A nervous bird," she was always calling him, running around the countryside or locked up in their bedroom playing his LP's as he tried not to scratch at the vicious poison oak that had savagely captured his body. She stepped out of her 2nd floor apartment onto the balcony over looking Commander's Palace.

The setting sun was losing some of its unforgiving heat, simmering itself reluctantly away into the oncoming night. The sun's radiating last breaths flickered through the majestic magnolia trees, making the thick oily leaves sparkle and glisten like street lights captured in wet crystal. Below her, under the canopy of tree limbs, several evening joggers passed by with sweating bodies slouching inward from the omni-present wall of moisture, their faces reddening into cartoon-size proportions.

Tomorrow, the musicians, in their fine black suits and matching old Cadillacs, would reappear in front of her building. They always smiled and waved as they smoked their cigarettes before sauntering into the restaurant with their instruments. She would hear their slow jazz floating out from the bustling dinning room windows, sailing through the shimmering leaves before entering her apartment, where she lay naked on her bed, cozy and safe and feeling the music soothe her busy, delicate body.

Ruth gripped the cast iron railing and felt some of the brittle paint flake into her palms. Thoughts of her childhood started to surface again. Diagnosed with diabetes at age 14 was nothing to sneeze at and she shuddered, despite the heat, thinking about all the long, nervous drives down to the hospital, during which her parents would fight the entire torturous trip. Worse were the rides when no one would talk at all. Then she would sit in the back seat, behind her Dad, blaming herself for the money they were spending on gas, prescriptions and lab tests. *Those damned tests.* They were the worst part, and it seemed like they didn't help much with anything anyway. So much of it was her own trial and error, trying to get the right amount of insulin to make it through another day, constantly afraid and always having to adjust the dosage every time she had her period, which kept her nauseous for hours at a time. On top of that, trying to avoid her father when he got drunk and started calling her a junkie because she wouldn't go anywhere without her constant companion, a shoe box decorated with Mardi Gras beads that protected her syringes and insulin vials. Even her own mother hadn't been supportive, eating herself half to death, seemingly more concerned in the neighbors' gossip and her own pathetic penances than in helping her daughter cope with the guilt of wrecking their picture-perfect Home Sweet Home. Mom could have at least helped with the injections, instead of claiming she was allergic to the sight of needles, abandoning a terrified teenager to rely on her younger brother, barely old enough to walk home from school alone. No wonder that when the needle daily pierces her skin, she thinks of him with his Artic blue eyes, freezing like a petrified rabbit every time she had a seizure and tried to convince him that everything would be all right as long as he knew how to stab her stomach with the six-inch needle.

Looking back at it all now, living at home was the scariest time of her life. A time when she slipped into fits of silent depression, clinging to the walls of their trailer home like the mold. The only way to fight back was attend nursing school. At least in the classroom, people knew what diabetes actually was and treated it without the crushing guilt trip her parents had thrown at her. It was on the college computer that Ruth learned how to calculate her daily sugar intake and discovered, to her amazement, just how many other people were diabetics. It was thanks to her teachers that she learned how to regulate and balance her own simple diet. She got so good at it that she could even sneak in the occasional glass of wine if she wanted to.

Ruth sighed and unwound herself from the lace window curtains that the breeze had swept out onto the balcony. She stepped back into her apartment and glided over to the cypress armoire. Taking out a pressed nurse's uniform, she held it against her naked body. For several minutes, she stood critically examining her twenty-four year old self in the full-length mirror, swiveling on the ball of one foot, as if checking the hem of a wedding gown. *Still cute as a button,* she thought. *No visible signs of damage yet. Still know how to make any mans head turn, especially those student doctors always hovering around me at work.* She slipped on her uniform and carefully flattened the starched fabric creases with the palms of her hands. After one more brief examination, she stepped onto the balcony again and relaxed a little. She loved living here. The Garden District had given her a place to call home, a place where she felt secure. The long hours she worked at Charity Hospital helped make her spacious place affordable and gave her the privacy she needed to breathe after work. She felt she fit into the bustle of city life, enjoying the camaraderie of being surrounded by hundreds of other anonymous diabetics who she knew were walking the same streets as herself and quietly going about their business, trying to make some sense of the challenges of life.

The evening air was filling up with the noise of insects mechanically rubbing their legs together, beckoning the return of the cooling night. The erotic scent of her neighbor's night blooming jasmine was inviting her senses to leap across the rooftops and jump onto the fiery carpet of fleeing clouds ablaze with pinks and oranges that dissolved the daylight into the pale skin of the moon. "That Irene!" she whispered, leaning over the balcony railing, before letting out a mischievous giggle. Down where the musicians usually smoked, a scraggly dog cocked its hind leg and was merrily peeing on the shiny chrome wheels of a parked with its engine running, stretched black limousine.

CHEMICAL SISTERS

Two green poker-dot Schiaparelli hats bob inside the rear window of a bumper-sticker-infested neon- red Chevy Sprint. With the economical 50-miles-per-gallon engine cruising on all three cylinders, Rachael and Rebecca, AKA R&R, AKA the Chemical Sisters were back on the road again. Merrily barreling down the deserted highway bound for the State Palace Theatre in New Orleans. The girls felt safe riding their trusty mechanical steed, known to all as Karma Queen, with its spotted-imitation-leopard-skin steering wheel and matching seat covers. The 14-hour drive from Athens, Georgia, had become a monthly routine that they now lived for. It was their dance-till-they-drop-then dance-some-more reward for kicking ass at college.

The couple had bonded instantly on the first day of classes like ants in a sugar bowl. Soon afterward, they were happily cohabitating in a cute shotgun house just off the main campus. Any tension emitted from their parents was quickly diminished when R&R pointed out that at least each one of them knew who they were sleeping with every night, unlike their nostalgia-driven parents who boasted about the promiscuous lifestyle they led back in their enlightened 60's student days.

R&R studied hard and partied hard. Their dynamic thirst for knowledge had given them a head start on the internet, and it wasn't long before they knew everything there was to know about the small but very raw rave scene in New Orleans. After several experimental weekend trips, they quickly became regulars among the after-hours clubbers who partied until they dropped at the Hurricane Hotel. And their intense yet likable personalities, woven with their deep love for the music, made the like-minded creatures revolving through the hotel respect and trust them.

Having made this long, night drive many times before, the girls knew all the safe spots for gas, where the bathrooms were not too creepy and the pimply gas attendants asked no questions. Places where two young girls, obviously out to party, could nibble on a fresh waffle before ceremoniously dropping a hit of Ecstasy in the dimly lit parking lot without being eyes too suspiciously. So that that by the time they arrived in New Orleans, the welcoming staff would slip them through the back stage door and transport them, along with hundreds of other ravers, into a high-pitched electronic frenzy.

Several freaky experiences had taught them how to stay cool with the bored cops and lone drunks cruising up and down the dark rural interstates of America. Often following the girls for hundreds of miles just because they didn't like or couldn't read one Karma Queen's in-your-face bumper stickers. For safety reasons, Rebecca's dad had insisted they carry a mobile phone. If push came to shove, the girls would make a distressed call to 911, hoping the dispatch would go to the very same cop who had been hounding them for the past sixty miles. And more often than not, the pursuing headlights would evaporate, sulking into the darkness like a beleaguered dog unable to chase an excitable march hare. Safe in their three-cylinder capsule, they continued into the night as the dense passing pine forest tried to absorb Karma Queen's headlights, making it feel like they were being hurled through an endless barrel of tar. The color of the land matched the hovering sky so exactly that it was only the glowing odometer that reassured the girls they where not sealed up in a vacuum of time. Everything was running smoothly until twenty minutes after their ritual hits of Ecstasy, Karma Queen decided to take a trip of her own, coughing, slowing down and then rearing up again.

"I think it's the fuel line," Rebecca said. "Might be some water mixed up with the cheap gas we just bought." Rachael nodded in pensive agreement, and they started patting, with the palms of their attentive antenna-like hands, Karma Queen's dashboard in encouragement.

"C'mon Karma Queen! Can you make it?" Rebecca asked.

"Where are we?"

"I wish I knew, but I don't think it would help much anyway. Not out here."

"Anything else you might like to add just to make me feel a little more secure, Rebecca?"

"No, but it looks like Karma Queen wants to say something!" They watched the speed odometer needle fall to a crawling pace of six mph. "We gotta get off this interstate ASAP. Is that an exit?"

"Never seen it before."

"Bunkie City?"

"Don't you just love these names?"

They signaled to exit the desolate miles of outstretched highway. Just as they hit the off ramp, Karma Queen gave out one last splutter before fading into nothing but a dimly lit ignition light. A few hundred yards from the stop sign at the end of the ramp, the car crawled to a halt.

"Come on, let's push her. That looks like a gas station or something over there. If it's open we can call Dribble A and get us a free tow. Hopefully we can still get down to New Orleans in time to catch the last dance."

JAKE

Several years older and a few parties wiser than his irresistible baby face would indicate, Jake burst the choking bubbles of domestic dysfunction and squeezed through the entangled snares of small-town boredom hoping to get lost and find some adventure down in New Orleans. His exit from the tower of babbling silence was accompanied by a hail of glass splinters falling like wedding confetti on his black, well-greased Mohawk after a shot from the double-barrel shotgun of RJ Cowen, forced into the role of reluctant step father in order to gain the hand of Jake's mother, a fine looking woman who, in the words of RJ, was and always will be the hottest piece of ass this side of the Rio Grande!

For sure, Gloria had all the right pieces in all the right places, but she was also a single mom with a hot-blooded, prowling ex husband who did not and could not comprehend the words *no more* or *divorced*, especially when a bottle or two of whiskey had slipped into his mind. Without a college education, Gloria's only opportunity for work in town, was punching numbers on a cash register or waiting tables and getting her ass pinched at one of the two local diners. When the judge refused once again to place a restraining order on her drunken husband, Gloria asked the amiable and balding RJ Cowen, who was acting as her legal counsel in an attempt to receive some child support, for protection. After a few preliminary interviews in and around the courthouse canteen, Gloria found all the emotional and financial security she ever could have dreamed of tucked away in the sturdy arms of her boisterous attorney. In fact, their honeymoon was so heated with mutual fulfillment that RJ merrily signed over half of his sizable estate to his dream-come-true-wife the following week. At last, Gloria felt she had found her knight in shining bed socks, while Jake felt himself falling into the emotional wayside, even more confused than the average 16 year old, trying to muddle his way through the twisted maze of adolescence. To compound matters, RJ and Jake clashed on just about every domestic and foreign subject imaginable. And it wasn't long before they had managed to carve up Gloria's new fantasy lifestyle into a mansion sized casket of tension, leaving the emotionally torn bride feeling like an undertaker stuck in the middle of two bickering individuals ruled by jealousy and petty resentment.

Jake had always been a social rebel, just like his old man, and in his mind, RJ represented the smugly secure arm of a failing, corrupt legal system. In truth, however, they both shared similar ideals, although neither would care to admit it simply because their abusive conflicts erupted more from vying for Gloria's attention than any high-minded social consciousness. To make matters worse for the evolving Jake, soon after the wedding, he witnessed first hand a deliberate accident involving his best friend, Matt, outside the local liquor store. Late one Friday night, a cracked-out frat boy, driving his daddy's convertible Cadillac, decided it would be fun to impress his cronies and run Matt over because he looked like a 'fag' dressed in a leather jacket with spiked green hair. Jake was in the store at the time, buying Red Bulls, when he heard the screeching tires and a deafening scream. Matt's head split wide open and a dismembered arm twitching against the Cadillac's dented, bloody grill greeted him outside. The scene became even more macabre when, hoping to flee, the drunk driver slammed his instrument of torture into reverse and once again, the vehicle's wheels tore over Matt's writhing and broken body. The sadist's escape plan failed however as the car crashed into the concrete pillar protecting the gas pumps, wedging the rear fender between pump and twisted piling. This, in turn, sent everyone, including the storekeeper, who had yet to dial 911, scattering from the scene, all justifiably afraid that the gas pumps would blow. Twenty minutes was too long to let time slip by in order to prevent Matt from going into a coma. For the next nine months, until the life support machine had to be turned off because his parents and their entire family had run out of money to pay the hospital and doctor fees, Jake lived with the guilt that it should have been him instead of Matt waiting outside the convenience store.

The final blow to Jake's low view of humanity occurred when the deceased's parents found themselves evicted from their two- bedroom home due to the mounting debt that resulted from the accident. All that the broken family could now afford was a trailer on the outskirts of town, owned and operated by the local salvage wrecker, who kept his junked cars and wrecking machines in the adjacent lot. Within a year, Jake witnessed the functional, unpretentious home turn into a derelict graveyard whose inhabitants had became morbidly depressed. Matt's parents had given up all communication with the outside world, including Jake even though he continued to try to bring some sort of social attention to this heinous crime by contacting national newspapers and social organizations with handwritten heartfelt letters. The last time Jake visited his friend's parents, they were suffering from excessive weight gain and manic insomnia, living on the proverbial potato-chip coach with a cable-less television bleating Evangelical channels, 24/7. It was during this time that RJ stepped up to the plate and joined forces with Jake, trying to glue together the broken remains of a shattered family. He freely offered his own legal counsel if they wanted to sue the driver's wealthy and politically connected parents. All was to no avail. When such a tragic and senseless loss of a child is unleashed without warning like a guillotine blade hurtling toward the block, the severed head quickly forgets the need for its pumping heart. All that remained for Jake was to listen to his own soul screaming, and before long, he was numbing the anguish by skipping school and taking more than his fair share of drugs. His impressive 4.0 plummeted in accordance with his self-esteem, resulting in a slew of verbal and abusive tirades directed by him at both the school principle and his own emotionally unequipped parents.

On the night Jake was shot, he was stumbling up his parent's recently landscaped yard in the late shadow hours after midnight. Everything was quiet until he tripped on one of Gloria's newly placed paving stones. Cursing his painfully sprained ankle, Jake managed to wake all six of RJ's prized Catahoula hounds, launching them into a pedigree cacophony of banshee howls that aroused the entire serene gated community. When the motion lights came on, dazzling Jake's eyes into momentary blindness, he angrily picked up a flowerpot and hauled it at one of the alarm sensors. The breaking pot sounded like a gunshot, startling the already nervous Gloria and RJ, who naturally thought it was Gloria's ex prowling around attempting to cause some harmful mischief. Filled with bravado to protect his wife and home, RJ came barreling down the stairs, loading his 12-gauge shot gun as he descended. Without turning on any lights, RJ saw a shadow move outside his Tiffany-replica double front doors, and a second later, he aimed his canon and fired. More out of panic than resolve, he quickly reloaded and fired again through the gaping hole of the shattered glass. It was only after he lowered his gun and the smoke had dispersed that he realized who the intruder was. By the time he stepped through the blown away remains of the doors, all he could see was a squirrel-like shadow limping down the oak-lined driveway and hysterical neighbors peering out of their bedroom windows, staring with dumbstruck amazement at his plump angry body, shaking now in all its naked glory. When the sheriff notified him several hours later that the police had safely picked up his slightly injured and very delirious son in law, all RJ could say was, "Could they keep his ass in jail and for a few hundred bucks more, throw away the damned key?"

Two days later, Jake hobbled out of the Sheriff's holding tank with his scalp crudely bandaged in heavy gauze and blotches of blood congealing along with his determination to hitch a ride to New Orleans. He had heard from another inmate in the cell next door that a bunch of 'ghetto punks' hanging out in the French Quarter were making their loose ends meet from hustling drunk tourists.

Hitch hiking though the almighty state of Texas is a daunting task for even the most hardened of travelers. It can take two mournful days on foot, just to get from one end of Houston to the other. In the blistering desert heat, dressed in his torn up jeans and deceased friends studded, blood stained leather jacket, Jake began walking with a self-contained fury across the gangplank of his own uncertain future, leaving his home forever, one more scorched soul searching for a slice of shade to wipe his sweat and lick his wounds.

ZANE

Scorched banana leaves curtained either side of a dilapidated trailer. Each windowpane had been duct-taped with an X, and from a distance, they looked like fading kisses found inside a washed out Valentine card. A flagless flagpole, beside the trailer's screen door, had a plastic flowerpot suspended with wire. The poinsettia that grew there several Christmases ago was long gone and had since been replaced with cat's claw spewing from the pot, up the flagpole and onto the trailer. When the heat reflected off the aluminum siding, the cat's claw looked like a web of cracks in a dirty pane of glass.

Inside the trailer, Zane was crouching in his bedroom like a nervous colt about to leap. His fingers sat poised on the rewind button of his portable CD player and a small set of headphones rested on his thatch of red hair. Above the TV babble, out in the front room, he could hear his father shouting something about his dinner being spoiled. The anger in his drunken voice made Zane's body feel clammy and suffocated, as if his nerves were choked in plastic wrap. To reassure himself that everything would be all right, he opened his wallet and counted the tips of the 20-dollar bills that his sister, Ruth, had been secretly sending him via her friend Irene.

Earlier that evening, Zane had found a blank sheet of paper and written down a list of all the people he knew before drawing a big heart around the list. He then scratched an arrow diagonally through the names, the force of the pen nib ripping through the paper. He had repeated this action until he had torn the sheet into pieces. It now littered the carpet like forgotten confetti. He looked up at a drawing his sister had made for him several years ago and that now hung on the wall above his head. It had inky fingerprint faces, pencil-stick-like figures and red dots for the eyes and ears, no recognizable mouths or smiles, crayon arms and legs and a gigantic tree sprouting mahny bluish-purple flowers from its branches. Behind the blossoming tree, a rectangle house with three windows of various sizes sat underneath a chimney issuing smudgy smoke. At the bottom right hand corner of the picture, an enormous five-legged creature with carefully painted blue and green stripes, grinned with the words *Ginger Cat* written above its head. Zane removed the picture from the wall and wiped the protective glass with his sleeve. Within the smudges of the smoke, he noticed for the first time the words, *I LUV U Zane*. He reread the words and wished he could press the rewind button on his CD player and start his world over again.

Without knocking, Zane's father entered the bedroom and staggered towards him. His father's head tilted sideways, as if a large weight were tied to his ear. Totally intoxicated, he fumbled to turn on the overhead light. Glaring down at his son, he placed his hands on his trouser belt and began to shout in a cruel tone of contempt, "You didn't go an' do it, did you? ... I am talkin' to you, boy! You didn't go and do it, did you?"

Zane remained crouching, staring at his sister's picture. He didn't want to look up at his father, hoping that if he didn't acknowledge his existence, the man might miraculously disappear.

"Look at me when I'm talkin' to ya. Look at me, I say!" His father slurred. Zane noticed some drying dog shit on the side of his father's boot as the room filled with a fearful tension.

"What? The rat got your tongue?"

"It's cat, Dad. C, A, T, cat" Zane replied.

"Don't you smart me boy! I told you, if you didn't go lookin' for no job today, you were outta here!"

"I did look!"

"Don't bullshit me. You've been sittin' here masturbatin' over your records again! I can smell it in your eyes. Your dick's goin' to fall off before long. Look at you, you queer son, did I rear a queer?"

"I looked in the paper, ask Ma!"

"You think you're so smart. Aren't you son? So damn smart for your own darn good!"

Zane glared up at his father, eyeing his flushed face and breathing in the alcohol oozing from the drunkard's pores. "I don't know, I just want to play music, that's all. Be a DJ or something."

His father stepped forward before kicking the front of Zane's portable record player. The leather toe ripped through the fragile woven fabric that protected the speaker and sent the player across the floor. "Play that, you lazy dope fiend!" he snarled.

Leaning over to examine the hole, Zane slipped his fingers through the weave, trying to see if the speaker had been irreparably damaged. He was breathing hard now, trying to contain the tears welling up. "I don't smoke no dope, Dad. Never have," he mumbled.

"Your lying to me again, son. What did I say about lying? Look at me, I said, when I am damn well talkin' to you!"

"Why should I? Don't ever like what I see!"

His father reached down for the headphones and yanked on their metal frame, causing the wire to pull under Zane's neck, forcing the boy to stand to avoid choking. They stood at eye-level, glaring at each other like a pair of rabid pit bulls. Zane's mother started shouting from behind the bedroom door, "Arlen! Leave him be. Come and eat something before you fall down!" Arlen slammed the door shut. "Shut up, Emma!" He hollered before facing Zane again. "What? You gonna hit me now? You couldn't fight your way out of a plastic bag."

Zane removed his headphones and started to walk past his father, but Arlen blocked his path with outstretched his arms and then began gesturing, "C'mon! Hit me, you scrawny little weed head. Hit me, I say! You're nothing but a ..." With his open palm he slapped Zane hard across the face, "Take that, you lazy buzzard!" The force of the blow sent Zane reeling toward the floor. He stumbled over the record player and fell to the carpet. His wrist twisted backward causing him to cry out in pain. Arlen cowered over him and grinned. "What? The CAAAAT got your tongue boy?" Unable to stop the tears marring his vision, Zane lunged at his father's legs, pushing the drunk off balance.

"Why you little punk!" Arlen yelled as his left foot fell onto Ruth's picture. His boot heel shattered the glass, and tore the fragile drawing. He then stumbled backward over a pile of loose records like a clown performing the splits. "You son of a bitch!" Arlen screamed.

Fueled with increasing anger, Zane pushed his father again as the boy tried to regain his own sense of balance. Arlen grabbed his son's arm, trying to stabilize himself. "Let go of me! Let go, you Bully!" Zane yelled as he latched on to his father's arm and started to spin Arlen around until the drunkard crashed against the wooden bunk bed frame. Arlen collapsed to the bed like a sack of old bones as his head crashed against the bedpost.

Shaking, Zane picked up his portable CD player and slipped his headphones back onto his ears. His wrist burned as if it had been dipped into a sink of boiling water. Ignoring his father, slumped unconscious on the bed, Zane turned the light out and exited the destruction of his childhood world.

ARLEN

Groaned, slowly shifting back into consciousness as thundering remorse rushed up through his nerves. In the half-lit darkness, he stared at his shaking hand. "You hit my son," he mouthed, gasping for air. Outside the bedroom, he could hear the toilet over flowing, the water draining itself back into the bowl with snake-like hisses. He wanted to rip the system apart, along with his own blistered heart, to wrench the cheap plumbing and all it stood for right off the thin trailer wall. "Always backing up," he mumbled, "Another god-damned thing I will never fix. One more constant reminder I'm stuck here shittin' my life away ... Emma Jane!"

The flickering glow from the TV projected against the back of the bedroom wall ghost-like shapes that danced in the corner of his half-closed eyes as if he were a sentinel absorbing all communication in the vacuum of his cursed domesticity. He could hear a preacher's voice drawn in a drawl, asking for money.

"How much does it cost to be saved?" The TV voice hovered inside Arlen's head like an annoying mosquito.

Aint she saved enough already? Arlen thought to himself. "Damnit, Emma!" He growled, as he lowered his right hand to the edge of the bed and felt the damp sheets with his fingertips. A gnarling ache raced through his spine.

"The hour is near my brothers and sisters!" The TV voice continued.

Arlen placed his left hand behind the hammer pounding his skull.

"Let us pray for the lost and lonely!"

He fingered a sticky liquid congealing in his hair.

"The book of Jonah!"

"Blood," he mumbled, "What have I gone and done?"

His throat seemed glued to its scorched surroundings. His gaping mouth tried to suck in air. He could feel himself choking like a flapping catfish yanked out of the muddy water.

"What meanest thou, O sleeper?"

He tried to spit to get the saliva going to moisten the hot ash burning in his mouth.

"They cast lots to see who ... "

He so wanted to dissolve the memories of the past half hour, the past half-lifetime, upon which he felt skewered on.

"For thou hast cast me into …"

"Enough!" he shouted. "Enough, I say!" He fell back onto the bed. The very same bed in which his son had slept the night before. "No more! … Please, no more!" he wailed, feeling the mattress giving way to the extra weight of his frame. The springs creaked as they tried to soak up his sweating heaving body that felt robbed of all life.

"If I could only close my eyes and start all over again." he moaned with both eyes shut.

"I am cast out of thy sight …"

"I need a drink!"

"Within me …"

"I need a … drink! Damnit … Emm Mer!"

Instinctively he lunged forward into the darkness, and then smashed his head on the slats of the top bunk. The wood bruised his skin and sent another nail hammering into his skull.

"Arise! Go unto …"

Jolted, Arlen remembered where he was is again and what he had just done. "Didn't I build this bed just after Zane was …"

"And covered him with sackcloth …"

"Cypress, from Papa's old barn. When was that?"

"Everyone from his evil …"

"Shit! I didn't even know my own son's age."

Lowering himself back onto the mattress, he could feel the angry guilt tearing its way up inside him, searching in vain for release. "Maybe 16 by now. Damnit. I really don't know anymore." He lurched forward, hitting his head on the slats again before falling back onto the mattress. He repeated this cycle again and again, each time hitting the slats harder until the bed frame and the floor beneath him started to shake.

"Doest thou well to be angry …"

He finally ceased his self-inflicted thrashing after a dozen blows to the head and with an outstretched hand fumbled for the door. Loose paint chips gathered underneath his nails as he scratched and clawed, trying to grip the door's lip and shut out the TV voice that continued to haunt him.

"Doest thou well to be angry I say ..."

His trembling fingers found the door handle.

"And also much cattle ..."

Arlen managed to pull the door shut with a slam, drowning out the preacher's voice with his own sobbing. He could hear himself crying, wanting the tears to carry him back into unconsciousness and forget the pain that had unleashed itself like an electric shock hot-wired to his skull. Digging up a belch, his teeth bit hard into his tongue. He could smell Emma Jane's perfume somewhere close by mixing with the acid of his own breath. The pillow wedged under his head felt as if it had been stuffed with old bones. "Are they mine?" he moaned, before noticing a fuzzy maze of fluorescent dots blinking three feet above his face. "Some kind of chart," he mumbled, "Stars of the constellations ... a thumb tacked star chart ... pinned under the slats. Torn and wrinkled by my bleeding skull." He tried to lift his head to get a clearer look. "Emma," he whispered. "Come see. ... Zane, I never knew. How could I? ... Look, there's Orion." Tears of remorse flooded his eyes again as his tangled mind, confused with too many unknowns, folded up like the petals of a poppy closing at sunset. Lowering his head onto the pillow, he slipped back into unconsciousness, sinking deeper into the nightmare of his own waking lifetime.

EMMA JANE

'Sounded more like a fancy show dog than a country,' I said. 'No problems,' he said. 'Just another routine mission'. He had gone on much worse ... Some joke that was! Had to go and volunteer didn't you, Arlen? Just couldn't stay at home with the kids. Oh no, not you. Always getting into the mess of things. That's what kept you going you said ... Still, you looked as handsome as ever, dressed in your uniform, boarding the plane. Made us laugh, those young 'uns, they did. What with bringing their skis and snowboards. Had heard about the great slopes, they said ... But it wasn't no snow you would cry about in the middle of the night, now was it? ... It was the frozen dust getting into everything. 'And I mean everything', you said. Ears, nose, mouth, even down ya clothes! And if you scratched at it, a nasty rash

would appear, kinda like Zane's, I guess. And the worst of it was that your orders were to not interfere, just observe. You know them Brass! Wherever there is a Russian, our boys have to follow! I thought we had gone and done fighting all them Cold Wars, I did. I mean, the ones we met down at the base seemed real nice to me and they sure liked the women, that's for sure. Always pinching ya bum they were! Couldn't get enough fried chicken and football either. More American than many folks I know around these parts and real reluctant to leave when their submarine or whatever it was finally got repaired. Offered to stay and work up at the docks, they did. Sure weren't in no hurry to go back home, not in my mind at least. I simply don't understand what all the fuss was about. Still, orders are orders. Don't we all know that one! It was those Taliban peoples you said was the problem. … Felt sorry for the Russians, you did. Having to mess with 'em all running around on anything that had four legs and screaming bloody Allah every time our boys so much as lifted a finger. Allah this and Allah that! With the men wearing them funny hats and dresses and never hearing of the word manners! Eating anywhere they liked with their bare dirty hands. Can you imagine such a thing? 'You couldn't trust none of them as far as you can throw them.' You said. Bloody murder trying to please em his Sarge told us later. … What's his name? … George, that's it. Crazy George, you liked to call him. A good old southern boy from Baton Rouge … No, New Orleans, I think. Black as Arlen's nails he was. One of them big fellows too. You know, with that sexy husky voice that sounds like Barry White. … Almost lost it with them, he did, that time you gone an' shot a wild goat and was cooking it up for supper with some of your Chef Paul's Magic Mix. … Never left the country without it. Oh no, not my Arlen. … Said you could eat anything you liked anyplace in the world as long as you had your hot sauce and Cajun spice mix! … That might be true, I say, seeing as I never left no country before.

They were just sittin' down to eat the supper you had roasted on an open fire when up charged a bunch of those religious weirdo's screaming about how the goat belonged to Allah and not to no Americans! They almost came to blows with you, they did. Should know by now not to mess with Arlen's meat. I tell you what. And then Sarge was trying to cool everybody down, asking them to come and join them. Oh no, they said. They wanted the goat back just as they left it, all alive an all! … I mean, come on! … Wouldn't take any kinda no for an answer. Wouldn't even take our American money either. You know someone's crazy if they don't take your money! ... I thought everybody liked our money. ... 'Not true,' says Arlen. 'More than half the world over there only deals with guns or yen.' 'Really?' I say. And you tell me who would want to live in a place like that.

My poor Arlen. Look at him now. It's alright, you just go an' rest, will ya? Forget all that stuff in that empty head of yours. ... Looks like you gone and knocked yourself clean out, you crazy thing, you. I'll go get a cold press and be right back. I mean, it's not like I ain't used to nursing you now is it. And don't you be worrying about your son. It's not nobody's fault we never stayed in one place long enough for him to know what he wants to do now, is it? At least Ruth went to nursing school. At least she's out working for a living and not slouching around at home all day playing them stupid records. Bless his heart! It's all going to work out, y'all see. Be back before you know it, he will. They always do you know. I just wanna know when you two are going to realize you're as stubborn as the other! After all, it was only joining the services that helped yours out. Oh, don't think I don't remember how you were when we first got started! ... Taking me out on dates at all hours and trying to get me to go to those wild parties where them black folks danced with whites! ... You do remember now don't you Arlen? The only way we were allowed to get married was cause you told my folks you had gone and signed up. Oh yes, those where the days. A pair of real life lovers we were back then before the kids showed up. I must admit, though, I liked all the family housing they went and gave us. Always had the newest appliances with a garden to look at from the kitchen window and plenty of social as well with the other wives. ... Well, until your accident, that is.

I wish you could see yourself! Sleeping like a big ole cuddly baby. Reminding me of the time I was about to have me another one. I had seen it on the TV and had dialed the numbers and everything. About to sell it to those rich folks at that baby center clinic place. I passed all the tests on the phone, I did. Healthy as a spring chicken back then. You said I could go and do it as soon as you got back from your last round of duty.... Still can't believe all that money they wanted to pay us for just one kid! Enough to put a down-payment on a house, it was. Even your pa said he thought it sounded mighty suspicious and would help find out if there was some sort of a catch to it all. You know, try and find out if we didn't have to give them their money back later or wake-up one morning and find the same kid on our doorstep, screaming and needing its diaper changed. You can't trust them fancy contract people no more! ... I must admit, though, we sure could use that 20 grand right about now. Don't you think, Arlen? A whole lot more money than we could ever save, especially on your wages. The only thing good was all the medical insurance and, come to think of it, look what happened when we you went and got sick! ... Oh well! ... Ain't worth crying over nothing we never had now, is it? ... You just keep them eyes closed and shut tight, Mister Arlen Spencer. I'll be right back with some fresh ice for that thick head of yours. ... Go on, get you some rest and stop all that fussing about Allah this and crazy yen that!'

SOME GUY UPSTAIRS

According to bar room legend, Jake's rites of passage into the ever rumbling bowels of the Hurricane Hotel began with the daunting task of hitchhiking through what he later nicknamed the Loathsome Star State. A bloody nightmare, consisting of beatings and shake downs under the sneering grimaces of several under-qualified law enforcement agents that Texas had stashed up its razor wire sleeve.

It takes one bad apple to spoil the barrel. And the only time Jake was given a brief respite from these illicit and uniformed rotten fruits was outside Austin when a truck driver offered to give him a ride all the way down to New Orleans as long as he went all the way down at the next secluded rest stop. When the time arrived, a mere 220 miles had crawled over the odometer and Jake found himself jumping out of the frisky trucker's moving cab, only to land in the self righteous arms of yet another "to serve and protect" goon who had recently graduated out of his diapers and was craving some action. The cop's thirst was quenched by rough cuffing Jake and pistol-whipping the belligerent punk's ass in the privacy of the backseat of his shiny new cruiser. So enthusiastic was the beating, that when he dumped Jake's limp body onto a deserted stretch of forlorn highway somewhere close to the Texarkana border, the uniformed Greenhorn thought he might have his first real, live dead body on his hands. With a rather macabre and over-zealous potential, the trooper then hauled ass with sirens blazing, trying to find his fellow graduates and share with them his first bloody experience. Unfortunately, before he could expound his auspicious tale, the speeding cruiser slammed headlong into a herd of stray cattle. Three hours later, his fellow cronies who got to witness a real, live dead body, ripped apart and strewn under the hooves of the nonchalant wandering cattle.

The following day, Jake had regained enough consciousness to stumble through miles of tic-infested pinewoods before falling into the arms of a slightly less militant state trooper, hunkering down in Northwest Louisiana. After another brief shake-down the fates took mercy on Jake's harrowing journey and issued an angel of mercy in the form of a nubile goth chick who pulled up beside the beaten boy as he stood propped up against a flashing, Men At Work sign. Somehow, she managed to carry his black and blue body into the padded velvet sanctuary of her 1976 GMC customized hearse. Three days later, when Jake finally opened his eyes, in the honeymoon suite of a nearby Best Western, staring at a badly rendered print of a steamboat tragically surrounded by wingless herons, he turned and gazed into the expanding irises of his mesmerized angel. With his usual charm and slow-moving drawl, he whispered, "Am I dead or in Heaven?" These words sent a slew of Cupid's arrows straight through his angel's larger-than-life heart and without another thought, she vowed never to leave Jake's broken-rib-or-two side.

"Am I Dead or in Heaven?" he repeated.

"You're only half dead, and we can arrange for a load more heaven!" whispered his angel, who then proceeded to peel the top bed sheet and lower her mouth between his naked groin, sending the mesmerized boy into an unreal realm of erotic bliss. That night and for the next six days Jake and his deflowerer intimately grew to know every part of each other's anatomy. Their ravenous fornication helping to heal Jake's wounds and quench, at least for the time-being, his angel's nubile thirst.

Like those of all sensitive young sweethearts, when their mouths weren't exercising fellatio and cunnilingus, they rarely opened unless it was to smoke cigarettes or order more iced beer and sandwiches from the hotel's room service, simply because neither one wanted to accidentally say the wrong stupid thing and ruin the whole unbelievable universe they had been thrown into. Surely we all can relate to such a predicament? Hasn't this situation happened to the best and worse of us? You must remember when a great time disappeared instantly with a slip of a nervous tongue, leaving your bewildered lover scrambling for his or her clothing before exiting through the same door they had first magically arrived through, instantly dampening the night's animalistic desires into a soggy insidious vapor reeking of stale cigarette smoke? Thankfully, neither Jake nor his Angel seemed to tire from performing oral sex, and on the seventh day, they reluctantly peeled apart their love-glued bodies and stumbled out of bed. No fig leafs in sight but plenty of used condoms littered the carpet and furniture, the Jacuzzi and emergency stairwell. After two helpings of breakfast, showers and tanking up the hearse, they began the last leg of Jake's unforgettable journey.

Jake leaned his bruised arm out of the car window. He could feel the cool morning breeze float up over his skin. Today it seemed for the first time in his sixteen years on earth that he felt wonderfully alive. He smiled at his driver then back at his own visage reflecting in the side-view mirror. Running his fingers through his Mohawk, he mentally began calculating how to engage in a domestic dialogue that would expand upon the limited, although intensely heated vocabulary of the past six days. Trying to perfect the persona of coolness, he peeled a Camel non-filter from his tattered shirt pocket and with the unlit cigarette dangling from his lips took a leap into hypersensitive space.

"What's your name again?" he asked as nonchalantly as possible.

"Molly. What's yours?"

"Jake."

"Pleased to meet you Jake."

"Likewise, Molly," Jake replied, checking his reflection to see if he was blushing. Feeling a little more confident, he continued, "The pleasure's all mine."

"Like Hell it is!" Molly grinned.

They stared at each other before bursting out with laughter. Finally, after thirty minutes of driving without either saying a word, Jake felt the ice melting, and it wasn't long before they were freely conversing about the ever-expanding universe that made up the day's youthful multitasking world. By the time they had reached the back roads flowing down to the Mississippi River, the starched seams of clothed awkwardness were well creased and ready to be laundered again. The puzzled facial expressions of the occasional onlooker, staring at Molly's vintage hearse as it tore through the slow-rolling vistas of overhanging oaks sensually veiled in Spanish moss, simply intensified their developing friendship, allowing the remaining miles, meandering through what is romantically known as Plantation Alley, to become an enjoyable memory neither would forget. Their laughter and growing affection for each other, oblivious to the mid day sun's enslaved shadows that for centuries had divided this rural landscape into the light and the dark, the shade and the sweat.

MOOSE

That Some Guy Upstairs! He can spin a yarn bigger than any of us! That's for sure! At least he buys his own drinks, though, and was sure as hell right about Molly. I will give him that one.

At five-foot-two-and-a-quarter and weighing in at a steady 98 pounds, she broke Jake's heart in a heavyweight class of her own. Packing a punch with knock-out proportions, the sole heiress to one of the South's largest and most profitable logging companies. Her parents, who tragically had been taken to a higher plane when their private plane took a permanent nose dive one stormy night someplace south of Denver, had left her 62 percent of the stock in their affiliated paper mill, slap bang in the middle of pine forest central: Woodville, Arkansas.

Her family had been one of the cornerstones of this sleepy rural town, and downtown several schools, the only bank and an expanding hospital, memorialized her surname.

Molly, whose real name was Myrtle—but I promised Jake I wouldn't tell any one—had also inherited her mother's bone-white skin and her father's knack for numbers, much to the dismay of the Logging Company's remaining board members, who, every quarter, felt the weight of her swift left hook when she would drive up to Arkansas to oversee the board meetings and ensure that the vast profits were allocated into the correct, designated hands, instead of the board member's fat pockets. Molly was not a greedy person by nature, perhaps because she already had so much, and this meant that large sums of money were often sent to charities and organizations she deemed worthy of supporting. One of the foundations she was presently overseeing was for the victims and families of high school shootings, a topic she could relate to both hypothetically and emotionally, teenager Angst and Melancholy being her permanent state of being.

As far as I know, Molly had skipped college, stayed out of jail and went straight into high finance. In drunken jest she would often mention her only and crowning high school achievement was founding a Marilyn Manson online fan club. When she moved down to New Orleans, her uncanny psychic entrepreneurship led to a series of midnight gothic-and-vampire-themed-tours in the heart of the French Quarter. For added authenticity, she hired real goth chicks and real vampire boys. Thanks to the timely revival of interest in everything ghoulish, Myrtle—I mean Molly.—once again struck gold.

The arrival of Jake seemed too serendipitous. Before she found him, Molly was almost at the end of her personal family planning venture, an enterprise she hoped would consume her life with something more valuable than her knack for numbers, something she actually wanted instead of just getting. Don't ask me why, but Molly desperately wanted to be a mother, and a single one, to boot because unfortunately, all the guys who turned her on were working hard to remain in a state of permanent adolescence. They were children for life playing 24/7 in the French Quarter bar rooms. Molly loved their raw aggressiveness in bed, but the picture of a unwashed male with ghastly hang over breath changing a diaper with hot cigarette ash falling onto her precious baby's forehead, always sent her scurrying back to her drawing room. You see, Molly had no intention whatsoever in rearing two infants, one 20 twenty years older than the other but requiring the same amount of attention. No indeed! A single motherhood with no tied connections with the male species was, in her mind, the absolute only way to go.

Then came Jake. No pun intended.

Clearly, he possessed the undesirable qualities mentioned above. However, he also possessed advantages that set him above all the other unknowing surrogates, and every time Molly and Jake were naked in the same room, there was no doubt in Molly's acute mind that Lust and Love shared the same damn moniker. In her "Sperm Donor" notebook, neatly penciled in under the page allocated for Jake, read:

Attribute #1 His charm-the-very-panties-off-you smile no matter what you just said.

Attribute #2 The size of his ever-ready mouthwatering cock.

Just thinking about these qualities sent uncontrollable wet flushes running through Molly's body. Genetically hot-wired with her father's pragmatic genius and her mother's nymph-like tendencies, she decided to switch off her motherhood mode as long as Jake appeared in a timely fashion, at least three times a day, tool in hand, smiling innocently and ready for work. … After all, at 24, she still had some time.

RUTH

The Bat Mobile, that's what Irene called her beat-up pickup truck, with its mud tires growling on the molten tarmac, hauling Ruth and Irene down bumpy, dirt roads with Nine Inch Nails screaming out of the speakers. Irene was a wild-card driver, constantly running red lights in downtown Bunkie City with a broken headlight dangling from the fender. The truck's floorboards were so rusted out that every time it rained, they would wrap garbage bags around their feet to protect their shoes from the back splash.

They had met at nursing school and it turned out they lived in the same trailer park, making it very practical to carpool, especially because Ruth's car was so unreliable and often sat at the garage for weeks on end because she couldn't afford the repair.

Irene and the Bat Mobile. It was easy to take her for a reckless fool, but she had enough smarts to know how to work those dirty old men down at the lodge. Never any hassle from those guys. Hell, she even managed to swing Ruth a part time job to help her pay the tuition and the endless piles of medical textbooks.

It had been Irene's idea to pick up a couple of young off shore workers from Old Prudhomme's Bar & Grill and drive over to the boat ramp down at the bayou. The night started serenely enough, the four of them smoking herb and watching the sliced reflections from the waning moon dance on the ripples of the dark swamp water. They had parked both trucks under a mess of wisteria that had wrapped itself around the landing's light poles, and even though it was late into the night, clouds of swarming insects were feeding from the potent pollen. The boys had gone back to their truck to discuss the plan of action, and Ruth was lying on a quilted blanket with her head nestled in Irene's lap, soaking in the stillness and enjoying the intimacy of her friend's warm touch.

"Just like that?" Irene said, pushing Ruth abruptly off her lap.

"Well, no. In a couple of weeks."

There was a long, uncomfortable pause as they watched a snapping turtle bob its head out of the water. Suddenly, emerging from a blanket of cypress trees, a large owl swooped down over the bayou, it's shadow sucking in the moon light. The turtle disappeared just as the owl's talons pierced the ripples of black water.

"You can come too," continued Ruth. "We can live ..."

"No, I damn well can't!" Irene interrupted. "You're going? Just like that?"

Perhaps Ruth was being overly sensitive because of the marijuana but she felt there was no need for Irene to be shouting at her like this. An awkward energy enveloped them, as if they were strangers meeting for the first time. Irene lit a cigarette. "You know I can't just leave!" she said.

"Why not? It would be fun!" Ruth tried sitting closer to her friend again, hoping to regain the intimacy they had shared just before she had told Irene of her plans to move to New Orleans.

Irene pushed her away again. "Why not?" she screamed, "Fuck you, Ruth!" She stood up and stomped back to her truck, opening and slamming the driver's door so hard that the vehicle shook and the dangling headlight rattled. Ruth could see the two boys laughing at the girl fight as she heard Irene start the engine and slam the stick shift into reverse. The tires slipped on the wet ground as the smell of burning rubber fueled Ruth's fears that Irene was about to leave her stranded with two strangers. "Wait for me!" she shouted, scrambling up the oyster-shell path, slipping and scraping her knees, trying to regain some sense of emotional balance.

"Come on, get your ass in here!" Screamed Irene, revving her truck some more.

Ruth had seen Irene angry before, who hadn't? But tonight she seemed to have spun out of control like the tires.

"Come on Ruth! Let's go!"

"What about your blanket?"

"Fuck that, as well!"

The early evening rain had made the roads dangerously slick as the Bat Mobile headed back to the trailer park. Soon, the truck was swerving uncontrollably around the tight, blind corners, its wheels barely keeping up with the engine. The speed of the driving and the anger in Irene's eyes was making Ruth feel nauseous. She leaned out the window, clutching the broken safety belt, hoping this nightmarish situation would somehow go away. Suddenly, Irene hit the brakes. The two girls lurched to a stop and Ruth hit her head on the truck window frame. Irene cut the engine. For several minutes, they sat in silence before Ruth dared speak.

"I'm sorry, Irene. I thought we—"

"Thought we what? "Thought we could just fly down to Party Central and have a real good time?"

"What's the matter, Irene? What's really going on, with you, tonight?"

Ruth's head was pounding. She thought she might throw up any moment. Irene reached into her bag before pulling out a faux-leopard-skin purse. Ripping it open, Irene carefully removed a photograph that was wedged between a dozen credit cards and handed it to Ruth. "That's what's the matter!" She said.

In the half-light of the dashboard, Ruth could see two beautiful, smiling girls. They were dressed, identically except the girl on the left was wearing a striped red ribbon in her hair and the girl on right was wearing a blue one. The portrait photographer had captured the girls looking slightly nervous yet obviously happy for the attention. "That's what's the matter!" repeated Irene as she placed a cigarette in her mouth before breaking down into hard, wrenching sobs, her body heaving each time she took a breath.

"They're beautiful," Ruth replied.

"Of course they're beautiful!" Irene mumbled. "They're my only smile in this shitty, forsaken place!" She sniffed and wiped the tears from her face. "Kelly and Sarah. Sarah's the one on the left." Irene tried to smile.

"I'm so sorry that I never knew," Ruth whispered, trying to offer her friend some comfort. Irene didn't seem to hear her and continued talking with the unlit cigarette dangling from her lips. Ruth stared at Irene, watching the cigarette begin to swell as it absorbed the falling tears.

"I was fourteen at the time," Irene continued. "In the sports gym … with Jerry Le Blanc."

"The mayor?"

"No you idiot. His son. … After school. Right in the middle of the gym! Never done anything like it before or since. God, it felt so exciting!" She faked a smile as her unlit cigarette broke at the filter and fell into her lap. "His rough hands and huge dick. Hurting me, it did. He kept apologizing the whole time we were doing it. He was as scared as I was and so cute—he blushed when he came." She paused and began wiping the crumbled tobacco off her lap in hard, quick swipes. "Tripped over his underwear, then started complaining about there being blood on them. What would his mom say? He kept saying." She rolled down her window and spat the damp butt out into the night. Turning to Ruth again, she took the photo and put it back in her purse.

"Jerry Le Blanc?" asked Ruth. "I thought he was in Memphis?"

"He is now! When he found out I was pregnant, his dad sent him up there. I didn't even know I was until it was too late. I think my mom knew before me. Can you believe?"

"Irene I am so—"

"What? Sorry? For what, Ruth? His old man paid for everything! He didn't want a scandal running out of my mouth and ruining his reputation, you know. How do you think I got the job at the lodge? He fixed all that up, you know. And why don't you think I ever get in trouble driving in this thing? Shit! He's so scared I'll tell the whole damn town.

"Where are they now? I mean …"

"Kelly and Sarah? At home with my mom. She looks after them most of the time while I work and go to college, saving every nickel, hoping to send them to a private girls' school down in Baton Rouge."

Irene started crying again. Tears of locked-up guilt and shame poured out of her eyes, spilling onto her face and into her lap. "It's like I'm a ghost here now, you know, Ruth? No one ever notices me now, but I feel so many eyes waiting for me just to crack up, wanting me to disappear, dissolve into thin air or drown in the bayou!"

Without warning, a heavy rain started falling. Large droplets bounced off the windshield, magnifying the darkness. The two girls stared at the raindrops squiggling down the glass. A few minutes later, another truck's headlights filled their cab with a sharp, yellow light. They could see the truck slowing down as it passed beside them, making them both shiver, before it sped off into the darkness.

"Come on." Irene said. "We better get out of here."

"If only … I didn't know Irene … I am so—"

"So what Ruth? Why should you care? You're about to leave, remember?"

They resumed the long drive into the night, passing the fields buckling in the beating rain. The one-good headlight barely cut through the dark, making the fields feels like an endless tunnel from which they could never escape. Razor wire, neon lightning, streaked across the black-ink-sky. Irene turned on her CD player, and Trent Reznor's primal voice welded with the storm, his powerful lyrics echoing a ceaseless endearment that some things can never change no matter how much we try.

Ruth slumped back into the passenger seat and dissolving into the music. Trent Reznor's song, *Hurt*, echoed into the night. For some reason, the lyrics reminded her now of her brother. What was he always telling her? Something about how some songs are like magical spells living in a divine lyrical kingdom. He believed that our lives are often mirrors of these spells and that everything we do, no matter how large or small, originated from the songs we listen to daily. "It's like everyday we are performing the song's magic through our own actions," He would tell her, "and we are all simply a collection of songs that lasts a whole lifetime. It's as if we're living inside one big musical box, living each moment a song at a time."

Ruth closed her eyes and began shaking. All of a sudden, the emotional events of the evening caved in around her. She could feel herself about to pass out. "Stop the truck!" she shouted. "Irene! Please! Pull over!"

Irene hit the brakes, swerved and pulled the truck along a muddy ditch. The truck started to sink into the soft earth and Irene could see Ruth's trembling lips turn blue.

"What's the matter Ruth? You look like death warmed up."

"Hold on a sec ..."

Ruth rummaged through her duffle bag and pulled out a shoebox. She tried to smile as she opened the box and grabbed her insulin syringe.

"What the fuck are you doing?" Irene shouted.

"It's OK Irene. It's only--"

"What the fuck? Are you completely crazy?"

Irene pumped her foot down hard on the gas, jolting the truck forward to get the heavy vehicle out of the mud and back onto the road. The sudden jerking movements made Ruth miss her vein, and the needle went deep into her thin arm before finding bone. She screamed, drawing the needle out before blindly beginning to stab into her arm again, desperately trying to find a vein as the truck continued to swerve out of control.

"Please, Irene! Slow down!"

"What's your fucking problem? You know I don't fool around with none of that shit!"

Irene regained control of the vehicle as Ruth took a deep breath, feeling the insulin entering her body.

"I'm a diabetic!"

"Your what?"

"A DI-A-BET-IC! I have diabetes!"

Irene looked down at the syringe in Ruth's shaking hand then back up into her frozen face. "Damn girlfriend! You OK? I never knew." She eased her foot off the gas peddle and turned the truck stereo down to a low whisper. Ruth took a deep breath and carefully placed the empty syringe back in the shoebox. She slid over the seat and tucked her legs under her chin. She felt damaged and violated. Resting her chin on her knees, she gripped the box and stared out the window into the dark rainy tunnel of night. She could feel her own tears streaming down her face, falling in a fury before disappearing like the raindrops wiped across the windshield. "Why should you care, Irene?" she whispered to her distorted reflection, melting into the rain-soaked miles. "I'm leaving, remember."

ZANE

Readjusting his headphones, Zane cranked up the volume on his portable CD player as a promise made deep within himself crashed and ripped into pieces of his own Destiny, taking on the form of a breeze filling up the vacuous night air. Without looking back, he conversed with the stars and galaxies of unknowns, filled with the hope that Destiny would blow his doubts away. *I didn't want to do this,* he whispered. *None of it, not one single drop.*

He was hoping Destiny would protect him from the fallout of emotions staggering his stride on the unlit road and shelter him from the miserable domestic silence that had grown into tangled knots in the damp pit of his stomach. He wanted to break into the here and now and somehow find a way to cool his swelling cheek and busted bloody lip. Whispering through the fields, he walked a little faster. *Don't turn back, Zane. Don't turn back.* To comfort his sprained wrist, he slipped his hand into his jean pocket and caressed the leather wallet with his fingertips. The contents of the wallet helped ease his overworked mind. The piece of paper with his sister's address made a light shine at the end of the unknown tunnel he felt he was journeying through.

Walking into another deserted mile, with the sound of critters either side of him, gnawing at the cut sugar cane, gnawing away his mother's blank face as he moved towards her, as he felt her arms reject him as she ran into the bedroom whimpering after Arlen. Gnawing away the memories of his former self as he looked around the trailer for something to call home before realizing that all the familiar markings were a mirage evaporating into his parents' fading shadow. He had been living in a slice of jagged time that chewed him up until he had enough courage to spit himself out and squeeze through the screen door like a hungry mosquito. First his nose, then his cheeks, then his scrawny body pushing through the wire mesh, squeezing out his awkwardness like juice squeezing from a lemon, permanently rearranging his adolescence into premature manhood. *Keep going Zane ... Don't even think.*

Walking from where he no longer belonged, with his father's words swarming above his head like hungry horseflies. Dive-bombing and biting his scalp, trying to take pieces of him back to the familiar. So many bits and pieces, so many failed words trying to pull him down to the graveyard silence of boredom and frustration.

Sweat soaked through his "Kiss This" T- shirt. Soaking up his childhood as the gravel road licked his heels, as he tried to suppress the tears. *I want to make my own,* he whispered. *Yes.*

That's what the wind is saying. Go now. Go make your own space with time.

Walking into the unfamiliar passages of his future Zane passed abandoned buildings, nailed and boarded up for sale, their derelict signage and obsolete commerce sneering at him through the peeling lead paint, wanting him to remain in their ruin. A cartoon bubble appeared floating above his head filled with his father's insults and rebuffs and all the misused words Zane had been subjected to for the past sixteen years of his life. He reached down and picked up a stick of willow. He flexed the stick and started whipping it up into the black ink-stained air, lashing at the bubble with its cacophony of letters. He sliced the stick through the darkness for another ten miles until he saw a familiar interstate sign, until he found his mark and the bubble of babble burst, showering him with a storm of malignant words that fell redundant at his feet.

He stood now at the edge of no return. Looking one way, then the other along a deserted stretch of highway, watching with an open mouth as car headlights ripped through the curtain of night and onto the road in front of him. His nerves ripped apart as the headlights, lit up his father's fallen words of abuse, littered on the ground. The car slowed down as Zane pressed the pause button, took a deep breath and kicked at the "get," stamped on the "out," and ground the "stay" back into the dirt.

CHEMICAL SISTERS

Karma Queen's fuel line had been blown out, cleaned and reassembled thanks to the garage beside the exit ramp. Thankfully, the place was open and that much to the Chemical Sisters surprise, a mechanic was on duty. He was a harmless-enough sort, as far as men go, with eyes bobbing through the thick lenses of his wire-rimmed glasses as if they were suspended in two miniature fish bowls. He was constantly shaking his head in disbelief at the idea of a three-cylinder engine. "Just can't figure out why GM would want to make such a silly thing." he would mutter underneath the hood. And no matter how much they tried to convince him otherwise, Old Man Morgan was sure R&R were the prettiest pair of Communists he had ever met.

Reds or not, his generous heart insisted he couldn't let them get back on the road "dressed like that in the middle of the night, especially in these here parts" without him making sure nothing else might go wrong with their car. Grateful that he was working at such a late hour, R&R agreed to let him give Karma Queen his full attention, even if it meant them missing some of their party in New Orleans. At least they would make it to the Hurricane Hotel safe and in one piece. And to top their luck off, Old Man Morgan also refused to charge them the regular price for his labor. "Glad to help out two strangers," he said. "Jus' don't go tellin' mah missus, tis all."

As harmless and helpful as he had been, R&R were glad to be back in the security of their Karma Queen. The Ecstasy they had taken earlier was really kicking in now, impairing their judgment and sending mixed signals to their synapses. One minute they felt slightly paranoid, the next overly ecstatic, and as rebellious as they might appear, neither liked to drive any great distance under any sort of drug influence. They were turning back onto the interstate when they spotted a lone figure stomping and kicking up a cloud of dust.

"He's cute!" Rebecca giggled.

"We don't have the room," Rachael replied.

"Yes we do. Just move all that junk off the back seat."

"You're right. One good deed deserves another, but what's he doing stamping his foot like that?"

"I don't know. Maybe he's trying to dance."

The girls laughed as Karma Queen slowed down beside the boy. Rachael rolled down her window. "You picked a nice time to be hitchhiking!" she said. "You running away from home or what?"

"Hi! … Er, where y'all going?" Zane asked shyly.

"Does it matter? Damn, what happened to your lip?"

"Not really, I guess. My dad."

"Come on, we are going to New Orleans." Rebecca said, acknowledging the weight and sincerity of his remark. "You're gonna be all right kiddo. We know a safe hotel for you to hide in. Y'all see."

"Thanks. A hotel, you said?"

"Yes, well, sort of. C'mon, get in before you fall in. We have a party to catch." Rachael stepped out of the car. *Boys are so goofy* she thought, watching with amusement as he tried to squeeze into the back seat of Karma Queen before apologizing for scattering their clothing.

"Don't worry about all that. Oops! That was a full bottle of glitter." Rebecca said.

"Sorry!" Zane replied, bumping his head on the door frame again.

With one foot in the car and the other out, he started to sway until Rachael grabbed his ass and pushed him over the front seat. "No worries," she said, "Just get in will you? It's creepy out here."

"Sorry."

"And no more sorrys. OK."

Rebecca stared up through the rear mirror. "Hey," she grinned, "your face is covered in glitter! That's too cute!"

"It is?" inquired Zane, feeling himself start to blush.

"And your clothes!" Rachael laughed. "Looks like you're ready to party now!"

"I am!" Zane said. "I really am!"

ARLEN

And I'm lying here knowing I'm dreaming with both eyes open and my arms and legs stretched out like a splayed star. My back is pushed up against a mountain of gravel eating dust, and I can feel a tongue licking me, starting at my toes and the soft skin between them, the tongue licks my wounds. The tongue feels coarse, almost rough on my skin, like a Velcro strap but not quite that sticky. I close my eyes and relax as if I'm partially submerged in a bathtub filled with soapy bubbles. I can see the words of my thoughts drifting up into the cracks of the peeling sheet-rock ceiling like puffy clouds from a fancy cigar someone once gave me for Christmas. The tongue glides over the inside of my leg before licking my groin and balls. I want to say it's Emma Jane finally getting horny again, but I know it's not her tongue because my cock hasn't ever been this hard before, so I lean back and imagine I must be dreaming within a dream. I can feel the long, licking strokes become more and more aggressive against my cock, like how those young girls lick in them porno movies I used to watch when I was stationed abroad. I moan and try to raise my arms above my head because I want to know whose tongue is making me breathe this hard and heavy, but I cannot move. I am stuck like when I was strapped to a hospital bed, so I panic knowing this isn't a dream anymore. I know it has turned into one of my nightmares pretending to be a dream, and I cannot close my eyes because if I do I will see a snow leopard staring into my face. I know it's a snow leopard because I've seen all this before, when I was awake and felt her whiskers and smelled her breath pinning me down into a cold mountain of shale. All I can do is try and forget I'm dreaming, knowing that when I'm awake, my nightmare will be the same. I must somehow forget to remember when the leopard opens her jaws that I must look into her mouth, past her teeth and tongue and into the cave of her guts. I wish I knew a trick to help me forget all this because I don't know what's worse than being awake in a dream or stuck in a nightmare pretending to be a dream. Perhaps if I pretend to close my eyes that are really open and continue lying here like I did that time on the side of a frozen mountain, waiting to be sucked up like a ball of dust spinning inside a vacuum cleaner, the snow leopard will go away and I will be able to dream about something else before I wake up and find myself stretched out on a bunk-bed with some pillows propped up behind my head, looking up through my fingers at a mess of stars.

I am able to reach up and touch the stars with my shaking hand. Touch all the constellations suspended in space. It comforts me knowing I can feel millions of stars, twinkling on my fingertips as if my hand is woven with them through Time. As I touch the stars, my mind feels connected to my thoughts, and for a complete breathe I imagine the stars carrying me through unknown galaxies, making me think, if this is a dream then why would I want to wake from it?

But I really don't want to think that at all! Because as soon as I do, a rifle butt starts hitting the back of my head. Forcing me to look away from the stars and stare at the end of the bed. It's my son's bunk bed I'm lying in, watching a figure approaching through the blue glow of the TV. The figure comes closer until it stops and hovers above me.

Once again, I'm not certain if I'm awake or supposed to be dreaming. I'm confused as to which part of my dream knows I'm thinking these thoughts as the figure goes from electric blue to a recognizable image of a man smiling. I know the man and his name is Peterson from Easton, Pa. He is offering me his outstretched hand, whispering, "You can use this Arlen. You can take my other hand, too."

I start to sweat. Trying to wake out of the part of the dream that knew I was thinking my thoughts would become a nightmare as soon as I wanted to stay dreaming. I know Peterson will remain at the foot of my bed, smiling, and, whether I like it or not, I must try to take control of my nightmare by saying, "Take your bloody hand away from me Peterson. Take it away, I say!" But he cannot hear me or will not listen because he is too busy biting into his other hand. Gnawing at his fingers, he whispers with a mouthful of flesh stuck in between his teeth, "Take it from me Arlen! ... Take my other hand!"

I am screaming in my nightmare again. "Give it to the snow leopard!" I say. "Give your hand back to her!" But my voice sounds like it is falling off the edge of a cliff, and Peterson remains at the end of the bed, chewing at his hand as if he is lost in his own dream and we are in two separate dreams inside my dream that is really a nightmare. As if the blood running down his chin is his nightmare inside his dream and no matter what we do, neither of us can hear the other until I reach for his hand and watch the flesh of his fingers slip off their bones like a silk glove. Now we both start screaming, watching his hand hold onto my hand as his hand comes away from his body. And once again I know I'm awake with my eyes closed, watching a nightmare that will never allow me to dream.

EMMA JANE

Excuse mah language, but after Arlen gone and left, we had to look where he went to, up in an atlas. A dust bowl bigger than twice the size of Texas it was, with nothing on it 'cept some mountains with a bunch of funny names. No wonder we could never get no answers about how they were doin' or what was goin' on or when they were comin' home. Just kept telling us everything was normal and routine and ya know when them brass says that, somethin's up. Sure enough, three months later, I get the phone call that he gone into hospital.

His pa had to close his welding shop and come up to look after the kids while I flew down to meet him. Some joke that was. More like a prison if you ask me. With all those bars and armed guards and security-buzzer stuff just to get in the place and Old Arlen looking as white as his bed sheets with those big leather straps wrapped around him like he was a parcel or something. Everybody treating us like criminals because they were so nervous he was about to get up and attack 'em! I mean, how could he? The entire time he was there, all he did all day was keep on apologizin' and mumblin' at his hands. Rubbing them on those messy PJs they made him wear, must have lost about 30 pounds, he did. What was they feeding him? I kept saying to the doctors, always running around, pretending to look busy before finally telling me there was nothing they could do and how sorry they all were. … Sorry for what? I kept asking! … It wasn't til I got him home did I realize what kind of sorry they were talkin' about. … Not speaking to anyone and sittin' on the couch like a stuffed statue, he did. Wanting nothing but the TV on and mah gumbo that I had to spoon feed him because he was dribbling like a baby for the first six weeks. And if that weren't bad enough, bless his heart, we go get that awful letter, all official an' rude like, saying he was being dishonorably discharged. I thought it was a mean joke after all the times he had gone off to—excuse me—God knows where. … I mean, he was always overseas, he was. Down in South America one year or over in Africa the next. Chasing more of them Russians, no doubt. … Did you know my Arlen was the only person who didn't get sick the whole time he was at work? Never once complained about his job, either, "Just doing mah duty, Emma." he would say. … Got enough medals to prove it, too, if you want my opinion. That purple one is mah favorite. But them brass are cold as fish, they are, you know, all smiles and in ya business one minute, then out on your ear the next. Oh yes! Next thing you know, we were evicted out of their housing! You try dealing with having to pack your whole house up and leave in the middle of winter, around the Christmas holidays, no less! I think they did that on purpose just to rub it in our noses some more, expecting me of all people to do all that drivin' in the freezing snow. Nigh on gave me a nervous breakdown, it did. No wonder I didn't have any mental energy left inside me when Ruth got taken with that diabetics stuff. Hiding in her room with them ugly ladybugs all day, brrrr! … Gives me the creeps just thinking about them! All those creepy-crawlies, crawling on top of each other. In and out of everything, living with her like that! And then we had to stay with his pa down here 'till he fixed us up this trailer. Just for a little while as usual turned into forever! Still, it's not that bad after I added some of mah special TLC. Just wished we had known we couldn't go to the VA Hospital, that's all. You don't really wanna know how much everything costs when your husband is dishonorably discharged. And me not being able to work cause all three of them always needed something. Thank goodness for mah parents, coming through with that money every month. I hated taking it I did. Made me feel like we was a charity case, but we made it, didn't we, Arlen? … You're still my hero. Yes you are.

Emma Jane stops talking to herself and wiped a bead of sweat from Arlen's clammy brow. She looked around the tiny bedroom, watching the blue glow of the TV cast shadows on her son's pile of LPs. Turing to Arlen again, she started running her hand over the cypress bunk bed frame.

Always good with your hands, you were, Arlen. And Pa says you're a damn fine welder. Fixin' all that farm machinery with enough work for years, he says now, that no one can afford to buy any new stuff. … Honest too! Paying off mah parents in no time even though they didn't want no money back. … And then me getting some part-time work at Harvey's Deli & Grocery, bringing home all that good expired stuff. "Nothing wrong with it, you said. They would only get in trouble if it stayed on the shelf Better we go an cook it than it go to no waste. Real ground meat and pork sausages. None of that cheap stuff, you know." Doin' alright, we were, until those nightmares of his started up again. And next thing you know, he's screaming and sweating and screaming some more at all hours in the middle of the night. Always something about dust and snow leopards, some kinda code I thought it was, til we saw the psychiatrist. … Not that he helped any. Felt more sorry for Arlen, being an ex-service man, himself. After a couple of sessions, he sends Arlen home with a bunch of pills that only made matters worse in my mind. … Shaking the whole damn trailer awake and then going into the kids room and waking them and hugging on them as he starts in with all his apologizing and crying. Scared the kids and myself half to death, he did! And then come next morning time, he don't remember a thing about what he had gone and done. Started getting more and more anxious that we were all ganging up on him and talking mean about him behind his back. That's when me an' the kids stopped talking around the house. I kept telling him it was his medication that was makin' him sick, I did. Finally, one night, he listens to me and takes them pills out of the drawers and stuffs all of them down his throat until he throws them right back up again. "Why not use the toilet?", I say. But you know Arlene, it's his way or the highway. What was left in the morning I hid under the bed until I could go and give it to mah neighbor, for a couple of bucks. After that, he admitted they made his stomach burn and drinking was the only thing that really helped calm his nerves in the first place.

Emma Jane slowly unbuttoned her blouse. She placed her hand over her bra and closed her eyes, trying to concentrate on two or three of the hunks she recently saw in one of her *Women Only* magazines. She leaned forward and pressed her body gently against Arlen. Sliding her fingers through his limp hand, she squeezed until her knuckles hurt.

None of them are as big as you anyways. ... Cant blame no one, anyways. ... What's the point now? ... Look at you sleeping. Wouldn't hurt a fly would you? ... I would drink, myself, if I couldn't git me no sleep. ... Like mah zzzzs, I do. Only time I can get some sort of rest from all the voices worrying me all day long. "Never enough this or never enough of that," they say. And our neighbors, laughing all rude-like when he comes home late. Always peeping out their curtains, they are. I mean, it's not like he pulls up into the wrong driveway every night, now, is it? And that Mrs. Granger, still has to go an' gossip about the time he stumbled into her trailer and passed out on her couch with all them sitting at the meal table, eatin' their supper and just gawking at him snoring away in their living room. Had to go and phone the police, she did, instead of simply walking a hundred yards and knocking on mah door. Had to get Arlen arrested for resistin' arrest. As if he hadn't been through enough already. A lot of fuss about nothin', if you ask me. I tried to warn that sheriff. "Don't make mah Arlen mad," I said. "You don't want to be around him, when he gets started." But that Sheriff wasn't doin' no listening, not to no wife, no indeed. Not until he was rushed off to the emergency room to get his bloody nose stitched up.

Emma lets out a sigh and closes her eyes. She can feel her head gently rising and lowering against Arlen's chest.

I know you're a real softy at heart, aren't you, my cuddly hunk of pillow? You go ahead and sleep, all night if you want to. ... Everything's goin' to be alright, just look at them sparrows in the good book they say. ... Don't you worry, come mornin' time, you won't remember a thing and we can start all over again. Jus' like we always do, jus' like as if nothing ever happened.

ZANE

Yeah ... Uh ha ... Sure ... Uh ha.
Way down. Way down.

Satchmo's immortal voice filtered through the Hurricane Hotel and trickled like rain falling down a clogged gutter into Zane's headphones. The Patron Saint of Jelly Roll was up and about cooking his magic, stirring the discombobulated protagonist into the gumbo of Nawlins. And in true tourist form, Zane greeted the Crescent City with an exasperated belch. A moment later, he tried opening his eyes, but they were nowhere to be seen. He felt nauseous and clammy, crumpled in a fetal position, wedged with his neck arched back, lying on something sticky. His limp, hungry body ached from saturated head to toe and for a several grueling minutes, he wondered if he would ever move again.

That lazy hazy river
Where we both can dream.

His confused mind punched in and began working overtime, trying to connect the dots, trying to evaluate his state of, *Where am I?* and *What is this place?* His eyes were in no hurry to help his questioning no matter how hard he tried to open them. In the darkness, he began groping around, inch by inch peeling his damp body off the vinyl couch like an oversized Band-Aid.

Throw away your troubles.
Dream a dream with me.

The giddy sounds of the Master Chef's trumpet continued bouncing from inside the juke box, swerving through the air before somersaulting across the bar room. The melody formed a series of invisible puppet strings that slowly raised Zane's head upright like that of a limp figurine. He had heard this song somewhere long ago, someplace buried deep underneath his skin. *Louis Armstrong*, he thought before slumping back into the couch, his reserve deflating like a soggy balloon.

A feeling of impending doom entangled his mind as he remained nailed to the couch, realizing that he was finally in the cosmic city of New Orleans. A city known for its elastic resilience, where the gumbo don't stop cooking, regardless of how low the flame might be. He took a gulp of stale air, listening to the piano as it added itself into the Roux, shaking in its own alchemy before leading the melody, limb by limb, and resurrecting his puppet-self back to life. His body began slurring in the bar room air until, at last, the gumbo seasoned enough and the spirit of Jelly Roll satisfied, the entire band kicked in and the puppeteer's strings let go, leaving Zane propped upright with his doll-like head tilted on the back edge of the couch. His washed out features gazed blankly toward the ceiling as he opened and closed his mouth, gulping like a catfish thrown out of muddy water.

How happy we could be
If you go up a lazy river with me.

The song on the old jukebox had finished, but until someone kicked it, the mechanical arm wouldn't release, leaving the needle slipping in the record's well-worn groove. Zane swayed as he tried to focus into the void of the half-lit bar room spinning at an elliptical 45 revolutions per minute. He raised his hand and, concentrating on his index finger, managed to bring the room to a halt. Satisfied that the room wasn't moving anymore, he tried breathing again only to realize that his tongue had been replaced with twenty-grit sandpaper.

Several streaks of daylight had managed to break through the aluminum-foil-taped windows and were cutting shafts of pale light through the ominous dark vacuum of the bar room.

Some of the light particles found themselves being sucked up into the ceiling with the cigarette smoke until a large, oscillating fan, nailed to the far corner of the bar, sent the smoke careening back down, creating a whirlpool mist in the middle of the dance floor. Zane tried to focus through the mist, his eyes following the hectic movements of the bouncing light, until totally dizzy he stared upward at the ghoulish whisper-thin clouds forming faces that appeared to be trapped and hovering just below the ceiling. Feeling nauseous again, he looked down and studied his boots. They were soaking wet, and the untied laces resembled a pair of squashed earthworms, dangling out of a soggy canvas tackle box.

"Hey! Looks who's coming alive!" a voice shouted from the mist.

"Welcome to the land of the dead!" another unknown voice laughed.

Zane reluctantly raised his head and tried to focus in the direction of the laughter. Squinting, he could make out twelve or so shadows hunched or propped against a bar, their silhouettes reminding him of a smoggy reproduction of da Vinci's *Last Supper*. One of the smudgy apostles floated toward him. "Here," it said. "Drink this." As if taking communion, Zane solemnly offered up his lips and sipped from a small plastic cup. Before the cold liquid had gone down his throat, he retched and vomited all over himself. "Sorry," he mumbled, wiping hot, soggy lumps from his mouth and chin.

"Oh boy," said the cup bearer, "You're a mess, lad. The Ship of Fools gone an' caught her another."

Zane could hear more grizzly laughter issuing from the bar as he began to wipe the rest of himself down. He felt a little better now, almost relieved. His eyes started to close down again just as someone kicked the side of the jukebox. Images of the night before began swirling like the bar room inside his stretched-out mind. He vaguely remembered arriving at the hotel with the Chemical Sisters and the wild energy on the dance floor before he was given some sort of pill, before dancing and drinking some more, before another song on the jukebox began to wind itself up, before Zane spiraled back into unconsciousness.

TREME

Grinning like a mischievous boy from one diamond studded ear to the other, Treme watched the sun climb slowly out of the Mississippi River into the gray muddy sky. He propped his bare feet up on the cast-iron railing of the Hurricane Hotel's third-floor balcony and, from this view, overlooking St. Charles Avenue, he could see the Crescent City Bridge looking like it was about to buckle and melt under the weight of the rising, flaming orb. He took off his shades and stared directly into the sun, trying to figure out just how big it actually was as it rose through the rain like a fiery, exploding bomb. "That's my kinda power," he mumbled, blinking into the sun.

Treme wasn't one to waste time or energy surveying the natural wonders of the world, but today, he felt he could appreciate the view, seeing as it was going to be the last time he would be hang out here, on his balcony. He covered his eyes again and tried to savor the relaxing moment. "Life doesn't get much better," he said to his bare feet. "All one, big, smooth groove. You just gotta know when to change the record, dat's all." He took a long, relaxed drag of his smoke and glanced through the balcony's metal floor. Between his legs, a black Ford was parked on the street. It had been there all night and now Treme was becoming highly suspicious of its contents. "Don't be messin' wit' me," he said, blowing cigarette smoke through the floor, "Not today!"

One more night of trading down on the dance floor, and he was going to walk away with enough cash to hook up with his girlfriend's cousin, who had just opened a nightclub in Miami. "How long can one more night be?" he beamed, baring a set of brightly polished gold teeth. "I'm gonna eat you up one day for breakfast, Mister Sun! You'll see!"

Known for never backing down no matter how crazy the situation, Treme was a street-smart professional. Born with a sixth survival sense for fishing out any narcotics agent or rival gang member trying to harm his big plans, he had become a respected member of the underground night scene. Through his music, he had made all the right connections without selling himself short, and six years of working his DJ gig to the max and selling anything deemed illegal by those high-minded folks who had nothing better to do than mess with his plans had resulted in his reputation as "Mr. Super Fly with the razor sharp teeth." Sure, he had been dealt a few blows in his time, usually by the make-sure-to-be-seen-in-church-to-get-a-political-ticket-folks who actually had their own lists of dirty laundry so filthy it didn't take long for Treme's attorney to uncover who was the criminal and who was simply trying to mahke it and who hadn't. Once all the "cards" were on the chopping block, so to speak, a truce always came to pass real quick-like, and after a few long-winded, plaintive words by his accompanying legal counsel and then a week or two of chillin' in his crib, it was business as usual for Treme, spinning his sounds and shuffling his deals deep behind enemy lines.

He took a sip of his Crown 'n' Coke, crunching down hard on a piece of ice. "Just play it cool, bra!" he said to a bunch of pigeons sitting on the red-tile roof across the street from himself and the parked car. "One more night, then I'm outta here!" His plan was to slip away after he had finished spinning his last set, around 4 a.m., then get Sophia to collect the rest of his money and meet her at his sister's crib down in the Lower Ninth Ward. If push came to shove, he would exit through the rear of the hotel and hop over the adjoining parking lot, even if it meant scaling a razor-wire fence. *What could be simpler,* he thought, sipping his drink again. Still, he could feel one of his "concerns" coming on, and Treme didn't like no concerns, especially the ones that went around sticking their noses and flashing their badges into his business. He spat his cigarette through the floor. "Who da fuck do ya think ya are, messin wit' mah plans?" he growled, as the red-hot missile bounced on the black LTD's roof. Crunching down on more alcohol-drenched ice, he flashed his gold teeth as the cigarette ember faded into ash.

ZANE

"Wake up, Baby Face!" a stale-breathed voice shouted. "Party's over! ... Hey, Snow White, wake up!"

Zane's consciousness slipped back into something hard that jabbed at his ribs. He peeled open his heavy eyelids and was greeted by a large, metal nose ring the size of a sliver dollar shining through a pair of flayed nostrils.

"You're a mess," the silver nose ring, snorted.

"I know." Zane replied sluggishly, trying to regain some sense of where he was. He stared into a pair of dark brown eyes that were surrounded by two black pools floating on a bald head, giving the impression of an emaciated, shaved panda.

"You want a job or not?" The nose ring continued. "Don't seem to me like you got any choice. Moose seems to like you."

Zane could hear unfamiliar voices laughing through the mist. "Who is … Moose?" he mumbled.

"You'll find out one of these days. Anyway, I'm sick of cleaning up this shit hole. It's all yours, sister! My tattoos never scab over properly here. Probably from all the friggin' funk! I'm outta this dump before I end up catching something contagious-like!"

"What's that in your nose?" Zane blurted. He was eye level with the silver bobbing dollar now. "Does that hurt?" he continued, eyeing at his own reflection staring back at him from the ring's smooth surface.

"Eh? Yeah, I can't put a bandage on them. They're supposed to dry in the air. Some joke that is, what with all the humidity an' beer an' piss! I think it seeps up into the ink when I'm mopping these disgusting floors. Just look at 'em!"

"Look at what?" Zane asked. "Your nose ring?"

"Of course it fucking hurts! What's the point of no pain?"

"I hate pain."

"Oh yeah? Well, you went and landed in the wrong place for that one, buddy! It's life, you know! A reminder that y'all just cattle. The chicks love it though. Being led to the slaughter before getting the big zap! If you know what I mean, wink, wink. Anyway, here's your key. The boss might be in around noon, if he ain't too messed up himself, that is. Tell him I told you to tell him to go stick this mop handle right up his tight ass! Twenty bucks to clean this shit hole just ain't worth a crap. It's not like the free room is any good anyhows, what with sharing a bathroom with all those screaming queens. Just isn't my scene.

Always doin' something to themselves, they are, in that bathroom, you know! Either playin' with each other's hairy balls or cleaning the jizz from underneath their nails. You'll see. Pubic hair and toenail clippings all over the place and not a sanitary towel amongst them! All I can say is be thankful none of them ever get on the rag!"

Aaron thrust the mop toward Zane, then continued breathing foul air into his face. "The rest of the cleaning stuff is behind the bar, in that back room. Watch out for needles. It's a right shooting gallery up in there. Fuckin' junkies every where these days. The toilets are blocked up again, too, thanks to that crazy Voodoo Witch. Somehow she managed to slip in here again late last night. I guess when everyone was so trashed, they couldn't tell their own ass from their face. In she shrank like an invisible germ sneezing out your nose!"

"Is she still there?"

"Who? What are you talking about?"

"The Voodoo Lady. Is she still stuck in the toilet?"

"Damn! What are you trippin' on? No, you idiot. She comes in here and stuffs handfuls of torn sheets from those Bible tracts of hers down the toilet so damn hard you can't ever get 'em out! And then pulls the chain. Not sure were she keeps getting all them Bibles from. Probably steals 'em from one of the hotels downtown."

"What's your name?" Zane thought to ask.

"Shit. I don't know. You can always recognize her when she comes in here. Anyhow, how many witches do you know, eh? She's about three-foot-six and weighs less than sixty pounds, one hundred percent Indian, you can't miss her." He stretched out his arms as if indicating the size of a fish. "And the plumber ain't worth a crap, either! No use you callin' him up. He only comes here when he's run out of party favors, if you know what I mean. That's how everyone gets paid around here, by the way. But don't go telling no one I said so. Boss gets mad if the toilets aren't clean. He says it's bad for business, so if I were you—and I'm sure glad I ain't—I would get your ass into gear."

"No, I won't. I mean, what's your name?" Zane repeated.

"What? Oh, Aaron. Why? What's up?"

"Nothin'. Just—"

"There's rubber gloves back up in there. You can get money from the bartender for paper towels and DrainO. Just bring the receipts back."

"I'm Zane."

"Whatever, dude."

Aaron slipped back into the mist. He kicked a beer bottle as his visage slinked across the dance floor. The bottle broke instantly. From behind the bar someone shouted, "Asshole!"

"Fuck you, too!" Aaron cursed as he opened the front doors of the bar room before disappearing into the daylight. For a brief moment, blinding sunlight streamed into the bar, lighting up the entire room like a hand-grenade flash. Then, as quickly as it had entered, the light dispersed, leaving the smoky darkness to settle again. The force of Aaron slamming the door had knocked the exit sign off the wall. Zane watched as it bobbed and flickered on two wires like a toy boat adrift on a smoke-filled pond. Finally, the sign came to rest twelve inches below the top of the doorframe so that whoever entered the bar next would have to duck or hit their head.

Outside the hotel, a streetcar rumbled along the avenue. From where Zane was slumped, the trolley sounded more like a train thundering through a collapsing tunnel than an innocent vehicle of public transportation. He could hear some bottles and glasses rattle on the bar and a Zippo lighter click open, but he couldn't see any flame. The bar felt deserted, though he knew there were people in there, somewhere. The jukebox had stalled again, and the only indication that there had been any sort of life in the place was from the tired, whirring sound of the fan and a square digital clock crammed above the bar, silently counting down the seconds to the next Mardi Gras.

The sunlight that had rudely entered the room a few moments earlier had finally evaporated, settling the mist so Zane's eyes could adjust to the heavy darkness. As he began to survey the surroundings of this stagnant catacomb, he noticed above the bar hundreds of Christmas lights emitting a faint, red, velvety glow. The lights flickered on and off at such long and random intervals that there were times when Zane would forgot they were even there. When they did come on, Zane could see through the stale cigarette clouds, a maze of broken air-conditioning ducts suspended with wire and looking like they were about to collapse onto the floor at any moment. In the torn, silver-insulated mouth of each duct, a pair of mannequin legs spewed out of the tubing. "Weird man." Zane mumbled as the lights flicked off again.

In the middle of the ceiling, suspended about ten feet from the floor was a large disco ball with vast patches of mirrors missing from its surface. The ball was spinning reluctantly, sixty degrees one way then thirty degrees the other. To its right, Zane could make out a pile of tables and chairs that had been thrown haphazardly against what looked like a makeshift stage. Next to the stage was a long corridor leading down to another dark passageway. "Well, I'm here now." he said aloud, gripping his hands tightly around the wet broom handle as if to reassure himself this was actually true. "Things could be worse," he muttered, trying to bolster his spirits. An outline of a payphone receiver dangling from one of the hallway walls came into focus and instinctively he went for his wallet. "Ruth," he said to himself, looking down at his clothing, stained with crusty vomit. "What a mess. She can't see me like this." He slipped his hand into his back pocket and rummaged for change. A moment later, he stood up frantically and almost toppled over from the rush of blood speeding into his brain. The broom handle flipped up and hit him square on the chin as if mimicking an old Laurel and Hardy skit. "Ow!" he yelped before realizing his zipper was undone and someone had removed his jean belt. "Why me?" he shouted into the void, trying to hold up his jeans as he begun searching for his wallet. First the back pockets, then the front, then the back again as his actions become more and more frantic with each failed gesture. He moaned and searched the seat of the couch before slipping his fingers down the crack of its torn and padded back...Still no luck. He was crouching now, gazing blankly under the seat, wiping away a slew of plastic cups and beer cans. The stench of the dance floor made him want to gag. He stood up and took in some air before searching his pockets again. Nothing. In an exhausted gesture, he sunk back the floor and kneeled among the debris.

"You looking for something?" a voice asked from the darkness.

Zane looked up in the direction of the voice. Squinting, he tried to make out who or what had spoken to him. "Um ... yes." he replied. "My wallet and my sister's phone number."

"You mean this?"

The Christmas lights flickered on. In the far right-hand corner of the room, behind the bar, stood a figure with an outstretched arm.

"Is it a wallet?" Zane asked hopefully.

"Yes! But there ain't no money in it! … Sorry. I already gone an' checked."

Clutching his jeans, Zane stood up and started shuffling toward the voice. He was desperately hoping that he wouldn't trip over his own loose laces and that the Christmas lights would stay on long enough for him to wade through the sea of broken glass. He lurched forward, and when the bar came into view, he dived and managed to grip its slick wooden edge. A sense of security overwhelmed him, and he thought for a moment that he might make it through all this madness.

Propping himself up at the bar, Zane looked around for the voice he had just spoken to. "Hello?" he said, as the lights flickered off.

TREME

Ducking, Treme stepped through the double windows into the kitchen of the Hurricane Hotel's loosely termed penthouse suite. He tip-toed over the piles of clothing and sleeveless vinyl disks and lit cigarette. His gut instinct told him that Aaron had something to do with the black car outside. "Don't go getting' no paranoia now." he said to a pile of half-empty Chinese food to-go boxes, "Not this close. Shit. No one here ever trusts no one here anywayz! Everyone gets a turn at being called a narc up in this place til something else happens, an' then itz someonez else ez turn. Itz like what Some Guy Upstairs always sez. Thatz just one of the deals of livin' here. Kinda healthy in his mind, makes us all equalz he sez!"

Until recently it seemed to Treme that Aaron had been behaving like a regular good dog, selling lot's of merchandize without the usual user excuses. "Wait a minute," Treme frowned, "Come to tink about it, datz all irregular in itself. He sure has been acting real suspicious-like the past couple of nights! That slimy, bald-faced punk-nosed mother fucker. He can move mah merchandize, though. Dat's the truth."

He rummaged through a pile of dirty laundry, searching for a pair of clean socks. "Aaron," he continued, "I'll go down an check on you real soon! Make sure he's got mah monies from last night and try an feel him out a little. For sure he must know how much I'm packing in." He stopped talking to himself and stared at a sock before sniffing it. "Damn!" he shouted, throwing the sock back onto the floor. "Wake up Treme," he mumbled. "So does everybody else 'round here. After all, you're the only dealer on these premises worth any-ting. Sure, they can always get a bag or two from the girlz, day or night, but why would ya want to be snortin', two-thirds bakin' powder and two-thirds rat poison up your nose? I know you're a slimy bird, Aaron, divvying up your own bags smaller than whenz I give 'em to ya, but I noze you don't cut 'em with nothin' nasty like bleach an shit. And the weekend crowd just eatz it all up. I mean it, Aaron. I'll blow ya balls off if you messes with mah plans. Damn! How come everything stinks up in here?" He rooted around for his gun. What he really wanted to do was fire off a few rounds, shaping one big X into the parked car's roof, just to see who would come squealing out. "Give them something to dunk their jelly donuts in," he smirked. "Then again, I'd better not. Better stay cool. Only one more night in this rat-infested dump an' then it's Miami Chan-Chan, here we come!"

Treme had been living off and on at the Hurricane Hotel for the past three years with few hitches. Most of the heat had been from the Tobacco and Firearms goons trying to bust the owner of the hotel for any lame thing their simple minds could think of. Often bringing in bus loads of fire marshals at 3 a.m. to check the fire extinguisher's expiration dates or arranging for a 16-year-old, eight-foot dude who looked like he had just turned 30 to ask the stressed bartender for a pack of smokes at the busiest time of the night, right before shift change, hoping to pop a lame-ass ticket on her for selling tobacco to minors. Then there was always the occasional strung-out-narc, for real with nothing better to do than rent a room at the hotel before trying to cash in on some chick-crazed coke action. They never hung around too long, especially after the "Girlz," had finished getting him all wasted and tied up in uncompromising positions, before waking up to find a Polaroid had been pinned to his limp dick. Nigh on illegal, in Treme's mind, but it worked smooth like clockwork and always sent the heat packing elsewhere, at least for a little while longer. Treme didn't much care for those girlz though, never was into any of their "funny stuff." "You're either a nigga or not," he would tell Martha if she started up with one of her love troubles. "Make up your mind, go on your instinct, and then do the opposite." Treme would snicker even though everyone at the hotel secretly knew he was actually very happy they were creating their rehearsed distractions. And in return for their services, he always gave them a "fair deal" if they were out of credit or buying his merchandise wholesale.

He put on his bathrobe and stepped over a pile of Popeye's containers. Kneeling down, he kissed Sophia tenderly on the cheek. "Just looking at her asleep makes mah dick hard," he said to himself. "Those lips of hers can do some damage, datz for sure! Never did understand mah brothers wanting any of that white meat. I like mine pure dark, inside and out." He stood up and tightened the robe, covering his throbbing log just as Sophia opened her eyes and smiled. "Hey, baby," she said.

"Hey, Sugar. You dreamin' bout Miami an' all them hot nights with your man?"

"Oh yeah." Sophia yawned and pulled away the covers. "That sounds nice. Why don't you come over here, honey, so we do some dreaming together." She patted the bed with her hand.

"I got me mah biz-niss to attend to. Some-tins on mah mind."

"What about puttin' some of that mind right here?" Sophia flashed one of her to-die-for smiles and turned onto her belly.

She leaned forward raising her ass up into the air and wiggled it, real slow-like.

"Baby, that's damn illegal in some parts I know." Treme whistled.

"Not in my parts!" laughed Sophia. "C'mon. Come wake me up a little."

Treme slowly took off his bathrobe and teasingly begin to flex his tight stomach muscles. Swinging his shoulders he sauntered over to their bed.

"Come an get me baby!" Sophia giggled. "Eyez ready for a dream or two."

"Eyez-err coming. Eyez-err coming.--What the fuck?" Treme looked down at his bare foot sitting in a broken Styrofoam container of cold mashed potatoes. The congealing gravy was already oozing between his toes.

"What's the matter, baby?"

"This place!" Treme cursed. "Thatz whatz der matter! Itz filthy! Looks like a bunch of white nigga's been livin' up in here!"

"I'll clean it up later, Sugar. Just for you. C'mon, baby, I'm getting' cold down here."

"You've been saying that for weeks. Shit, Sophia! I got gravy in mah toes!"

Sophia started laughing. "Let me suck 'em clean for you."

"Damn girl. You're one hot bootieed vacuum cleaner."

"You complaining, Mr. Treme? I SAID. I'll clean up. An I's will! But first, you gotta pay the room service."

Treme hobbled around on one foot. Using his bathrobe, he wiped the cold gravy off his feet. "I ain't complainin' none," he said. "Just got things on mah mind. That's all." He slipped onto the bed and straddled Sophia's warm body. Leaning forward he kissed her smooth back and neck.

Sophia moaned. She raised her knees and whispered up to him, "Quit all that thinkin' will ya? And just for a little while, love me like your momma!"

MONA

Pulling down her stained, leopard-skin panties, Mona perched herself on the ripped-vinyl, cigarette-burned, floral, padded toilet seat. She took a deep breath and, leaning over the seat, picked up a beaded handheld mirror that Some Guy Upstairs had made for her 21st birthday. "When was that now?" she said to her oval reflection. "Six, maybe eight weeks ago?"

Today wasn't starting out too well and Mona knew that had to be fixed, real quick. Last night's frolicking antics, like every night, lately, had not helped matters either. In fact, the blur of events had come to a dismal crash-landing, with her usual ungracious style of taking advantage of male bodies, whether they were in a comatose state or strung out on the couch known to all occupants of the Hurricane Hotel as the Ship of Fools. Mona knew she just couldn't go on behaving like this forever, but in the mean, lean time, like every other morning for the past two years, the only way to prevent this all from happening eternally was to continue doing it just a little less often. In this way, tonight would never seem as bad as last night or the night before. Such was the confused-mind logic of this beautiful angel.

Using two razor-sharp fingernails, Mona plucked a plastic bag from her bra. She carefully spilled the crystal-contents onto the smeared mirror. Rummaging thru her bra again, she found another bag and flicked it hard from her wrist before inspecting it in the blue light. Nodding to herself in agreement, she mechanically opened and poured the powdery contents next to the first pile. She leaned over from her vinyl throne, opened the medicine/shoe/panty hamper, and blindly searched through the mixed contents until she found a pair of tweezers. With another outstretched hand in the direction of the sink, she removed with her pinky and thumb a chewed up plastic straw from a lipstick-stained plastic cup that also held a congealing pink concoction and a semi-submerged rotting slice of lime. She ran the straw between her purple-smeared lips before carefully wiping the straw dry with a piece of crumpled napkin that had been stuck to the sole of her platform shoe for most of the prior evening. Somewhat exhausted from all this activity, she peered down at her reflection and watched in horror as her face began puffing up like a porous raspberry sponge. She opened her mouth, began examining a large silver ring pierced through her tongue, and was relieved to find no pubic hair wedged between it and her favorite fleshy organ. This observation made her smile and glance into the bedroom, where her favorite collection of organs was starting to stir on the bed/couch/stage.

The amount of privacy that Mona required for her morning ritual depended on how manic she was feeling as a result of the night before. Today, total seclusion was an absolute must, so she braced herself on the tilting commode and kicked the bathroom door with her heel. As usual, the door merely ricocheted against its warped frame before slowly squeaking back to its original, non-private position. She stuck her tongue out at the door hinges, shrugged her shoulders, and with the same foot began sliding an overflowing box of shoes/cosmetics/clothing toward the door. Once the box had made contact, Mona raised herself off the toilet and kicked at the box until a two-inch gap remained between her and the ever-present outside world. Dissatisfied but realistic, Mona knew this was the maximum amount of privacy she would ever get during her lifetime and, leaning back, exhaled an exhausted sigh of completion before lighting a cigarette.

"I think it must have been seven weeks ago," she mumbled, before making four heaped lines of cocaine/baking powder and four thicker lines of crystal/meth. Her eyes where trying to focus on her eyes trying to focus on the eight lines. Shyly, she began whispering to them one of her many memorized nursery rhymes;

Everyone's a Meanie
And Mona's a little ho!
Guess all of you
Will just have to go!

She placed the burning cigarette on the edge of the bathtub and watched with satisfaction as the ash fell into a pool of something growing inside the tub that she would rather not have to think about cleaning up. Checking that her privacy was still quasi-satisfactory, she leaned forward and snorted two lines of coke/baking powder and then immediately two lines of crystal/meth.

Mona jolted her head back like a wild horse breaking free from its reins as the mixture scorched her blistered sinuses. Instantly, her bowels opened, releasing first an enormous expanse of gas, then two loud squirts of liquefied feces. She tilted her head back to the mirror, feeling the warm liquid sliding out from her sore anus and let out a sigh as a few droplets began running down her inner thigh before reluctantly finding most of their way into the toilet bowl.

Breakfast of champions
Sounds like a scam!
Cause it ain't what you eat
That makes Mona shit!

Mona relaxed with a sense of achievement as another burst of hot liquid exploded and discharged itself, causing the cracked toilet to creak on the buckling, stained linoleum floor. She looked down between her knees and mumbled to herself, "One day, I'm gonna fall right through this dump."

A zigzag line of black ants appeared. They were following the rusting plumbing down the damp, peeling sheetrock wall before nonchalantly crossing over the few feet of blue circa-1970s flooring. Mona watched the ants and felt herself hypnotized as her eyes followed the insects' early morning sojourn into her world. Several minutes later, they disappeared beneath a broken brick used to prop up a clawless, footed bathtub. As Mona contemplated the ants' exit, she was filled with a euphoric combination of relief and dire loss, a sad and common malady for the likes of Mona, who was diagnosed as an overweight anorexic. Without further warning, she burst forth in a resounding flurry of verse, causing the half-awake Martha to scream at the bathroom door: "Shut the fuck up!"

Crushed once again by Martha's seemingly lack of compassion for her lyrical talents, Mona lit another cigarette. After taking several long, hard drags, she carefully balanced the cigarette on the side of the bathtub again alongside a row of butts.

She picked up the tweezers from the top of the hamper and hunched back over the beaded mirror. Tears welled up inside her four eyes as she plucked at a nest of nose hairs. Concerned that a runaway tear might land in the remaining white powder, she finished them off before rocking herself on the commode, flushed and filled with an absolute sadness that the ants had left her all alone to deal with the logic that each day tangled up her beautiful childish mind.

I wonder who y'all be,
Laying down there in wait for me.
Maybe some hideous hunk
With a two-foot hard on trunk,
Waving his magic at me.

Casting Mona under his spell
Like a misplaced millionaire
Or a hero amputee,
Cumming all over my crucified body,
Someone as emotional and perfect as me!

JAKE

"Here, smoke this!"

"I don't smoke no dope."

"You do now."

Jake watched Zane nervously take a hit and instantly gag. Zane coughed again and then took another toke. He passed the joint back to Jake and felt a calm numbness fold over him like a love letter being sealed in an envelope moistened by a sweetheart's lips.

"You're a mess," Jake said.

"I know it. Anything else? I lost my wallet."

"I know. I found it on the floor of the bar room this morning," Jake reminded him.

Zane slumped back onto a barstool and stared at his distorted reflection in the mirror behind the bar. "Wow. That's strong stuff. Thanks, I guess."

"No problem. Take some more. It'll help you get through the next couple of seconds, help organize the rollicking pace of the Hurricane Hotel! By the way, Jake's mah name and guess what's mah game?"

"I'm Zane. Well it was last night." The two boys laughed as Jake continued, "The Old Ship of Fools got you real good, didn't it?"

"What's the Ship of Fools?"

"That fair-weather friend of a couch, over there." Jake pointed into the mist. "That red stick of vinyl tongue you passed out on."

"Whoa, I don't think I can remember that far back. Why the name?"

"That's easy. Don't you feel just a little bit foolish this morning, or what?"

"I get it."

"Finally. If it's any consolation, it's happened to the best and worst of us. Just don't go getting caught with your pants down twice. If you know what I mean. People will think you like it that way."

"I'll try. Pleased to meet you, Jake." Zane offered his hand.

"No problem. I don't shake no hands, though. Nothing personal."

Zane placed his hand back on the bar and then contemplated his fingernails. He was feeling relaxed, all things considered, and as he watched Jake return from the cooler with a couple of beers, he felt almost mellow.

"Have a beer. It will help with the sandpaper in your mouth. On the house."

"Thanks. Don't mind if I do."

For several minutes they sipped in silence. Then Jake said, "Tastes good, eh?"

"I think so," Zane relied, waiting to see if his stomach could handle anything else. "What's all this?" he pointed at the bar top.

"Recycled Mardi Gras beads. Some Guy Upstairs made it somehow. That's him down there at the middle of the bar, daydreaming with his tape recorder. Made it in exchange for a bunch of rent and a pound of the old Coca Cola. It's been in magazines an' shit like that." Jake wiped away a pile of plastic cups and emptied an overflowing ashtray onto the floor, then pointed rather proudly at the cleaned section of bar top. "Look, here's yours truly, in all his glory. Pretty cool, huh?"

Zane wiped away a foggy film of sticky alcohol, trying to make out what it was Jake was referring to. "It's an orange octopus," he finally remarked, rather surprised.

"Sure is!" beamed Jake.

"Looks more like you than you do!" Zane laughed.

"Funny one, aren't ya?"

"Used to think so until all this happened. Did you say you had mah wallet?"

"Here you go. I had it drying out behind one of the coolers."

Zane opened the soggy leather wallet and produced a scrap of mushy paper.

"What's that? A ticket?"

"It used to be my sister's address and phone number."

"Where is she? Maybe she's in the phone book."

"Down here someplace. I doubt it. She's a nurse and has to be careful, you know."

"You'll find her," Jake said, offering some much-needed encouragement. "A nurse you say? Where? Charity Hospital?"

"How did you know?"

"I was just guessing. They say it's the best place in the world for gun-shot wounds and overdoses. I wanna check the place out someday. Is she cute?"

"Yes. Very. Why?"

"Just kiddin'. Lighten up now, will you! You're gonna be all right. You'll see. I can tell by looking in your eyes that you aren't no asshole. But first things first, right? Clean-up time! What you say? I got some extra clothes in my room, and you can use my shower if the ladies have invaded yours."

"What ladies?"

"Martha and Mona. You'll meet them soon enough. Don't listen to nothing Aaron says. He's been acting weird lately. Word is he's a narc. Then again, that don't mean too much around here. After a while, everybody will think you're one, too. It just goes with the territory. As for the hotel boss, he's actually a pretty cool dude. Straight up, you know? And if he don't spot you some cash, Moose at the end of the bar will. Just tell him you love the Irish! You do, don't you? Hell, they both helped me get back on mah feet after the ex went and threw me out."

"Why'd she do that?"

"Can you believe it was because I couldn't have her baby?"

"You don't look like a family man to me. No offense."

"Stranger things have happened. Let's have another beer. Enough of my domestic bullshit."

"Thanks. My clothes are starting to feel like cardboard. Another beer oughta help."

They finished their beers and grabbed two more for the road. Zane followed Jake across the littered barroom. "I'll clean up this mess down here and the bathrooms for you," Jake said. "Today feels pretty slow, and I don't like sitting around doing nothing. You just deal with yourself and the rooms upstairs. OK?"

"What rooms?"

"Upstairs. You got your key Aaron gave you, remember? We got about thirty rooms, I think, maybe a few more, maybe less, I don't really know, it seems like they keep disappearing then reappearing."

"Where do they go?"

"Oh I don't know. Some get strung out, some disappear into another dimension, kinda like the folks staying in them. What do you expect? You're in the Hurricane Hotel! Here we are." Jake opened a battered, broken-hinged door and motioned a curtsy. "Ladies before gentlemen," he grinned. "I'm talking to you Ms. Zane. Welcome to the Pleasure Dome!"

SOME GUY UPSTAIRS

Where have I seen that face before? ... No. ... It was. ... Yes! ... When was that? He wasn't wearing. ... No! ... How come I can't ever remember a name, only a face? ... What did Jake say? Come on! Shit! It was only a minute ago! ... That's right! Zane, I think he said. ... Kinda cool sounding, like a hand coming down on a mosquito. Maybe he has an older brother. ... No, I think it must have been his. ... Well,

well, well. This might be my lucky day! Look who just walked into the barroom. If it isn't old what's his name. ... Hi there. ... Shit! What'd you say your name was again?

MOLLY

The temporary housing arrangement Molly had offered Jake when he first appeared, with two broken ribs, quickly changed from "a couple nights," to semi-permanent. She didn't really care how long he stayed. After all, her three-story home had plenty of room to be alone when she needed to work, and Jake seemed house trained, aside from his laundry, which she simply refused to do. He became a pleasing distraction from her numbers and the idea of not having to go to a bar and pick up another loser just to get laid for a night. The fact that he could be part of her spawning project quickly became Attribute #3. And for all his rebel rousing and chest strutting, Molly found him to be quite the idle homebody, preferring a good book to TV and fresh meat to fried.

After several months of congenial cohabitating, Molly softened a little, and Jake found himself enjoying her family-owned and-operated mansion—paid for in cash, she would always add never being one for loans—historically preserved, smack in the middle of one of the most romantic spots in the world. Their nights filled with sensual delights from the exotic cuisines whose salivating ingredient's wafted through the cobbled streets, cooled by the soft breezes blowing off the Mississippi River. They would aimlessly stroll until 4 a.m., immersing themselves in an architecture that seemed to smooth and caress every crease of their minds and bodies, both lost in a time when waking at noon to the smell of coffee and beignets from Café Du Monde seemed like the most important routine of the day, a time when everything seemed possible, when they believed they were free to leave anytime they chose.

Magical days turned into magical weeks, then months. Molly worked her numbers while Jake tinkered with neon lighting. It became apparent that he had a natural genius for design, and Molly supported his new interest with enthusiasm even though electricity terrified her. Everything was going according to her detailed plan until Jake, supported by the Uptown Cocaine Club, started exhibiting his neon and glasswork in local galleries. Before long, he wasn't coming home at night or the next day or even the day after that, and pieces of Molly's gothic, antique silverware began reappearing in the French Quarter antique stores. She often left her safe with a few hundred dollars stored for cash-flow purposes unlocked, but after Jake started on the cocaine it became apparent he was skimming off the top. Fights and accusations broke out, resulting in drunk fights and fierce denials. The more Jake immersed himself in his new drug habit the more his qualities disappeared and just as happens during any extended use hard drugs, Molly woke up one morning to the realization that both Jake's smile and his cock had vanished or were buried so deep within a nervous body, she barely recognized either of them. So she went directly to Plan B. She removed most of the money from the safe, hoping it would regulate his drug consumption. Then she took herself off the pill, quit drinking, and, after three months sober, fucked Jake's brains out at every available opportunity, often when he was comatose. After sixteen weeks of this rather sordid, regimented routine and no hint of a baby appearing, Molly went to her gynecologist with a sample of Jake's intoxicated sperm. A week later, in the very same office, she received the lab results indicating that it was, her egg that was infertile, thanks to a rare hereditary disorder that had lay dormant for a few generations.

Molly's way of grieving such a cruel and unfair fact consisted of taking Jake back emotionally under her clipped and torn wings. Her relentless cajoling to quit his habit finally sent the two to a month-long rehab/vacation to a clinic/resort in Barbados. After a thankless week of Jake carousing until the mid-morning hours when he would appear only to grab a few hours kip, Molly booked the next available seats home to New Orleans. She flushed his door key down her toilet, kicked his ass out onto the very same 4 a.m. streets where they aimlessly bathed six months prior.

Trying to expel Jake's lingering presence was no easy matter, and Molly finally set a large, silver platter on the family dining room table, lit all the candles in the house, built a large pyramid out of her maternity books, and garnished the four-sided triangle with her shredded sperm donor notebook. She saturated the entire offering with lighter fluid, leaned over the table on tipsy-toes and ignited the evaporating fluid with a lit cigarette held tight between her painted lips. An hour later, when the cathedral bells struck 12, she dumped the smoldering ashes into a brown paper bag, walked to the local cemetery, scaled the perimeter wall and sprinkled the ashes beside the grave of her beloved adopted mother, the Voodoo Priestess Marie Laveau. Exactly one month later, after consulting oracles and financial portfolios, she dyed her hair neon red and went into real estate. Before her first fiscal year was through, Molly had bought and remolded six large French Quarter condominiums, netting a gross profit of a mere $10 million.

"Fuck it all, I say. Some of us are just cursed with good luck!" she said to herself, on her way into The Abbey Bar, having just made another killer deal. "And why am I flirting with this thinks-he's-so-cute-bartender, pouring me my early-morning wake-up-call Bloody Mary? Hell! At 24, I still got me some time."

ARLEN

Funny how many times a day history has to go on repeatin' itself in our little unnoticed routines. I mean, every morning I sit here and take mah dump, remembering as a kid how we used to play battleships with match boxes swimmin' in the bottom of the toilet bowl after we had gone an sipped on some of Pa's black coffee. I would never have thought back then that every time I took mah trousers down that would be one of the few things I ever seem to be able to remember! That, and Sarge screaming out his orders about mines and how we need to get into single file, three feet apart, an' keep our eyes on the ground and not on our neighbors' ass. Shit, there it goes again. I'm not sure what I ate last night and sure enough, there they were, a whole mess of APMs or in Emma Jane's terms, anti-personnel mines. You know, those nasty little buggers that are spring-loaded like but-

terfly wings and look so simple and innocent that hundreds of kids all around the world pick them up out of the dirt thinking they are cute plastic toys until their little curious fingers go and trigger the springs and off goes their half their face or arm. And the worst part is that this is happening all the time, right now, as I speak. I guess we were lucky that the mines we stumbled on were made in Russia and not from Sweden. They're the worst ya know, and what's up with that? I always thought they were supposed to be a neutral country. Anyway just because our mines were Russian don't mean they were the ones who had gone and dumped them right in the middle of nowhere, by the truck full, off the edge of a cliff, and not just any cliff either. No, sir. It had to be the one we were climbing halfway up. The same cliffs that if you stood still long enough, the loose shale would make your feet start sliding all the way back down to the bottom. You could have heard a pin drop with the amount of noise we were making trying to get into single file with the evening light not helping us none neither. It just kept getting darker and darker, real quick-like, you know. One of those low-cloud an' overcast evenings when you couldn't even find the moon if you tried and everything was startin' to turn into one big blotchy gray, the same friggin' gray as our little butterfly-exploding friends who were just hanging out, waiting to cripple our asses. I can tell you, after several months of doing not much of anything, the sudden change of mental tactics took a little while to kick in mah brain. For sure, we were professionals, and in my mind, the best in the world when it came to getting' the job done, but living for months like a band of gypsies hadn't made us any sharper either! So all of a sudden you got a bunch of guys that can barely see in front of their hands climbing up a steep, slippery hillside acting like a herd of mountain goats until our adrenaline and everything else you had left in your tired body kicks in making you feel so pumped up with life that you feel like you're one with the universe and nothing is going to stop that feeling because there ain't no feeling like it known to man or beast. And once you're on that plane, you make damn sure you're gonna stay there, even when the rocks start fallin' into your face, forcing you to improvise and crawl on all fours with your head up the next guy's ass. But this time not no three feet away. I mean up his arse! So that you don't get all that grit driving you blind crazy and distracting your ability to concentrate and hug the ground like it was your mother, praying to every thing you ever wanted or thought you might want, knowing you're still only two-thirds up that cliff and inching through the absolute gray. … I tell you what, this rain, it is really comin' down outside now! Pa says cousin Judie says that they're already talkin' 'bout evacuating some parts of the Gulf Coast, and her motel is gaining business, booked up solid for a week already. She says she has never had that happen before in all the years she's been cleaning. Of course the weather channel is predicting this is the big one, but they always say that and you know them TV people will say anything to keep their ratings up. Still, I wouldn't want to be livin' down there right now. … Where's the toilet paper? … Before long, we were prayin' to the guy above us, hoping he didn't go and slip, when in the corner of my eye I see something move like a white flash of lightning streaking across the sky. I don't really know what I thought it was, but it sure made me jump and holler down to Sarge, who says, "What you shouting about?" and when I look back up the mountain, the white flash has gone an' disappeared. So I raise my arm to point where I thought I saw something and suddenly a wild cat the size of a friggin' Japanese car jumps out of a hole and straight over the top of mah head, its long tail brushing across my face as I shout again, "What the fuck?" and start slipping down onto the soldier below me. Bless his heart. After all these years, I can still remember a few things, like the smell inside a pair of brand new leather boots and his name.

EMMA JANE

Every morning I can hear him shavin' an' doin' his evolutions, promising this and pretending to be quitting that. Just wish you could hear yourself, that's all, Arlen, cause we know you don't mean none of it. Oh, it's not that I don't love you or the kids anymore. It's just I get so tired all the time no matter how much sleep I get. I guess after all the times you spend everyday, wipin' their bums an' blowin' their noses, hoping they're going to turn out OK and be productive parts of societies without even a thank you for all the baths an' snacks an' new pairs of shoes they're always sayin' they need. … Sure I love 'em. They're mah sweet little cherubs. But there's only so much a woman can give each an' every day of her self sacrificing life, especially cause it never seems to get any easier the older you get. I mean, when I was younger, I could handle Arlen always being away and us constantly movin' houses an' not being able to stay in one place long enough for mah kids to go to school to study to achieve their goals. ... Well, that's what them nosey teachers kept sayin' to me, like they knew best or something! What's wrong with them playing with themselves all day long at home, I say, except for the fact that they're always ganging up on you when it's time for bed time or to wash their hands before supper's ready. I know if I had to do it all over again, I would've gone an' got me a tape recorder with a few commands on it, because you tell me how many times a day did I have to say, "Don't do this or that or else." Think about it. How simple my life would have been if all I had to do was go an' press a button every time I wanted them to do anything right. But I ain't no machine, now, am I? Not me! I is all woman. Just ask Arlen. He'll tell you about when he used to come home from leave and how much I missed him, and who could blame me! What with him God knows where doing his service, all we just wanted to do was eat seafood and curl up in bed. Ain't nothin' wrong with that, except those kids would always be waking us up in the mornings saying they were hungry an wanting this and needin' that and Arlen wasn't in any hurry to get out of bed an' feed em because he was exhausted and supposed to be on leave, he said. So I was the one left making the breakfast everyday an' not just any breakfast either, I might add. They all wanted eggs an' biscuits with mah special homemade gravy an' pancakes with molasses on top and who wouldn't you say. But I tell you what. You try feeding them like that on about four hours of kip after me an Arlen had finished with our haymakin' and TV watchin'. Cooking plain wore me out, especially when they would come in our bedroom at all hours of the night wanting to sleep, cuddle up in our bed, and be all nosey about our haymakin'. Sure I didn't mind it when Arlen was gone, but he got real mad when they would climb into our bed when he was at home. I can't blame him for shoutin' and hollerin' at them about privacy and personal space. You would think them kids would learn better, but oh, no! They just tried even harder, they did. Thought it was some kinda big joke, waiting until we were fast asleep before creeping back in like a pair of roaches sneakin' 'round in the dark. And then everyone was awake again, makin' us all mean and cranky the next morning with me trying somehow to keep them from killin' each other because the kids were screaming, "Mom says this" and "Mom says that" and "how come you says we can't but she says we can?" Trust me, that made Arlen as mad as a half-dead hornet til all I could do was sit down and watch me some TV, prayin' he would disappear down to Old Prudhomme's Bar & Grill and go and cool off for a while. ... But you know Arlen and his little whiles. They can last three whole days, leaving me to start prayin' for real this time, getting' all worried about when he came home all he would want to do was sleep and not help take care of the piles of unopened envelopes that come into our house, day in an' day out, regular like clockwork, even on Sundays now, thanks to them special postal bread truck men who somehow manage to knock on mah door with their certifiable letters exactly when I'm tryin' to use the phone and get past a bunch of machines on the other end of the line so I can speak to a real voice who sure don't speak no proper English. ... You tell me how are you supposed to take care of any kind of business like that with your kids raisin' cane, danglin' around your neck, makin' you so upset they finally patch you through to someone who can talk, but first they insist on tellin' you about your reconnection charges and late fees that you gotta go an' pay on top of the regular bills, and that just gets me madder than Arlen until all I can do is start my own yellin' at the operator, "You can damn well keep mah lights," I tell em. "But trust me, you don't want to be in mah house when there ain't no cable goin' on the TV."

THE CHEMICAL SISTERS

They originated from Upstate New York, and like so many other migrants enjoying milder climes, wore their "New Orleans: Proud to Call it Home" bumper sticker with pride. Their unprecedented claim to subterranean fame, which resulted in Some Guy Upstairs adding their portraits to the hotel's beaded bar top, remains a highlight of conversation whenever anyone sits down to recount the adventures found in the bizarre chronicles of the Hurricane Hotel.

According to barroom legend, it all began when a certain unnamed domestic airline, announced it was laying off its entire suspected-to-be-gay work force, including most of its pilots and a whole bunch of stewardesses, on the pretext of the airline's diminishing amount of massive profit. But everyone knew that the airline was really trying to promote a newer, clean-cut cooperative image as part of an aggressive marketing strategy to increase sales throughout the Bible Belt. When the Chemical Sisters caught wind of this via the Internet, they decided to go into action. Fueled with the belief that sexual harassment, regardless of gender, is simply not acceptable and by the fact that who you choose to cohabit with is no one else's God dammed business, they quickly came up with their own aggressive strategy.

Within a week, they arrived at the airline's main terminal, and after a quick surveillance infiltrated the offensive airline's catering provider. Disguised as a pastry chef and a dishwasher, they added large-dropper quantities of Ecstasy to the snack and dinner rolls just after the gooey hot dough had been taken out of the ovens to cool. Everything went according to plan, and soon after several planes took off with trays of warm, tampered, yummy bread, nothing short of pandemonium broke loose.

The first indication that something was amiss in the now overly friendly skies happened when the pilot for a routine cross-country flight insisted on detouring and refueling in Hawaii. Once his wish had been successfully granted, he made a detour out of the Northern Hemisphere before landing safely a few thousand miles downwind on the remote oceanic isle of Bowee Wowee. When the plane was finally located several days later by a Chinese fishing vessel, the crew and passengers refused to leave their paradise until they had finished belly dancing and drum circling in the local islanders' month-long harvest celebration.

Another plane, bound for Vegas, ended up in the outer regions of the Arctic Circle after the passengers had become mesmerized and then filled with heated compassion while watching an obscure documentary about the plight of an endangered species of snow rabbit. Collectively, the passengers and crew felt it was their solemn responsibility to bring international attention to the plight of these fuzzy wuzzy bunny rabbits. They organized themselves into bands of vigilantes and were dropped off at specific points where the rabbits were known to breed, thus ensuring, in their beautiful minds, that they would be able to offer complete protection for the furry offspring of these twitching-nose-long-hair, frozen carrot eaters. It was only after they had landed in the blistering snow that the rather dreary fact that they were all dressed in summer casino attire looked to make their crusade impossible. But, after a series of long negotiations with the local Eskimo population, which was extremely concerned that it would have to clothe and house these insane, invading bunny rabbit protectors, the Canadian Mounties were called in and managed to send the lovable, frost-bitten vigilantes back-packing to the American border. It was recently reported that they have now founded a rather bizarre, long-eared religious sect somewhere in Upstate New York, just west of Albunny.

The wildest story, according to all the air traffic controllers who were working that most memorable of kite-flying days happened, quite naturally, here in New Orleans when a charted flight containing leaders from several religious organizations experienced an epiphany of such magnitude that everyone on board believed that the Second Coming had actually happened several months prior and that the new Messiah was hanging out in the French Quarters, having way too much fun to inform the world of his Divine Cosmic Presence.

After several prayers of devout laughter, they spoke in unanimous tongues and came to the conclusion that their old beliefs were a complete and utter hoax. This freeing realization, fueled with a few more dinner rolls and gallons of ex-communion wine, sent them scrambling among themselves in search of a new deity to worship and in a bold nose-dive descent from thirty thousand feet, their plane landed totally unscathed on the street-car line running along Canel Street. When the police finally showed up, they were greeted by a boisterous horde of naked evangelists who claimed they had spoken to the Messiah who proclaimed the need for a year-long Mardi Gras, and where the hell was Bourbon Street anyway?

The fact that everybody on the affected planes were all having such a great time made R&R's plan look like it might tragically backfire, with the puritanical airline gaining off-the-chart ratings. Thankfully, though, several next of kin of the partying passengers threatened to throw such a large class-action lawsuit into the airline's fat lap that its frightened stockholders, with no lead on what or who had caused this casualty-free flying circus, sacked their CEO and the entire board of trustees. And a month or so later, in a very savvy PC move, the new board unanimously approved the airline's new motto: "We Fly With Pride."

As for the CEO, rumor has it he was last seen dressed in combat attire selling taxidermy glass eyes in the remote hunting regions of the Great Lakes.

SOPHIA

Peeling slowly off the bed like a dripping wet kiss departing a pair of hot lips, Sophia wrapped a damp sheet around her sweating body and watched Treme step into the shower. "What's he goin' to sing about this time?" she whispered, feeling her stomach tingling. "I like his smell just the way it is." She sighed, stretching her body across the covers. "And for all his toughness, he's a teddy bear under the covers, aren't you Treme. Almost shy you are, always letting me do whatever I want with dat hot body of yours. I could go all day, I could, especially when you make me lean back and hold my ankles like dat."

Adjusting the bed sheet around her ebony-smooth waist, she sashayed over the drink-stained carpet and into the kitchenette. Opening the refrigerator, she soaked up the cool air before running her metallic-purple fingernails over her soft nipples. "Miami Chan Chan here we come!" she laughed, watching her nipples jump back at her. Rummaging through the overflowing refrigerator, she pulled out a Biggie Size root beer and sucked hard on the plastic straw. "Almost as long as mah man's," she giggled, tasting the cold, sugary fluid on her tongue. "I got me a keeper for real this time. If I started from his toes and made my way all the way up, there wouldn't be enough hours in the day."

Looking around the hotel room, she kicked at a pile of dirty clothing before turning over a pair of satin boxer shirts with her bare foot. *Not bad for a sister who was born and raised in the projects,* she thought, flicking the shorts across the room. *Her girlfriends were always telling her that. That, and how lucky she was.* "Well it has nothing to do with no luck," she mumbled. "I worked it, you know! … Everything! From mah nails on down. Everything has to be just right and all in its proper place. It's in the little details, ya know, like the Good Book says. I don't shake mah booty for just any man, I don't, especially all those wanna-be gangsters thinking they're staring in a MTV music video. I know, I know. But Treme is different. He's in a class all by himself. A real gentleman's gentleman he is, and related to Sidney Bechet, no less."

Cramming the empty root beer cup back into the refrigerator, Sophia sauntered over to the love-stained bed. *Sure, I'll get this place cleaned for him, use the cleaning guy—what's his name?—give him a surprise before he has to go an' DJ tonight.* She dropped her bed sheet dress on a half-eaten pizza and fell onto the bed. *I can't believe we're really leaving. Clean the sheets, too, down in the laundry room. Got some quarters in my purse, I think. … Where was that now? … I guess this place is a mess, but we spend so much time in bed.*

She wrapped herself around a pillow like a satisfied cat. A thick cloud of hot steam wafted out of the bathroom and settled above her head as she pulled the covers over her naked body. "I'll clean up real good for you, baby," she whispered, listening to Treme singing above the noise of the shower. "I've gotta look after mah man, just like the Good Book says."

TREME

That Sophia. She's got the booty to die for. Wouldn't be here now if it wasn't for her!… Always ready for me when I get off mah work, always got a kind thing to say. Not like those other sisters, complaining and bein' so needy. And God, what an ass! … Thank you for giving me the idea! … Thank you for telling me while we were getting down where to stash the money and mah merchandise! … Thank you for giving me the divine inspiration and soul power to walk on outta here and keep mah plans rolling! … Man, this showers sucks. You'd think that for all the money I spend I could take me a decent shower. What does these white niggas do? I guess they don't clean themselves too much. … I'll stash it under the sink in the garbage bin. No one would ever think of looking in there. And cover it up with some of Sophia's empty root beers. … Too sweet for me. I like mah Crown an' Cokes. … Wash 'em out first, cause I ain't like them other niggas. I like mah money clean. Got a smell unto itself. Almost sweeter than Sophia. … All thirty grand of sweetness. … What the fuck now? Where's all the water pressure gone to? I pay mah rent! … Will have to talk to the owner again. He's cool enough, never too much trouble. I just don't know what finger he stuck up those Feds ass though. Someone needs to tell him to take it out and wash it real good. It's only a shitty hotel he owns. If they want something to go and bust up, why not start with City Hall? Now, that's a thought. Maybe that parked car is after him again, but I can't be taking no chances, not tonight, not with it being mah last night an' all. No one's going to stop me goin' out with a bang! I ain't no wimp-limp-dick. If these be Feds in that car, I'll shoot their punk nigga asses to wherever the fuck they came from. Then play me a real long hard set before splittin' town. Anyway, I ain't got enough on mah person for any kinda real jail time. I knows exactly how much is legal to carry around. Gotta keep to the plan. … That's better. Now, where's the shampoo gone to? Sophia! Sophia! Shit! She can't hear me! Probably gone back to bed again. I ain't complainin' though. Always ready for me when I need her. I wonder if I'll miss anythin' here at all? Mostly mah Ma, but she'll be OK. We can fly her down for the weekends, although I knows she won't leave no Nawlins. Never has. Not even in no hurricane. Always stays. Says if you leave you never know what your gonna come back to, an' chances are someone will try an' say your house can't be lived in no more or worse, you don't own it no more even though it's all paid up for thanks to the old man, bless his heart. Died out on them oilrigs, he did. Believed in insurance all his working life until the day he died. Thankfully mah Uncle Lee had the old man's insurance papers all locked away in his safe. All paid up, and you can't fuck with Uncle Lee. When they weren't goin' to pay Ma, Uncle Lee took his Forty Acers and a Smith and Wesson right down to the insurance office, right down there on One Shell Square. Walked past security and up to the eleventh floor, straight past the secretary and stuck that pistol right between the insurance adjuster's eyes. Showed him, he did. Wrote the check for the full amount on the spot, right there and then. But that weren't good enough, not for Uncle Lee. Oh no. He made the adjuster go with him all the way back down the elevator and out past security into his car, drove all the way up to the bank and cashed it himself with a loaded gun sticking in his ribs. ... Right across the avenue at the Whitnee. Makes me laugh every time I sit on mah balcony thinking about it. ... "Never can trust no white man still after all these years," he says. ... Still, some niggas out there try and do though, get a little taste of that white meat, and it rots out their belly! Next thing you know, they turned into ghosts and preaching about protection. Shit. Ain't no such thing as protection down here. You think we don't know whose real and who ain't? We got the same wide screen TVs as y'all, mother fucker! That's the biggest joke. Everybody thinks we're so damn stupid. Mark mah words. All that complainin' an' secret prejudice an' shit gonna catch up with y'all one day. We all gonna get a college education, and whose gonna do the dirty work then, huh? Whose gonna mahke the roads and clean the sewers and turn on ya cable an' lights? Better start learning some Spanish real fast, is what I say. ... Shit. Looks like the handle to the hot water is about stripped out. ... Better tell the owner to get someone in here to fix it. I should ask for some rebate money back, too. But he always lets me slide. Got the hook-up. That's what this world is all about. Connecting the dots and hook-ups. I'll use some more of this fancy soap I got for her, spread it all over mah body, then put on mah Old Spice to cover up the smell. Can't be stinkin' like those girls down at the bar. ... .A nigga got to stand on his own two feet, even in the shower, especially if I ain't got mah gun handy. Can't be worryin' about leavin' it up in the room 'cause chances are Sophia will go an' blow her own head off. She's just like a kid when it comes to guns. Another reason why I ain't in no big hurries to be flyin' down to Miami or any wheres else real soon. Fuck all that flyin' shit. I feel naked if I ain't packin' mah little piece of Shuggie Otis. Now where's the clean towels at?... I cant be standin' out here all day like a dumb-ass nigga all naked an' shit, because that's when your ass get in trouble. I swear, that Sophia.

MOLLY

Lighting up a cigarette, Molly watched the rain overflowing from the flooded gutters onto her bare feet. Her morning Bloody Mary, combined with the rain, were making her horny again. "It sure seems kinda strange out here today," she mused. "Doesn't look like it's going to stop anytime soon, either." She leaned over the cast-iron railings and felt the cold, dripping water bounce onto her bare neck before dribbling over her nipples. "What I could really use is a hot, hard body to massage me!" she sighed, petting the water with her fingertips.

Below her, the cobblestone streets, usually bustling with commerce, were deserted except for a few determined locals battling through the rain and unsuccessfully dodging the rising puddles en route to Matassa's Grocery Store, where they could restock their personal bars and, if they had any spare change, gather up some last-minute emergency provisions like an extra carton of cigarettes or a six pack of Bic lighters. At the end of the street, the tap-tap-tapping of hammers frantically hitting nails clamping sheets of plywood over storefront windows seemed to be beating to the rhythm of the Marilyn Manson song, shrieking out of her bedroom.

Trying to cool herself down, Molly tilted her head back over the railing and for several minutes let the falling rain splash onto her face and run over her body before disappearing between her legs. "It has to be long and perfectly smooth," she moaned, crushing the soggy cigarette into the human-skull ashtray, nicknamed Jake. Glancing one last time at the flooding street below her, she disappeared into the main room of her house that legend has it is one of the oldest "Ladies in Waiting" chambers in the Americas, built specifically for the French landed gentry for their daughters to be available to court and entertain potential husbands. It was on this very same balcony, according to every tourist buggy driver whose pony and carriage daily clattered past her house, that during Mardi Gras, these enslaved-to-high-society daughters would throw down handkerchiefs or beads to the drunken masked-male elite who paraded by on horseback. Molly always liked to point out that several centuries later, the symbolism of this ritual was very much alive every Fat Tuesday on Bourbon Street.

Without drying herself off, Molly opened her laptop and read the latest weather report. It wasn't her skin she was thinking about now. It was Jake's. Over the past couple of months, she had not been able to get him out of her mind. Even though she had tried to dismiss her thoughts as pure insanity, his ghost seemed to be following her into every dive bar she frequented, and somehow their final, last breaths together had dissolved into the seductive ripples of Eros' Pool.

Being a woman of action and not reaction, Molly decided that the approaching storm was a good as time as any to venture out of the French Quarter and take a cab Uptown to the Hurricane Hotel, where Jake had been living since their separation. If nothing else, she tried to convince herself, if the storm everyone was predicting actually hit, she could make sure he was safely tucked away inside her writhing body.

ZANE

Slipping, Zane fell into a foul-smelling puddle as he fumbled up the dimly lit stairs. His mind was spinning out of control from all the information his boisterous guide was relentlessly bestowing upon him. Jake's enthusiasm amplified Zane's exhaustion until he felt sure he was about to pass out again. Jake, oblivious of Zane's state of mind, continued to point out all the rooms where the full-time residents stayed, as opposed to the rooms that were semi-vacant if any one was foolish enough to rent one. Usually, an unsuspecting foreign tourist, looking for a cheap alternative to the YMCA or an unlucky traveling rock band whose tour van had broken down or been stolen. Jake went on to mention that, because it was the height of summer, most of the vacant rooms were officially off limits, as all the full-time residents had the air conditioners, and this state would probably continue for at least the next six months or until some cooler weather dared to show up.

They had just reached the second-floor landing when Treme came bounding down the stairs, muttering something about mother-fuckers and parked cars.

"You seen that no good white nigga Aaron?" Treme shouted.

"He just left, maybe a half hour ago." Jake replied.

Treme turned his head a full 180 degrees. "What woz dat?" he said, backtracking up the stairs. "Ya saw him leave? Where did he go?"

"Hell, I don't know! What's the matter? He owe you money or something?"

"Who said dat? You getting in mah business again Jake?"

"Whoa! Hold on, Treme. Calm yourself down will you? This here's the new cleaning guy. Good people! I can't say the same for Aaron, you know! He had such weird vibes."

Zane was cowering behind Jake's shadow. The sudden presence of an angry six-foot four black man bounding down the stairs like a berserk cannonball and obviously packing a gun was the absolute last thing his wound up mind could handle. Treme turned and peered over Jake's shoulder. "Who's dis skinny-ass punk?"

"Zane," Jake said, stepping out of the way. "Zane, meet Treme. Treme, meet Zane."

"Shit, brah!" Treme sneered. "For a cleaning guy, you sure are filthy lookin'. Why don't you start with cleanin' up yourself?"

Treme and Jake both started laughing as the frightened and bewildered Zane blushed. "He got hit up by the Ship of Fools," Jake said, "Going to hose him down right now."

"Be sure to wash his ass real good." Treme snickered. "No idea where Aaron was going, eh?"

"Maybe back to his girlfriend's in the Bywaters."

"Girlfriend? That nigga straight?"

"I don't know, Treme. You know me! I always tried to avoid him. Calm down, will you? You're making Zane here real nervous, and we don't want him to get the wrong impression, now, do we? Not on his first day of class." Jake patted Zane on the shoulder. "He's got a heart of gold, really, haven't you Treme? Remember. Shines like his teeth. See?"

Treme leaned forward three inches from Zane's nose and grinned, baring a set of gold teeth.

"Hell of a DJ, too. Best in the house, ain't that right Treme?"

"Whatever, if dats what they say," Treme replied, eyeing Zane suspiciously. "You don't drive no black car do ya?"

"Who? Me?" Zane said, confused.

Jake stepped in again. "Listen, Treme. Did you hear about the film crew coming to town? Some Guy Upstairs says he has it all lined up. They're down at the bar right now. He's getting' lit up with some producer-looking dude, talking about reality and shit. Going to have cameras and a film crew and everything here. You know old SG, can bullshit better than anyone."

"Cameras!" Treme hollered. "What the fuck is goin' on today?" He pushed the two boys out of the way and bounded down the stairs again.

"See you on the flip side!" Jake yelled. "Hey, Treme! Maybe you can spin some records for those film people, become an overnight success!"

"Shit, Brah, I'm already a star in some people's minds."

Jake laughed and started walking along a narrow corridor lit partially lit by a window that had several torn, stained bed sheets stapled to its peeling frame. Occasionally, the bottom corner of one of the bed sheets would let out a faint flapping sound, like the noise of a broken pigeon wing helplessly beating on the sidewalk. "C'mon Zane." he said. "Oh, Treme's alright. Just a little crazy, that's all. But then, who isn't in this town, right? Just stay out of his business, and he'll soon warm up to ya. Got an angel for a girlfriend, too. That's always a good sign. She's so fiiiine looking! Sophia shines like his teeth. Pretty wild, eh? Ever seen gold like that before?"

Zane shook his head.

"Treme told me one time," Jake continued, "something about carrying your gold on the inside of your person instead of the out, less likely to have it robbed when ya sleepin' in your crib. Crazy don't you think?"

"What business?" Zane asked nervously.

"What? Oh, I'm sure you'll find out soon enough," Jake chuckled. "Don't worry. OK. C'mon, I'll show you your room then you can take a shower. I got some old clothes someplace around this dump."

Zane was having major second thoughts about the whole cleaning up gig. From what he had seen so far, the entire contents of the Hurricane Hotel appeared as dangerous as a hand grenade without a pin, and all the lifeless bodies crumpled up like soggy pieces of cardboard made him feel like the place was haunted with crazed ghosts unable to free themselves into a calmer and saner realm. Everywhere he turned, he saw demented spirits who somehow knew they were eternally plastered behind the flaking walls or trapped and chained under the buckling floorboards. Aside from the living ghosts, there was trash littered on every available surface issuing foul odors that could be seen wafting along the corridors like dry ice. The caustic smells of the smoke clouds where singing Zane's nose hair and making him want to sneeze every thirty seconds. Jake even appeared to be morphing into some weird swamp creature, his ghoulish shadow stretching up onto the ceiling as if he was crawling on all fours along the peeling plaster walls.

They walked through the smoke past several closed doors, and in between cloud bursts under the strained light, Zane could make out from the rusted stains and badly patched nail holes some of the old room numbers. Room 26 had been painted with diagonal black and white strips, and someone inside was singing. Thumb tacked into the press board door was a scratchy, barely legible handwritten business card:

MONA'S & MARTHA'S
CUM AS YOU ARE
COCK & TAIL LOUNGE

Jake stopped outside the door. "Here we go!" he said. "Your new neighbors. That's Mona singing one of her nursery rhymes."

"Who is Mona?"

"Let's find out." Jake took a hefty swig of beer and knocked on the zebra-skin-painted-door.

"Shut the fuck up!" a voice screamed from inside the lounge. Zane jumped behind Jake's fiendish shadow. "It's only Martha," Jake laughed. "C'mon. Don't be shy." He polished off his beer and knocked on the door again with his empty bottle. "Martha!" he shouted. "Guess who!" Without another word he opened the door and brashly walked into the room. "Guess who," he said again. "So glad you could make it. Martha, meet your new neighbor, Zane."

MARTHA

"Hello, Jake! Welcome. What brings you *up* so early?"

"Martha, meet Zane. Zane, this is Martha."

"Hello Mar—" Zane said, peering sheepishly around the door.

"And whooo might I ask are you, Mr Cutie Toot? My, what a mess we are today. Had a good night, I can tell. Been a naughty boy, have we? Well that's all right. Martha doesn't like clean boys, anyway, unless of course they're a little ... Oh, never mind. Please doooo come in."

Zane froze in the doorway. "Thank you, er, Mar—" he mumbled.

"Maharthaaa! You know, as in the wonderful priestess who was so wrongly sent to the slaughterhouse. That ghastly jail. So very very wrongly accused to spend time with all those rather hairy-looking Amazonish women. But that isn't the real reason why I chose my Martha. No indeed. Do you know what it means? Do you, Zane?"

"Goddess of the night!" Jake blurted, laughing as he sat down on a chaise lounge virtually unrecognizable thanks to a heaping pile of clothing. "Have a seat, Zane. She won't bite, not this early in the morning."

Martha raised herself from underneath the covers slowly and propped her throbbing head on a larger-than-life-size animal that resembled a one-eared Eeyore. An uncomfortable silence ensued as Martha and Jake stared at Zane, trying to read the boy's inventory as he stood half in and half out the bedroom. Martha decided to break the ice by lightly patting the edge of her bed with the palms of her brightly painted, finger-nailed hands. "Says who?" Martha giggled. "Hello. Anyone home? Anyway, as I was saying before I was so rudely interrupted, Martha means Mistress of the House or Wondrous Lady, in Aramaic. Does etymology interest you, Zane? As with all meanings of Life, names fascinate me. The distressed sister of Lazarus, you know, who rose from the dead. That's how my life is. One big rise from the dead. My earthly father wanted to name me Methuselah. Hebrew—Not that I am—meaning man who was sent, but where? That's always been my question. Martha doesn't like to be sent anywhere. Jake can vouch for that. Hell, no. Martha enters!" She squinted and stared into Zane's confused eyes. "Do you understand, little man? Do you, Master Zane?

"I think so." Zane replied, mustering the courage to enter the room and stand on a pile of torn-up hair-color boxes heaped in a pile on the carpet like the beginnings of a Boy Scout campfire. He cautiously sat on the edge of Martha's bed as she continued rapidly talking at what seemed like a million words per minute.

"Please Do sit here. A tad bit closer. That's so much more home like My, you are a young un. Are you Greek? I adore Greek men. All those Herculean orgies and wildly hung, hoofed beasts. I must admit, you look more like a Zach than Zane to me. After all, he was the father of John the Baptist, Zechariah, that is, struck dumb because he didn't or couldn't believe. Bless his heart. You're not a mute, are you?"

"I don't think so. I'm from Bunkie City."

"Oh my God! You poor poor thing, you! Mona! MONA! This little sensitive elf is from Bunkie City! Monica is her real name, but don't ever call her that. I much prefer Un Monifa! I'm the unlucky one in Yoruba. Oh, Un Monifa, are you alive in that bathroom? We have company out here. Don't start your day being a party pooper. Ha! Ha! Talking of parties, Jake, be a doll and hand me my handbag would you? Over there, under that minx!"

Jake began searching for what he thought might resemble a minx while Zane looked around Martha's bed chamber. From carpet to ceiling, her room had been covered with stuffed animals crudely nailed and stapled to the walls by their squishy limbs and ears. In every corner, the crucified animals were several layers thick, giving Zane the Doraphobic impression that he was inside an inverted ball of dried cat hair. Martha with amusement watched Zane staring at her furry womb-like creation. "Its aptly named the Fluff Room." she said. "A rather insidious classic around these parts, wouldn't you agree? Oh dear, are you bored with etymology, Zane? What fascinates a wreck like you? Do you indulge in phobias? You do rather look like the type!"

"Found it!" Jake shouted, triumphantly waving in the air a large glittery purse. "Give this to Martha," he said, handing Zane the bag before letting out a sigh and slumping back into the chaise lounge, exhausted from his search.

"Cool bag." Zane said.

"Thank you my dear! Yes they're recycled Mardi Gras beads, a gift, well, sort of. Actually, more like a trade with that industrious lunatic across the hall, you know. My, look at you! From Bunkie City, you say? Are you sure you're not mute? I'm guessing, of course, but are you suffering from a little Venustaphobia? Is that it, Mr. Zane? Do you fear beautiful women? And what are you gawking at now?" She ran her hands over her two silicon tennis balls. "These? Yes, they're real. You can touch them if you like. The first time is free. Twenty grand a pair. I think I got them on sale. Oh, my little Hedonophobia, that's a lot of, well, never mind that. Shall we proceed? Personally, it all started as an altar boy."

Martha was now talking so rapidly that Zane was only catching every other word. But rather than appear rude, and feeling glad to be sitting down again, he gave his best shot at looking like he was listening.

"Until the priest diagnosed me with Christophobia that is! Shortly afterward I was condemned for being Papaphobic! And that pretty much did it for me. It ran in our family, you know. My earthly mother was Anthrophobic, nothing nice if your entire wardrobe happens to be funded by the largest florist in town—you must have seen our delightful green house on the Avenue? Well, you might not. Sent her to de Pauls. It did! That was where I first realized I was Gerascophobic. All that drawling and messy pajamas. I just had to run somewhere. Mona! MONA! What the fuck are you doing in there? Now she's a case study for you. Drowning in an uncharted dysmorphic ocean, that one. Totally cast adrift, bless here heart, lost to the rude and uncaring winds of Cacophobia, like most of the world really. Don't you think? A bunch of mindless sheep, grazing in a Eleutherophic minefield. Oh my, how depressing. Life just can't be all that." She let out an exasperated sigh and pretended to wipe a forlorn tear from one of her heavily painted checks. She took a deep breath and was about to start up again when Jake interrupted, "Did you know they're making a movie downstairs?"

"Who is they?" inquired Martha.

"You know, that Some Guy Upstairs. He's talking to the producer right now. There's a film crew coming an' everything."

"A FILM crew? You mean reel-to-reel cameras an' shit?"

"Yes. Where's your ashtray?"

"You're probably sitting on it. MONA! Get your finger out of your ass! Mona! For fuck's sake!"

Zane opened his eyes and fell off the bed. He had been drifting in and out of sleep during Martha's last monologue. For a second or two, as a thousand plastic animal eyes stared menacingly at his, he thought he was dreaming a real-life nightmare. Martha pretended not to notice and continued yelling at the closed bathroom door. "Did you hear that, Mona? I know you haven't done us all a favor and accidentally cut off your head. What am I always saying? Hollywood would come searching for me one day!" She broke off her tirade and began sniffing the air like a deranged bloodhound. "I don't mean to imply," she said, shoving Zane off the bed again, "but would you mind staying down there? There's a good pup. I'm glad you're not suffering from Automysophobia. Ever heard of showers? I'm sure there's some soap laying around here somewhere. Please don't mind me. I've seen enough, well, not really. Look out Mona, wherever you are. I'm sending Mr. Bunkie City Boy in. There you go. Shoo fly, shoo!"

Zane reluctantly stood up and looked pitifully at Jake for assistance.

"Good idea Martha!" Jake laughed, prodding him on. "Your room is next door anyway. Not like you won't be seeing a lot of each other."

"Excuse Me? You're living here? With us? Oh, my precious little Bunkie Boy!"

"I thought I told you!" Jake said. "Zane's the new cleaning guy."

"He is? Well, he's off to a good start smelling like that. I'm confused, did you go and dispatch that awful errand boy Aaron? The exalted one, my ass! Did he, Jake?"

"He sure did!"

"Oh my! You're my new unsung hero. Sit down again. Here, let me help. There you go. Smells like me, personally. Why didn't you say something earlier, Jake? Oh, my harmless little Eurotophophic. You need some help." She began rummaging through her handbag until she found a small plastic bag. "Jake," she summoned, "go into the bathroom and get the mirror from Mona. There's a dear. Sit a little closer, Zane. We'll fix your precious little Bunkie self right up and then you can shower and be all clean and fun again."

Martha raised her head up to the ceiling and began issuing what seemed like a prayer to the animals gazing blankly at her. "Oh Mary, mother of us all, thank you that I, Martha Mladen, derived from the Slavic Mlad—you know, our family name, meaning quite literally young stud—Van Duessen, the third, woke up this morning as alive as I went to bed. I put it down to bottled tomato juice in mah vodka – God, what is she doing in there? Just kick the damn door down, Jake. I have no idea if she's alive anymore! That, and sex with strangers, at least a dozen times a night." She chuckled to herself, staring at Zane. "Wouldn't you agree? Oh dear, perhaps not. Finally! Thank you, Jake. Did you see any form of life in there? Now then, this won't take long. Jake, hand him one of those towels you're sitting on. There we go. You can go right on in. Please don't mind Mona. I really think she's had it this time. Here, before you go, hold the straw like this. That's right, you're a natural. Take a deep breath. Up, up, and away. ... Don't blow back! Oh well. Here, try again. We have plenty where that came from. There we go, my wounded waif. ... Yes, that's it. Sniff, sniff! Oh do put that green tongue of yours some place else, Jake. Of course, I'm not going to forget you, but we do need to hurry, can't be wasting the day talking in bed. I know my entourage must be waiting for me downstairs. Mona. MONA!!! I really am leaving you this time!

Martha finished off the bag and started patting Zane on the knee. "My little homeless egg, help yourself to any of the clothes on the floor. Just, don't touch the dresses in the armoire. They're still rather hot—After your shower that is. Are you ready, Jake? For heavens sake, you're such an insatiable piggly-wiggly at times. MONA! I will continue praying for your life to evolve!"

Martha leapt from the bed and wiped her smeared nightdress on an equally stained bed sheet. After a quick examination in the mirror, she grabbed Jake's arm and pushed him out of the room. "Arise!" she shouted, strutting down the hallway, waving her arms in the air as if swatting an annoying fly. "Arise, I say! Thus spoke what's his name!"

MONA

I'm gonna run away again. I am. You'll see. ... And what will you go an' do then huh? You're not the young, sweet thing you used to be. Not running around, anymore, turning all those boys heads' rock hard. Oh no! ... And you know it, don't you Martha? Getting scared of a little old age, aren't you? I know you've gone an' done a lot for me, but there's only so much abuse a girl can take. I know you want to help with my operation, but how much did you say we needed? I think it was sixty grand, but I can't even remember the name of it. You're the expert with all that medical crap. Dr. Martha, my ass. Telling me it's a simple procedure and all they have to do is take out half my stomach and that it's the only way to stop me from getting fatter. Shit, look at me. I don't eat a damn thing and still put on these slabs of rotting flesh. ... Wait. Lips suction, or something like that. ... Without any scars. Like I mind them. They can scar me all they want to, and none of them will hurt as much as you with that vicious tongue of yours. 'Yes! I can still hear you out there, holding court in your fluffy stuffed kingdom. And of course it has to be Jake. Got something going on, those two have. I can smell it from here. One of these nights I'll catch 'em and, what will she be saying then, my mistress of the house? Oh my God! ... That isn't, is it? ... Yes it is! What's he doing here in our bedroom? ... I thought. ... Shit! Who invited him up into my room? The nerve of it all! Don't expect me to be giving you your money back, little man. I did feel bad about taking his ID though. How was I to know he was only 16? ... I know, I can leave it at the bar when I get dressed. Oh, will you just look at him? Just as cute as I remember. Shy little red-haired bird, and hung like a horse, you know those skinny ones. How can I get out of here with-

out him seeing me? Shit, Martha, stop screaming at me. Yes Martha, of course I'm still here. Why don't you just hush up and quit your verbal diarrhea? Who do you think you're trying to impress with all that etymology nonsense, that's what I want to know! No one I know really cares where his or her name comes from. No one around here uses his or her real one anyhow. A name is just like a tattoo. You try an' scrub it away but your mind won't let it go unless you burn it out, and then you're left with nothing but another nasty scar. A name has too many reminders of the people who named you. I mean, look at mine. Monica. What kind of name is that? Sounds more like an old-fashioned pair of sunglasses than a princess.

I cannot believe he's sitting there like a little Tootsie Roll on my bed. Doesn't look old enough to be in here, if you ask me, and that's saying something. More like kindergarten with someone holding his hand, and where did Jake go?... He didn't leave him alone with her, I hope. ... What was he thinking? Then again, he ain't too big on any thinking. Good grief, Martha, why don't YOU shut the fuck up? But you just can't, can you? I know it's because you're so scared that if you ever stopped that ranting of yours you'll drop down dead. Lazarus, my ass. How many times have I heard that one? Why don't you tell them your real name? ... See !... You're just like the rest of us, full of some sort of bullshit secrets. You just pretend yours don't stink, that's all. Do you, Michael? Yes, Ms. Smarty Pants. With a capital "M" for "Mother." ... Remember? You told me when we fist met. How long ago now was that? I had just turned seventeen and run away from home. Gotta laugh. It wasn't that far of a run. I could hardly call Midtown to the French Quarter being on the road or anything. One bus ride. One way. Still, no one ever found us, did they? You picked me up on Decatur Street and took me to your third-floor, fancy French Quarter apartment overlooking the A&P grocery store. How time flies. I loved that place. I really did. Every morning we would wake up and hear the street musician's buskin below us as we drunk our coffee on your balcony, or should I say gallery, as you liked to call it, with all your ferns and flowers sprouting everywhere. I will always remember you dressed in your satin red chemise, pouring cold water on top of those obnoxious tourists below as you watered your plants. "Oops," you would say. "So sorry!" And both of us half wetting ourselves, laughing before I would go to the French Market and bring home some of those juicy fat Creole tomatoes. ... WHAT NOW? Why *can't y'all just leave me alone to reminisce about my life in peace? Leave me with my tomatoes and how we would curl up in bed and squeeze them all over each other. Remember that? You were like one big lollipop, back then. We had some good times until those ex-TV celebrities showed up and started buying all the buildings and turning them into condos. We were paying $450 a month for six years and then all of a sudden we get one week's notice. No renter's rights down there. Out on our asses. And then the fucks were charging $1,200 a month and didn't even paint the place. I still miss it, though. Maybe we can go back there someday. Maybe after we make some money. Maybe you'll light up some candles again in our bedroom with those big French doors wide open to catch the soft midnight air. That's what I loved about you. Your internal romanticism. Kept yourself away from all those parties and was never into people just popping in. Not like now.*

Oh no, here we go. Now she's started her phobia routine. How boring is that one? You're such a bore Martha, you haven't noticed little Bunkie Boy has gone and fallen asleep. Too busy running your mouth about me again. You're just like my mom at times. Never paid any attention to anyone but herself all her life. … Not that I care. The bitch! Leaving me and my sister at the Schwagasteinos grocery store just before New Year's. … You could drink in those grocery stores back then. And all the shopping carts had ashtrays on them. Not that long ago, actually. Gotta hand it to old Mr Schwagastein. He sure was a clever old buzzard, because the place had a full bar and was packed every day. Real nice looking too. None of your cheap stuff for Mr Schwagastein. Right next to the meat section at the back. He knew how much people loved to shop, especially in the heat. Open from 6 a.m. to 12 p.m. and the best place in town to pick up a roll of toilet paper and a margarita to go. Mom would pop out for a stick of butter and four hours later come home smashed and still no stick of butter for the potatoes. Bless Dad's heart, always trying to fix it. "Mr. Lucky," his buddies would tease him at work because he still had all his fingers and thumbs, and very little else! Mr. Lucky! If only they knew. Him being a pipe welder an' all, and a real good one until they shut down his union. … Said it was their own greedy fault. But was the first to admit that working conditions jumped from semi-dangerous to life threatening as soon as the unions left. He ended up having to work all the way across the bridge at the shipyard over in Nawlins East.

That was okay until they went and made it illegal to drive without any car insurance. You know how much car insurance is down here? Almost as high as Brooklyn. Go ask mah dad if you don't believe me. How was he supposed to pay for car insurance and buy all the groceries and pay for mom's drinking and the rent, what with the price of gas going up and Mom always so smashed she couldn't keep a job together even if she tried. Too busy trying to get down someone's pants? At least that's what my sister's friend's brother found out a couple of years later when he ran into her at Jazz Fest. … Anyway, Dad being the good man that he is decided he would stop driving until he had enough money. He didn't want to break no rules, he said. … "Them rules are rules," he was always quoting us. … Damn shame because we had one of those Cougars Mark IIIs. Such a beautiful car, with an engine bigger than the trunk and tons of room for us all come summer vacation time. We would all pile in an' go down to his sister's house in Ocean Springs. … What a ride! With them real leather seats and electric windows. I can still remember them hot summer days with me and Sis cleaning it for him on the weekends. We loved leaning over all that warm metal and bubbles covering our bodies. Got us both going in the back seat. Ahh, that back seat. It was bigger than our bed! Dad, loved it, too. "No use getting a smaller car," he would say. "You'll see. If we go get one of them foreign little buggers, then the price of gas will just triple." And he sure wasn't going to buy no non-unionized Japanese tin death-trap with their twenty-five miles per gallon. "I like mah eight miles just fine," he would say when Mom started up on him about not being able to afford to drive anywhere.

YES, Martha! … NO! I am not sleeping in here. Just zoning out all your phobia crap is all. … What now? No way. You're not coming in here, Jake. Leave me alone. Damnit, here's the friggin' mirror. Now get out! Leave me to remember when our last family Christmas was and Dad's ride to work got sick with the flu and because it was a holiday he couldn't get a bus across the bridge. So he decided he would drive to work, and of course it had to be when one of those motorbike cops was snooping around and stopped him on the interstate before throwing him in jail. I mean, come on! That's mah old man we're talking about. He hasn't even smoked dope a day in his life and now he's locked up because of a traffic violation. They pulled the usual crap on him. Wouldn't let him make no call or nothing. No wonder those human rights groups are always after their asses. Kept him in there for over twenty-four hours just so they can get that bonus from the city. And for what? No insurance and an expired brake tag and a lost car registration? I mean, they made him out to be such a criminal, on Christmas Eve no less. And of course it had to be the only day Mom decided not to take a drink. "Where was he?" She kept saying, getting madder and madder until she starts tearing down all the Christmas decorations. Then she's flying around the room like a bat outta hell, knocking over the tree an' giving the uncooked turkey to Dixie, who got sick as a dog. Ha! Shit, it cost more for the lawyer than the ticket. Poor Pa. He just couldn't understand what the world was coming to. "No one has any respect for anything or anybody," he kept saying. Worked everyday of his life since he joined the Marine Corps, at 18, and look at him now, thrown in jail without any rights. I mean, think about that for a second. Every friggin' day! ... How many hours is that? I work a couple of eight-hour shifts downstairs at the bar, and I need me a vacation for the rest of the month. Sure they're long shifts, but all your life? And of course, when he came home and saw what Mom had done to the house and Dixie lying on his mat all sick and yelping, he went all quiet-like again and waited till Christmas morning, after we had opened our presents, then he went and packed all Mom's stuff in the Cougar and drove it into Lake Pontchartrain, right there by the marina. Boy did she throw a fit until he threatened to dump her ass in the lake, as well. She shows up, a couple of days later, to borrow some money, and storms back to Mr Shwagasteinos. with me and Sis in the shopping trolley. She got so hammered at the bar that she took off with the butcher, forgetting we were still in the shopping cart. Then the store went and closed, with me and Sis left inside. "This might be fun with all the free cakes and ice cream," I thought, until the alarms went off and it was our turn to go downtown to central lockup. That was the maddest I ever saw mah old man. He threw such a fit and we haven't seen her since. Bless his heart. Getting all depressed afterward, playing his Louis Armstrong LPs all night and day. He loved that Satchmo, had all his records and a whole bunch of them seventy-eights, too. We didn't mind the music as long as he was happy because we knew he loved her real bad. Just couldn't live with her, that's all. ... I just wished I hadn't got caught smoking pot at school right after that. Got him all silent again when they suspended me and then I had to open my big mouth and ask him, "What's the matter? Louis Armstrong smoked marijuana his whole life, and if he can smoke, why can't I?" "No he didn't," Dad said. "Yes, he did," I answered back. "I heard it on WWOZ! If you don't believe me go and phone the radio station." Well that did it. Dad stopped playing his records right then and there. … Hold on. … Where are they going now? What the fuck? They're all leaving, except for the little Bunkie boy. … No way! He's getting' undressed in my bedroom. Shit! He's coming right in here! … Fuck! Fuck! Fuck! I can't have him recognizing me like this! C'mon, Mona, think of something, will you? Damnit, this will have to do! Just cover yourself in the shower curtain. Thank God we never got it together enough to put all those silly little clips on the rod. … There. That's it. Boy does it smell funky. Shit, here he comes. Might as well come straight on in, why don't you? Don't mind me in all your glory. Take your damn shower. See if I care. … No, that's the cold, you silly little man. Just wish I had a better view because it's sure getting hot and sticky under this smelly plastic sheet. Get in, will you? … Great, now you are splashing my feet. Probably with that big cock of yours. Can I soap it up? Ha! Damn! I need a cigarette. But I can't smoke with a shower curtain over my head now, can I? Nigh on suffocating under here it is! Hope you feel a whole lot better. And don't think just because you're pretending not to see me under this curtain I can't smell the difference between Martha's autumn peach and my seaweed rose shampoo. Shit, I think I'm going to faint. I was feeling bad about taking your wallet earlier this morning, but I sure as hell don't anymore. … Peaky Boo! Oh, little man! I know you're playing with yourself in mah shower now. I know you'll probably want to go an take a dump next. I can see it all now. Him dumping on me dumping in this dump. Give them something to talk about downstairs with all their new movie friends. I bet they're having a whole lot of fun without me. Oh dear, I just realized I haven't pulled my panties up. How embarrassing is this? … That's it. Enough is enough. I'm outta here. I'm not gonna sweat no more for no kinda man.

TREME

Destined for another world, Treme leapt down the hotel stairs like a landslide. Deprived of another night's sleep, his frenzied thoughts were filled with leaving the madness of the Hurricane Hotel ASAP before the whole place blew up and messed with his plans. He tripped on a loose piece of carpet, and as he fell realized he had only left New Orleans once before in his brief time on earth. *And when was that?* he thought, picking himself up off the floor.

At the foot of the stairs, he opened the door to the bar and heard the familiar crackling of skewered laughter spewing out of Some Guy Upstairs' mouth. "That SG," he muttered. "I remember now. Talking to those two tourists from Germany,—or were they Swiss—who had accidentally stumbled into the hotel, delighted and intoxicated to have found an insane piece of the vibrant New Orleans jigsaw puzzle, unrecorded and off the charts." He was just about to enter the bar room when a flash back transported him to the exact same day one year ago.

"Yes. And this my friends," SG was gargling, "is a direct descendant of the blood-curling, sword-swashing, high seas-buckling Jean Lafitte, the Pirate, one of the founding fathers of our displaced and ever resilient city."

Treme sat at the bar as the two tourists started buying everyone drinks. A sheet of LSD appeared from SG's back pocket and was ceremoniously divvied into quarters. Soon after, Treme was playing his new role, flashing his gold teeth as he stood on the bar slicing the rising cigarette smoke with an imaginary cutlass. The Swiss tourists weren't totally convinced he was actually a real-life pirate until the first wave of LSD kicked in and SG made them both huddle up next to Treme as he raised his T-shirt and revealed the same gun he is now waving in the air. The tourists were sold, lock, stock and barrel. After a quick exchange of money, with no questions asked, they followed Treme into SG's beat up prospector van, bound for the deepest, darkest and meanest swamps Louisiana had to offer. And according to SG's history books, the home of Jean Lafitte's buried treasure.

They set off at high noon, navigating through the city and onto the interstate before journeying another sixty-odd miles to the tranquil tourist spot of Spanish Lake, with SG driving and ranting to the tourists about twelve-foot-long water moccasins and wild Cajuns cannibalizing soldiers like in the movies. Everything was going down real smooth until, after paying an over–the–top cash deposit, they boarded the canoe. Then time slipped a gear, and it became apparent that neither SG nor Treme had ever ventured near, let alone on, water except to take the occasional late-night joyride across the Mississippi River on the Algiers Ferry. Unperturbed and selfishly determined, SG finally got everybody somewhat situated without totally loosing it staring at his watery reflection. Treme sat at the front of the canoe directing traffic, with the two Swiss tourists in the middle, guarding the ice chest and Treme's favorite possession: a beaten up Boom Box, circa early 80's. Captain SG, sat in the rear, tripping his brains out. By the time they had heaved and shunted the canoe away from the slippery bank, all four boys were laughing hysterically until the canoe rental man pointed to a pair of paddles, propped up against the bank. "You might need these!" he snickered, not caring if he saw his splitting-at-the-seams twelve-foot junk of a canoe or its contents ever again.

After shunting back to the bank and picking up the canoes, the intrepid explorers were back in the water, avoiding their reflections. "All Aboard! Engine's running! We're cooking with gas now!" said Captain SG, trying to sound upbeat. "Cooking with Crown more like!" shouted Treme, staring at his gold teeth reflecting in the murky water.

"Yar! Yar! Yar!" replied the two tourists nervously.

The day-trippers had been canoeing for almost an hour when everyone agreed it was time to find some shade from the relentless overhead heat and blinding glare of the sun reflecting off the water. They paddled into a narrow canal lined with tall marsh grass and shrubby trees whose twisted bark and limbs were laced with two-inch thorns. As they paddled deeper into the canal, something scraped along the bottom of the hull and sliced it open like paper cutting a finger. The canoe came to an abrupt halt and started sinking into the black muddy water.

"Shit. What was that?" shouted Treme, spilling Crown and Coke all over his jeans.

"Probably an alligator." replied SG, unsure what was going on until he noticed the water filling up the canoe. "Quick, someone grab the ice chest. We're leaking like a sieve." The water had already made its way over their feet when the chest started floating. The tourists stood up and shouted in stereo, "SHITZER" before diving head first into the swamp.

"Where do you think you're going? Are you crazy? What about the alligators?" yelled SG, watching semi-submerged tourists, half wade, half lurch, through the grimy water and disappear into a maze of tall grass.

"Fuck 'em. That's more Crown and Coke for us." Treme grinned.

"You're right. Now then, how do we get outta here?" replied SG, pointing to the thorn-infested bank. "If you just step out and pull the canoe up over there, then turn it around, without the extra weight, I think we can make it back. Just watch out for them thorns."

"Fuck you too, SG. I ain't putting mah feet in dat shit."

"You're kidding me."

"Oh yeah, why don't you do it? You're the friggin' captain."

"Because you're at the front of the canoe!"

"So what's your point? Why should I have to get out?"

Water continued to flood the canoe as they bickered. Finally, SG moaned reluctantly, "Okay, I'll do it." Treme stood up to let SG pass and the canoe capsized, sending them both flaying into the water. "What'd you go and do that for?" said SG, spitting out a mouthful of black marsh. "What are we going to do now?"

"Brah, just hang on," said Treme, scrambling to his feet.

"To what? A friggin' snake?"

After much fighting and a lot more cussing, they righted the canoe, and pushed it onto the bank. Out of breath and shivering, they emptied the water, climbed back into the canoe and surveyed the terrain.

There were no houses or streetlights to be seen. In fact nothing familiar at all, just miles and miles of grass bending in the faint hint of a breeze.

"Well, least we still got our beer," said SG forlornly.

"I guess. What about the boom box?"

"It's still here, lodged under the seat, soaked through, I imagine."

"Oh well."

"Oh well."

They sat slumped in their marooned canoe like a pair of disgraced hounds, contemplating as best they could the inner meaning of their dilemma. This lasted for about a minute until they both realized how terrifyingly quiet it was. In fact, they were in a weird space called the Sound of Silence, a place that doesn't go down very well for most New Orleanians, the quietness that means your cable bill is way past due, or WWOZ is off the air and if you don't get your music fix real quick, your soul will freeze over in 96 degrees of shade. They were no longer afraid of alligators, snapping turtles and slimy snakes. It was the heavy noise of quietness that was gnawing away at their nerves.

SG instinctively grabbed the boom box and stood up in the canoe. "Fuck this!" he shouted and pressed the play button on the dripping player. Jimi Hendrix's guitar wailed out from the waterlogged speakers.

"What the fuck? I thought that was gone an' trashed!" Treme laughed.

"You know Jimi!" beamed SG, "Life after death, baby!" He cradled the boom box close to his chest as if it was a newborn infant and cranked the volume, strutting up and down the canoe like a demented, headless chicken. "Voodoo Chile" ripped through the swamp waves. A moment later, with paddle in hand, Treme was accompanying SG from the other end of the canoe. For sixteen glorious minutes, they jammed with Hendrix's alchemic guitar that escaped the drowned cassette and echoed through the swamps, sending a mass of every living and some non-living creatures fleeing into the air or scurrying into the water. The dancing boys grinned, watching angry four-headed herons flapping and startled headless owls screeching. Tree-climbing alligators boomed as a hundred legged nutria rats gnawed the fingers off a flying crawfish. Clouds of feathers were falling and forests of leaves floating as thousand-year-old snapping turtles dove deeper into the mud. Before long, the entire ecological system had woken from a sleepy summer afternoon siesta and was moving into the anarchy of a confused spring.

"What's that noise?" Treme dropped his paddle and waved at SG to turn off the music.

"What noise? I don't here anything except—"

"Hush, will you? Turn it off!"

"You mean Jimi? No fucking way, man."

Treme grabbed the boom box and threw it into the water. "Listen. I can hear something. It sounds like some kind of engine."

Treme tried to focus on the emerging sound. Something was definitely puttering through the ruckus of the swamp, getting closer and seemingly swallowing up the confused landscape. For the first time since they had left the Hurricane Hotel, both boys became totally, paranoid.

"Shit! Do they have cops out here?" Treme asked as he frantically rummaged through his soaked jeans pockets.

"Hell, I don't know." replied SG. "Probably. They have helicopters and million-dollar planes, satellites and armored tanks these days. Why not shitty little motor boats? Good a place as any, off the streets, right here, in the middle of fucking nowhere."

"Duck!" Treme whispered nervously. "Too late. I can see two heads over there. See em? I think they've seen us!"

"Shit! They're wearing uniforms! Get down! Get down!"

They both squatted like two naughty Boy Scouts taking a dump. "Oh well," SG sighed. "It won't be the first time."

"They don't look like no cops to me," Treme said hopefully. "They're wearing camouflaged suits an' shit. Maybe they're Marines."

"Out here? This place doesn't have any oil fields, does it?"

"I don't know. Wait a minute! They're ... yes, they are. Women!"

The motor boat slowed down. Before it pulled up alongside, an elderly women stood up and yelled, "What in heaven on earth's name do you two louts think you are dong out here? Making such a senseless racket. Don't you know these parts are protected?"

"From what?" blurted SG, dumbly gawking at two alligators dressed head to foot in combat fatigues.

"From what!" the other women joined in. "This area is part of the Audubon Nature Wildlife Reserve, and you're trespassing. Don't you know those eagles are an endangered species?"

"Er, sorry," SG replied sheepishly. "What eagles? No, we didn't. Our canoe—"

"Oh hush up when you're being spoken to!" continued the first woman, "Look up yonder. There's one of their nests. See? And you two hooligans are disturbing their natural equilibrium." She furiously wagged a finger that seemed to be transforming into a six-foot water moccasin. "Look at the pair of you! Only content when you're destroying God's greatest gift, Mother Nature." She bent down into her boat and produced a notepad and pen. "What are your names?"

"Our canoe," pleaded SG. "It drowned. Sorry, we didn't mean to—"

"Enough! That's what everybody says when it's too late in the day! Sorry doesn't save those eagles now, nor, I might add whilst I'm on the subject, this entire precious swamp."

"Sorry," repeated Treme, totally overwhelmed.

"Another sorry! Is that a "Sorry there's hardly any clean air anymore" or a "Sorry we have no more drinking water?" It's always "Sorry this" and "Sorry that."

"Ma'am, what are y'all talking about, if I may humbly ask?" SG said, desperately trying to get a grip on the situation as the water moccasin fingers reached for his throat. "God fuckin' help us," he mumbled.

"What was that?" barked the other alligator. "None of that language around here. Do you know who we are? I guess not. We're from the Audubon Natural Institute of Preservation, part of the ornithology team studying this rare moment when bald eagles are finally reappearing and nesting, after a forced hiatus of almost 15 years!"

"So things are looking up," said Treme, bursting into uncontrollable laughter.

"Well of course we have to look up. You don't look down at birds do you? Well, you two might. It's fool delinquents like yourselves that have nothing better to do than come out here and disturb the ecological system. Chances are you'll never grow up and before long, you'll continue blindly contributing to the dumping of unnecessary consumerism into our sacred waterways."

"That sounds like such a waste," replied SG, who was laughing so hard now he thought he was going to pee in his soggy jeans.

"Stop that, while you're not even close to being ahead, Mr. … what's your name?"

"SG, and this is Treme. Pleased to meet you both. Its good to know there are people as scary as yourselves fighting out on the front lines, preserving the glory of these endangered eagles. Why bald? That sounds so, well, rude, don't you think?"

"I will let you know one thing, Mr. SG. Your flattery and sarcasm is what's making this world a hopeless cause. I just hope what's left of your consciousness will one day realize that if we don't do some—"

"Look!" shouted Treme. "It's one of those bald mother fuckers. Oops, sorry. They're coming back to their nest."

A thousand pairs of eyes turned skyward and watched as a nonchalant eagle landed on what looked like a crown of thorns.

"Yes, there is a God. Now *please* make this Acid go away," whispered SG, bowing his head solemnly and staring at his muddy shoelaces, which resembled a pair of slithering "There's another one of those eagle things," blurted Treme again. "Shit, I mean, they're fucking everywhere."

"That's the mother. And we will have none of that foul language around here."

SG started laughing uncontrollably again. He didn't care whether he peed in his pants anymore.

"What's so funny?"

"Fowl," replied SG, "around here. Get it? Oh God, someone please get it." He was buckling over now, preparing himself to be devoured by the camouflage alligators. Instead, they scratched their noses and started laughing. Then, all four of them were creasing up, the two boys ragingly, the two women ever so politely.

"Can we all go home now? Please?" SG pleaded. "Were from Nawlins. Our van is at the canoe rental shop. I promise we won't come back here."

The alligators started whispering to each other as they fanned themselves with their tails. "That's out of our way. We have our own landing at the reserve's headquarters."

"Oh please. Pretty Please, with sugar on top?"

"You're not on the run, are you? Not a pair of fugitives or renegades?"

"Not really," said Treme. "I'm a bad-ass DJ, though."

"No Ma'ams!" interrupted SG. "We just wanted to experience how the other half lives."

"Well, you're up to your waist experiencing it now," laughed one of the alligator as they started gesturing to Treme. "Fetch me your line."

"What? Out here? You don't look like the type. I do have some back in the van."

"Rope!" shouted SG. "They mean our rope. R O P E."

"Oh, I have some of that, too."

SG pushed Treme out of the way before throwing the soggy rope attached to the end of their canoe to the women. "All aboard," he said, taking up the slack.

"No way," said Treme nervously. "With those two?"

"Now or never," said one of the women, "Don't forget about them alligators. Almost feeding time."

Holding onto each other, the boys maneuvered into their rescuer's flat-bottomed boat. One of the women said, "Not another peep out of the pair of you, or it's back into the bayou. Is that understood?" She revved the engine and skillfully steered them through the canal into the main body of water.

The LSD the boys had taken, was settling down a little now, creating a stimulating poetic equilibrium, amplifying their senses so it appeared they could feel the trees breathing and the water molecules dancing. The sun was setting over this primal landscape as they sat awestruck by the Spanish moss draped over the lightning-battered cypress trees with their hundred-year-old bark smoothed with time so it reflected like vertical, organic mirrors the bright pinks and reds of the evening sun. A cooling breeze began ushered them on as they glided through the floating fields of water lilies. The luscious petals of the lilies took on the intensity of the sunset's gold and yellow hues, resembling floating tongues of fire rippling across the lake's shimmering skin.

"The Indians who lived here long ago say these trees dance at certain times of the year," one of the women whispered as they passed a cypress that was more than ten feet in diameter. "Wow!" exclaimed SG. "And look over there. There's a tree growing out of the middle of an old one. This place is prehistoric,"

"Good observation. You're correct. Much of the fauna here is some of the oldest known to man. This whole area dates back to the pre-Mesozoic era. The cypress tress are a mystery to all who study them. Their knees, as we call them, can grow up to twelve-feet high and continue growing even after the actual trunk of the tree has been cut down. That's right. Growing, not as one might think, into another tree. They continue growing as knees. There's a lot of speculation about what their function actually is. Some say they collect water, but no one really knows except they're as tough as any old oak."

"They look like elves or dwarfs or some weird friggin' aliens. I mean, look there's some over there parading around the trunk like its Mardi Gras or something." SG pointed out, just as a gray heron swooped low over the boat, turned and passed over again. They could hear the beat of its six-foot wings as it soared up into the shimmering tree line. "That's so friggin' cool!" Treme said, noticing that he was actually starting to feel comfortable with his surroundings. His body movements and gestures seemed to be more natural now, and he playfully flapped his arms as if he were a Heron. It felt like the entire cosmic universe was integrating inside of him and every time he breathed or blinked his eyes he was melting into a remote portal of time lost in the past.

The boat glided on as the creatures of the day silently morphed into the shadows of the night. The women continued sharing their expertise, enjoying their students' enthusiasm and wonder at the hidden mysteries unique to these swamps. As their bony, ring-less fingers pointed this way and that, the city boys felt a warm connection within themselves for the two women and this majestic environment. They sat closer together, humbled and aware that something bigger than themselves had invited them into its exclusive club and then given them the best seats in the house for this once-in-a-lifetime performance, a show that did not need any kind of applause, an exhibition that they could partake in just by breathing and appreciating the millions of years of rehearsal time needed to make this unique moment a living masterpiece.

Dragonflies were beginning to appear and feed on the mosquitoes. One lighted on SG's hand and, for what seemed like hours, the boys studied the insect's intricate stained-glass wings and translucent, vibrating blue body. They were blown away that they could see through the eyes, which rotated a full 180 degrees. SG suggested they take the insect home as a pet.

"What would you call it?" Treme asked.

"Delicate Balance," replied SG.

"Brah, sometimes you can be really drippy!"

By the time the little boat had turned the last watery corner of the bayou, the sun had vanished into the rising full moon. New noises from flying frogs and hairy crickets were filling the night air. Cosmic fire flies danced above the water, in the light of the moon. Inspired by the night's movement, the women started to hum a tune. After several minutes, SG said, "Hey, I know that song. It's an Irish traditional, isn't it? Moose is always singing it at the bar when he gets all nostalgic like."

"Who is Moose?"

"You'll meet him one of these days. How does it go again?"

The two women started singing as their boat glided underneath an over-hanging live oak limb that was covered with furry porcupine snails. Feeling at home with these natural mysteries, it wasn't long before all four of them were singing like a band of cannibalized sailors;

Step we gaily on we go,
Heel and heel
And toe for toe,
Arm and arm
And row and row,

All for Marie's wedding

After an uneventful docking and an exchange of farewell pleasantries, SG asked the alligators if they had a business card for his records. The women promised to sign them up for the institute's newsletter. The alligators looked at the address SG gave them, and then into his constantly puzzled eyes. "Hurricane Hotel," they said. "On St Charles Avenue, no less. That's the prettiest avenue in this whole wide fleeting world!"

SOME GUY UPSTAIRS

For all his multitasking faults, Some Guy Upstairs was best known for his skeptical and cynical attitude toward life, brought on by his relentless and often ruthless search for the elusive fame. On the few occasions when he thought such a thing was within his grasp, he would become too distracted to focus on all the details needed to accept the path of one's own Destiny. This sad fact resulted in his darkest drunken hours. He wallowed alone at the bar and babbled into a tape recorder a slurred barrage of what ifs, and if onlys. Such dismal depths of self-pity forced his bruised ego to drag itself back up off the floor and sober up a little before striking out again in hot pursuit of yet another object or thing that seemed impossible or too elusive to achieve. Some Guy Upstairs suffered from an oversized ego and a lack of self-esteem. In his warped and complicated mind, the pursuit of the unachievable was a far greater and more saintly activity than working steadily with the manageable. Rather than be like the rest of the crowd, which in his mind was stuck in the mundane details of life and having far too much fun, he would set himself up so that the lengthy preparation required for one of his unachievable pursuits would become the main focus of his attention just long enough for everyone at the bar to know what lofty ideals he was about to wrestle with. Of course this form of martyrdom lasted only until everyone wised up to his antics or, as happened more often than not, a newer, more complicated pursuit entered his mind. Being a lazy sod, SG would then resort to total drunkenness until he forgot what it was he was actually preparing to pursue. After a week-long binge, he would wake up in a pool of his own urine, look around the bar room, and start the process over again, ranting about how he was going to quit whatever chemical substance he had overindulged in as part of his preparation, blaming the drug usage as a reluctant necessity for his saintly quest. The rest of the residents of the Hurricane Hotel were content pursuing absolutely nothing and for sure weren't about to quit any damned thing anytime soon, making a point to avoid Some Guy Upstairs like a bad case of the crabs. All this resulted in SG spending most of his miserable, martyred life alone, without so much as a shadow to keep him company.

It was in one of these semi comatose states that SG discovered his one, true companion, a cheap-ass battery-operated cassette recorder that he found in a local Goodwill store. Consoled by his new friend, he would waste away hundreds of hours babbling into its built-in microphone, devising a series of unanswerable questions that he boasted could never be answered. It wasn't long before SG became a Zen guru at this form of logic, believing unanswerable questions brought about greater wisdom than seeking actual answers or solutions. In fact, he was the only person at the Hurricane Hotel who was able to question the absolute impossibility of nonsense over and over again, the kind of guy who smokes forty cigarettes a day for thirty years and then asks, "Why do I have lung cancer?"

Prior to his arrival at the Hurricane Hotel, Some Guy Upstairs kept himself out of the mainstream by holing himself up in a sketchy part of town known as Central City, an area filled with abandoned warehouses, dilapidated storefronts and businessmen picking up transvestites. He lived from chocolate daiquiri to chocolate daiquiri, crapping in a bucket on his abandoned building's roof. His only contact with the outside world was a concerned neighbor who squatted in the building next door. He let SG use extension cords for lighting and occasional cooking. Most of the time, though, SG lived dismally dark and hungry, diligently working on his pursuit of rejecting self-fulfillment.

One freezing and starving December day, he woke up shivering and half-sober to discover that once again, someone had stolen his extension cords. For some reason, this petty theft became the sign he needed to abandon his search for hidden meaning in self-induced misery. He threw his porn collection onto the deserted frozen sidewalk and staggered the three dismal blocks to "the other side of the tracks." After a re-evaluation of his disheveled life via a forty-eight hour binge, at the Abbey, he stumbled uptown into the Hurricane Hotel armed with just enough cash for one month's rent in the dingiest room available. He hasn't left there yet.

Quasi-traumas in the local art scene and his simpatico relationship with the manger landed him a few privileges, one a commission to cover the fifty-three-foot bar with Mardi Gras beads in exchange for several months' rent and a lot of pharmaceuticals that were buried so far under the counter that it took a professional safe-breaker to access them and haul them into his room. He would mix dangerously large concoctions of whatever he could shoot, snort or swallow. After a hefty self-administered dose, he would remain locked up and undisturbed for weeks on end. No one in the hotel really knew or cared what he did in his room, and that suited SG just fine, as it gave him something to brag about when he reappeared at the bar needing a prescription refill or every other Sunday, when he would join the other denizens for a well-deserved liquid brunch. During these luncheons, the residents would engage in heated debates about the plight of the universe and who had recently got caught catching whatever from sleeping with whomever.

Just like everyone else living in the Hurricane Hotel, it didn't take Some Guy Upstairs long to resign himself to the simple fact that he would never be happy even once he became famous and that the closest he would ever come anyway was to spin out the rest of his yarn dislocated from any iota of reality. Living in this dingiest of hotels, with its twenty-four/seven bar felt like the perfect place for him to wallow away. At least here he could ask as many unanswerable questions as he liked, knowing no one would bother to try to answer them. At least at the Hurricane Hotel, he could enjoy the company of like-minded aliases who simply couldn't handle all the instructions found on the back of a detergent box.

ARLEN

Looks like I need to pick me up some more paper on mah way home from work tonight. ... If I go, that is. ... Maybe I should just stay here and think about quitting all this booze and acting out stuff and try and find me some real help because every time I sit on this toilet all I see is them little clouds from the mines disappearing into the gray falling night. All I can see is Peterson's outstretched arm and me trying to help break his fall before we both start sliding, and that Tharwatt noise bursts in mah ears. That's the sound, you know. Not some fancy-ass gun shell slaabang. No sir. Just a flat-out Tharwatt. Kinda like a mean hog fart, is the best way for me to describe it. I don't think I realized it was a mine then, but instinctively, I went to the ground with my eyes glued shut to mah sockets. I was holding onto his hand as more mines exploded and some one below me screamed for a medic and the next thing I knew I was on my feet, scrambling up that cliff slope as quick as I could. I remember the back of my legs felt like they were going to tear themselves loose as I slipped a foot before making two. Someone told me later that I passed about ten other men, but I swear I never saw shit. Just had one big red star in front of my eyes, pounding inside mah skull. I could feel mah helmet strap twisting around my neck, choking me until I yanked the fucker clean off with chunks of hair an ear all stuck underneath mah fingernails. I wasn't stopping for nothing. I was getting up that mountain with that one big pounding mother of a red star pounding in front of mah eyes. By the time I got to the cliff ledge, another thirty mines had exploded, taking out half our unit in less than ten minutes without one single round of bullets fired. It was downright fucking crazy. So many screams trying to figure out what the fuck had just took down so many men.

I was coughing up bloody mucus—and I've never smoked another cigarette since—staring up at the sky, trying to see if any of those stars were laughing down at me. But they were all hiding in that thick gray soup of a night as I kept blowing out hot air before bending down and breathing in cold before leaning back up an blowing out hot again. ... Down an' cold, then up an' hot. Trying not to shit in mah pants as the rest of our unit scrambled over the ledge, shouting and screaming and kissing the ground we were trembling on, all of us heaving like bulls with our gear half gone because several men were missing the limbs that our gear was once strapped to. Then Sarge came running up into my face from outta nowhere. It seemed like he just dropped out of the sky with the laughing stars and was in front of me with claws in his eyes, ready to rip mine out. He was yelling so hard his spit was making me blink. I remember trying to back away from him, but my feet just froze on the spot. I don't know how long we stood there with him shouting, but it stopped as soon as he looked down. Then I looked down at what it was he was looking at, and the world went silent because wrapped around my arm was Peterson's hand, wriggling like a lobster. Its claws had embedded themselves into the top of my wrist and the hand's thumb had gone right through my palm. Blood was squirting everywhere like jets of red, warm piss, pissing all over Sarge's and my face until the world got real loud again and I could hear Sarge screaming about how I had gone an' fucked everything up. He kept on yelling, but all I could do was stare at the hand with its nerves and muscles wriggling like tentacles trying to feel around for the rest of its arm. That's when a rifle butt whacked the back of mah skull, and for the life of me, I ain't been able to remember much else since.

EMMA JANE

All your gruntin' an' wailin' in the bathroom, Arlen, only reminds me about the money it costs these days to go out an' eat, especially at that McDonalds, it being the only place left open after they went and closed down your sister's little grill an' snack-bar. Kept their prices low until they was the only ones left on the block, and us all pretendin' like we don't know what's goin' on and still eating there until they put the prices back up. It's like what Arlen says about them fast food chains, "When you take the kids with you, it costs you twenty bucks just to fart in the place." And he's right, you know. But it's still a treat. And don't you remember for the longest time that eating out wasn't even like close to an option, what with him and then the kids getting all sick on me. Falling on their backs like a set of drunken dominos. You'd think if they were all lying in bed, you could get a little more rest in yourself, but that ain't the case at all. It just gets worse because now you got to be runnin' around three times as much an worrying even more than usual. First Arlen then Zane if I remem-

ber right, with all them gooey ointments covering his body because of that Poison Oak mess, itching all day an' night until his skin got raw and started bleeding onto the bed sheets. … That's when we took him to that fancy health doctor who says, smiling all the time at me, it will take sixteen years for all that poison to completely work its way out of my son's system. Well oh no it won't I say to him! You'd better find something to make that happen a whole lot quicker because you tell me who do you think is going to wash all them stains out of my son's clothes an' bedding for that long! It certainly won't be your smutty stuck-up nurse trying to push us out of your sterile office into that waiting room with her spaceship music sounding like who knows what. And then his nurse starts telling my Arlen that if he threatens the doctor again she'll go an' phone the police on him, leaving me in the parking lot to tell my only son that he had better start learning how to use mah washing machine real fast-like. But you know them kids. They don't listen to nothing you say. And mine ain't no different because he just starts wearing the same old clothes all day an' night, moping about the house and lookin' like he had gone and fell in a bucket of pork grease. Stubborn bugger just like his father. Then Ruth goes an gets diabetes just to keep him company. Starts having to take all them injections. … I mean, I hate needles. I'm allergic to 'em. They make me faint. You know there's a proper name for my condition, but I can never remember what's it called, and as usual, no one else seems too interested in worrying about it, only worried about themselves. So I go an' tell Ruth, seeing you're at home all the time now, you can start washin' them dirty bed sheets for Zane just so you know what I've been doin' for more than half mah sacrificing life. … And wouldn't you know it, that's what she does without ever complainin' once, just to make me feel bad, I bet.

Sure, we did have some good times to remember everything by. You know we got all the photos right there in that album I got as a wedding present. I just think it's the simple everyday stuff that beats you down, though, even if you got lots of family around. No one really wants to deal with your kid's problems because when you show up with one of them on their doorstep, asking if they wouldn't mind looking after it for an hour or two so you can go get your nails done or buy a new toaster or get back on that damn phone, everybody looks at you like you're crazy. I swear, it's enough to make you want to quit life an' go live on top of one of those mountains or someplace like that.

I would get miserable living there after a while though, 'cause I like me a warm body to snuggle in bed with at night I do. I think that's mah problem! It always has been. ... Well maybe that and maybe my weight. But you know what? When the kids and Arlen start to gang up on me and get mad because I enjoy an odd dozen or so doughnuts or drink me a case of diet cokes a day, I just refuse to listen to all their "That's bad for your health" anymore. All I hear is myself saying, "Guess what, you guys. I put up with y'all for too damn long already, and now you can at least let me have a moment to relax an eat a bag of potato chips, snuggled up with the TV and a nice one of them magazines that Arlen gets so jealous of," ... I mean, silly ol' fool! That's why I go an' hides them under the sofa so he won't get all upset. Thankfully, he ain't done no cleaning his entire life and wouldn't even know there was such a place as under the sofa or in between the bed mattresses. Not too domesticated is my Arlen. I mean, he only cooks when he's come back from fishing, and now that he's working with his Pa, I have to make him an extra plate of lunch every day or else he goes and spends all his money down at the Dixie Mart, chatting up those cash register girls I bet or cutting up with the truck drivers who are always slipping a couple of beers in with his po' boy. And that gets Pa real mad because he says its stupid dangerous welding half lit and he ain't going to pay for no insurance for a mahn drunk on the job! ... Does it ever stop? ... I guess not! I keep prayin' it will, but now I ain't too sure what it was I was prayin' for because I don't know where Zane has gone an' run off to or when he's goin' to come crawlin' back home. I'm pretty sure its illegal for a sixteen-year-old boy to be out roamin' the streets all night which means the Sheriff will have to find him sooner or later, and then Old Mrs. Granger will have yet another thing to talk about—like ain't she get nothing better to do? Must be nice, I say, having so much time to sit around and talk about everybody else's problems. Oh well, at least I got me mah health.

Arlen! Hurry yourself up and get out of the bathroom, will ya? If you ain't going to work today at least you can go watch some of the weather channel for me so I can pee before cuddling up with mah magazines an' maybe doze off for a little bit longer. Maybe I could even have a dream about getting me enough sleep so I ain't so dog-tired all day long. I mean, it's not like mah mind don't need some rest now.

ZANE

Prying open the splintered door of the claustrophobic nightmare known as the laundry pit, Zane was greeted by empty detergent boxes and soiled clothing falling on his head. It took almost an hour just to clear a path into the tiny room before he could transform the moldy abandoned clothing, stuffed in garbage bags or crammed into every available nook or crevice, into neat piles, ready to be laundered. Whatever concoction Martha had given him earlier had hot-wired his senses into an anxious productive energy that he now diligently applied into this semi-mindless task of rummaging and sorting through the discarded wardrobes of the hotel's misfits. As he picked through the bags, he discovered numerous items of clothing that would actually fit him, including a pair of silver-painted lace-up leather boots and a red rubberized T-shirt, both perfect for cleaning up the slimy muck in the bar room which he really hoped someone else was dealing with.

Zane started whistling. Possessing a few items he could call his own made him hopeful that everything might actually work out just as Jake had predicted. He whistled a little louder, thinking about his sister and how surprised she would be to find out he already had a full-time job and a place to live.

As the drugs wore off, though, an ache for food nagged him, and Zane wondered if anyone at the hotel ever ate anything beside drugs and alcohol. There were signs of food everywhere: A disposable décor of trampled Popeye's Chicken boxes with varying degrees of rotting meat lay scattered throughout the building, a decomposing reminder that an outside world might actually exist. He was about to look for something to munch on when he discovered a pair of working washing machines and an industrial dryer hiding under the garbage bags. The machines had been rigged, so that anyone who wanted to use them didn't need handfuls of quarters. Next to the machines was plastic shelving, containing quasi-clean towels and half a dozen unopened boxes of laundry detergent. This sign that an organized life form had existed at the hotel raised Zane's spirits even higher, and as his enthusiasm grew, his hunger disappeared. Soon he was merrily washing, drying, folding and neatly stacking the entire filthy contents of the laundry room, separating the colors from the whites and playing the sock matching game between loads.

The industrial dryer had heated up the closet-size room into a baking oven, and an itchy sweat broke out all over his body as if he were running uphill for a speeding bus. Behind the washing machine was a small window that had been painted shut. The glass was smeared from years of grime, and it fogged out any daylight trying to enter. After a cussed struggle that cost several scuffed knuckles, Zane pried the window open. Festering hot, musty air escaped into a thirty-degree-slanted rain as he leaned out and gulped fresh air. From his vantage point on the third floor, he could see the low-lying New Orleans skyline stretching for miles to the east. Row upon row of single-story shotgun houses stood neatly spaced, occasionally divided by dense patches of live oak trees. He watched the hammering rain saturate the flaking asbestos roof shingles, turning the crumbling material into thick, slick mats that looked about to slide off their wooden frames.

Lighting up a cigarette and leaning across the washing machines, Zane exhaled the smoke into the wet, saturated air. The confused smoke tried to backtrack into the dry laundry room. He playfully waved his hand at the smoke, watching the exhausted vapors gently rise before plummeting with the falling rain. The windowsill was covered with a thick layer of crusted pigeon shit. As the rain drummed on, beating a primal rhythm, the hard, crusty surface softened, then expanded, then started to crack and finally transformed into a delicate translucent watercolor, floating over the ledge of the sill before vanishing, revealing a smooth cypress frame resembling freshly hand-planed wood.

"Wow! Dis place looks great! ... Will you come up an' do mine next?"

Zane jumped, hitting his head on the bottom lip of the window. He slipped off the washing machine and landed on a garbage bag stuffed with dirty clothes, and the bag split, spewing nasty smells into the freshened room. Perfectly framed in the doorway stood a tall woman with skin that shimmered like wet tar. The visage wore a white-sequin bra with long, baggy sleeves and a matching pair of see-through flared trousers that clung to her thighs as if the material was soaked. Zane guessed she was about twenty years old and noticed her hips sway every time she breathed.

"What's up wit you, all open mouved like dat? That's rude, you know?"

"I'm sorry," Zane blurted. "It's … just. I'm Zane, and you must be Sophia?"

"How'd ya knows mah name?"

"Jake said you're a real fine piece of ass. Shit! I mean—"

"Stop while yaw ahead." Sophia interrupted, frowning before laughing as Zane tried to gather himself from the pile of stinking clothes. "Dat white boy Jake. Did he also tell ya I's Treme's piece of ass?"

"I'm sorry! I didn't mean. … Pleased to meet you. I'm Zane. Oh, I just said that. The new cleaning guy."

"What happened to da old one, Aaron?"

"He left this morning."

"Dat's a shame. I was goin' ta pay him to come clean our crib for us."

"I'll do it!" Zane blurted again, raising his hand like an overzealous schoolboy.

"Will ya?"

"I would love to."

Sophia looked around the transformed laundry room and ran her multi-ringed index finger lightly over her ruby-painted lips. "An how much ya gonna charge me?" she winked, "for doin' what you done in here, dat is?" Zane started to blush the color of his hair. "You're blushin'," Sophia laughed again. "That's too cute. I was goin' ta pay Aaron a tweenie. … Will that work for yous?"

"Oh yes!" Zane begged, biting his lip to prevent himself from drooling. "Sure thing. Whatever you say, ma'am."

"What ya say?" Sophia placed her hands on her hips. "Did I just hear … I ain't yours or anyone else's ma'am. You can take dem kinda manners eleswheres, you hears?"

"Sorry." Zane blushed again.

They stared at each other for several minutes, listening to the vibrating sounds of the washing machine simultaneously kick into spin cycle. The dryer hummed.

"It's alright," Sophia finally said. "Chances are you don't mean no nothing by it. Just to us sisters down here, that sounds like Aunt Jermima condesendin' bullshit." She studied the transformed room again. "You do theese sheets an' towels, too?" She placed a hamper full of dirty laundry on top of one of the garbage bags. Zane could smell her as she stepped into the room. He got off his knees. "Sure," he said. "Just leave them there. That's perfect. I'll do them for you on my next load."

"Sees ya later, then." She let out a teasing smile, laughing at her effect on him.

"Sophia?" Zane bleated. "Sophia?"

"Yes, Sugar?"

"Where's your bedroom?"

"You mean my crib?"

"Yeah."

"Fourth floor, front of the building, penthouse suite. Just go on in. Excuse da mess! Just teasin' ya. I'll leave the door open. Pile dem clean clothes on mah bed. I can make it later. Still got me a little time left."

"Gladly. Whatever you say, Sophia."

"Oh, here's the tweenie. Don't spend it all at once." She peeled the cash out of her trouser pocket and handed it to him. Zane could smell her again, a primal scent of pure sexual expression. "Martha sez they're makin' some kinda movie downstairs. Ya knows any-ting 'bout dat?"

"I heard something. Ahhhh!" Zane buckled over. His legs had cramped themselves stiff, knotting the calf muscles and shooting pins and needles up his inner thighs. Totally embarrassed and trying to divert Sophia's attention, he pointed at the window. "Is there a hurricane coming in?" he asked, hobbling to stand upright. "It's raining like crazy out there."

They watched the rain fall like nails. The heavy droplets bounced off the windowsill into the laundry room and splashed onto the back of the hot dryer before evaporating into a rising mist.

"I don't know no nothin' 'bout no hurricanes," she replied. "We're goin' ta Miami tomorrow to start working at da Chan Chan club. Ever heard of it? It can rain all it wants to up in here," she laughed and started walking out of the room.

"Wow, that sounds nice. Are you leaving with—"

"Treme? Of course! He's mah man, remembers?"

Sophia left, and Zane scrambled to his feet. He let out a shrill whistle. "Damn," he said, shaking his head and rubbing his cramped legs. "Jake's right about that Sophia. She sure is F I N E." He grinned as lustful thoughts of being alone with her in her bedroom raced through his mind. He stared at the empty doorframe, sniffing the air like an anxious puppy, trying to commit to memory every inch of her ebony goddess body. He could hear her laughing down the hall, something about funny white boys, as he surveyed his work in progress before cramming another pile of damp clothing into the dryer. "Oh man," he smirked at the rain. "Man, oh man. That Treme sure is one lucky fucker."

MOOSE

Hitting a classic Sunday brunch buzz, Moose could hear Some Guy Upstairs, or SG as everyone liked to call him, slurring away his thoughts and insisting he alone was talented enough to be director, editor and sound man, all rolled into one, for the producer Dude's documentary film about the rave scene, a low-budget piece of history to be filmed right here in the heart of New Orleans, at the State Place Theater. From what Moose could ascertain, SG and the producer had met at the State Palace a couple of months ago and recognized one of their own as far as how much bullshit he could spill out. Their bond was sealed after the producer told SG that he had recently seen some of his artwork on a reality TV show that was filmed in a nearby funeral home. This piece of ego-stroking trivia inspired SG to invite the producer to the Hurricane Hotel for cocktails next time he was passing through. At the bar, SG would introduce him to some of the wackier freaks of the after-party rave scene. "You never know," SG said, "Maybe this could add a whole new spin to the partying!"

Serendipity struck with a heavy blow when the producer's lighting man went AWOL late last night. The film crew finally found him passed out in the back seat of a black LTD that was parked outside the hotel. When the producer showed and found SG tying one on at the bar, he joined the drunk for those promised cocktails. What he didn't know was that SG had a knack for getting whoever he was talking to as inebriated as himself, and in less than an hour, the two were cutting up in a heated discussion about the moral dilemma facing today's misguided youth. In their opinion, it stemmed from the absence of classic spaghetti Westerns being studied in high school.

Several cocktails later, SG turned the conversation to himself, waffling on about all the ideas to make the rave documentary more dramatic. He tried to explain how his ever-spiraling mind was exploding with animated storyboards that could translate the multiple layers of complexity in the Hurricane Hotel. Even though SG knew none of the hotel residents really liked him, he felt confident, with the right amount of ego stroking he could get every one of them to give an Oscar-worthy portrayal of their beleaguered and dismal lives.

Blah, blah, blah. SG's mind raced on, calculating how to force the producer's loaded hand into hiring him right on the spot and secure his long-awaited ticket to the glittering cosmos of Hollywood. He was just about to expound on his first theory when Treme bounded across the dance floor brandishing a pistol in the air like an excitable child waves a rattle at its mother.

"Treme!" shouted SG. "Perfect timing. You seem to be rather rattled. Have a drink and meet the producer dude. Dude, meet Treme. Did you know Treme is a direct descendant of the sword-swashing—"

"Fuck dat bullshit!" Treme yelled Treme, standing over the producer with his gun pointing between his legs, "What ya doin' here? You a narc, or what? If you are, I'ma gonna blow your white limp dick straight up your black nigga ass. Who ya tink yuo is comin' here an' messin' with mah business with all your cameras an' shit? This place ain't no public restroom."

"Hold on, Treme!" SG interrupted. "This here's a real producer. He's cool. And you know, from Hollywood an' shit! Gonna make us all Super-Size Me stars!"

"Oh yeah?" Treme replied skeptically. He backed away from the producer's face just a quarter inch.

"That's right. A sense of calm is needed to …" SG was scrambling for words. All he could imagine was the producer returning to Hollywood without him. "He's joined us to make a documentary about how … you single-handedly found your cousin's gold, and after, you gave it ALL back like the intense hero you really ARE, to the correct authorities an' shit that is. Of course, they said you could keep some in ya mouth. Show him your teeth, Treme. Show him that hero smile of yours." SG gulped in some air before yapping on. "And PUL-EEZE … put that gun away. There's a good boy. That's so much better. Thank you."

Treme reluctantly lowered his gun as SG lit a cigarette. "Have the bartender mahke you one of those Crown's you like so much. Shit! What am I talking about?...I am the bartender. There we go. Every one take a deep breath and just fuckin' relax. By the way, have you seen the Chemical Sisters lately?"

SG leapt over the bar as Treme sat down next to the sweating producer and stuffed his gun back inside his jeans. "Yeah," he said, eyeing the producer up and down again. "They were up in here late last night. Why? Who wants to know? Is this guy for real or what?"

"Okay, good. Yes, for real, Treme. That means I think the whole cast is here."

"What cast you talkin 'bout now, SG?"

"The movie cast, Treme. The movie! Like I said, we are going to make a friggin' film, and you're going to be the star, Treme, a real live star!"

SOPHIA

Dem white boys. Tink dat they're so smart wit' these little remarks an' tongues sticking out like they's dogs in heat. Don't have no respect they don't! Tink they's can win ya overs wit' all dat fancy talk an' big words. Then, as soon as ya give 'em your sugar, they drop ya like a hot plate of bacon. I's seen it all before . All the womens warns you 'bout 'em at church. They says, "Look out for dem white mens. Tink you just got off dat boat an owe dem someting other dan a day's wage." Sure wished I's listened when I had dat troubles wit' mah daughter after the good Lord came an' took her away from me. Wish I'd listened to mah heart an' not dat lawyer who says he was going to help me sues dat hospital when all his wanted was to get insides mah pants. ... And he did some. ... How was I's supposzed to knows no better? Me being seventeen an' all an' not tinkin' straight cause I felt soos vulnerabe tryin' to recovers from dat loss of mah sweet little three-year-old dying in dat hospital bed. ... You tell me how many babies are born with ... what's it called ... complications, I tinks. ... It's not like we can go for regular checkups an' find out for ourselves anywheres, now is it. There ain't too many places you can take your children for no free checkups unless ya goes to one of dem Uptown crisis centers. ... An' den there's always the forms dat dey make you fill out before you can get da treatments for free. Mah ass! A week later you go an gets a bill in dat mail, dats for the lab results, they says. Their part was free but not da place where they take your blood to be tested. An' you had better pays it or else they start sendin' dem nosey welfare peoples 'round your house looking for problems. I mean, you look an' see for ya self down here. There's more hospitals an' clinics for cats an' dogs than therse are for us sisters to take our babies to be inspected. Not dat I is sayin' no cats an dogs are bad but don't go exspectin' me to go arounds an' be all smiles when yous start complainin' to me none cause I's isn' in no hurryies to go an serves you dat extra ketchup on your hamburgers an' French fries when you be drivin' through mah resturants all rude an' demahndin' your lunch in a hurry! Oh no. Don't even tink about it. An' when we complains about the lack of medical helps we don't get, it's years later someone finally shows up right 'round election time sayin' they will change everyting if we get out an' vote for their sorry ass. And guess what? As soon as we gone an' voted them back in office, they say we's complainin' too much and dats the problem wit' us black folks. A burden, everywhere in der country because we complains too much. And I says what you talkin' bouts? When was der last time you checked yourselves in der mirrors? Then theys get all rude again like all dem doctors at dat hospital who said I gone an' gave the wrong food to mah sweet Daniella, but in mah heart I knew dat theys gone an' given her the wrong kinda medicine without checkin' what kinda blood she was born wit'. ... I mean, you don't rush your child to no hospitals to go an' get it worse than before it went in now. Dat's what dat lawyers kept sayin' to me, anyway. Dat an' how he would help me for free if I's sit on his side of dat fancy desk of his. You know, before I knew it, I was on his lap listenin' to him keep tellin' me how much his important work costs per hour an' hows he could make it so much better for me if I's only help wit' his loneliness. All I knows is he gone an' made matters a whole lots worse because after da second time he gone an' done it to me, I went an' told mah Pa. ... I means, I was so scared 'cause he was threatenin' me dat I had to pay for his services now. An' who's gonna listen to a seventeen year old nigga wit' a three-year-olds dead baby? So I's had to go an' found me some protection real quick-like. It didn't take me but a couple of days to find mah pa hanging wit' his Indian brothers under der overpass. Kinda funny it was because he didn't go an' recognize me straight off because I had all grown up and it had been over six years since I seen him last. But when I tolds him 'bout his granddaughter dyin' in dat hospital an' dat no good lawyers whose always smiling on dem billboards all over town, mah pa just about got a war started, he did. What wit' him taking his Flambeaux torch to dat lawyers fancy office an' den his own blood an' kin brother goes an arrests him 'cause he works wit' dat same lawyer's brother. Tell me what's dat all about? I mean, he's one of da biggest dealers in our neighborhood. What gives him the right to arrest mah pa simply because he got himself a police uniform from the cleaners? Dat's what's gets everyones so angry down heres, wit' one brother fighten' against another brothers all der time. Mah Ma says them politicians do dat on purpose to keep us all divided up just like dat big grocery store dey developed right in da middle of her old neighborhood. Tore down the building she been livin' in for forty years an' sent her to dat cheap housin' out in Nawlins East. Has to stay theres not knowin' no ones. You can hears our pastor talkin' bouts it at church if you don' believe me none. That's where I go on Sundays now for real ... 'cept when I's wit' mah Treme, of course. I like church. It was Reverend Gordon and his sisters dat was der ones dat got me dat job working in dat pharmacy. They were so kind an' understandin' 'bout mah daughter an' everyting. Dey say it happenz all da time an' dat I shouldn't go an' feel no guilt about it. He told me all I gots to do is have respect for mah self cause no one else'll do dat for you.

Der job was goin' fine til me and Ashanna got caught sneakin' out dem birth control pills and handing dem out for free to our sisters an' cousins. I still don't knows what all der fuzz was about. After all, they were out of experation date an' even dat pharmacist said himself in court dat they would be thrown out anyways. … Well, we said, "Why waste 'em?" We knows how much they cost a month an' all dem tests you have to go an' get just to get the rude doctor to proscribe dem for yous to take. "How can anyones afford dat?" I said to der judge. "It's not like welfare pays for any of it." No wonder we's all getting' pregnant at high school! Looking back at dat now, it was a good ting we gone an' got caught, I tink cause I wouldn't have met mah Treme down ats the jail dat night. I knew right den an' there when I saw him he was mah man. … Still remember him runnin' over to's me an' whisperin' his lawyer's phone number in mah ear. Der whole times dem cops was beatin' on him with dat metal chair. I tell yous what, dat just made me remember his number more somehow, it did. An' sure enough, after three days when they let me make mah phone call I could still remember his number because his whole family came wit' dat bail bonds money right aways. And tinking of mah man, I can hear him now, cutting up at the bar. His voice always makes me glow inside like electricity flowing through a light bulb. No white boy ever does dat for me. You can clean mah room an' dats dat. Stick wit' dem white girls an' good luck because theyse jus' as bad as their men. … Hangin' on to mah Treme when he's supposed to be workin' all night. Tinkin' all dat hot lick lick on dat dance floor is goin' to impress him, some. I mean, I can't blame dem none. Just look at dat white music they have to listen to all der times. Not like you can get up an' dance to any of dat screamin' hate stuff and wailin' country. Still, I always gotta be on mah guard. Especially after I caught dat trixie c what's-her-name hangin' all over Treme like he was her pet monkey, getting' him excited 'bout how her rich daddy was in der record bizness an' ignoring mah feelins like they didn' matter none. Well, I gone an' shown her some of my own bizness I did. I don't have dees expensive long-ass nails for nothin', you knows. The next time we's was alone on da dance floor I's started getting' real close to her like I was her friend or something and pretendin' dat I's didn't even see her holdin' onto mah man in der DJ booth. I waited til she was all smilin' an' re-

laxed an' den grabbed her between her skinny-ass legs like she was a Mardi Gras coconut thrown by King Zulu himself. Then I squeezed down there real tight. … Kinda funny it was, watching her turn red then blue then white an' screamin' in public like a mad preacher man. … Martha told me later after the girl had gone an' passed out dat they had to take her no-ass white butt to der hospital. Good, I say. … If it was the same one as mah sweet Daniella, I bet she's still there. That was the only time I gone an' got mad wit' Treme. … Told him if he ever messes wit' an more of dem girls I was gonna do it to him next. … I have to laugh. He pretended like he was all mad, sayin' no womens talk to their black mens like dat. But he knows as well as I do who takes care of his eggs and' bacon. Eventually, he calmed down, and the next time we were makin' love, whispered in mah ear that he only liked his meat dark. Still, I's a little worried 'bout what's goin' to happen down in Miami, but I got a few tricks he hasn't seen none before. An' once I gone an' shown him how cleans I gone an' got his apartments like he asked for, he's gonna know how serious mah lovin' for him really is.

RUTH

Appeared from under the warm bed covers and stretched her self-semi awake. She glanced at the clock, turned off the alarm before it could shriek at her and stared out at the heavy rain. Lying in her bed, looking up through the open French Windows, she felt as if she was in a tall tree with the dense blanket of clouds moving through her hair. Today, the clouds reminded her of the times when Zane and she would go on summer vacations at her grandma's house in South Carolina. "Looking down from those tall trees," she whispered, her eyes closing again. "Shouting up us on Sullivan's Isle …" She pulled a pillow over her head and drifted back into a restless sleep.

Grandmother lived in an old rambling house built by the army for one of the Captains stationed there just after the Civil War. Mom always said that Mama had come from old money but lost most of it during the Depression, but I never did understand what that really meant. It sure didn't feel like any kind of money to me, new or old, especially as Mama was always talking about how she would have to leave the island to go and live in a trailer on the mainland because she couldn't afford the rising property taxes. Kinda creepy, that house was, now come to think of it, with all those crucifixes and embroidered Bible tracks, framed on the walls, saying how sweet the home is and bless us for this and that. The whole place reeked of mothballs, and the ghost-like sheets covering the furniture and piano made me shiver every time I brushed up against one. "To protect their pristine and delicate condition," Mama would say, even though a set of heavy blinds and curtains were drawn over most of the windows, which remained closed all year round.

I wasn't much into sand myself, but the salty air was good for Zane's skin, even though it would turn as red as his hair no matter how much sun-block I applied. We would spend hours making sand castles with moats filled with buckets of warm ocean water, drawing smiley faces in the sand with sticks waiting for the incoming tide to wash it all away. ... That was my favorite part. ... That and the giant Pelicans flying so low across the water you could hear their wings beat as we tried to touch them with our outstretched hands. Everyday, we would watch the birds following the big container ships, gliding in and out of Charleston Harbor. The ships seemed to be moving so fast that one minute they looked like they were mobile islands and the next, a pencil line being erased over the horizon.

Every year we were told we had free reign of the house except for Mama's bedroom. Even on rainy days it was out of bounds. Of course, this made her bedroom the most exciting and sought-after place to explore in the entire house, and whenever we saw an opportunity, we would sneak up the three flights of stairs only to find the bedroom door locked. Even at night, Mama would lock herself away while Zane would make up stories about what went on in the secret room. He was always trying to scare me as I lay there pretending to sleep. We both agreed that she must have a really big secret hidden in there, perhaps it was a black lover chained to the bedposts or a weird animal from some mysterious jungle that ate children for dinner. Most likely, it was where all that "old money" was hidden. Zane said she must have a toilet in the room or a secret passage to another part of the house because we never saw her enter or leave other than at meal times or when she went to Mass.

A sweet old lady named Gracie pretty much ran the entire workings of Mama's house. She would clean and cook all their meals before taking out piles and piles of china that was never used and meticulously clean each piece, then carefully place it back in the glass cabinets. Once a week she would polish the endless drawers of silver, and on Fridays, she'd dust the entire floor-to-ceiling library. Gracie did all the laundry and shopped on the mainland every morning before she came to work, except, of course, on Sundays, when she was given the rest of the day off after driving Mama to and from morning Mass.

It was Zane's idea to climb one of the tall Pine trees to see if we could peek into the window of Mama's mysterious room. … "Give her a surprise." he said as we raced back from the beach to the Pines standing in front of the house. They were so tall and straight, their pretty bark looking like blocks of chocolate ready to be eaten. On windy days, the branches would swirl through the air, dancing to the sounds of the ocean waves crashing on the shoreline. On quiet, hot summer days the leaves would gently sway back and forth like hands waving to someone living on the moon, casting deep, dark, blue shadows that stretched across the entire length of the lawn.

Zane started climbing first—a real monkey show off, he was, proudly demonstrating how I had to wrap my legs around the tree trunk in order to shimmy up the tree. How old was I then? ... fourteen? ... No, twelve, I think. … Up we slowly climbed like a pair of determined snails. Sure wasn't easy without any low branches to pull yourself up with. I will always remember how the pinesap stuck to my fingers and clothing, giving off such a strong, yet refreshing, scent. When we reached the first of the branches, Zane leaned over and pulled me safely up so we could see the window of Mama's secret room. The fresh-smelling sap was making me feel giddy as we snuggled our backs against the thick tree trunk. "Let's wave and say, Hi." Zane said, exhilarated by the height we had just climbed.

Mama must have seen us climbing from her bedroom because as soon as we started waving she came rushing out of the house below us like it was on fire or something. Her skinny, withered arms were flaying like matchsticks thrown into the wind as she ran hollering with her dry, coarse voice. "What are you doing?" she yelled. "Have we no respect?"

Next thing Mama was underneath the tree peering up at us. Her face was getting redder and redder, all knotted and mean look-

ing. Zane couldn't help himself from laughing, teasing her that they were stuck and could she phone the fire station for a ladder? I started laughing, too, trying to calm the fear I felt looking down into Mama's fire-filled eyes. For what seemed like hours, she shouted and we pretended we couldn't hear her. Both Zane and I felt wilder and wilder as strong gusts of wind began to blew through our hair and swayed the branches to which we were clinging for dear life!

"If I have to climb up there and get you, I swear, you wont be able to sit down for a week!" Mama shouted. She was looking so mad now that I thought she would sprout horns and wings and fly up and grab us with her claws. "Go get a ladder!" Zane shouted back again. But Mama wasn't listening to anything we were saying now. "I swear! I'll beat the pair of you like a filthy rug til Sunday!"

Reluctantly, we climbed down to face her wrath. You had to hold on to the tree trunk for with every ounce of your strength, which surprised me because I thought climbing down would have been easier than going up. I was holding on to the tree with every part of my body, even my fingernails, hoping a piece of the bark wouldn't tear off and send me falling twenty feet to the ground. As we inched our way down, Mama's voice got louder and louder, but I was so glad my feet were back on the earth that I didn't care if she beat us or not.

As soon as we were standing in front of her, Mama cuffed Zane's ears with her cane, glaring at me and saying that I should know better. She swiped at Zane again and he ducked out of the way of the lashing stick and started to laugh uncontrollably. She struck him on his back next, yelling in our ears, "Look at your clothes. Look at your clothes!" Then her cane struck him hard across the face and Zane let out a whimper like a lame dog. Holding his cheek, he looked at me and froze. Mama's cane struck him right across his hand this time but he just stood there, looking at me like I was a ghost or something. Again and again she thrashed his face with the cane, getting angrier as Zane stood unflinching like a statue being hit by a feather. Only his eyes changed, becoming blurry and swelling up with tears. "Zane!" I said, "Move out of the way. What's the matter? You're making me scared looking like that. For God's sake Mama, stop hitting him!"

She stopped her thrashing and glared at me again. "What are you both looking at me like that for?" I said, before Zane pointed down to my skirt. "What's that?" he whimpered as tears streamed down his raw cheeks. Mama rushed over to me and yanked my arms up into the air. She lifted my skirt with her cane, and I could feel myself becoming weak and dizzy as I tried to shake my arms loose. Mama started grinning at me before I bent down and saw a drop of crimson blood trickle down my inner thigh.

"Grandma." Zane screamed, "Ruth's bleeding from the inside out!" He ran over and held me, trying to stop my shaking as Mama straightened out her long black dress and hobbled across the lawn toward the house. "Grandma! ... Grandma!" Zane shouted again, watching her stooped figure become swallowed up in the heavy shadows of the trees. Finally, I screamed, "Mama!" and she stopped and looked back at us. All we could see was her pale face peering through the darkness of the trees shadows. It was a face without a body, bobbing like a peeled potato in hot, dirty water. She raised her cane and pointed toward me. "That will teach you!" she yelled. "That will teach you, my dear!"

"Grandma! What's wrong with Ruth? Is she dying?" Zane hollered. He was crying now, and I could feel my stomach becoming all knotted as I smelled the warm blood trickling out of me. "What's wrong?" he shouted. "What's wrong with my sister?"

I fell faint to the ground. I remember watching the trees sway above me and the clouds pass through the leaves. Then Mama was standing over me. "That's her punishment," she laughed. "That's your sin for disobeying God!"

Ruth opened her eyes. Her body felt clammy and hot. She pulled the top sheet off her bed and realized she had been petting herself in her dream. Her panties were soaked through and in a rush, she looked down to see if she was bleeding. "I'd better hurry and shower," she said to a bottle of water on her nightstand. "Time to work." She touched the bottle with her fingers and stroked the condensation running down onto the nightstand. She could feel the water mixing on her fingertips with her own wetness. "He will be all right," she whispered, rolling her fingers over her thumb. "I'll call Irene tomorrow."

MARTHA

"Reality. It doesn't exist anymore," Some Guy Upstairs yelled, standing on top of the bar, desperately trying to get some attention. Below him, the barroom was exploding into its usual mayhem as both film crew and hotel residents guzzled gallons of cheap booze.

Perched at the bar under SG, studying her nails, Martha basked in the bedlam. *Excuse me, my voluptuaries,* she smirked to herself. *Stop right there, while you're not even close to being ahead! And please, Some Guy, close your mouth while you're at it. Your tongue is wagging like too many pricks I know.* She pressed the pause button in her mind and slugged down her gin. Belching, she pressed her mental play button again. *You mean reality used to exist but somehow stopped? When was that exactly? Was I busy in the bathroom or painting my nails? I just can't for the life of me imagine missing such a calamity.*

"Of course it does, SG!" shouted the producer, confused as to why he was unable to focus through his camera. "What a comment. It's just that everyone has their own reference to it, that's all. Take Reality TV, for example."

My poor sweet souls, continued Martha. *Look around this dump, will you? All of them begging for attention like a pack of stray dogs that just found a pedigree bitch. As if they know what they're doing. Faking those smiles like that. Ready to tear each other to pieces at the first hint of a way outta here. And that film dude with his Sunny Side Up tight-fitting T-shirt, teasing us all like that, and trying to coax us into believing our torn shards of existence are really worth a crap.*

"Reality TV? Are you crazy? Whose reality are they trying to portray? Certainly not yours or mine," SG replied, polishing off a shot of pink, sticky liquid and throwing the plastic cup into the air.

Certainly not yours, that's for sure. What reality do you think you're on anyway? And while you're trying to figure that one out, tell Mr. Producer Dude over there to stop reading me like that! What's his problem? You'd think he's never seen a sister with a dick before. Spare me, please. Take a deep breath for about an hour, would you, right there in the bottom of your beer glass. What makes you think we want your kinda of reality around here anyway? As if our delicate minds aren't warped enough. As soon as I saw his tight Hollywood ass strutting in here like he owned the place, look out I said. The new Messiah is descending to save a gang of Nawlins lepers. Don't you know the reason why we live in this sown up back pocket of a shadow, rotting in our rented tombs is because we have grown skeptical of any form of reality ever existing at all? We live here because we're just a bunch of not-so-sweet smelling petals that have fallen off the back of a rosebush, forever banished and strangled in weeds, growing in the safety of darkness, quasi-content like a mushroom sprouting out of cow dung. Oh, I hate to be so crude, but all you need for a lifetime membership in this dump is some spare change and a clean rubber. Is that too confusing for you, Mr. Spick 'n' Span? Does that thorn cut too deep?

"Anyone want to sign up?" Martha shouted across the room just as a plastic cup landed in her lap.

"That's for sure!' Jake replied, trying to engage in the reality debate. "The people in them reality shows don't seem like they're real to me. For one thing, they're all so professional, like they have real jobs or something."

"What ya talkin' 'bout now, Jake, you idiot?" Treme burst in. "I got me a full-time job. Anyway, what's workin' got to do wit' becomin' famous?" He pushed his way toward the camera, baring a set of gold teeth.

Martha picked the plastic cup from out of her lap and carefully spits her gum into it before tossing it back in the air. *Fame,* she grumbled to herself. *That foul-tasting breath exhaled by an illusive twisted angel, that forbidden fruit, rotten to the core and eaten with maggots. Sure, I'll take a bite. Who wouldn't? … Excuse me? Go right on ahead and push in front of me, why don't you? What you goin' to do with your fame anyway, Treme? Buy a car that goes bling, bling? Or give your folks a silver-plated leaf blower for Christmas? Ha!*

"I agree with Jake. I mean think about it," said SG. "How can you be living in a real reality on reality TV?" A puzzled expression came over his face as the same plastic cup he had tossed in the air some ten minutes ago landed on the bar. He looked up at the ceiling, scratched his head, then continued. "Let me give y'all an example. You're in the bathroom, and you notice you got this big old embarrassing zit about to burst on your chin.

Meanwhile, the camera starts to roll. You're not going to act natural now and go pop it, are you? Of course not! Instead, the whole time you're being filmed, you're distracted from acting real because you're worried about how ugly your chin looks and wondering when the camera crew will leave so you can go find a safety pin."

"What'd ya say?" Treme asked, polishing his gold teeth with his shirtsleeve. "You ain't filmin me in dat bathroom. Dat's mah private bizness! I always knew you were a sick mother, SG!"

Typical, Martha thought, watching a plastic cup with gum attached to it roll toward her ashtray. *See? That's exactly what I mean, a REAL reality. We have to break everything down to the grossest of simplicities here, don't we? Pick at a zit, my ass. Is that the best you could do? Are you trying to impress that producer dude again with your pseudo-political social correctness? .You want reality around here? Why not talk about how half the time there isn't any toilet paper in any of our rooms, let alone clean towels, soap or sheets. No wonder we have to slink down to the bar at all hours, dripping wet. I mean, you try drying yourself off with a couple of paper napkins and see what reality you find yourself living in.*

"Everything you do in front of a camera can't be real simply because there's a camera filming you," the producer said. "Is that what you're trying to say? Well, that's what makes or breaks a film, isn't it?" He paused and blinked as if he had some dirt stuck behind a contact lens. "The greatest directors can convince you that what you're seeing is for real. They touch your hearts and make you believe the film is a reality. They can make everything you see feel real again. Make you believe you're connected."

"Woo hoo!" Martha whistles, standing up to address the degenerate congregation. "Hey you, Mr. Producer Dude, don't go getting your knickers in a twist now. Aren't you getting a little too profound for us slops swilling in disillusion? Take my advice: Stay awhile before you touch anything sharp. Can't you see? We're all actors on this stinking stage. Playing any role you want us to, as long as you can pay, that is. We're nothing but an over stimulated cast, too busy to care or think about the real consequences of anything close to reality, real or other wise. All of us, hooked on some useless thing or other and self-medicated into believing that if we behave and follow the reality spoon-feed to us, we have the chance to become the absolute best and therefore deserve anything we want. We seem to believe we're entitled to be the best director, best cast, best screenplay all rolled into one. Only trouble is, we keep forgetting one vital part, a part no one ever cares to mention. I mean after the rehearsed perfect sex, perfect wedding, perfect kids protected inside the perfect picket mortgaged fence, do you even know what the hell I'm talking about? Look around! I hate to be such a downer, but isn't it getting a tad hotter out there? Doesn't the idea of paying for clean drinking water seem, quite frankly, rather odd? I mean, unless you don't plan on getting wet when you're taking a shower or brushing you're teeth or, worse still, soaking in the tub!"

Martha had run out of breath. She looked around the bar room like a self-proclaimed preacher waiting for a resounding "Hallelujah." No one was listening. Dejected, she slumped back onto her stool and slugged down more gin as her thoughts dribbled on. *Oh stop it Martha. Come on. Out with it! The Text my loves, the Text! Aren't we destroying the one thing that binds us all together, the only thing that enables us to exist here to begin with, the one real thing that every one of us walks, sleeps, eats and shits on? And not just in here. Out there, too. Oh my ravaged and pillaged Mother Earth, promise me one simple thing: Out live us all, will you?* She lit a cigarette and starts burning holes in the plastic cup next to the ashtray. *This is what we have become, isn't it? A bunch of selfish pimps, willing to sell our disillusioned selves to anyone who wants us. Thanks to some presubscribed reality, we're back where we started, minus a few thousand tons of ice caps, scrambling around in one big over-devolved soap opera. Every one of us told how to feel, act, cook and clean and kill, all of us believing that if we pamper our own selfish needs, some abstract miracle will protect us from the real reality of what is really going down. Isn't that what we want anyway, to be protected from reality by introducing a perfect, precious and immortal fake one?*

Some Guy Upstairs jumped down from the bar, laughing hysterically, and pointed at the producer. "By the way, talking about reality, how's that acid? Kicking in yet?"

"What acid? What the hell are you talking about?" the producer replies nervously.

"The acid I slipped in your cocktail. About an hour ago now."

"You're kidding me, right?"

"Alas, dear friend."

Martha laughed uncontrollably as her mind ran off with another one of her epiphanies. *Dear friend! My ass! Some joke that is! No such thing around here! The only time that comes close to reality is when we want something! How's that for a jab of reality for you?*

"Come on Martha." SG yelled, slapping her on the back and pointing to the empty bar stool in front of the camera. "Get yourself up there!"

"Oh, it's my turn? Well about time!" She pulled her shoulders back, puffed out her chest and sniffed at the awaiting camera. "Let's mix things up a little, shall we? Change the roles around, don't you think? I want to see those wonderful hunks from the not-so-silver screen role-playing my reality. I wonder who's sophisticated and enduring enough to translate all of my subtleties. Nick Nolte? No, I have it. Of course! Harrison Ford. What a hot ass on that one! Although I must admit, I've never seen him play anyone I can honestly relate to. Oh well, put on some lipstick, Harry, if you want the role of your lifetime. I'll loan you my heels, we can smoke a few J's and then you can come do me right, Sister. Oh this could be fun! What do y'all think?"

"About what?" SG muttered, throwing a cigarette-burned plastic cup into the air.

"Oh, never you mind. How about Al Pacino," Martha continued excitedly, "with a little weight gain, portraying Mona? Get yourself a toilet to rehearse on and God knows the rest would be easy. I can see it now: Scar Face Mona descending through the fiery gates of the Hurricane Hotel with a golden Oscar strapped between her legs! What? And who are you, wagging that microphone at me? Of course, I'm ready. Do you have a mirror I can borrow? I have to check on my nose hair. Be sure to get my better side, now! There's a doll. I'm the one you've been waiting for. Just like in the song, you know. Remember that slice of reality and everything else will work out just fine. Excuse me, Jake, you impatient fool! Step aside. This is my turn to give these cameras what they really want. I mean it, Shoo fly, before I break your balls! Sure, I'll take another drink. A little less on the ice this time. What's in it anyways? Neat scotch? Why not? My obvious choice would be Tom Hanks. Just kidding, Jake. How about Sean Penn? Glad that makes your imbecilic mind feel better. Now run along. Let's see. Please, not quite so close with that thingy of yours Mr. What's Your Name Producer's Butt Boy. Thanks, that's a little too far back, don't you think? No, of course you don't! Tell me, have you ever done this before? Well act like it, will you? More to the left. The LEFT, I said! That's better. Just a tad closer? What's that? These, under my dress? What sort of question is that? Of course they're real!"

MOLLY

Fidgeting in the back seat of an idling cab, Molly watched the meter tick over. For a hefty tip, the driver had allowed her to smoke in his cab while she listened to the rain drumming on the taxi's roof. After another cigarette and the fare paid, she stood underneath the sagging awning of the Hurricane Hotel, questioning her reason for being back here. It took another ten minutes and yet another cigarette before she pushed on the heavy, broken-hinged double doors and stepped into the hotel's cavernous bar room.

James Booker's soulful rendition of "Junco Partner" greeted her, along with the confusion of swirling cigarette smoke. The stale, acrid smell of moldy booze singed her nostrils, and she wondered if this dive had ever been cleaned in its life. Above the sound of Booker's spider fingers crawling over piano keys, Molly heard Jake's laugh. She wiped herself dry, regrouped her nerves and homed through the smoke-screen in search of his voice. As soon as she saw him slouching against the bar, joking in his usual care-free manner, her heart unwillingly skipped a beat, and right then and there she knew all over again why she had been missing him way too much.

Jake was busy in animated conversation with Martha, discussing who should portray her delicate and sensual goddess-self for the upcoming movie. He glanced over his shoulder and noticed, drifting toward him through the hazy fog, a familiar ghost. He slugged down his drink and before Molly had the chance to turn and run shouted with an exceptionally mean voice, "Shit y'all! Look who Lestat just dragged in!"

Martha, following Jake's eyes, witnessed a stunningly fragile looking goth chick float toward them, dressed in fishnet stockings, matching arm-length gloves and very little else. The only evidence that this petite creature was alive was the slight glimpse of redness trying to penetrate through a pair of porcelain-smooth, powdered checks. Jake turned back to the bar and cursed, leaving Molly standing like Frankenstein's virgin waiting to be dipped into a vat of boiling electricity. Martha, sensing the awkward situation, gave a friendly look of curiosity before bleating out in her usual graceful way, "Oh my ghoulie gurlie wurlie! You must be Jake's earthly betrothed. What philophobic hell awaits such a dear in these unreachable catacombs of life!...And WHO are you, really, my fair and dark nymph? ... Oh my, I am so jealously envious of your nine-inch heels! Please do sit down. We need to talk."

"You're friggin' kidding me!" Jake growled, staring at Molly's reflection in the mirror behind the bar. He frowned, realizing that all folklore ended right here and now because, in front of his very eyes, the prettiest of all blood-guzzling vampires really did exhibit a reflection.

"Oh hush a bye baby," Martha said, slapping Jake hard on his back. "Just look at her will you? Enough to cure any puritanical Protestant's ithyphallophia, I must say. Come. Come. Here, my dear, have Jake's seat." She shoved him off his seat and motioned Molly to sit down. "He's been keeping it warm for you for eternity. Did I catch your name?"

"Molly," she whispered nervously.

"Dolly, you said? ... Oh My, I knew it!" Martha began fluttering her hands in the air as if shooing away an annoying fly. "A fellow sister, if ever I saw one. Oh, Dolly, what a name. I myself nearly dipped my beautiful crown of thorns in the christening waters to rise with such a virtue. Oh, Dolores. What a meek and succulent virgin, you are. Jake, you should be ashamed. Look at this perfect resemblance to the Blessed Mary herself. I'm sure, oh mother of all sorrows."

"It's Molly. M O L L Y." Jake grumbled, pulling up a stool and noticing how Molly had become totally captivated by Martha's fawning.

"Pardon me?" Martha belched, slugging on her cocktail before continuing. "What was that? Molly? Of course! How rude of you, Jake, for not introducing us formally. You're such a dragon at times. They say the Vikings invaded our cursed and heathen country long before Wal-Mart ever existed, and looking into your cold and heartless Norseman eyes, I must say ..." Martha lost her train of thought as she lit a cigarette and patted Molly delicately on her shoulder. A few puffs later, she was back on track: "Molly on the other hand—look at her if you dare—a sweet visage of Miriam, another Mary, I might add, a sweet sea of bitterness. Well, another theory says stoic rebel. Yes, that's so much better suited and how perfect you two are matched. Draco the Mohawk Monster rising out of the impish sea of sensuous rebellion, oh my! This is history for the bathroom walls. And speaking of such heroic themes, I have to pee. Anyone care to join me?"

"No thanks," Molly laughed, watching Martha exit before nervously placing her tiny hand on Jake's knee. "Hi, Drack-O. That woman certainly knows her Etymology!"

Jake glared back. "What are you doing here, Molly?" He wiped her hand off his knee as if it were a flea.

"I came to see you, see if you were—"

"Oh yeah?" Jake interrupted. "If I was what?"

Molly hesitated. She hadn't seen Jake this angry before. Crazed on drugs, yes, but not acting as a caged animal scorched with boiling water. She lit a cigarette, and then handed the pack to Jake. He noticed that her hand was shaking as he held up his lighter. *Damn it!* he thought, watching the flame illuminate her porcelain face. *What is she doing coming back here?*

They stared at each other's reflections in the mirror, smoking in nervous silence until the Christmas lights blinked off. In the partial darkness, Molly mustered the courage to continue. "Because I wanted to see you. There. That's what!"

Suddenly, Jake jerked himself onto his feet, sending his stool crashing to the floor. "Because what?" he yelled, as cigarette smoke blew out of his nostrils as if he were a dragon sailing on the sea of bitterness. "Because you need another prick to make you a baby? Oh, don't look so surprised. You didn't think I knew, did you? Well I do. I found your—what was it called? –fuckin' donor book. Oh yes! And your pathetic little remarks. What was I again? Your personal cute punk dick?" He was leaning over her now, and Molly thought he was about to pick up his beer bottle and smash it across her head. "Jake, please sit down. I'm sorry. I am so sorry!"

"Bullshit. Rich bitches like you are never sorry! You're all the same!"

"Jake! I *said* I'm *sorry*, okay? If you must know, I can't ever have a baby anyway. So there. How's that for a last laugh? You can feel so much better now, can't you? I just wanted to see you. That's all. It was obviously a bad idea. I gotta go."

Molly stood up but was immediately pushed back down by Martha. "And where do you think you're going, my vampirish Queen of the Rebels?"

"Martha. Please, not now!" Jake said, feeling like a total shit as he watched Molly trying not to cry.

"I will have none of this!" Martha insisted, restraining Molly as she tried to stand up again. "Now then. Where were we?"

As if on cue, SG walked over and took their refreshment orders. A few moments later, without so much as a quarter exchanging hands, he poured them one of his favorite concoctions, Alligator Butt Juice, he said, winking at Molly. "A necessary dietary supplement around these parts, you know, consisting of large quantities of cheap tequila with a dash of iced pink lemonade and, of course, served in a plastic cup."

"Yummy for your tummy," Martha laughed.

"And good for the nervous digestion," SG added, "especially now, that we're all going to Hollywood!"

Several Butt Juice shots later, Martha resumed the conversation. "My almighty I! If this isn't a lover's tiffie-wiffie or what, I swear. Why don't we all just—"

"Shut up, you disturbed trouble-maker!"

"Well, I must say, Jake. That's a little better wetter! Glad my charming self and a load of cheap booze can finally warm up your little heart. Actually, I'm the one who has to leave. My services are needed elsewhere, via that cute cameraman. Seems like I made the audition in the bathroom! Can I trust that you both are not suffering from any more mahlaxophobia? Just one look at you, Hon, and I know you haven't get any phallophobia running through those ice blue veins of yours. Let me check down there for you real quick-like!" Swooping her hand down between Jake's crutch like an owl chasing after a field moose, she groped and winked at Molly. "Those heels of yours are most definitely working, my sweet wench of the wetlands! Let's compare edible thongs next time I wear one! As for your fledgling here, no ithyphallopholia to report so far! If you need assistance, please don't hesitate to call. My number is scratched on every public bathroom wall in this far- from-industrious city, male bathrooms, that is. Anyway, I must be off for real this time. I can feel the need for an audience coming on, and I must find Mona because looking at you two love birds is making me all weepie-eyed weepies!"

With a series of elaborate gestures, Martha placed Molly's hands snuggly in Jake's lap and Jake's hands neatly in Molly's. Satisfied that her bonding ritual would not fail, she made the sign of the cross backward and examined Jake one last time to check for any lingering traces of medorthophobia. She was about to exit when she noticed Zane standing in the middle of the dance floor, wrestling with a garbage bag. "Oh my sweet stare of gothic owls," she said, clutching her throat as she lusted over the nervous boy creature of divine youth. "All I ask is that you pray, next time you're tied up or on your knees, that one day, I, the queen of all self-inflicted sorrows, can resurrect my trusty nurse uniform and heal that walking visage of Saint Sebastian,—from Bunkie City, no less—from all those heavy plastic burdens lying now at his feet. Do pray, I say, that when those nasty, cold, needle-like arrows pierce his oh-so-young and supple—my tongue alone and heaven forbid not Mona's—will be blessed enough to lick every little one of his tender wounds back to life so that he sees in his own resurrection that I am truly the one he must cherish and …" Her thoughts drifted off into a sordid daydream.

"Anything you say!" Jake said.

"Who's the cutie?" Molly inquired.

"Oh spare me, will you? That's the new cleaning guy, Zane. He's too young for you. Well, maybe not. Damn, Molly, that feels good."

"I know," Molly whispered, unzipping his fly.

THE CHEMICAL SISTERS

The girls had completed the thankless task of taking water samples from the Mississippi River, and were ready to seek shelter from the pummeling rain. All through the sunrise they had watched the sky slowly darken, and by mid-morning the ominous slab of low-lying clouds had ripped open a steady, heavy downpour. Instead of the usual busy commerce of boats bustling up and down the river, all they had seen today was a lone barge grumbling its way south through the stone-gray water. Unbeknownst to R&R, most of the up-river vessels were gathering at the mouth of the Gulf, waiting to see if the next Coast Guard report would force them to limp their way over to Galveston and to avoid the venerable path of what looked like an exceptionally large storm heading straight for the Crescent City.

Earlier that night, they had dropped Zane off at the Hurricane Hotel and danced around for a while that merrily baptized the pair and their fellow ravers' in the living music of hip hop. R&R always made sure plenty of people noticed them, just in case they ever needed an alibi before slipping out of the hotel and heading across town to the levee. Under the security blanket of a 4 a.m. fog, the two unsung heroines would then bravely infiltrate the chemical plant's property. The plant was known for its blatant disregard for the Environmental Protection Agency's policies. After cutting through the razor-wire fence, they would stealthily slip past the snoozing security guard and then lower themselves off a loading dock into a moored vessel. They'd place the contaminated liquid in glass vials and store them in a plastic frame once used to hold hair rollers. After all twelve tubes had been labeled and sealed, they'd be transported to R&R's homemade laboratory after a few hours of sleep, back at the Hurricane Hotel.

During the night, the two girls had worked efficiently and quietly, recording the speed at which the river was flowing, the temperature of the water and the exact tidal time when each sample was taken. It was a tedious process that required a determination and sense of sacrifice of one's own precious time for the common good of others. To date, they had discovered more than two hundred chemicals inhabiting the Mississippi River. More than half the chemicals they'd found were known to be carcinogenic, according to the extensive lists and resources on the Internet. Of course, some local government regulations were available to the public up in Baton Rouge, but R&R felt that all the chemical plants in the lower river region were given cart blanche to dump whatever they wanted whenever they wanted, and to hell with the rest. It's no wonder that this area was known as Cancer Alley, and to the best of R&R's formidable knowledge, the only other local group trying to keep tabs on this ever-increasing toxic nightmare in New Orleans was a small pocket of dedicated scientists and underfed graduate students working out of their own labs at Tulane University.

As they worked through the early-morning hours, Zane's name arose on several occasions, and they both agreed to monitor him during the next couple of months to make sure he fit in with the other hotel residents; at least most of them had started out the same way as he had. R&R were thankful that the crowded dance floor had been exceptionally friendly last night, offering the young boy a good taste of what the Hurricane Hotel was all about. Unfortunately there had been no signs of any interesting boys to amuse and somewhat occupy the sisters today. No big deal, really. After all, boys were so low on their totem pole, even if it had been six weeks since their last intimate encounter with one. Sure, Zane was a cutie but, he had lack of experience written all over his pimply face, and neither of the girls was in the mood to give him their free sex tutorial, with its strict guidelines of how to use the multitude of contraception devices that are absolutely necessary these days to ensure the utmost protection from all those nasty deadly viruses living in just about anything liquid.

It was generally known that R&R found boys rather dim as they pranced around with their egos hinging on a rather silly looking organ that bulged between their jeans. Not that these girls didn't like attachments; on the contrary, they were very found of them as long as they were actually detachable and could be scrubbed and sanitized before and after use. As for the older men who stumbled into the bar after midnight, chances were they were married and out late because of a domestic squabble, or worse still, away from the family on a business trip. The schlep these graying losers gave the girls about how sexually experienced mature men are, invariably made the sisters physically gag. "You want experience?" one of the girls would invariably say. "Then come on up to our private Cock 'n' Tail Lounge!" This usually sent the guys running back to his wife. The more zealous lecher who had determined that he might have a chance with a cute pair of girls, would be led drunkenly upstairs to the waiting lounge, where they'd strap the excited male down on a bed, remove his pants and underwear, dim the lights and crank up the stereo. In the loaded, chaotic darkness, the Chemical Sisters would leave through the bathroom adjoining the next room. The ever-hungry and eager Martha and Mona would then replace the sisters. As the guy came, believing all his fantasy prayers had been answered, Mona and Martha, somewhat satisfied, would untie him, turn the lights back on and watch the bewildered and embarrassed guy try to flee, pant-less and cursing, from their lounge, pursued by a chorus of rabid laughter. Even on the Internet, the lusting male species was not safe from R&R. Using chat room names like Wet 4 U and Cum 2 Me Daddy, they would get an unsuspecting candidate all worked up, giggling to themselves as they listened through the audio or visual feed to the moans of how much he loved them or could they suck whatever it was he was holding harder baby. Just before his self-induced climax, the girls would announce that their ex-marine Dad had just walked in and was eager to know who was corrupting his precious twelve-year old daughters. For R&R, the male homosapiens were a sad and sorry species, a species way down low, practically off the chart, of their food chain of existence.

Rebecca was holding the hotel doors open for Rachael and a bedraggled youth who had just stumbled out of a parked car. As they followed him into the bar, they noticed he was carrying a microphone in one hand and a battery pack in the other. A series of wires attached to the battery were trailing along the wet dance floor. After shaking themselves dry and adjusting their eyes to the smoke-filled darkness, the sisters could see, standing on the middle of the bar, Some Guy Upstairs dressed like a scarecrow and unable to keep the crows from devouring the crop. Directly across from him, Martha, Mona, Sophia and Treme were fighting over who should pose in front of a producer-looking dude who was holding a digital camera. Further down the bar, Jake and Molly, seemed to be totally distracted by their own intimate conversation. When the soirée looked up in unison to see who had entered their Sunday-afternoon pantomime, they raised their assortment of concoctions and hailed the Chemical Sisters with, "Here comes the Hurricane Hotel's very own Intelligent Design!"

ZANE

I been at the right place,
But it must have been the wrong time.
I been in the right place,
But it must have been the wrong song.

The growling voice of Dr. John echoed through the barroom and into Zane's headphones as he dragged the overflowing garbage bag onto the dance floor. It was obvious from the wreckage of broken beer bottles, crushed plastic cups and strewn underwear that no attempt to clean up last night's partying had been made after he first woke up on the Ship of Fools. *When was that?* he thought, before realizing he had absolutely no idea as to what time of day or night it actually was. It was as if time had managed to lose itself as soon as he had entered the Hurricane Hotel, with the seconds fleeing from the minutes—possibly running upstairs and locking themselves in the derelict rooms—leaving the deserted and confused hours, congregating at the bar, bickering as to what to do next. "What a mess," he said, staring at the sea of sharp and sticky trash he was precariously stumbling through.

I've been in the right vein,
But it seems like the wrong arm.

Oblivious to the trash, a half-crazed cacophony of hotel residents were laughing and cutting up along the bar, their heads bobbing and twisting like a sedge of drunken herons, every one of them primping and ruffling their tail feathers before taking a turn in front of a producer-looking dudes digital movie camera. Next to the camera, SG was flaying his arms and gesturing like a condemned prophet who was possessed, waving his hands at an obliviously hung-over youth who was swaying on a bar stool and dangling a microphone above the nodding crowd's heads. The youth resembled a nauseous and pale statue, reluctantly fishing, trying to catch a Mohawk here or purple wig there. Across from him, a sagging and lopsided, silver umbrella, bandaged together with duct tape and wired onto a metal tripod, stood on top of the bar. Inside the umbrella, a blue neon bulb was smoking and failing miserably to brighten the scene.

I'd have said the right thing,
But I must have used the wrong line.

Zane stood in the shadows, laughing at the amateur moviemakers engrossed in the rehearsal for instant fame. He had never seen anything quite this animated and found himself mesmerized by their anarchist theatrics, filled with an array of cliché gestures juxtaposed against a blatant disregard for any sort of thespian technique or style. Both cast and crew were totally self-absorbed, lost in their own make-believe worlds, yet innocently oblivious of that tedious and obvious fact. *What a wacky stage I've gone and found myself on,* he thought dragging the bursting garbage bag across the dance floor. *I'll finish my cleaning and then go join in.*

He had just reached the middle of the room when he noticed that Sophia was waving to him politely. He let go of the bag and returned the gesture. "Hello, Sophia!" he said happily.

"Hi ya. Uh, Zane was it?" Sophia asked, giving him one of her million-dollars-to-die for smiles.

"I've cleaned your bedroom—"

Before Zane could finish his sentence, he noticed that Treme had stepped away from the camera and was glaring at him "How'd you know her name, white boy?" he shouted. "How'd you know her name, I said."

"We met upstairs," interrupted Sophia nervously. She stood up and grabbed Treme's arm, trying to restrain him from confronting the boy further. "In the laundry room. He's harmless, Okay."

"Oh yeah? Well tell him to stay out of my business!"

"Sure I will, Treme!" Zane said, embarrassed now that the whole crowd were staring at him and his overstuffed garbage bag. He noticed Jake motioning towards the exit door. "See you in a few," he said to Zane, before turning around to face a ravenous looking goth chick whose hands were busy massaging something in Jake's lap. Zane nodded back and, with a gesture of frustration, yanked hard on the garbage bag. A ripping noise issued from the bottom of the bag. "Shit!" Zane exclaimed, noticing that a broken bottle had sliced the bag's stretched and thin skin.

I been in the right world,
But it seems wrong, wrong, wrong.

By crouching and wrapping his arms around the bag, Zane managed to bear hug it safely to the end of the room without too much of its contents leaking all over him. With what was left of his strength, he wrestled with the heavy doors until he forced the rusted, spring-loaded hinges open just enough so he could throw the bag out onto the waterlogged street. Trying to protect his heel from the closing door, he lost his balance and fell face first on the garbage bag, which exploded, spewing its rotting contents all over the sidewalk. "I don't believe this is happening," he shouted at the nonchalant rain, and in a state of exhausted frustration, he crawled on his hands and knees over to a plastic chair propped up against the wall of the hotel and protected from the pounding rain by a canvas awning that was tied loosely to the first-floor balcony. Inside, he could hear the crowd resume its frenzied laughter as Dr. John's herculean piano fingers wound down another sacred song from the spirit of Jelly Roll's inventory of make do commandments:

I been in the right trip,
But must have used the wrong car.
Been in the right place,
But it must have been the wrong time.

Lost in the rain, Zane could see a streetcar trundling towards him. Through the dense corridor of live oaks, the trolley's soft interior glow shined like a window of warm light attempting to flee from a curtain, drawing in the charcoal night.

ARLEN

Swaying over the toilet like a reluctant pendulum accepting the weight of time, Arlen's forehead and nose press against the mirror cabinet. His trousers and pants sat around his knees, covering his unlaced work boots, which were nailed to the floor. He opened his eyes and in the mirror saw Emma Jane eating a box of Krispy Kreme donuts. Beside her, Zane was wearing headphones and had his hand down his jeans. Next to him, Ruth had her sleeve rolled up and was injecting her arm with a syringe.

In front of them was a large desk, behind which sat three men. Two of the men were in army fatigues and the third a doctor's coat. On the desk sat a stack of *Women Only* magazines that the men would refer to while interrogating Arlen, who stood in front of the table, in the middle of this stage. Bright florescent lights flooded the stage, blinding Arlen so that he had trouble focusing and didn't know whether the officers were questioning him or his family. Every time Arlen addressed the uniformed men, he saluted, exposing his privates. Throughout the interrogation, all three officers yelled at him in curt, cold sentences.

"You do know why you're here, don't you, standing in front of us today?" the first officer asked.
"Yes sir!"
"You know how important this meeting is to both your and our well-being?"
"Yes sir!"
"You know this is a necessary procedure for us to evaluate how you will be discharged?"
"Yes sir!"
"You do know the difference between dishonorable and medical discharge?" Ruth asked.
"Yes sir! I think so, sir!"
"You are aware of the severity of the charges brought against you here?" the second officer asked.
"Yes sir! I think so, sir!"
"For the record, no pun intended, is there anything you would like to add to your testimony?" Zane inquired.
Arlen stared down at his unlaced boots, then up at the officers who now also were stuffing their faces with donuts.
"For God's sake man, stand still!"
"Yes sir!"
Arlen slowly stretched is left arm to eye level and concentrated on his shaking hand and said, "Can you remove Peterson's hand before I am discharged, sir?"
"There is nothing there but your own hand, Arlen. Would you like us to remove that?" Zane asked.
Arlen stared at his shaking hand once again. "NO, sir!"
"Take note of his request," the first officer commanded, to which the second officer said, "Note taken."
"Is there anything else you care to add?" Ruth repeated Zane's question.
"I did see a snow leopard, sir!"

"Snow leopard or no snow leopard, you disobeyed orders, and twenty men are now dead." the first officer stated.
"Twenty-one, sir!"
"Twenty-one?" the voices inquired.
"Yes sir! I am dead. Correct, sir! This is hell, correct sir!"
"You're not helping your case here today." The doctor commented.
"How can I help it, Doctor sir?"
"By addressing your remarks to the courtroom with some sense of responsibility, for a start!" Ruth shouted.
"Does this mean you will not remove Peterson's hand, sir?"
"This is totally absurd, there is no hand. You know that, and we all know that! Your tactics here today are as lame as they are hostile. Lame hostile men are dangerous, Arlen, a menace to what we stand for! They have to be purged, flushed down the toilet, and scratched off the record!" the first officer yelled.
"Remark scratched. Gentlemen, might I say that this seems to be an utter waste of our valuable time. Can we conclude?' Zane requested.
"We have no option than to discharge you from all your duties," the first officer told Arlen.
"Honorably or dishonorably, sir? And how come our cell phones never worked over there but theirs did, sir?"
"Enough," Ruth said. "You are an insubordinate pathetic fool!"
"Yes, sir!"
"You are discharged! Dishonorably! Now get back under the rock you pathetically crawled out from! Get out of my sight before I have you thrown out!" the first officer yelled.
"Yes, sir! … Sir?"
"What now?"
"What shall I do with Peterson's hand?"

The toilet flushed.

EMMA JANE

"Arlen Spencer, the third! What are you doin' strutin' in my bedroom like a crazed Cockerel, wakin' me up in all God's glory? An' just look at you. With that big ol' soldier of yours standing at attention like that!"

Arlen was dancing in demented circles around their bedroom, mouthing the lyrics of an old blues song by R. L. Burnside. He flapped his arms like an overfed turkey and wiggled his bare, pimpled butt at Emma Jane. A beaming smile seemed to be tattooed on his half-shaven face. "Ima gonna change sweet Emma," he sang. "I'm gonna change all over I am."

They both laughed as Emma Jane rubbed the sleep from her eyes and slid her *Women Only* magazines under the pillows. "What are you doin', Arlen?" she said again, yawning. "Am I dreaming? Is that one of Zane's records you're playin' all loud an' all? What happened to the TV? We haven't forgotten to pay the cable again, have we?"

Arlen didn't seem to be listening. "Emma Jane," he beamed. "Don't you remember this song? We used to go hear him live down at Fred's Chicken Shack on Friday's. Before we left ..." His voice trickled back into the song like rain falling down a gutter.

"I can't say I do, Arlen. I can't say I do." Emma Jane said. "Arlen?"

"Yes, my butter-drenched sweet potato."

"Are you okay?"

"Yeah, I think I am."

He stopped dancing and stood in front of the window, watching the rain. For a moment, they listened to the heavy droplets falling in time with the beat of Burnside's guitar before cascading over their gutterless roof. The song finished, and Arlen slumped onto the edge of the bed, his joyful mood compressing with the buckling bedsprings. "I'm so tired of all this fightin' Emma,." he sighed, looking out of the window at the low-lying clouds.

"What fightin' you talkin' 'bout now?"

"Everything fightin'. Every breath of the day fightin'. Mah thoughts fightin'. Mah dreams fightin'. Shit! I can't even take a dump without there being some kinda fight goin' on. That's what fightin' I'm talkin' 'bout Emma. It's like every second I wanna make it all go away an' find some rest. You know, I was born with it in mah blood, but it makes me so damn tired an' exhausted all the time now."

"I do know what you mean, Arlen. I been layin' here thinkin' the very same thing myself."

"Well, I'm gonna try an' stop!"

"Are you? An' how you gonna do all that?"

"I don't rightly know, Emma. I'm scared to try. Does that sound crazy or what, coming from my fat mouth. Like if I stop ..." He paused and lowered his head.

"If you stop what, Arlen? Go on."

"I'll keel over and rot like an old bull put out to pasture, standing all alone in the hot sun doin' nothing 'cept goin crazy, listenin' to the flies bitin' at mah ass all day long."

"Arlen?"

"Yes."

"Have you been drinking again?"

Emma Jane was sitting up now, her bulk propped up with a ballast of pillows. She hadn't heard Arlen talk about quitting like this before. Angry and ranting at the world, yes, but today he seemed so happy and carefree when he entered the room, and now, all of a sudden, he had switched into someone utterly dismal and withdrawn. It was as if some kind of unanswerable question was nagging at his soul. She leaned across the bed and playfully ran her fingers over his back. "I almost forgot how big that ol' soldier of yours was my sweet honey dipped banana split."

Arlen didn't notice her comment or her fingers caressing figure-eights on his back. He remained consumed in his beleaguered thoughts, focusing on the raindrops as they squiggled down the window like transparent worms. Finally, he spoke again. "Not sure what happened to me today while I was sittin' in the bathroom an' doin' mah daily rituals." His eyes transfixed on the watery worms like a mesmerized child's. "Maybe it was hittin' Zane last night. I ain't rightly sure. I never hit mah own kin before. Don't believe in that, I really don't Emma. Jus' like mah pa you know. But something inside of me felt like it wanted to erupt and explode like a bomb an' at the same time I felt all blocked up and twisted from feeling like I had flushed away another day of my life."

"Have you tried mah dried prunes?"

"What was that? No, Emma. There wasn't no need because when I gone an' woke up, everything felt like it had changed inside me, and now I felt a whole lot different, kinda weak but stronger at the same time. Do you know what I mean?"

"I think so. Kinda like when you throw up, all hungover in the morning, and then say you feel so much better and where's mah beer."

"Yeah, something like that, except I don't want nothin' to drink today, at least I think so. Oh, I wish I had a way of expressin' mah words rightly. I mean, whatever it was that has gone and passed through me immediately made me want to run after Zane and Ruth and say I'm sorry."

"Ruth, Arlen?"

"Yes, Ruth, too."

"Ruth?" she repeated, before glancing up at a small, faded rectangular section of wallpaper. "You haven't mentioned Ruth's name since you called her a junkie and then made me take down all her paintings of body parts, remember? 'Cept for the one in their bedroom, and you gone an' broke that last night."

"I remember, Emma Jane. Oh God, what have I gone an' done?"

Tears swamped his eyes, rolling down his cheeks and falling off his chin into his naked lap. "What have I done? Can you see now why I'm so scared? If I don't stop soon, I know you're gonna leave me next." He stopped crying long enough to look into Emma Jane's eyes. "How is she doing?" he whispered.

Emma leaned over and pressed her body against his. "Now you go an' calm yourself down, you hear? Nobody's gonna leave no one 'round here. It's all gonna be all right, you'll see."

"How can it be?"

"Well, for a start, Irene's mom says Ruth's doing real well-like, busy down at that hospital in Nawlins—"

"Hospital?" Arlen interrupted. "Is she sick again?"

"No, she's a nurse, remember? Been one for a couple of years."

"Has it been that long? Do you think she'll ever ..." Arlen started crying again. His hands were shaking violently from a combination of raw suppressed emotion and the lack of his morning pint of vodka. "Emma?" he whispered.

"Yes, hun?"

"I'm still scared."

Emma cupped his hands over hers and smiled, wiping his wet face with the fringe of her nightdress. She drew him closer, nestling his trembling hands in her bosom. "Hush, now," she whispered. "You big ol' bear. Hush now, I say."

He could feel her heart beating against his fingertips as they sat in silence, listening to the rain and shyly glancing into each other's eyes like lovers nervous of their first kiss. Finally, Emma Jane spoke. "Arlen Spencer, just you don't be listening to yourself no more, you hear? You ain't been scared of nothing your entire life! Who said quittin' all that anger an' self hate stuff is easy? Shit! If you think forgivin' yourself is like runnin' an errand to the Dixie Mart, think again, cowboy. Anyways, being scared isn't such a bad thing if you use it right. Why do you think I go to church? Most anybody I know can't do it alone or by themselves. I know I can't. By the time the good Lord's day gets around to bein' Sunday, I know I'm 'bout to go an' loose it myself."

"It's not about no religion, Emma. It's—"

"Who said going to church is about any damn religion? That's not it at all. I don't know what all them religions are half the time anyway. What with all that Hanukkah an' Allah an' Day Late Saint stuff. Seems to me it's all the same thing in the end. No, Arlen, I'm not talkin' 'bout religion. You don't have to be told where you're goin'. After all, how can anyone really know what happens when their time's up anyways? What I'm talking about is bein' with a bunch of other folks you know are about to loose it, too, and for some reason being 'round them makes me feel so much better, like I remember I'm not alone or somethin'."

"I'm goin' to talk with Pa later today. He's always tellin' me about Old Stephens at the feed store. Says Stephens stopped all that booze an' acting out after the judge took his license away the third time, told him when he got out of jail he wouldn't be drivin no more ever again so there was no hurry for him to lessen his sentence. Pa says he's as happy as a catahoula rolling in a mess of cow shit now, says Stephens is just glad he ain't gone an' killed no one before when he was drivin' drunk all the time. And if Stephens has to walk everywhere an' not be runnin' riot in that fancy-ass truck of his an' still be all happy-like, Pa says he must be doin' somethin' right for once in his lazy life." Arlen stopped talking and smiled at Emma Jane. "Do you think I can do it, too, Emma? Do you think I can stop all ma fightin' with myself?" He closed his eyes and hugged her again. "I don't think I can. I don't think I can stop."

"Arlen Spencer!" Emma Jane shouted, pulling herself away and glaring into his eyes. "Listen to your dumb self! Will you stop all this mournful self-pity right now and look at me? That thick-headed skull of yours needs to shut up an' listen to what I been sayin' to you."

"What?"

"I mean, just plain listen and don't do no more of that thinkin'! Open your eyes an' look 'round at the world out there. Look at all the mean and terrible things we keep on doin' to each other everywhere, what with murders an' layoffs an' corruptions an' all. If bein' nice an' likin' ourselves was so damn well easy, do you think this world would be as messed up as it is right now?"

"I don't know. I haven't ever thought about it like that."

"Well I damn well have! It's a struggle, and an endless one at that. Look at me. I ain't no perfect text-book example. I gotta fight every day just to be right with mah self. I gotta fight just to get myself outta of bed sometimes. Sometimes, that's the biggest fight of all."

"Can I do it Emma Jane? Can I?"

"You, Arlen, can just about fly to the moon and back before suppertime if you put that bull-horn brain of yours to work and just for a minute stop thinking'. I don't know how many men I know have gone an' gone through what you gone an' done. I bet there aren't too many alive that aren't scared someway or other. Least you already got a start with a good job with your Pa."

"And you, Emma. Don't forget you!"

"Oh, Arlen, you old softy. You know I'm always here for you."

They held each other like long lost friends. Arlen was about to speak when Emma placed her finger over his mouth. She let out a mischievous giggle and batted her eyelashes. "Now, then," she smiled, "why don't you go an' find another one of them ol' records. Maybe Mr. Barry White or somethin', an' hurry right on back, you hear? Let's see how many push ups this here soldier of yours can still go an' do."

ZANE

Slumped in a plastic chair outside the hotel, Zane's mind was lost in the haphazard events and people he had encountered in the tiny slice of a day. He glanced at the mound of trash disintegrating in the heavy rain and felt he was frantically trying to connect an abstract series of dots into some semblance of an orderly picture. A melancholy feeling seeped up through his skin as he wondered if he would ever see his sister again. "Least I still have my ID," he whispered into the rain.

Up and down the avenue, the live oaks had turned charcoal black and resembled giant spiders with sagging limbs lying in wait in the pools of flooded grass. The dense blanket of cloud in the evening light made the brick buildings opposite the hotel look like they were constructed from thick globs of fleshy paint about to drip from a life size canvas, precariously propped against the skyline. Zane leaned back in his chair, fumbling for his smokes, and let out another exasperated sigh. Suddenly, a voice boomed from the darkness. "You can't go leavin' no trash like that, not on dis 'ere fancy sidewalk, rain or no rains. It's illegals in dis fancy part of da citee!"

Startled, Zane looked up to see a tall black man wagging a thick cigar-like finger at him. He had sat across from Zane in another plastic chair, also sheltered by the hotel awning that had started leaking heavy droplets of cold rain through its saturated and bursting seams. Zane noticed that the man's clothes seemed magically dry.

"What's da matter? Ya never seen no black mans before?"

"Yes I have!" Zane blurted awkwardly as he stared at the stranger's enormous hands, that were attached to arms of equally muscular proportions.

"Well act like it, why's don't ya? An' close ya mouth before someting falls in it."

"Yes, sir. I mean, sure thing." Zane blurted again.

The stranger was wearing a long-sleeve red and blue horizontally striped cotton shirt buttoned up to the neck and a pair of faded, baggy jeans that hung over an enormous pair of laceless sneakers. On closer inspection, Zane could see that another pair of soles had been carefully stitched over the original ones with heavy black twine. The man's head was covered partially with a blue and white bandana knotted at the back and slanting at a forty-five-degree angle, and perched on top of the bandana was a black baseball hat with "Saints" stitched across the front in bold gold.

Zane, uncertain what to do next, took a cigarette from his crumpled soft pack and stared back into the rain.

"You got a light, Mr.?" the stranger asked, withdrawing a cigarette butt from his shirt pocket and attaching it to his lower lip.

"Sure." Zane replied. He offered the stranger a fresh cigarette from his pack along with his Zippo. The man placed the new cigarette behind his ear and fired up the butt. "Damn big flame you got goin' on there!" he said, examining the lighter. "You in da army or what, Son?"

"Naw," Zane replied, laughing at the idea. "But mah Pa is, or was, I should say."

"Mine too!"

"My name's Zane."

"Jessie, or jus' plains Jess to yous."

"Pleased to meet you, Jess."

"Oh yeah? An' how do you knows dat?"

"What?"

"I said, how come ya so pleased to meet me? Ya don't knows me from no Adams!"

Zane wasn't sure how to reply. The man was making him feel very awkward. *It would help if I could understand a word he's saying,* Zane thought. *But he seems friendly enough'*

The rain was now striking the canvas awning so hard that Zane felt like he was inside a kettledrum being beaten by a thousand pairs of hands. He inhaled on his cigarette, enjoying the hot, damp smoke filling up his lungs and making him slightly dizzy. His body relaxed and he sank further into his chair. *How long have I been down here now?* he wondered. *It sure feels like time has disappeared and been replaced by a blanket of warm fog that has wrapped me up into a ball and sent me off bouncing into another world.* Even the cars crawling along the avenue seemed to be moving in the same slow-motion state that Zane felt himself slipping in. He watched the passing cars shimmer like splashes of electricity cast from the street lamps. Their windshields were covered in rain no matter how fast the wipers flayed across the glass, so it was impossible to see if anyone was actually driving the cars. Zane's head nodded as he tried to focus on a chicken bone floating into the gutter. "Guess I better go find another garbage bag," he muttered, half asleep, to a bobbing chicken wing.

"I guess ya had gone an' betters." Jesse replied, leaning back in his chair and watching the young boy.

Zane disappeared into the hotel just as a streetcar rumbled to a stop directly in front of the building. One of the passengers, a girl, it looked like to Jesse, was staring right at him as the car started up again and trundled past the hotel. "What's she lookin' at?" he muttered, as a cold shiver ran down his spine. The car disappeared into the rain. "Everywhere you go, peoples have to stop an—" Jesse cut short his sentence. His eyes were fixed on what appeared to be a small college knapsack buried under a pile of crushed, Big Gulp root beer cups. Instinctively, he looked up and down the avenue, rubbing his large hands together before standing up and stepping out into the rain. He gently kicked the sack with his oversize sneaker. Suspiciously surveying the avenue one more time, he bent to pick up the bag when the hotel doors burst open and a grinning Zane emerged, triumphantly clutching a new garbage bag as if it were a rabbit he had shot and was now posing for the standard hunting lodge photograph. Quick as a flash, Jesse booted the sack back under the trash pile before slumping himself into his chair.

"Found one,!" Zane said happily.

"Me, too," Jess replied, shaking himself dry, but locking his eyes on the garbage pile. He leaned back into his seat and casually lit the new cigarette with the Zippo.

"Hey," Zane shouted, "that's mine."

"No it ain'ts!"

"What? Yes it is. I just gave it to you."

"Sees. I told ya."

"Told me what?"

"Ya jus' give it to me. Ya jus' said so yourself."

"What are you talking about? I—"

"I's talkin' 'bout dis lighter. Sit down a minute."

"No!" Zane shouted. Anger and frustration mingled with exhaustion made his head feel like it would spin off his body and bounce along the drowned sidewalk. Sensing the boy's despair, Jess motioned for him to sit down again. "Lizen, kid, to some frees advice. Ya just gone an' got yaself off dat banana boat, now, don't ya?"

"What banana boat? I just want mah lighter back! Please, sir."

"Hey, nows. Calm yaself down. Easy, I says. Jus wait a minute. It'll save ya a whole lots a troubles later."

"What will?" Zane slumped into his chair totally defeated. He thought he was about to pass out.

"Livin' 'eres in Nawlins."

"I don't see too much living going on at the moment, just a whole lotta folks dying real slow."

"Dat's everywhere in dis 'eres countrys." Jesse interrupted. "It's jus' we have a lot more fun doin' its down 'eres. Now lizen, never be givin' no lighter to no ones that's asked ya for a light. Sees." Jesse held up the Zippo as if to show Zane what he was talking about. "No lighter's, no foods, no spare change. See?"

"Why not?"

"Cauze if ya dos, ya settin' yaself up for some serious troubles."

"What do you mean?" Zane was totally confused.

"I mean is, if I's ask ya for some change an' ya goes an' gives it to me, I can see wheres ya wallets at. If I stops an gives you mah left over food, I knows da place you gone an' eats in an hows expenzive dat places is an' wether it's worth me robbin' your ass or not, soos I's can go an' eats theres myself."

"Shit, you're gonna rob me now?"

"Not unlez if ya let mes." Jesse laughed. He seemed to enjoy confusing his young audience. "Rules number ones. Just cause I's black don't tink you 'ave to helps me outs. That's what da tourists who get into troubles do. They don't behaves like that when they'res at home. Ya don't see 'em sneakins about in their own town and lining up to help theirs own poeples now dos ya? For some reason, as soon as theys get down heres they wants to try an' helps us. Makes 'em feel like theys parts of da local color, I's guess, but we can sees it's the wrong kinda helps, sees? We don't need ya sympathys an' quarters. Dat don't pay too many bills, now, does it? Seems like no outsiders been helpin' us before, so why's ya gonna try an' starts now? Just makes us suspicious you gonna try the sames shit as you gone an' done to our Indian brother an' sisters." Jesse stopped talking and, content with his words of wisdom, puffed on his cigarette without ever removing it from his lips. He leaned forward and, firmly holding onto the Zippo, lit Zane's fresh cigarette.

"Thanks."

"You're welcomes. As I woz sayin', we beens lookin' after ourselves since mah papa's papa woz gone an' told to get off dat cotton fields an' fend for hisself. See, when wes quit bein' slaves we become problems, which, dependin' on which sides of the propertys lines yous an' I's are on, woz either not so long agos nows or so far back dat a lot of folks wanna forget to write it in da historys books. Now, I ain't sayin' I knows everyting because everyones gots to have problems, right? Because if we had no more problemz we wouldn't needs no more politicians, you dig?"

"Does this mean you're not giving me my lighter back?"

"Alls I's sayin' is, don't take no ones frees help from a stranger 'cause ya gotta be suspicious of theirs motives. Saves ya a wholes lotta troubles in da long run!"

Jesse finished his speech and took the cigarette from his mouth. With his large fingertips, he rubbed the end of the burning tobacco until the fire was extinguished and then placed the half-smoked remainder behind his ear. He looked down at the trash pile, then back at the exhausted boy. "'Ere's ya goes," he said, handing Zane the Zippo.

"Thanks."

"Yours welcomes."

Zane put the lighter back in his pocket, finished his cigarette and reluctantly got out of his chair, searching for the energy to open the new garbage bag and fill it with the old trash. He looked at the pile before stepping out into the rain. His clothes soaked through, instantly, and the new garbage bag whipped shut in the rain. Cursing in the blinding wetness, Zane began the torturous "Doubling the Garbage Bag," dance.—An exceptionally twisted dance we all have experienced on way too many occasions. You know the one, when you're trying to fit a broken garbage bag into a new one, and for some reason the new bag just doesn't want to open, even after you've found the right end, and once you have opened it, the old bag seems to be twice the size of the one you're trying to put it into, so that before you know it, both bags split. –

Jesse watched the knapsack as Zane danced. "You needs some help?" he said.

Zane stopped, looked up at Jesse then back down at the pile of rotting chicken bones. "That would be great. Thanks."

Jesse stepped out into the rain and stood over Zane and the trash, his towering frame protecting the boy from the deluge. "You sure?" he asked. Zane nodded, and a moment later, Jesse's dexterous fingers had expertly opened the garbage bag and he was on his knees, shoveling the soggy, slimy mess into a neat pile. "Hold dis end," he said to Zane.

While Zane was holding the open bag and wiping his eyes from the rain, Jesse, with one large thrust of his extended leg, kicked the bag under the parked car. A few minutes later, with all the trash in the new bag, he sat in his chair and, using his own lighter, lit the cigarette butt that had miraculously stayed dry.

"Thanks again, Jess." Zane said gratefully, before disappearing around the corner of the hotel in search of a dumpster.

"No problems," Jesse replied, finishing his cigarette. Then, in one lightning-fast move, he jumped out of his chair, bent down next to the car and snatched the sack. He opened it quickly and whistled, and then dissolved into the thick blanket of the rain-drenched night.

RUTH

"May I?"

A dripping-wet young stranger was motioning a request to sit next to Ruth even though there were a lot of empty seats on the streetcar.

"It's a free country," she replied before turning her attention to the workers repairing a section of the trolley tracks in the pounding rain. The trucks flashing yellow lights were suspended in the droplets of water running down the window. Another set of droplets that encapsulated a large antebellum home draped in the leaves of the live oak trees chased after the yellow droplets until they merged and ran off the window together. "Squiggle giggles," she whispered to her reflection.

Most of the time, Ruth enjoyed riding the streetcar, any public transportation for that matter. She didn't even mind waiting in the rain. The waiting seemed to slow everything down and give her a chance to become part of the day again. Quite often, she was the only person in uniform on the streetcar at this hour except for a few elderly women finishing off another long day of tending to the needs of the Uptown kids. Ruth would watch the women lightly fold their weathered hands into their laps, as if praying, before dozing off, one by one. Just before Canal Street, they would all open their eyes, check their handbags and exit the trolley before crossing the road and continuing their two-hour journey back to their own section of town.

"You're a nurse. That's cool. I like uniforms. Where do you work?"

"Charity Hospital, the emergency room."

"Can't believe there's a hurricane heading this way. Seems so crazy out there."

Ruth watched her squiggle giggles dissolve in the reflection of the young boy's face. *A Hurricane,* she thought. *Why hadn't she heard about that today? How could she? … She had to sleep the better part of the afternoon and had woken before the radio alarm went off. A computer was going to be her next purchase, one of those compact laptops instead of the one she had to use at the public library. She had to stay better informed, stay more up to date with what was going on. She could afford one now that her college loans were almost paid off, even with the rising cost of her medication. No credit cards for this one. Always liked to know what's coming in and going out.* "A hurricane, you said?"

"Yeah. I think it's the big one, you know, heading straight for us."

Ruth hesitated. She didn't know why she had engaged in conversation with this stranger. It wasn't like her at all.

"Well I ain't leaving. Looks like a lot of folks aren't either," the stranger said. "They always say it's going to hit us, you know. Then that warm water from the Mississippi shoots it off west somehow up through Texas. They can have 'em all if you ask me. You going there now?"

"Where, Texas?"

"No. To work."

Ruth didn't respond. The idea of a hurricane was making her anxious. She rubbed her hands together and studied the stranger in the reflection of the window. She guessed he was about 21 or 22 years old. He wore a striped wool cap, and blond dreadlock extensions spilled out of the hat onto his neck. A worn-out long-sleeve cotton checkered shirt and a pair of converse shoes with torn jeans set him off as either as a drop out or worse, one of those trust fund babies she occasionally ran into in the bars.

"I play music," he said.

Ruth turned and glared at him, hoping he would get the hint and leave her to drift back into her domestic thoughts. "That's nice," she replied curtly. Just as she was about to look back out the window, she noticed in the corner of her eye a black case beside his feet. Before she could stop herself, she blurted out, "What's that?"

"What's what?"

"That, in the case?"

"This?"

"Yes, that!"

"An oboe case, with an oboe inside it. I play down on Frenchman Street with a bunch of other dudes. It's really cool. You should stop down there some time. It's a lot of fun, if you know what I mean." He winked and leaned his wet shoulder against hers. "We're playing there tonight, as a matter of fact."

"As a matter of fact, I have to work." Ruth pushed his shoulder away.

"Well so do I, but not all the time."

She knew she had made a big mistake interacting again with this guy. Hoping to end it now, she repeated, "I HAVE TO WORK!"

"Excuse me? So do I you know. At the Gumbo Place. Almost every morning, if I can drag my ass out of bed. Wink, wink! Nudge, nudge! Say no more, as they say. I'm a prep cook down there. Some say it's the best gumbo in the city, but I'm allergic to seafood." He started laughing at himself. "Kinda funny being down here and allergic to seafood and all. Where you from? I'm from Connecticut. Come to think of it, though, they have a bunch of seafood on the East Coast, too." He let out a snort. Ruth faked a smile. "That's okay," she said, feeling slightly bad for yelling at him. "Some say I'm allergic to sugar and that exists pretty much, everywhere."

"Really? You a diabetic or something?"

"How did you know?"

"Your wristband. My mom's sister, she caught it several years ago."

"Did she?"

There was an uncomfortable pause as the streetcar came to a slow stop. They both took the opportunity to watch a group of overweight and underdressed tourists, soaked to the skin, board the trolley. After a long exchange of words, the tourists complained to the nonchalant conductor about why they had to pay again and why couldn't his machine give them the correct change for their dollar bills. Several minutes of bickering ensued until they finally had all their quarters figured out thanks to an elderly man, who professed to be blind and who had just happened to have a pocket full of loose change.

"Thanks to the kindness of strangers," Ruth whispered to herself.

"What'd you say?" The young musician turned and leaned a little closer. Ruth could smell him now. One hundred percent musty sock. "Anyways," he continued. "As I was saying. There's a hurricane coming and—"

"Yes," Ruth interrupted. "You've already said that, and that you're not leaving. And that there's an oboe in that oboe case of yours. And that you play down on Frenchman Street. And … what else? Allergic to seafood. Did I miss anything!"

"Prep cook," he sneered.

"God, you just don't give up, do you?"

Ruth pulled herself closer to the window. She could see the Hurricane Hotel approaching in the distance. She gazed with silent fascination at the Expressionist mural painted on its facade. The faces of the dancing, larger-than-life-figures seemed to jump off the walls, creating a hypnotic-cartoon effect and a delightful contrast to the rest of the pristine, solid buildings lining the avenue. Under the hotel's awning, two figures were smoking cigarettes. Ruth gasped as one of the figures got up and entered the hotel. *Could that be?* Her mind raced. *No way. Why wouldn't he have called me first? I have to call Irene.*

"That's a great late-night hangout."

"What?" Ruth turned, confused. She had forgotten about the annoying voice now sitting almost on top of her. For an instant, she thought about jumping off the trolley and chasing after him.

"Best coke in town. We should go there one night."

"What?" She repeated, still trying to decide what to do next.

"We should go."

"Jesus! I heard you!" She clasped her hands together until her knuckles went white. She could feel the stranger's breath contaminating the side of her face. "Okay, Okay, you've got three more stops to convince me why I should have to continue listening to you, so you'd better get started, because I know you will."

"Whoa, you're for real, huh?"

"First stop, coming right up, and not soon enough!"

The stranger smiled, folded his arms and said, "I believe men and women are created equal and in the eyes of the universe, color and gender are not issues."

"Second stop, almost there."

"Shit. Excuse my language. Music is the purest form of expression. It is a gift from the universe for all the world to enjoy. That's why we have ears, you know. How am I doing?"

"Why the oboe?"

"Oh man, the notes you can reach with it, makes your whole body feel like you're alive. Not an easy instrument to learn, I might add. It's all in the breathing, just like sex, but it blends in so well with a saxophone or trumpet, and my folks never gave me—"

"Three, time's up! And, as the old saying goes, see you on the flip side, dude. Excuse me, this really is my stop."

"But, I don't even … your name?"

"Why?"

"Because I like you!"

"You don't even know me."

"I can tell you're lonely, and—"

"A contagious diabetic. Now shove off."

Ruth pushed her way past the stranger and strutted off the streetcar. She turned to face the moving trolley and could see his nose and face pressed against the glass like a demented circus clown. *Creepy,* she thought, and walked briskly down Canal Street, wrapping her wool nurse's coat tightly around her petite frame. She took a couple of deep breaths. *He was right. It does feel strange out here tonight. I'll talk to the hospital security guards. They always seem to know what's going on.* In the distance, Charity Hospital loomed as a shiver ran through her body, forcing her to look back over her shoulder. The rain was coming down so hard that it was impossible to see if she was being followed or not. She shivered again, pulled her coat tighter and started to run.

A few minutes later, she stepped safely through the hospital's revolving glass doors. Glancing at her medical bracelet, she sighed. *How many times a day do I have to check my blood sugar? No more talking to strangers, Ruth. You certainly don't need yet another prick in your life.*

JAKE

"What was that?"

"What was what? What are you talking about?"

"Outside. I heard something, sounded like a gun shot."

Jake jumped up from the mattress and leaned out the window.

"Nice butt!" Molly giggled, pulling the bed sheet over her own naked body.

"Shit, Zane. I knew something was up."

"Hey, where do you think you are going? Get back in here! I haven't finished with you yet. Jake. What's the matter? ... I mean it, get back here this instant."

"Shut up, Molly!"

Jake scrambled to put on his jeans and t-shirt before running down the hall.

"Your shoes!"

"Fuck 'em!"

Outside in the flooded parking lot, Jake could see Zane flopping about in the rising water like a snared fish. Blood was leaking out of his left leg as he tried to prop himself up against a dumpster. A bullet had penetrated his thigh and continued through both sides of the dumpster until lodging itself in the hotel's wall.

"What's going on here?" Jake yelled, running over to Zane. He saw a flash of metallic in the air. Then he saw Treme.

"I said, where is mah money, you stupid little punk? Who da ya think you are, messin' wit' mah plans like dat?"

The blinking overhead lights were made the gun in Treme's hand shimmer like a sparkler on the Fourth of July.

"I told you, Treme!" Zane wailed. "I haven't seen your bag. There must be some kinda mistake."

"You're the only mistake 'round 'ere, white boy. Now, are ya goin' to climb back in dat dumpster or am I gonna have to cap your ass again?"

"Please, don't shoot. I'll climb. I'll climb!"

Zane writhed in the water, desperately trying to turn his shaken body upright on his good leg. He got on his feet and limped like a barefoot child who had stepped on a nail.

"What the hell is going on here?" Jake shouted, trying to regain his breath. "Shit, Treme!" He placed his arm around Zane's sagging shoulders. "You gone and really shot him!"

"Stay outta this, Jake! He gone an' stole mah money. That skinny-ass punk. I'ma gonna nail 'im to dat dumpster where he belongs. Fuck 'im for fuckin' wit' mah plans."

Jake was desperately trying to assess the situation. He noticed Sophia standing next to Treme, clutching his arm and holding an umbrella over her head. "Sophia," he shouted. "Talk some sense into him, will you?"

"Jake, I think he did steal it, I swear." Sophia looked as frightened as Zane did. "He gone an' cleaned out our room, and then it was gone."

"What was gone?" Jake looked back at Zane. "Did you?"

"Yes, but no. I never saw no bag of his, I swear! Shit, Jake. I'm scared. My leg. ... Am I going to die?"

Jake could see the bullet hole in Zane's jeans. Blood bubbled through the pierced, singed fabric and ran down his leg into the floodwater that covered his shoes and ankles. He looked at Zane's horror-stricken face. The frightened kid's cheeks were as white as cocaine, and his lips had turned anti-freeze blue. Trembling from shock, Zane's eyes were glazed over, staring blankly, like a blind man. "No, you're not goin' to die," Jake said as reassuringly as he could before turning to Treme again. "Shit, Treme. Where was it? Someone call for an ambulance. Sophia!"

"No one's callin' no nothing. It was in da garbage under the sink, an' he says he emptied it. Now there ain't no bag or money. I mean it, Jake. Get outta the way. Don't be messin' with mah plans. I just gonna plug—"

"Hold on, Treme. Hold the fuck on." Jake lowered Zane gently back to the ground, propping his shaking frame against the side of the dumpster. The water was up to Zane's waist now as he shivered violently. "Don't go floating away on me. I'll be right back. Hang on, okay?"

The sharp, rusted lip of the dumpster sliced Jake's stomach as he plunged head first into the soggy, rotting garbage. "Doesn't anyone have a flashlight?" He gagged, trying not to heave up his guts. "Anything at all?" He blindly pushed trash around with his bare hands, groping for anything that felt like a bag. He searched for several minutes until the smell and the futility forced him up for fresh air.

"Find it?" Treme shouted.

"Hell no. I need a flashlight."

Jake stood in front of Zane, shielding him from Treme, and tried to regain his bearings. He pulled globs of congealed mashed potatoes from his wet hair. To his left, he could see Martha, Mona and the Chemical Sisters yelling at him to move away from Zane. His gut told him this was one big mistake about to explode into an even bigger one. *Maybe the bag really is in the dumpster,* he thought. *Maybe Sophia has stolen it.* His mind raced with possibilities. None of them seemed convincing or close to hopeful. *Maybe Treme has just gone insane. It's not like this would be the first time.* All he felt certain of was that Zane was innocent. "Poor bastard," he mumbled, pulling more rotting remains out from his hair from the failed dumpster-dive. "Fuck this. I'm going to get an ambulance."

Treme fired a shot into the air. The hot lead spun up, over the hotel then descended, and lodged itself twelve hundred yards down the avenue, between the eyes of the unflinching bronze statue of General Lee.

"If anyone else moves, I'll send 'em weres I's 'bout to send this nigga punk. And for the last time, Jake. Stay outta mah business."

"Look, Treme. I'm going to find a flashlight, alright? Everything will be all right. We'll find your money. I'll be right."

"You ain't goin' shit! You either get that punk back inside dat dumpster or you're gonna join him."

"You know what? I was inb middle of having some fun with mah girl and—"

"Your girl? Shit! Don't make me laugh. I thought you was Martha's blow-up doll."

"Fuck you, Treme!"

"NO. Fuck you, bitch."

Treme fired again. The bullet whizzed past Jake's ear, singeing the side of his skull. He could smell burned hair and his face felt like it had been dragged along a gravel road at high speed. He rubbed the hot blood across his face and slowly walked toward Treme. To the left of him he could see the Chemical Sisters running after him. Treme blindly fired off another shot. The bullet spun past the girls and across the avenue, boring through an empty parked car and into one of the large windows of the Whitney Bank. The shattered glass set off both the bank's and the car's alarm.

The madness deafened the rain-drenched streets as Jake threw himself at Treme and grabbed his legs. The two boys toppled into the water, wrestling like giant crabs. Treme freed his arm and hammered the butt of his gun into Jake's exposed back, cracking several ribs. Zane hobbled toward the fray until Sophia, wielding her umbrella like a splayed baseball bat, hit him square across the face, knocking him unconscious just as the Chemical Sisters pounced on her and sent all four of them toppling over the skirmishing boys. Semi-submerged, the human pyramid writhed in the water until Treme's gun fired two more shots. A frightened calm descended over the twisted mass of limbs.

Sophia was screaming now as the Chemical Sisters began peeled Jake's limp body out of the human wreckage. She tried to stand up, swinging her broken umbrella at anyone and anything that got in her way. Martha socked her straight in the jaw with a karate kick, forcing Sophia's head back onto Treme's motionless body.

"Someone get an ambulance!" Martha yelled, yanking the umbrella out of Sophia's hand. "And for Jake's sake, hurry up!"

SOME GUY UPSTAIRS

A fender-bender-beaten-up Dodge van slid to a halt beside the pile of crumpled bodies. The driver's door swung open and SG fell out. "Forget the ambulance," he yelled. "Come on. Pile in." He wobbled around to the back of the van and, after opening the rear door, frantically shoveled handfuls of Mardi Gras beads onto the flooded parking lot. Confusion filled his mind as he remembered loading the very same plastic treasure into the very same vehicle only a few months earlier, after the final Fat Tuesday parade, in the very same parking lot.

A crowd had gathered in the pandemonium as Martha and Mona lifted the choking Zane out of the water and eased him into the van. Molly and the Chemical Sisters staggered behind them carrying Jake, his pale limbs dangling like a portrait of an emaciated victim hanging from a cross. Blood trickled from his mouth as they lowered his crumpled body into the rear of the van.

"What about Treme?" SG cried as he ran over to Sophia, who was cradling her lover like a sleeping infant.

"Back off, white boy. Leave us alone!"

"We can't just leave him!"

"You ain't touchin' nothin' no time soon!" Sophia yelled as she groped around in the water in search of the gun. "Y'all done enough damage already."

"Sophia, it's me, SG. I can't leave him."

"I mean it. Back off!" Sophia was pointing the gun at SG now. "Please, SG, leave us be!"

The producer dude emerged from the safety of the crowd and tried to stop the Chemical Sisters from closing the van's side door. "We need more footage!" he yelled. "We need so much more!"

Martha sprang out of the van and with one of her notorious vice grips, grabbed hold of the producer dude's balls with her long nails. He fell to the floor with an agonizing scream. She snatched the camera from his hands and hurled the priceless footage of the afternoon's events into the murky depths of unsalvageable eternity. "Film this, dick head," she yelled, scrambling back into her seat as SG started the van, trying to regain control of the situation. He sucked hard on his unlit cigarette, which was drenched and unraveling from his lips. "Hold on," he shouted, slamming the vehicle into gear. Without checking for oncoming traffic, he launched onto St. Charles Avenue. The van hurtled across the flooded medium, sending everybody's heads against the ceiling. Jake let out a tortuous scream, begging for someone to stop the motion. "Hold on, big guy!" SG mouthed SG as the van bounced over the trolley tracks and made a hard left. Flooring the gas pedal again, he glanced into his rearview mirror at the sea of shell-shocked passengers. He could see the outlines of their heads bobbing in a morbid wake of silence. "Bless Jake's bleeding heart," he mumbled, ignoring another red light as he spat the soggy cigarette onto the dimly lit dashboard. He could feel his mind melting as he tried to adjust to the mechanics of driving. Glancing at the mirror again, he studied his dilated pupils, a pair of scorched, cracked saucers about to implode into the depths of his skull. The cigarette slid off the dashboard and landed on his wet boot. Martha, sitting in the passenger seat with Mona on her lap, wiped condensation from the windshield. "Thanks, Martha," SG said, looking into the rearview mirror again and praying into the burnt keys of his soul, "Someone better be awake at Charity Hospital. You hear me, Sweet Jane? Someone has to be there, rain or no tripping rain!"

TREME

Dat Sophia! Always full of dem surprises, she is. Just listen to her singing up there like an angel running away from heaven. An' I didn't know ya spoke no Spanish. What's dat, you said? Oh, excuse me. Cuban, you say. Well, I didn't knows dere woz a difference. ... A song by the Buena Vista Social Club. Well, it sure sounds beautiful.

A song your grandmother knew, before she left the islands as a free woman of color. … Dat most have been a along time ago.

I tell you what, Sophia, dis Miami Chan Chan place sure looks just da same as mah Ninth Ward, what wit' dem porches an' barbecue pits an' no street lights workin' at night … Ever noticed dat, have you? Uptown, they have lights working all over da place like you're cruisin' around in a flood-lit football field at Christmas or someting. But not down in here. Not in the Lower Ninth. Ain't even one on at the end of the block to let you know what street you gone an' got your ass lost on. Tell me what's dat all about? No wonder everyone's so scared an' shooting at dere own shadows. It's like we're livin' in a cave or something. … What you sayin' now, Sophia?… Yes keep your fingers running through mah hair. It feels soothing like dem guitars I can hear in dar backgrounds.

I knew ya would understand. No matter what it takes, ya can't be havin' no one messin' with mah plans, because if they do, it's all over wit'. … Once you hesitate, peoples can smell your weakness an' you're just another lost brother who has sold out before you're old enough to own your first car.

Hey, is dat mah cousin Eagle Wolf comin' to see us off? What a surprise! Yo, Bra! Look at him dressed so fine in his indian costume with his feathers ripplin' like gold leaves in a breeze. An' all dem different beads sparkling like broken glass on da street. Could loose myself for hours inside his costume, I could. You knows peoples want ta pay thousands of dollars just to owns onesz day do, but cousin Eagle Wolf knows better, don't he, Sophia? He says if someone wants to pay that kinda money, you know it's worth three times more than what he's asking for it. … Man! It's the whole tribe out parading, now. Look at dem wailin' an partyin' like it's Super Sunday or something. I respects dem, I does. Dey don't listen to no one's fabricated rules either. Did you knows one of dem costumes takes a whole years to make, wit' da wholes familys an' grandparents an' cousins an' children sewing on it. Dat's what I call real art, Bra. An you tell me dem folks ain't hard workin'. Shit. How many hundreds of hours a day is dat?

Sophia, I have to admits dis raggedy-ass wagon ain't what I was expectin' to be travelin' in through these streets. I means no offense to no ones, but that pony looks like it's worked all day down in dem French Quarters in da middle of August or someting. I was expectin' one of dem silver Rolls Royces wit' white-wall wheels an' shit like der one King of Zulu rides around in on Fat Tuesday. Oh, wells. Did I tells yous, your voice sounds like sweet guitars strummin' through my veins. Even if I don't understand no word of dis song, you're singin', it's helpin' me figure out mah next set of plans. An baby, maybe you could find me a blanket or someting while I lie here doin' mah tinking cause I is shiverin' really colds now. … An' baby, I tink I is goin' to need some help getting' up all dem flights of stairs so I can getsz mah records together for mah next gig. You knows what's funny? I feels like I's got so much more music inside of me dat I want to play. … I swear, I's do, Sophia… I swear, I's do ……

RUTH

The fluorescent lights overhead flickered more off than on as Ruth followed the doctor through the maze of people gathering in crowded corridors and overflowing from the waiting rooms onto the flooding streets.

"Nurse, I need your assistance. We have another problem."

"Right away, doctor."

"Talk about an emergency in the emergency room, what with the backup generators failing. We're basically operating in the field down here."

"It seems that way, doctor."

Behind them, a ruckus broke out as the ward's doors swung open and a mob of hysterical misfits stumbled forward with a limp body held above their heads. The doctor blocked their path. "Excuse me. This is a restricted area. You are not allowed in here without—"

"Zane!" Ruth shouted. "Is that you?"

"Ruth! We have been looking all over for you. We need help."

"What's the matter? Your leg. What happened?"

"Nurse!" The doctor interrupted before noticing the blood pouring out of the suspended body's mouth. "Good God, that boy looks like he's bleeding to death! Find a Gurney! Over there. That's it, gently, gently. Lay him down."

The speechless posse wheeled Jake through the rising chaos, searching for an empty bed as the doctor walked beside them ordering the crowds to make way. He examined Jake. "This is not looking good," he muttered under his mask. "What a mess, and by the looks of things, it's only getting a whole lot worse."

Ruth located a vacant bed at the far end of the ward, and they carefully lifted Jake's body off the stretcher onto the sterilized bedding. "Who are all you people?" the doctor asked as measured Jake's vitals.

"We're his ... relatives, and I'm a trained and overqualified doctor," Martha replied.

The doctor glanced at her and growled, "Sure you are, and I'm General Sherman. Listen up! I'm in no mood for jokes at such a critical hour. I've trained as a military doctor and served an extra three terms of duty, so I've seen and heard all the bullshit I ever wanted to and then some."

Martha didn't flinch at his remark and confidently proceeded to tell the skeptical physician of her own medical training, naming the doctors she had studied under and the medical fields in which she had specialized. She then gave the doctor several secret signs known only to those sworn on the Hippocratic Oath. Somewhat satisfied with Martha's credentials, the doctor addressed the rest of the ramshackle posse. "How did you all get in here?"

"There's no one at the reception desk," SG blurted out.

"What about security?"

"Look around, doc. What security?"

"This situation is impossible."

"I know," Martha interrupted. "That's why we're here, offering our help, doctor. What else do you have?" She looked at Jake and let out a mournful sigh before diagnosing the patient as drowning in his own blood from a punctured lung. The doctor agreed with her prognosis and let Martha and the other "relatives" stay. He then instructed Martha to assist in setting up whatever basic life support, suction tubes and medications the failing hospital could provide, hoping the dying lad might have a slim chance on the next available operating table. The lights flickered off again as someone down the hall collapsed into maniacal screams. Reluctantly, the doctor and Ruth left Jake's bloody bedside.

"These places depress the crap outta me," Mona said, peering past the plastic curtain and then down at Jake. His once thick, dark hair drooped over the pillows like soggy watercress.

"No shit," Molly whispered, shaking as she held Jake's hand. A few minutes later, Ruth returned and stood over Zane, who was sitting in a chair beside his friends with a pool of blood and water forming at his feet.

"Who's that?" SG yelled out, pointing to Ruth. "She's cute!"

"That's my sister," Zane replied protectively.

"Pleased to meet you, I'm SG or Some Guy Upstairs for short. Hang on, I'll be right back."

Ruth knelt in front of her brother. "Hey, you," she said. "What you gone an' got yourself into this time? Better take off those wet things so we can take a look at that leg of yours."

"Sure thing, Sis. You doin' all right?"

"You tell me. Yes, I love it down here. It's not normally quite this crazy.—This might hurt—They say there's a hurricane on the way—seems funny, me giving you an injection."

"I guess so. Ouch!"

Ruth expertly cleaned, stitched and bandaged up her brother's leg. A few minutes later, SG stumbled back inside the curtained room carrying a large box. He has a plastic bag tied to his belt. "Got some supplies, guys," he said. "Man, this place is about to blow."

"Tell me something we don't know already. What you got in there?" Mona said, pointing to the bag.

"It's candles. I was going to do an installation piece down at the Circle bar. ... Well, that doesn't matter now. ... Here. Y'all grab some, and Martha, take care of this, will you? I traded with one of the orderlies." He handed Martha the plastic bag filled with vials of Demerol.

"This sure isn't no Valium!" Martha exclaimed Martha. "What do you think we are, elephants?"

"Since when did you start complaining, *Doctor* Martha?"

JAKE

I could use a large swig of Tom Waits right about now. ... Filling me up with his rattle-tattle-clinking piano, sounding like a demented gang of wind chimes shaking bones and cursing through my veins as gargling voices dig into my skin, realigning my heartbeat into a slugging jab, punching through the alleyways and the graffiti-crazed mayhem of a world filled with disposable lives.

Sing to me, Tom. Sing to me now! As I dangle on your chords, suspended like a puppet stuffed with crow feathers and the slaughtered words of tin-can battles rattling on flagless flag poles whose rusting wires flap like the clinking chains of slaughtered love. Comfort my ears! Shed my skin! Let your orchestra of stretched strings screech over the muddled rooftops, knowing that I'm not afraid to take another first step and break free from these wings pinned inside a stagnate specimen box.

Don't cry for me as I begin again. Don't cry, I say. Up here, I'm worthless and lacking nothing. Up here, I'm able to howl into the desert of limbo. See how my body writhes in the wrath of eternity, twisting upward, past the walls of manicured screams, like the burnt flakes of a lost love's letter!

Oh Molly, Molly, Molly! I can only thank you like a moth thanks the flame. Thank you for the very first time your galaxy of delights, dripping wet between your silken legs, opened for me, giving me the strength to Pogo through the great abyss and smash the wasted what ifs, sending them reeling into a land bleached by a sun bred in Texas and suckled with vultures spitting out Amarillo. Watch me, Molly, as I fall higher and find the words to strengthen the hopeless and crush the hours floating in pools of self-denial. Let anarchy rise! Rise out from Molly's legs! Let's cherish all our first times that make the memories of a lifetime. Break the spells spewing from a caldron of boredom and lit by self-righteous fires. Let's worship the moments blown by headless winds and feel every fleeting second.

Don't breathe, Jake. Don't breathe, not until I've slugged down another iced fifth of rhythm and ground these chords into the ashes sprinkled over mystical pyres. Seep into me, reassure me like a whisper echoing through a canyon of rusted schemes and demented false starts.

Rage on! Rage on against the grime of the beaten souls reflected in the cathedral's stained-glass windows. ... Roar as I spit out dirt, clawing my way through the moldy belches of commerce. ... Reach in and pull out my heart. Keep it from beating in the vaults of tattered time. You see, I have staggered into a song and come out the other end without regret. Not once did I let up or let go as I scratched music onto blood-stained walls, as I copied your verses, your words, your prophetic visions on the peeling plaster of deserted dreams, not caring if I shared my plate with rats picking the scabs off a jailer's fat ass, not caring as long as I had music entering my ears. ... Can't you see? I am hitch hiking my way into another first time, knowing that my blood will dry in the sewage of busted expectations where the vulture's shadow floats above a scorpion's sting. I have hobbled, bruised and aimless, into the fists and shriveled cocks of uniformed bullies, whose anger I already miss. Can you smell them now? ... So close that it seems like yesterday. ... Wait, another door is closing.

Oh, you pretty ones. Thank y'all for protecting me with your perfected dysfunction, ticking away on the floating clock of time. Let your confusion skewer the world we can no longer crawl out of. Will you join me now as I slash and burn a few million bar codes and blow out the borders that pierce our tongues? You know our flesh becomes plastic as soon as we are born ... so recycle. Transform all senseless sorrow into a song no one can understand. You have seen the crows circling. Circling over the thankless hours with their beaks eager to peck out the eyes of youthful abandonment. And still we pity the man who prays to be saved.

Oh my beautiful angels, rub your genie lamps against my flesh. There's no more everlasting to be found in this disposable age. ... Faster now, it's all been used up. So use the unusable and rub me, baby. I want to bust out the same way I came in. I want to break free screaming, biting and kicking. I want to enter another first time, severing the umbilical chord with a fucking hard on.

ZANE

The besieged hospital staff and doctors worked around the clock, doing their humanly best to prevent the eruption of anarchy. In the hot, murky corridors the desperate and bedraggled, seeking shelter from the storm, continued to arrive, their lowered heads and crumpled bodies looking like abandoned shadows. Fear herded them onto a ship's plank of shell-shocked disbelief before forcing them to disembark into a sea of uncertainty. Zane noticed, instead of chains brandished around their feet, many wore sneakers without laces with neon lights blinking at their soles and heels.

The busted air conditioning had made the clammy air so stifling that Zane felt wrapped in a coarse blanket of sticky itchy fog. A constant bead of sweat trickled down his furrowed brow and over his eyelids, blurring his vision. The pain medication Ruth had administered earlier as she cleaned, plugged and stitched his wound had made his limbs feel heavy and at the same time sped up his thoughts into a frenzied whirlpool of confusion. He sat silently in his underwear, trying to focus on the flickering shadows cast by the candles floating out of the Jake's curtained cubicle. He watched the elongated forms rise to the dim, pastel ceiling then spiral through the narrow corridors and disappear into the soggy darkness. Their fleeting, nervous energy reminded him of Jake's living shadow, which he had followed only earlier that day into the Hurricane Hotel.

Absorbed in the shadows, Jesse's words churned inside the young boy's mind. The lines of scared people made him realize that there wasn't anything as frightening as finding oneself without a home. Compassion rose from him. *Ole Jesse was right. These people are not the ignorant savages he had read about on flyers he saw posted at home every time David Duke and his cronies rode through town. ... These people had experienced a crueler side of the coin, and they knew many saw them as merely a problem, not part of a greater progressive solution. ... Better to live in the safety of being invisible than try to break into a world haunted with prejudice. ... Shit, if he was honest with himself, the real reason he hadn't paid too much attention to what Jesse had been saying was that the old man was black and had looked worse off than himself. ... Just look at his shoes and the way he picked up the rotting garbage with his bare hands.*

Zane melted down. Nothing seemed to make sense anymore, not a damned thing. All his teachers tales that he should feel proud to be part of the richest and freest country in the world seemed such gross lies. He wondered whether nomadic people were better off than these crushed, homeless souls trying to survive on broken sidewalks paved with what felt like uncaring prosperity. What confused Zane the most, though, was Jess' remark about not trusting anyone who tries to help you, even when you're down and out. There seemed something very corrupt in this remark, some kind of broken link in humanity's chain. *What forces could make a person feel and believe such a thing? Zane wondered. What past circumstances had driven Jesse to make such a hopeless comment?* For Zane, it wasn't a question of pointing a finger or laying the blame. He was still too young to become bitter and jaded. Everything he had experienced today was just making him unbearably confused, causing his mind to flounder with so many unanswerable questions. In too short a time he had heard the voices of too many scars itching beneath his skin, too many self-doubts gnawing their way through his innocent heart. All he wanted to do was vomit up the past twenty-four hours of his life and then go hide in a dark corner, purge the images from his memory onto the sanitized hospital floor and smudge them into the linoleum tiles with his bare feet so he might be able to start again.

"Hiya, Zane. You okay?"

He wiped his eyes as the Chemical Sisters appeared, followed by a band of giggling children.

"I think I'm finally loosing it."

"Why?' Rebecca asked.

The Sisters pulled up chairs and sat on either side of him, and he spilled out all his fears and confusion, crying his way through the events that had hurled him head first into a bottomless puddle of despair. He cried and talked, then cried some more until he felt empty and hollow. The sisters sat patiently, listening like concerned teachers. When he was done, they Zane that this apparent hopelessness was part of the challenge we daily have to respond to in life. The only advice they could give him was to never be too quick to hand out judgment on a fellow human being, regardless of race or color or creed. "It will eat away your humanity and drown all consciousness!" Rebecca said. "Just remember the words of our hero, Madame Eve Curie—"

"Words don't seem to mean anything anymore."

"Bullshit. Nothing in life is to be feared. It is only to be understood."

He faked a smile as Ruth and the doctor came in to check-on Jake. The doctor pulled back the curtain. Zane and the Chemical Sisters, followed by the children, stood up and joined the rest of the Hurricane crew, who were weaving about a few feet from their friend's bedside. The doctor announced that it was time for them all to bid farewell to their friend. Unbeknownst to this valiant, nodding, night watchmen, Jake had passed away several hours earlier. A wall of sadness caved in over the crowd as Martha removed Jake's oxygen mask and ceremonially kissed his dry, purple lips. She kissed him again, then jumped back. "Doctor!" she exclaimed. "Oh father of all my medicated sins, look! Jake is crying!"

Streams of tears were rolling down the deceased boy's face.

"Impossible! Let me have a closer look," replied the doctor, leaning forward and wiping Jake's cheek. "Well, blow me over. They certainly look like tears to me but they're drying into some sort of ... Astonishing ... amber-like substance. I can hardly believe it, and ... look at that. There's an insect, a tiny ladybird, frozen inside each tear! Nurse, what do you make of this?" He asked as he placed one of the amber beads in Ruth's palm.

"Oh! It's my very own Lazarus, risen from my breath! ... Just a kiss, just a kiss from my own martyred lips! Awake, I say! I, Saint Martha. Please, I'll have no more delusions cast at me from this doubting world! Someone tell me what was in that Demerol. Doctor, I must have some more! Perhaps that is the trick to saving this world!" In a swan-like dive, she swooned into Mona's arms, who stepped out of the way to let her sister's fainting saintliness crash onto the hospital floor.

"How can this be?" Ruth spoke. She turned one of the tears over in her palm and read aloud. "Made in China."

An excitement erupted around Jake's bed. Music began trickling through the hospital's loudspeakers. The toe-tapping, finger-snapping, torchbearer of The Spirit of Jelly Roll, the man who invented Mambo piano playing filled the air. A round of applause, if you please, for the one and only Professor Longhair!

I went down to St. James Infirmary
To see my baby there.
She was lyin' on a long white table,
So sweet, so cool, so fair.

"I'll make a cast of my favorite organ and bronze it, no silver," Molly smiled, slipping her necromantic hands under the sheets.

"Stranger things have happened, I'm sure, although in all my years of medicine, I can't think of one," the doctor said. "Still, for all the merriment, this lad is most certainly dead, and I have to send his body down to the morgue. This bed is desperately needed. Nurse, where's the orderly? Oh, and what Demerol?"

Oh, when I die, please bury me
In my ten dollar Stetson hat.
Put a twenty-dollar gold piece on my watch chain
So my friends know I died standin' pat.

"Doctor, the morgue is flooded. There's no way of getting a body in or out of there," Martha interrupted as the Chemical Sisters flung themselves over Jake's body.

"Is there anything I can do to relieve some of your confusion?" Mona asked, slipping her hand down the doctor's pants.

"He's coming back to the hotel with us. It's been democratically agreed," said an ecstatic SG.

"We shall take Jake back to the Hurricane Hotel, back to where he belongs," Mona exclaimed. "It's bad enough he had to die in such a place, let alone rot. Excuse me. No offense, doctor, but this place is way too clean."

"I think I can relate," the doctor said, slowly pulling her hand out of his pants.

Jake's tears dried up and Ruth distributed the amber beads to the happy, open-mouthed children. "Now run along, my precious miracles," Martha said, picking herself up off the floor.

"Go show your parents and the rest of the world who I really am!"

"We'll prepare his living corpse for burial or resurrection, or whatever comes first." SG stated, and in an uncommon display of organized comradeship, the Hurricane crew wrapped Jake's body in the bed sheets. Fearing further chaos, the doctor disappeared into the corridor as Ruth sat down next to her brother, who was fumbling with his bootlaces. "How are you doing?" she said.

Zane looked into her eyes and realized for the first time that neither his sister nor anyone else could help him connect all the dots he had experienced in the past twenty-four hours. He wobbled to his feet, feeling his wet clothes cling to him like a protective second skin, and for a brief moment, the surrounding insanity seemed to melt into the harmony of Professor Longhair's voice growling out the final verse of his "St. James Infirmary Blues."

Get six gamblers to carry my coffin,
Six chorus girls to sing me a song.
Put a twenty-piece jazz band on my tailgate
To raise Hell as we go along.

Zane found a glimmer of solace in the thought that Jake would be amused by the idea of no one really knowing if he was dead or alive or better still, neither, preserved in a limbo that many in New Orleans work hard to maintain. Zane wondered what would become of Jake's larger-than-life spirit as it began the next oddest of odysseys, parading on the swaying shoulders of his fellow journeymen, bound for the safe haven of the Hurricane Hotel.

"Are you going to be okay?" Ruth asked, watching her baby brother's childhood evaporate into the puddles beneath their feet. She smiled as he checked the flame of his Zippo. Staring into his eyes again, Ruth searched for clues that would remind her of the young boy she had once known. "Where are you going now?"

"I don't know. I really don't know."

Leaning forward, Zane kissed his sister's cheek as if he was late to catch a plane. He hoped that time wouldn't check out and leave him stranded without the hope of ever meeting his future. His body staggered under the weight of the destiny on his shoulders as layers of his former self, peeled away like old paint blistering in the sun. "I don't understand anything anymore," he whispered.

"Look around. Who really does?" Ruth replied, trying to smile. "What about your headphones?"

Zane stared at Ruth, then at Jake's empty bed, then back at his sister again. "I don't need them anymore," he said, letting go of her hand, "I think it's time to make my own music."

Ruth hugged her brother again. "You know where to find me," she said, "just in case you ever want to."

Zane forced a smile. "Sure I do," he said, as he wobbled out of the hospital and into the rain-soaked madness of his own bewildered carnival.

PART II

ROUND ABOUT NOW

08:00 P.M.

Ladybugs and carrot noses seem like funny things to be listening to when you're stark and tripping out in the Hurricane Hotel, wading across a flooded dance floor waist high in a tepid soup of stinking lake water with a tape recorder dangling around your neck. I can feel its two-bit boot strap tightening around my throat as I play back the voices of a distant past, trying to decipher who or what decides which memory is salvageable or what must be trashed.

I mean, it's not like this has ever happened to me before, breaking and entering an abandoned building whose fractured architecture scared the meanest of shadows away. I'm alone now except for these haunting memories pouring out of my mind and staring me bluntly back in the face. Can you see them? Out they pour. Out through my eye sockets like sly old water moccasins, slithering over my face and wriggling into infinity, a carnival of snap-shot images rearranged into a deranged slideshow, distorting the present into recognizable shapes of my haphazard past. Ouch! What was that? Something just took a bite out of my ankle. Nothing like losing your balance in slimy rising lake water. Just hope I haven't cut myself too deeply this time because you know this water sure isn't anything close to squeaky clean. No bottled spring water here, I can at least guarantee that. This sure ain't no aqua-blue swimming pool in some fancy weekend home, not like wading in a tropical shallow end, sipping on a cocktail with a pair of shades on your head and a bunch of nine-foot naked blondes tanning themselves on shimmering, imported Italian tile. I wonder if it was the edge of the stage. I guess I'm lucky, though. Things could be a whole lot worse. I could be trapped outside, lost and forgotten on the broken streets, anchorless, with nothing to drink, surrounded by a mess of pissed-off snakes and mean old rats, all of them ravenously mad because their beloved sewers have gone and backed up, forcing them to relocate real fast. Trust me, down here, in these lower depths, when it floods this bad, they will come right at you. With all their biting and gnawing and wanting to scramble up your back or down your pants like you're a floating island or something. And when it's raining this hard, you can't really see where you're trying to go. You just gotta bee-line it with some kinda abstract belief there might be higher ground on the other side of town, with your arms out waving and mind gone cursing, hoping you don't fall into one of them exposed sewer drains. ... Can you imagine the water rising this fast? With so much pressure, it can pop off a one-hundred-pound metal grate like flicking a bug off your arm. Pop and off it goes.—Sounds like a brand of vodka I know.—Pop n Off.—All heading down river, I can only suppose!

08:20 P.M.

Where was I? ... Oh yes! ... How quickly we seem to forget. ... Let's not get too distracted now, not when we have only just started. Just because the water is spinning me around like a rubber ducky after the plug's been pulled, try and concentrate, press the play button on that tape recorder of yours. ... Go on, what's stopping you? Focus on who is telling the story. Listen to what has already been said. Press it, I say! ... There we go.

She would watch those bugs for hours, she would, clouds of red and black insects swarming at sunset, ushering in the waking of winter. She hadn't seen that many before, thousands of them, invading the house and crawling over the furniture and congregating in the dingiest of corners like stubborn sheet rock dust. All huddled up together trying to keep warm and acting like you weren't even living there at all. I mean, you could wake up in the morning and fall out of bed and find one had crawled into the cap of your toothpaste. You could twist off the cap, squirt out some paste, brush your teeth, gargle and rinse, inspect your nose hair, twist the cap back on, and wouldn't you know it, that cheeky, sleepy bug hadn't even moved or made a sound. Simply loved them, she did. Started collecting them in her bedroom, just be-

fore she was diagnosed with diabetes, some time around Christmas, I think, round about the same time our old man came home all beat up and twisted, telling us he'd lost both sides of the war. … She started talking to them next and giving them complicated medical names. Lucky fellows, if you ask me. I can still see her now, rubbing their little red and black shells with her delicate fingers, not much bigger than them ladybirds themselves.

Hey now, what just happened? I thought these were new batteries. Hold on a sec, let me take the back off the recorder. Let me wiggle and jiggle my finger a little. I hope they didn't get wet, because I sure as hell didn't bring any spares. Don't panic, take a deep breath. Try to be thankful there are no red ants up in here. They're the worst you know. You can see a nest of them coming straight at you, floating on a plastic flower pot or dancing on the lid of a garbage can. They must have some kinda weird, internal radar because just like them snakes, they can make a ninety-degree turn, no matter how fast the current is flowing, and before you know it, you're totally covered in them nasty, mean, biting buggers. I hate them, I do! They can swim underwater and still bite like a fucker. Someone told me they came from Texas. Go figure. Hold on, I can see the door leading up to the rooms, and my tape recorder is working again. What did it just say?

… and then it snowed.

08:45 P.M.

Come on my ole body bag and all! You can help open this door. I knew there was a reason why I had to bring you along. You're part of the contract. You're part of the deal! For real now. Can you see the stairs through the peep-hole glass? Come on, help me give this door a shove. It's not like we have all day now, is it? It's not like I'm waiting for Santa in the middle of August or something not quite as surreal. Stay focused! Force the door open and keep replaying the story!

A real little Picasso she was. Scratching away the hours, drawings her new-found insect friends. She'd carefully scribble a few lines that miraculously became an enduring face or an ephemeral body, always contemplating what she had drawn, with her cute little frown crowned in blonde curls, then taking any old marker and drawing arrows above their heads. With a medical dictionary she stole from school, she'd dissect and name them with human body parts. I gotta laugh! When it snowed, everything looked so neat and tidy, so perfect and empty, just like the back of a postcard you want to mail to your lover before you dare write anything stupid on it. The landscape became so quiet you could actually hear yourself think as I followed her footprints through the crystal calm whiteness, wearing those gigantic rubber boots our mom had bought at the thrift store. No one knew what thermal was back then, let alone snow suits. All bundled up so tight, we were, like a pair of fluffy little condoms, with our determined, freezing blue hands building larger-than-life snowmen with chestnut eyes and soggy carrot noses.

Finally, I've managed to jimmy open this warped excuse for a door. At least now I can take a look at what's gone and cut up my ankle. It sure feels like something is still gnawing away at it. You know you don't have time to examine your feet when they're totally covered in black, foaming turd water, especially if you're out on the drowned streets, melting in the rain. Out there, you're way too busy trying to avoid splintered slabs of two-by-four pine, torpedoing below the surface like nuclear missiles ready to slice you up like you're an overripe tomato or something just as squishy. I must admit, all this strenuous exercise means I need me a stiff drink. It's high-time to gulp me down some more of that Crown I borrowed from the bar. Here we go. That's better –Are you sure you don't want some?

09:12 P.M.

Man, this place reeks of the unforgiving forgotten! Some kind of toxic odor is permeating the walls and my nostrils, making my head spin like a lopsided ceiling fan set on high. Thankfully there isn't any sign of water on the first floor yet. Sure is weird being the only one in a building filled with so many reminders. I know I should probably rest and take care of my ankle, but if I remember correctly, this is the part on the tape where her father looses it and starts calling her a junkie. I sure would like to show him a thing or two, one day, but I can't even go there, right now. I know she has to wear a bracelet in case of emergencies everywhere she goes, even at night when she's sleeping. She told me one time that when the metal bracelet hits something like a table or a wine glass, it makes a clinking noise, reminding her of her father's voice dangling like a chain around her neck. Hang on. That's odd. All the doors to the hotel rooms are wide open. How many rooms are there again? Twenty four, I think. Hey, all in one day, you can stay in a different room for almost an hour, all in one day. How come I never thought of that until now? Maybe I should try it next time. What am I talking about? What next time? Who am I trying to kid? Take another slug of Crown, why don't you? That'll help fix anything other than the solution. And while you're at it, maybe I can find some hydrogen peroxide. There must be some lying around in one of these bathrooms. Then again, this place wasn't known for its hygiene, now was it? Come on, ma old body bag, let's quit all this talking to myself and just do it. Let's fix up my ankle and figure out a game plan. What's that? … Sure what the heck. … You can procrastinate on this stinking, slimy stairwell for as long as you want. Why should I care if the carpet reeks of stale piss and booze? It wouldn't be the first time I've nodded off here, and it's not like we're going anywhere anytime soon. Maybe while I'm sprawled out I can reminisce a little longer about ladybirds and blonde curls, fingertips and carrot noses.

10:00 P.M.

Slurring down, speeding up, slurring down some more, it's like my mind is driving through a ruined city in the middle of rush hour traffic and I'm staring blankly out of a windshield cracked by an ex-lover's heel. I thought by now I could've gotten a little farther, seeing as I haven't even made it up to my old room. But hey, now, don't run no red lights, and let's not get too depressed about my general lack of progress, not now, not when we know what happens once depression kicks in. Let's do our best to avoid the downhill trip with a tormented scream trying to burst out of a zipped-up mouth. Let's do whatever it takes to avoid smudging out any trace of moonlight lipstick as you fog up the mirror with your sagging breathe of cornered, stale air. ... I mean it, don't go there again. Don't let depression distil your mind and zap your strength. Don't let it make all your thoughts become disposable and useless like a friggin' wet lighter tearing up my thumb. Anyway, it's already way too quiet to start loosing it. And you still have all these stairs to climb. Listen to me! Forget about your ankle bleeding gooey lady bugs. Don't lookdown. Do something to take your mind off your mind. Play the other side of the tape. Play it now, before ...

Slipping into toxic lucidity, that's about all I can remember, crossing over Lake Pontchartrain, cramped in the back seat of their car, Karma Queen, I think they called it. Driving us into the heartbeat of New Orleans I could feel my senses rushing out the window and floating into the air like an escaping balloon, rising above the scorching tongues spat out by the chemical plants, licking the tip of the crescent moon. Rising above the dancing, flesh-like fires burning the shadows of night, so high on adrenalines from the idea of finally living down here, I felt like a boil bursting on your bum, a sticky wet dream come true. This is it, I kept saying to myself. This is it for real now, man. And they were playing music on the radio station I hadn't heard of before, WWOZ, the life line of the city, a raw, living brass band beat injecting straight into my veins, tattooing my memory with some primal-sounding ink, instantly toe tapping and habit forming and as natural as, say, smoking a cigarette, all those slipping and sliding musical notes delicately repeating themselves over and over, day after day, kinda like a record needle sticking into the grooves of life. You dig?

10:22 P.M.

Wanna hear something really weird? ... Probably not, but I'm going to tell you anyway, my old body bag and all. This water hasn't stopped rising ever since we broke in here. So? Can't you see? Are you blind? It's not making a sound! Can you tell me what's that about? I guess not! I sure as hell know it's coming in and it doesn't look like it's stopping anytime soon. But for the life of me, I can't hear it seeping up the walls. All I feel is a pounding pressure in between my ears, as if I'm lying flat-out in a tightly built box, realizing the air is being slowly squeezed out, or worse still, suspended upside down in the deep end of a pool, having to hold my breath for as long as I can, knowing that when I come up for air a swarm of horse flies are going to sting my face real good.

Snap out of it, will you? I knew you should have grabbed another bottle of Crown from the bar. What was I thinking? I thought two bottles would be enough. I know I can't drink these days, not like I used to. Too much booze just doesn't cut it, makes everything seem sloppier than it already is. Anyway, excuse me, would you mind telling me just how many voices are inside that skull of yours? ... Good question. I'm not really sure, but I kinda like the company. Just remember what the doctor told you the last time you felt this way. ... What was that? I can't remember. ... Take a few of those horseflies outta your ears and listen! "Too much mixing ends up in too much grief. Trust me," he said, "from one old junkyard dog to another. Woof, woof. No mixing and matching the hard goods with your booze, not a good idea, not in this place, at least, not with your track in your arm record. Worst dope in the country down here, and laced with who knows what. Narrow down your choices if you want to keep on trucking. Either take the bad crap and nothing else, or may I prescribe a little dose of Get the Hell Outa Dodge. Might save your life someday." "What about you?" I said to him. "You're pounding down shots and shooting up in the bathroom every twenty minutes." "I don't count," he said. "And why's that?" I said. "Because I'm already dead!" he said. "Oh yeah? So can you tell me how the dead feel today?" I said. "Pretty good right about now," he said, "But you know nothing lasts forever." "How do I know you're not faking it," I ask. The doctor got real close up in my face. "Look into my eyes, Sunny Jim," he said. "I don't see anything wrong," I say. "See," he said, "That's exactly what I'm talking about!"

10:44 P.M.

Can't you quit all your gobbledygook and get up off the floor? Do something. Take your finger off the pause button before them batteries run out.

Not much else to say, except maybe how the light of the moon cast dense, purple shadows over the silent swamp, making the landscape feel as if it had been removed from time, like when you find yourself in a waiting room where all the windows are kept shut, but every now and then, without a sound, the curtains gently move. At least that's what it looked like to me as we exited over the bridge. Gotta laugh, thinking back at it now. Every time one of the girls said something, I could feel myself squirming, bashful and awkward, like one of those dwarfs being kidnapped by a pair of rebellious Snow Whites. All I could do was stare out the window, try to act tough admiring my busted lip the size of a Creole tomato.

Hello. What's happening now? I think I know where I am and then Zap! Every couple of seconds I blink and am hurled into a another slither of fractured time, a fragment of space that feels cut up, pasted back together, then sliced up some more. Too much movement inside my head. Even these floorboards won't sit still! They just will not stop rolling, up and down, in a sea sick, wave-like manner. Their ripples are trying to hypnotize me as I rest my head on a wooden lake that once was covered with carpet. And from this angle, eye-level with the uneven, nauseating floor, I can see clumps of pea-green carpet fluff stuck to hammered tacks, running alongside the walls down the whole length of the corridor. And for some reason, they remind me of a spotty- faced child, awkward, quiet and calculating with a bag of old nails in his hand, making an organized trail along the terrifying, busy sidewalk until he reaches a house, where he hides in a room impatiently waiting for the moon to touch the tips of the live oak leaves. Only then, can he sneak back outside and put his muddy boots back on. Only then can he retrace his rusty trail all the way back to the circus, all the way back to the excitement of playing hooky with the clowns.

12:00 A.M.

I blame these giddy distant voices for making it impossible for me to stand up straight. Even when I have made it this far, all the way up to my old room. Oh, don't be fooled. I crawled. ... Number thirty-seven, just for the record. Knock, knock. Do you mind if I fall in? Hey, now! The key is still where I left it, nestled under the trash can. Now is that a good omen or what? Not that I need it now, the key, that is.

Sure am feeling thirsty again. Maybe it's all this thinking about how far back a memory can travel. I mean, do they really fade away or simply keep on echoing indefinitely inside the skull and the only reason we can't remember them is the fact that the mind becomes so walled up from the drudgery of daily routine, numbing us up, so to speak, like painting a red-brick wall red. Is it possible that the purest of memories become clogged up like dirt in a drain and the only way to clean it out is to have something unmanageable and totally out of control burst into our existence and jack hammer the red-painted wall? I don't know why, but for some reason, all this memory talk is reminding me of the times when my sister and I used to take two empty cans of tomato sauce—See I am off again—with real meatballs and tie them to a mess of string over by the abandoned saw mill. It always took so long to unravel that string. Why was that? Why does string eventually knot back up again, no matter how neatly you try to wrap it?

12:06 A.M.

We finally got inside my room, the royal we that is, me, myself and my old body bag and all, safe and sound. Can you believe the inside feels like I never left although for sure a lot more of the old plaster has caved in. Everything in the room is sprinkled with a fine, needle-sharp dust, makes the place look almost clean or recently kissed by a delicate morning mist. I heard that back in the day, this old plaster was mixed with an arsenic and lime binder. Makes you want to breathe a little softer now, doesn't it? Sometimes I would wake up in my bed and see a fine film of dust covering the bed sheets. No not that! I know what your one-track mind is thinking. My face would itch for a week. Doesn't help if you paint over it either, it just keeps on flaking, no matter how many coats you apply.

I really should sit down before I spill down. Moving a little too fast for my own good! Did you ever find anything to write with, Mr. Body Bag and all? I mean, what are we going to do when the batteries run out? What do you mean you don't know? Stop for a second and assess the situation. Hey, why don't you go stretch out some more string? And while you're at it—Hang on—well, blow me over! There's my old typewriter. I'm surprised no one went and snagged you, my sweet Lettera 22. How I've missed you, baby! You been doing all right? Shame about your ribbon but maybe you can help me figure out what is really going on with all this unraveling and knotting up of memory stuff. In or out of my mind, you know I never was any good at long-distance relationships. You do know that, don't you? ... Hello! What have we here? I can't believe some one left a roll of unused toilet paper. A miracle waiting to happen, on top of the desk Mona gave me. Good old Mona! Have you got any string that needs twisting? I wonder where you are, my succulent demonic angel. Did you know that every night we would get tragically lit up like a pair of damaged fireworks before she disappeared and mooched around the bar, creating another one of her masterpieces in mindless observation. She told me she was trying to capture on film all the insignificant details that no one remembers how to act out anymore. I remember helping her real good one time. Right here on this very same floor, comatose for three days straight, I was, unable to move and in a babbling stupor while she filmed the whole damn thing, curled up on my bed like an amused kitten. When I finally came around, she said I had given her the performance of a lifetime. Only wish I could remember what I said. I wonder what happened to the film. I hope it didn't get washed away along with the rest of my mess!

04:44 A.M.

I have to stop passing out because my ankle is bleeding bloody lady bugs. I have to figure out a way to crawl onto my bed and focus on how much is left to do. I bet I can use that toilet paper if I write real soft. Now that's a great idea! What's that? ... You really think I should take off these wet clothes? Look how the color has faded. It's as if they were slam dunked in a tub of hot bleach overnight. Can someone tell me what's actually in this flood water? Anyways, I'm getting tired of them constantly interrupting me. Who? My clothes, stupid! Who else? You can probably use that curtain to dry off. And while you're at it, can you pull up the floorboards? I think I left my old rig and spoon underneath one them.

05:11 A.M.

Oh, that's so much better. You look like a true, wandering Bacchante, demented without purpose and all set for the eternal, edible parade. Might I suggest that before you play the next tape, you wrap that shower curtain around yourself just a little tighter? You don't want to be catching your death of cold now, do we? Perhaps another bottle of Crown can slur you back into life. I can't believe you gone and drowned one already.

05:12 A.M.

Is that tape recorder of yours running away with itself again or what? Oh, it is, is it? … Okay, so you really want to know what it's like to be a hot shot DJ, eh? The mother ship of all pearls, the life of the party. Well, you can start by handing me my drink and be thankful you're not hung over like this everyday, or stuck in an airport for that matter, with all those tight-ass security inspectors wasting your precious time, trying to bust you for who knows what. What's with those dudes, anyway? I know it's a shitty job, but haven't they ever heard of smiling? And straight up, can you tell me, do I even look like a terrorist? Isn't it just a tad, bit, too obvious? They just don't like my attitude. Always making me late for that high-paying gig in smoke-free Singapore. Then it's more of them, standing around with their same non-smiles, trying to do the same damn thing. I mean, are they all related, or what? Because six hours later, they finally release my ass with just enough time to connect to that frantic overnighter to the industrial bell tower of a Berlin bat house. Sounds real glamorous, does it? Is this what you wanted to hear? I must admit, I do get tired of people thinking that a DJ isn't a real job! … You gotta a light? … Thanks! Now then, let me get back on my sloppy, hobby horse! Let me tell you something. A big shot DJ isn't like when you're in a rock'n'roll band. You don't have none of them roadies lugging your tonnage of equipment around all day and half the night. It's nothing like that, not even close. But the real kicker is you often don't know if the crowd you're about to play to even knows who you are, let alone digs your grooves, especially when you're playing abroad. It's yours truly up there on the stage sweating buckets and leaning like a collapsing tower of Pizza because you're always dog tired from having to sit around and wait half the night in a crumpled-up dressing room because you don't come on stage until the 3 a.m. dude has finally signed off. And when you do finally get up there, chances are you're going to find yourself with a pissed-off sound man ready to quit or wanting a blow job. But do I care? Hell, no! I'm the life of the party, remember? Standing in front of so many beautiful bodies, all of them perfect and happy and high on everything you can imagine you might possibly want. And right then and there, as you start doing your own thing, you can feel your adrenaline is popping out of your veins, knowing you've got to get it totally together without no kiss-your-ass-back-

up band to cover your ass. You're on your own on this stage, Bucko, with a sea of sweating perfect angels writhing below you, all of them expecting you to send them to some far away nirvana and never come back again. Talk about pressure. That's why you've got to do all that homework between flights, listening to hundreds of hours of other people's tapes and remixes. ... Why? Because each city –Hell, every club—has its own sound that everyone dances to. Might tweak you out just a tad, don't you think? And if that's not enough, you do realize you've got all of the first three minutes to convince a sold-out house that is ready to party until they drop that what you're making them listen to is exactly what they must have. I mean, they could be paying $200 just to get into the joint, and it's your job to make them so friggin' happy that they don't remember a damn thing the next day, except of course, how fantastic a good time they all had and when can they come back and do it all again. ... Fill it up for me will you? ... And don't forget the vampire promoter sets it up that way, always making sure it's your neck on the line if the gig doesn't slide down real smooth like a cool pint of Guinness on a sunny shamrock day—Ahhh! I sure could use a few of them right now, couldn't you?—No advance payments in my world either, Bucko! What's that? Are you kidding me? Of course I love it! Up there on stage you're on top of the universe. You're the man, spinning those humping crowds of gorgeous, sweating bodies around your twisted little fingers, tweaking their minds into new dimensions. It's like primal space travel and you're the rocket ship, their real-life in the flesh Flash Gordon, sending them out of their minds to some far away space station in search of Barbarella. Sometimes I just gotta laugh at how crazy it all gets, though. I mean, all that traveling and security shit, trying to keep it together and at the same time you're like a living , lightning rod, connecting the crowd like a bunch of lost dots ... How do I do it? ... What do you mean? ... Oh, my reputation! ... You really wanna know? You wont go telling tales out of the barroom now, will you? Promise me on Hurricane Club's honor! It can be our very own eensy, weensy, cross-your-heart-and-hope- to- secret. Okay, tell it like it is Mr. Super Fly DJ, Mr. Rub A Dub Tub.

All I use is an empty plastic water bottle and, of course, a whole lot of dumb nerve. The night before you're going to leave, wrap up your emergency stash real tight-like with cling film or plastic wrap. I always carry around a box of disposable plastic gloves. Those yellow kitchen ones work just as well. Then submerge it in a glass of hydrogen peroxide with a little bleach added for good measure. Don't pick at it for the rest of the night, you know, like a zit on your chin. Come next morning, lo and behold, you remove your stash with a new pair of rubber gloves and cram it real hard into the cap of the plastic bottle. Ram that sucker, good and tight! Personally, I don't use no tape or nothing. I try to keep my life simple. That's my motto. Then refill your bottle with regular old tap water and zipper dee dip, you're on your way to the airport. No, silly I'm not going to say it's a fail-safe ticket, in fact, in emergencies, I've used toothpaste caps. Chances are you'll edit this out anyway, but take a look next time you're waiting to board a plane. Count how many dudes are strutting through security and sipping on plastic bottles. Of course I have to bring it with me, are you kidding? You try taking a sixteen-hour flight straight into a hotel room that looks exactly the same as the one you were in the night before without so much as a moment to relax before yours truly is back on the dance floor and expected to create another intoxicated, four hour set. ... Sure, you get to party afterward, that's all part of the job, and anyway, after all the work you've done making everyone transcend with your solid, fat, prime rib rhythms, you damn well deserve a little R&R! ... What's that? ... Oh, I see, you want some too. You're as bad as the rest of them. Well, you can partake, only if you can tell me who invented the candlestick. Do you know? Why? Because, I'm seriously thinking about getting some personalized for my next tour, you know, handing them out to my fans with my mug shot stamped all over them, maybe with something like, "The Crowning Light" or the "Light of the Party" etched into the glass. Pretty cool, eh? But where were we? ... Oh, yes. Before you can close your eyes again, you're off to the next gig. It's like you're always pretending you're a bird, fluttering up a stewardess or two. Better have it well wrapped, that's all I say. ... You're, kidding me, right? ... Of course you can't trust the shit they hand out back stage or in the dressing rooms. For one thing, you've often got the squeaky-clean sponsor breathing down your neck. And you know he wants your blood before you can even can think about driving downtown to score any of the hard stuff. I can guarantee you're so strung out from all them night-before parties that you're going to need something when you finally show up for work. Trust me, I learned the hard way. ... What? ... You really want to know?...Well, I remember one time trusting some punked-out foreign dude who didn't speak a word of English, all smiles and bongo-wongo, he was. One of those can't-pronounce-your-name types but knows how to say, "Got a light?" with a perfect American accent. He knows you're disparate enough to take anything that comes gift-wrapped in a piece of plastic. Read my lips: Use your own dope. It's not like you can stop in the middle of your set and waddle off back stage with your finger stuck half-way up your ass, screaming that this shit you just scored ain't worth a crap, and fetch me some toilet paper because the stuff I just took is running down my leg!. Oh no! I'm not going to let that happen again. Twice was enough, you dig?

07:38 A.M.

That's the end of the batteries but I'm not going to panic. Maybe I can hot-wire the tape recorder to either side of my skull and see if I can fathom out what's really going on, because I have no idea how I managed to wake on the Ship Of Fools, floating on the dance floor, gaping at a revolving disco ball. I'm absolutely, totally confused as to the precise realm of time I am presently stuck in. I know something has collapsed, but I'm not sure what. I only hope this doesn't mean that the inevitable like-it-or-not has finally approached, castrating my search for an illusive opening to exit these thoughts. I know that the last time I checked in, I was dissecting my room and deciphering a cure for successfully proving why everyone's brief lifetime shouldn't be judged by a few isolated snap shots that quickly become distant, deceptive and fleeting. Maybe if I start unraveling the cassettes and eating the tape I can find the solution and know where this is all heading. ... Wait! There's something moving, over there. Is that who I think it is? Ahoy! Over here!

08:00 A.M.

There you are, my ole body bag and all. So glad you could join me again. How's the water temperature today? I don't feel so moribund when I'm stuck here with you. And before I forget, let me tell you how happy I am, knowing you can float! Maybe between the two of us we can drift away from these snake-slithering questions that are determined to suffocate me. I swear, if I could I would fire up a flare and ram it down my throat. You know I would roast their slimy asses before eating them in Hell.

??:??

What was I thinking coming back here like this? There was nothing in my contract that said time would check out, propelling me now into a denser state of numbness, groveling around with the remains of the displaced misplaced who cannot for the life of them figure out a way to escape. Maybe, I missed a clue scratched on the hotel walls peeling with toxins and stained with shadows, smeared with bloody footprints. Maybe if I can crawl into that beer cooler, this gnawing silence will scurry away and forget who I am as long as I promise to keep my big mouth shut. Maybe then I can wriggle my way through this soggy mess I seem to be wrapped up in. At least if I outstretch my fingers, I can feel the wet steel of my Zippo rusting beside me. At least without any notion of time, I can't tell if I'm slipping backward or forward, early or late.

0?:??

I feel so much lighter now, thank you. What a great idea to duct tape one of my eyes shut. Instant relief, halving all those unanswerable questions that were running out of me like a bad head cold, too much sniffling, dribbling down my nose and chin.

When time checks out, it really does leave you hanging, skewered and awkward, dangling on a hook like a worm waiting to be cast into the unimaginable depths of who knows what. "That's why most suckers love to fish," Martha would always say. I hope she's okay, although the last time I saw her, she wasn't feeling so good. She told me that always happens when you get locked up for months at a time. The isolation forces you to implode and do just about anything for the crumbs that feed your half-baked world. I hope she makes it seems such a lame thing to say. Not to change the subject, but have you been noticing the shadows lately? They resemble a thousand pairs of hands with razor sharp nails, reminding me of Mona's "The Needle Jumped Into a Burnt Spoon Nursery Rhyme." It's rather too crass to repeat during this thrown-together timeless, vigil. Anyway none of this is helping me figure out why every time I think about what I should be doing next, there's some kind of delay that lasts way too long until my thoughts slip back into this vacuous state where nothing ever gets done and everything remains the same. Chances are y'all be telling me next how all my delicate scribbling on moldy toilet paper wasn't worth a crap and how I was beginning to resemble one of those sultry, sensitive, poetic types loitering in a coffee shop sipping organic iced tea as I weave through my tempest of self-induced woes, dribbling after school girls, winking with one eye shut.

00:??

Tell me, old body bag, what kind of picture would you take, lying flat on your back looking up through a pin-hole tear in the roof? Can you capture a splintered soul ascending into Hell with a mouth so damn dry it feels like I slept with my head in an oven before some bright spark threw a lighted match down my throat, smiling and waving, trying to sell me more junk with that perfectly rehearsed, "Have a nice day?"

Don't ask me how, but I'm back in my room again, vacantly staring into a void so perfect and blue without a cloud in the sky, reminding me of paradise slapped on billboards in every ghetto of the world advertising Bacardi Rum. And when I lift my head up off the floorboards to examine what has yet to be written, I can feel myself splitting in two. One part is so ready to leave. The other, is disparately begging to stay, forcing me to realize that when the rusty needle breaks in your vein, your bloody footprints might be the only record you have of ever having been anywhere at all. And wouldn't you know it, they're rapidly fading as I speak, disappearing into the stained carpet, soaked from the faucets, spewing out raw sewage, issuing a stench, making me gag a few dry heaves more.

I never thought running out of time would be so banal. It's like being suspended after school and forced to write down a thousand trillion question marks on reams of blank paper, forcing me to question a world that has spun out of control into who knows what since I don't know when.

00:0?

You own me big time, as I scurry up a broken ladder like a demented rat fleeing a sinking ship, scrambling into this well-constructed imitation gas chamber filled with 120-degree humid air where I can smell what's left of my lungs sizzling like a rasher of pork flesh frying in a skillet. And that's after I barely escaped from the room below, contaminated with mosquitoes, swarming and sucking all over my wounds.

You try it some day. You try breaking through a roof built with two-inch thick pine, hard and wooden, public-school-plank pine. You try busting through hammered-down tight coffin pine, William Faulkner pine, nailed shut with a hundred thousand steel needles longer than my fingers, making it impossible to pry anything open because the whole damn suffocating furnace has been sealed up tight from the outside in!

Burning up, that's all I can say, with an itchy sweat from the glass fiber dust clinging inside my nose and ripping up my throat until I can't breathe anymore, forcing me to tumble back down, soaking and choking and bleeding from the scratching, leaving nothing to regroup except a few measly drams from a hot bottle of Crown. And that makes me mad, knowing I'm about to run dry in so much water. So, I muster up the energy to climb back on in, to war and cuss and make a few holes, one brittle splinter at a time. Ignoring the boiling roof-tar paper that's eating away my fingers with its gooey black jam sticking to the skin underneath my nails and melting my pores.

Burning up! Is all I can say, as I clench my fist and punch through the shingles, showering me with scolding, asbestos rain. And be sure to remember the entire time I'm up there, my neck is breaking and my spine is cracking from leaning backward, straddling the rafters like a demented clown, praying he won't step onto the soaking wet plaster and fall through the ceiling into the locked-up closet where a long, lost friend, the cliché skeleton, hasn't seen daylight since the Saints won the Super Bowl.

Burning up! And now I know why the locals always say, "Don't ever forget to leave a hatchet in the attic," although, what I really need is a nuclear-powered space suit pumping cold, fresh air into my heaving, burnt lungs with a warp-factor-five light beam strapped to a hard hat as I work a portable chainsaw, ripping the roof wide open instead of fumbling in the dark with a broken wire hanger and some useless items from an out dated wardrobe no longer recognizable because I'm almost blind in one eye while the other remains securely duct-taped shut.

Burning up! Every time I breathe, rawness boils inside me, wanting to erupt with volcanic proportions as I am forced to understand why a worn-out mop and broken broom are our nation's symbol for rebirth.

00:00

How much farther can a blind man see? Beyond the splintered rooftop horizon, fires burn through the magnolia trees. Their century old roots strangle and drown in the stagnate brine of flooded lake water. An orange mist settles in the thick, brittle air, consuming the city's broken tomorrows, rekindling the ashes of what is barely left standing to float on past as I try to comprehend all the bits and pieces of all the nicks and knacks, the never ending bills and paper-trail reminders that taped up so many lifetimes, trying to keep them precariously glued together, floating underneath me now, everything floating without time, lost and insignificant, like our endless lists of post-dated assurances and paid-up premiums unable to insure the alive and the kicking, the shaken and stunted.

How much farther can a blind man see? With my body dangling off balance like a wounded pigeon, perched on a hacked up rooftop. The loose asbestos tiles scorch my ass and evaporate a puddle of uncontrollable tears, flowing down the gutter as my soul connects with the passing wreckage of a world I can never fix. Have I mentioned this before? I can't quite remember. There is someone I should pray to, but I can't think who!

You know, it's as hot on this rooftop as it was in that attic I managed to crawl out of a few timeless seconds, or was it months, ago. Isn't that right, my old body bag and all? I must say, you are a trusty friend, sitting patiently beside me like a well-trained pet that has lost its leash. You're looking pretty good, all things considered, although you could use a little more color in your lifeless cheeks. Well-fed though, stuffed with so many crumpled sheets of wasted words, stained with mouthfuls of reminders and fistfuls of memories scribbled out of place with a splinter from a broom, my crudely carved nib dipped in dried ladybug juice. Your loyalty has convinced me that all that is needed to remember the past is to recycle the future and start all over again.

Damn it, will you just look at this mess? Remember it everywhere. An apocalyptic toxic puddle of Disneyland proportions reflecting the unforgiving sun, shaped like the decapitated head of the late Marlin Brando as he hisses out Kurtz's immortal last words amid the confusion and screaming of a forgotten 60's protest song, igniting a rage within me that I've run out of excuses when the last drop of Crown slipped down my throat and the borrowed rusty needle broke in my vein, forcing me to accept that no distorted reality fueled with whatever I shot, snorted or swallowed will ever come close to this broken key that has snapped inside the lock of 200,000 displaced tomorrows.

Can you hear that, above me now? Above the coffin rooftops, helicopters are circling like a pack of mad vultures. I hope they stay this time and quit taking photographs. I hope they begin to rescue the stranded and bewildered, the torn and undone, the innocent living in the poorest of civilized nations who never knew the word "security," let alone "serenity" because they were unable and unprepared to escape from the chaos and the sun's blistering heat, bleeding over a wasteland, drowned beyond recognition.

Hush now! Hush now! Can you? No matter how insane displacement might sound, at least for a little while, there will be no more messages to delete or stamps to lick, no more envelopes to seal the remixing of hours that we tie ourselves up in like misplaced balls of endless string. Maybe for a second or a fraction sooner, we can show a little love for the unfortunate ones we preach about caring for. Maybe this will force us to break bread with a stranger before I zip myself shut like I promised y'all I would.

Hush now! Hush now! Hush Now! Listen to the Mississippi beckoning us on. Calling me to return to where we all first came from, letting us know the circle is complete. Helping me to understand there is nothing wrong with ending at a new beginning.

Hush now! Hush now! Hush now! Let me rest like a snow flake on a puddle of tepid lake water. I think it is round about now that I must slide off this rooftop with my old body bag and all. Oh, didn't he tell you? This was the only way I could leave without repeating the same old mistakes, over and over and over again!

Hush now! Hush now! Hush now! Will you cast off my unanswerable questions and see if any solutions can float. I have fulfilled my contract. I can return to the dirt. So be my guest, I must insist, and let me jump, my friend. Jump, back into the skin!

PART III

A Little Later On

ZANE

Tick, tick, ticking. Loose gravel lodged in the tires, clicking with the rhythm of his manicured nails. Tick, tick, ticking. Rising out of the cracked, baked earth, the unforgiving heat is blistering the landscape and dissolving the clouds into pools of vaporous jellyfish. Breaking the horizon, scattered islands of pecan trees, with limbs splintered from lightning, bow, defeated and on either side of the rutted stubble road, the tips of scorched fields sway like slow-moving hands. "What am I doing coming back here like this?" Zane mutters, stubbing out a cigarette and vacantly watching the smoke curl around his tattooed fist. Thoughts of turning back filter through his mind, creating tension and stretching his nerves like an elastic band strung between two parting points. He bites his fist and feels bone against tooth as he tries to quell the gnawing sensation squirming in the pit of his empty stomach.

"Where the hell are we, boss man?"

"Not that far now. And I am not your boss!"

"Sure thing boss."

Zane digs deep to force out a smile. He had almost forgotten there was another person in the car. He stares back out the window and notices perched on a sagging barbed wire fence, a band of crows pecking with demented fury at a bullet-riddled POSTED sign. Their sharp beaks unconcerned whether the fields are private or bankrupt, busted or abandoned.

The limo hisses past endless miles of sugar cane and rice fields that have bellied up or are going to seed. More land for sale, more shot-up signs, more broken families for hire, more endless pecking, more, more, more. All too familiar reminders of a new world order that has gone berserk, ransacking rural America before vomiting back onto itself.

"Say, Brah!"

"Yes Boss?"

"Why do you keep calling me that?"

"What?"

"Your boss!"

"Man, who's drivin', an' who's sittin' in da back seat chillin' with his bling bling fingers an four-legged furry coat. Wearin' his mirrored shades, soakin' in da AC an totin' on a smoke?"

"You're a poet and don't even know it." Zane chuckled. He could feel the driver's eyes staring at him in the rear view mirror.

"Shit Brah, weez born wit' dem words in our mouths!"

They both laugh, forcing Zane to relax a little. He likes this driver, with that Nawlins soul about him, that never quite sure if you're really loved or despised kind of soul, warm, embracing soul that can conceal the distrust of your very existence, a soul Zane felt was life affirming and part of the city's unforgivable beauty.

A cell phone obnoxiously vibrates in Zane's pocket, breaking his train of thought.

"Look out, boss man. Time to get back on the clock!"

"Tell me about it."

For someone riding high on the waves of the communication gadget age, Zane wonders why he always despises these phones as much as he did. *Maybe I really am old school. Maybe I'm only happy with a simple turntable and a bunch of loose vinyl, winging it from gig to gig. Do I really need suitcases full of computerized, digital, over dubbed, loop-to-loop, phone fax machines? What made me decide they were so damn cool and necessary to begin with?* He thinks.

Buzz. Buzz. Buzz. Every time he feels the phone vibrate it reminds him of what's-her-name, back East, going through the finger moves, demonstrating the endless commands and options these intrusive objects own. Of course, he had enjoyed the one-on-one tutorial between the twisted sheets of another rented room, but these days it seems the shapeless voices always want too much from him, all at once, all right now.

Without warning, as if rising out of the dirt itself, a pick-up truck appears, barreling, toward them.

"Look out!" Zane cries.

"What the hell?" his driver shouts, slamming the brakes before steering the limo to the side of the road. "Man, what kinda place is this?"

The truck speeds narrowly past them in a cloud of dust.

"It's our welcome home committee," Zane replies, shaken.

"Oh yeah! That ain't no welcome in my book."

Zane fumbles through his record bag for a small, silver case and gestures to the driver. "Here, want some, help calm the old nerves?"

"You're kiddin' me right? Out here?"

"Are you sure? Colombia's finest."

"Naw. Not when I'm on duty, boss man. That stuff will kill ya, ya know."

"Some say it already has."

Zane opens the case and removes a silver straw. He snorts a large bump of crystal white powder. Feeling the driver's eyes boring down on him, he snorts again. The powder burns through his sinuses.

"See, dat's exactly what I'm talkin' 'bout."

Zane sniffs and wipes his nose. "What exactly is that?" He takes another bump, then reluctantly closes the case.

"Look at you. Ya got da whole world dancin' on your fingertips, wit' chicks up your ass, Mr. Hot Shot Music Man. Yours truly, the one and only, Mr. Fly Himself. An' all ya can say is you're already dead. What's your problem?"

"It's a long story," Zane mutters, in no mood for a lecture.

"Well look around, will ya. We ain't exactly goin' anywherz anytime soon, now are we? This place feelz like card-carrying DUKKKE country to me. You got anything better to talk about?"

"You're safe with me. Times have changed."

"Shit. Now you're really trippin' on me!"

Zane wipes away a filmy red residue from his nose and lips. "I wish I was," he whispers, examining the bloody mucus on his fingertips.

The silent miles unveil more silent miles like a tattered curtain opening across an abandoned stage. Curled up in the backseat with his coat wrapped around him, Zane drifts in and out of sleep. He notices a church surrounded with a gravel moat, standing alone and vaguely familiar. The pristine, red brick, painted white shutters and spiked steeple pierce the blue eye of the sky, giving the building an aura of cold detachment from the surrounding landscape, as if it had recently landed from some far-away world where everything worked and had an order unto itself and was now ready to battle with the indifferent chaos of the unforgiving dirt. Zane shivers, "Broken voices of men, broken arrows of time."

"You said something, boss man?"

"Oh, nothing. Only a few more miles now, just a few more."

Metallic statues bruise the skyline, obsolete farm machinery rusting into the color of the earth, testaments to man's labor that this land has soaked up, spat out, then soaked up some more. These rusting mechanical dinosaurs were once part of Zane's childhood playground, his silent getaways, his personalized tattoos of who, he once was. Their immobile presence challenges him now with a secret language of his past, forming in front of his eyes like inked-in-the skin images that can't be washed away no matter how many years have passed, convincing him that he is traveling backward in time and space, journeying to a place he has known, endured and is forced now to remember, a slice of personalized time when these metallic bones had transformed him into a gun-slinging outlaw, Snoopy and Batman all rolled into one, a bloodless battleground where he had fought invisible aliens and overweight cops trying to capture his prehistoric flying machines.

Zane's eyes close down again as he travels backwards. Back into fractured moments spent slashing wasps' nests. With the same sticks, he redesigned mounds of fire ants growing out of bloated tires. He drifts towards a place where he found his first dead bird inside a chunk of transmission casing. With cupped hands, had carried its fragile, rotting form home before placing the lifeless bird under the trailer, where he would patiently watch it decompose into the damp shadows. Later on, he would bleach the tiny bones and tie them back together; creating a flying creature he could call his own. A dream catcher that he attached to the top of his bunk bed with an old shoelace so that at night he could stare at the featherless bird silently swiveling above him until he fell asleep to dream of being carried away on the creatures back bone into unknown constellations.

Zane bumps his head on the window and opens his eyes. He had almost forgotten where he is and where he is going. He lights a cigarette and watches the exhaled smoke blow about the limousine. His thoughts remain lost in his childhood, the times he was spiked, jabbed and torn by the loose metal spokes falling out of the collapsing farm machine's wheels, remembering with a sense of wonder how he would pick at the rusted, brittle splinters buried under his skin as he listened to his parents argue about the date of his last tetanus shot, before sending him to the thrift store for more mud clothes to tear up in. It was at the local *Vincent De Paul's* that he first discovered music. He had found old LP's stashed under a pile of *National Geographic's* smelling of mold, a vintage gold mine of vinyl that he started to collect and horde under his bed even though he didn't really know what to do with his treasure except enjoy the art work on the sleeves and the titles of the songs, unaware that the power of music was already silently inserting itself into his life. He found something rewarding in owning what no one else seemed to want. A few years later, before she started nursing school, Ruth, came home with a portable record player. So many memories tick inside his skull into the here and now, mixing up his mind before easing their way out like a splinter rising up from the skin. Emotions trickling out of his pores like the poison oak he would constantly scratch at. "Gotta laugh," he whispers. "Look at me now, making my living scratching vinyl around the world. People even carry my record cases for me…Oh Mr Fly This! … Mr Can't Touch That! … My Main Man Zane, where the hell are you going?"

MARTHA

Reluctantly crawling out from underneath the bed, Martha scrapes her cheek on something sharp encrusted in the booze-stained carpet. Lately, all this displacement stuff has left her fragile self overwhelmingly discombobulated. "IT! … IT! … IT! … I guess it had to happen," she bemoans. "I guess it got the better of me, watching her rise above the grimy deluge of the streets as if she was the reincarnation of Mother Teresa herself, working it, sixteen to eighteen hours straight, and then back again the next day. Always there now she is, down at that emergency shelter, if you can call a couple of sagging soggy tents and a temperamental generator the Red Cross."

Today, like everyday it seems, lately, Martha is having a time of it, and she knows it too well. Her emotions feel like they're being constantly battered against a rocky coastline like a splintered piece of driftwood. *What where they thinking closing down Charity Hospital like that? A flood of biblical proportions comes torpedoing through the city, nigh on destroying two-thirds of it, and someone has the smarts to think there isn't going to be anymore sickness, bullet wounds or broken limbs running around! I know the place was old, but that hospital has saved more lives than Jesus Christ.* She raises her head off the carpet and wipes a slither of toenail clipping from her cheek. She examines the way the nail polish has stained the miniature crescent moon with a deep, metallic purple. *It kinda looks like a delicate piece of sea shell lost without a beach to call home.* She sighs again, studying the nail for a moment longer before grinding it back into the carpet. *Whose dazzling spark of a cost-effective idea was that one? I heard the suicide rate is higher than the murder one now. Think about that while you gobble down your Cheerios. I'm sure it's thanks to all the stress caused by closing down public institutions that people for generations have grown up familiar with. Oh comrade Martha, don't get me started. I'm stressed out enough as it is. … Damn it, where's my Flurazepan!*

With way more effort than it should take, she pulls herself to her knees and stares at the silent, vacant bathroom. *Just look at her, would you. She's finally gone and totally lost it in my mind. What's got into all these people leaving me? I mean, she treats those displaced kids like they're her own kin, always got one of them in her arms, she has, cuddling it between her tits, playing with it, smiling at it with that ghoulish smirk of hers. Wouldn't be surprised if she hasn't figured out a way to breast feed them by now, poor little buggers, having to put up with her cooing ga-ga nursery rhymes. You're not going to tell me there isn't some kind of law that says only normal people can volunteer, emergency or no emergency! I don't see her volunteering to lift one of her sausage fingers to help me in my moments of crisis! Typical, like I don't have a million disasters going on all at once.*

Martha props herself up against the edge of the disheveled bed and reaches for a half-empty bottle of tequila. *Deserting me like that.* Nodding her head back and forth, she tries to relocate her concentration. She rips the plastic caps off the dozen prescription bottles strewn on a milk crate beside the bed. A few seconds later, she is swallows mouthfuls of Zyprexa, Klonopia, and Laical in mixed quantities and no apparent order. "My own natural disaster!" she wails, washing the pills down with heavy slugs of warm Mexican booze. "Always too busy with it now, she is. Never complaining about it, just excepting it as an opportunity to give something back to this forsaken world." With indignant satisfaction, Martha finishes the booze, belches, and throws the empty bottle at the bathroom door. "I mean for fuck's sake, we are talking about the same Mona, aren't we?" The bottle bounces off the door and onto the carpet and stops beside a pair of beaded platform shoes. "After all I gone an' done for that bitch, she goes and abandons me and moves across the hall, wanting her own privacy, my ass!" Staring at the tequila bottle, then at the bathroom door, then at Mona's shoes, Martha feels like a vulture deprived of a carcass. "Okay, get a grip. At least your daily prescription is finished with. At least I can resume my..." Her words slow into a chaotic slur. A sudden wave of depression hits her like a slap in the face. "Like what has this City ever given me except a load of bitter sweet heart ache?" She forces herself to her feet and stares into the cracked, full-length mirror propped up against a zebra-skin-painted wardrobe that spews out clothing. "Damn it, it and more fuckin' it!"

For several minutes, she tries to focus on the many sets of mascara-smudged eyes staring back at her. *Something unexplainable is going on inside of me! Some sort of demonic seed has gar-*

mented in my soul and is sprouting diabolical thoughts. Ever since that cursed hurricane I feel desperately misplaced. Get a grip Martha, take a friggin Valium!

Her body sways like a tethered buoy on a restless ocean. From the neck up, where the mirror is broken, she resembles a Francis Bacon portrait, from the neck down, a headless figure painted by a child. "Great," she wails. "What a masterpiece. You can't even get your reflection together! Let alone..." Tears swell as she wipes away the smudged mascara. "Not sure if I can define it anymore. Not sure if it really exists, and if it does, isn't it one big lie? ... An orgy sized lie, a calculated disguise designed to entice me back? Can someone please tell me what a young girl is supposed to do with so much emotional upheaval flying around? It's like that damn hurricane never left. ... It's like ... Oh, fuck it! ... Don't forget your Amphetamines."

Martha mimics a scream at her reflection. "Oh, my God, what's happening to me now?" A thick cloud of butterflies expels from her mouth and swarms above the mirror. She screams for real. Again, no sounds as butterflies continue to spew from her mouth. *This cannot be happening, not now. I haven't even had my Ritalin yet!*

More butterflies appear, flying away from the mirror and landing on her naked body, rapidly covering her from head to foot as she tries to scream again, then again and again, widening her mouth with each failed attempt, hoping that somehow her voice will overtake the butterflies. In minutes, her entire, shaking body has disappeared, covered in a fluttering array of electronic greens, yellows, and reds. "Get away from me, you ghastly fluttering fiends, get away!" Frantically she tries to wipe them away. "Who do you think you are some weird chemical concoction that has formulated into an apocalyptic nightmare? More like one of those gruesome tie-dyed costumes from an outdated 60's commune. Oh, spare me, please. I can't be seen wearing such a thing!"

Martha stands paralyzed, numb in horror as the insects rise off her body and circle the ceiling before dispersing through the broken window. In their mouths are bite-sized pieces of her flesh. A state of panic breaks through her drug-induced delirium, overwhelming her as she jumps trying to catch the fleeing insects. "Get back here, you pesky thieves, get back here!" Every attempt to trap the insects' fails as her flesh disappears, making her more and more crazed. Ruthlessly, she slaps her body, trying to squash them against her skin. Forcing her eyes closed, she claps, slaps, and then jumps again. "It's just a bad dream," she wails. "You know, all I got to do is change the dosage. Tweak it a little. Maybe add a few more Valium and less friggin tequila. I know, let's half the dozen Xanax. Think it through girl, you're in the trade! You shouldn't have gotten rid of the Prozac, I say. They said there might be side effects. Drop the Zoloft. No! Damn well double up on all of them. There you go, y'all see, everything's going to be just fine, I swear."

Martha opens her eyes. She can hear the bedroom filling up with her own maniacal screaming. In the mirror, staring blankly back at her is a skeleton with its red bones picked clean of flesh.

MOOSE

Without moving his head, Moose sits like a motionless stick insect on his personalized bar stool. He stares around the empty bar room and, for a moment, his watery eyes deceive him and the bar fills up with familiar faces. *Damn shame, it was,* he mutters to himself and a row of plastic cups lined up in front of him. *I spent the last ten years of my life sitting on the same barstool, day in day out, sipping ma draught beer an' staying out of everyone's business, just like the rest of us, and they come in and want to close the place down because a hurricane is blowing through. You'd think they'd have a lot more important things to do than mess with us, not like we haven't had no hurricanes happen before in here, now is it? Take a look around this dump. Is there anyone who hasn't gone and lost everything to begin with? Is there anyone here who isn't already complicated with their own natural disaster? And besides all that, where are we supposed to go if they shut this place down, anyways?*

He sips from a plastic cup containing 25cent draught beer before continuing in his low, crusty, smoke scarred mumbling, *As I was saying, they come in all official-like, telling us it's for our own health and safety reasons. Well, you tell me which one of us has the time to be worrying about our health! That's the trouble these days with all them government-bureau-types. Just because they marry your sister's cousin's brother, they think they can go around sticking their noses in everybody else's affairs. And for what, you tell me. It's not like they walk in and make anything better, now is it. It's not like they say, "Hi my name is So and So, and I'm related to So and So, and I'm here to help fix your problem." On the contrary, they make matters worse, from what I've experienced, insisting you need a permit for nigh on everything nowadays. Mark my words. First it was a permit for gambling. Next, it will be for breathing the air. And the only consolation we citizens have down here is at least we know who your momma is.*

Looking up from the plastic cups, he raises his hand and motions to the end of the bar. "Hey Mona!" he shouts. "How about another round of drinks, if you can ever get off that damn phone of yours?" He spits on the floor and mutters to himself, *It might seem like I ain't got nothing better to do all day, but trust me, there's always a reason to stay holed up at the bar, minding my own business like. I mean, look at me. I managed to slip off their books for the past twelve years and still collect my social security thanks to them ponies down at the racetrack. Made me enough to go and retire early, just in time I might add, because sure enough they started raiding our gambling joints and shutting down our cribs for--what was it they tried an' called it?--illegal tax invasion purposes or some such official jargon like that. What a joke! If y'all want to see some real tax-invading going on, take a stroll down to city hall at lunch time an' watch what them counselors and school boards are driving around in. I mean it! Go see who's sitting on whose laps in them fancy restaurants. Then, while you're at it, time their lunch breaks. Hurricanes or no hurricanes, someone's doing all right.'*

Mona slinks up to Moose as if hypnotized. She places another draught beer on the bar and, without saying a word or taking any money, slinks back into the darkness. Moose tips his cap and continues mumbling; occasionally glancing over to the dance floor as if expecting someone he knows to walk in. *At least I made me enough to keep me comfortable in case of one of those emergencies or rainy days. And while we're on the subject of rainy days, I never heard of such a thing, have you? Escorting us off the premises like we were a bunch of criminals or something, without so much as a finish up your drinks lads. "To go where?" I kept saying, but all they kept saying was "Board the bus." "Board that school bus," I say. "No way! I ain't no nigger!" So then a fight breaks out, and they personally have to throw us onto the bus where we go and sit for half the day waiting for a driver to show up. Well it didn't end there, oh no, not on your life. When the driver did finally show, he goes an' tells us someone has gone an' siphoned the diesel out of the gas tank and he ain't driving no wheres. Then everyone shouts and another fight breaks out, until them army officials jump on board and escort us back off the bus, herding us like a bunch of cattle over to the Superdome in the pouring rain. And if that isn't enough to pull your chain, once we get there, they make us line up outside the building for another half a day because we all had to be frisked for our weapons. So I say to them, now soaking wet and all, "How long you plan on keeping us locked up in this dump without water and food?" I mean, I might as well have stayed where I was. Least it was quiet at the bar. At least there weren't no hungry babies crying all the time and everybody ready to rip each other's eyes out because they were so friggin' scared, but no one knows nothing until the Superdome roof starts leaking all over the joint and all Hell breaks loose because we're all starving and getting sick, crammed up for I can't remember how many days, sweating our butts off with no toilet paper or water to wash your hands with. Then we start hearing reports about how everybody's too busy on their vacations to do anything to help us. Trust me, once we heard that one, the place got real scary real quick-like. The entire Superdome felt like it was about to blow up into a bigger storm than any hurricane that had happened down the street. So they start opening the gates and shouting through some loud speakers that we are being evacuated out of town. After all those shenanigans, I can assure y'all I wasn't going no place else, free helicopter ride or no helicopter ride, so I sneak out all quiet like a shadow in the dark and make my way back to the hotel only to find when I get back here, all traumatized and everything, that the place has been temporally shut down. Apparently some joker broke in during the storm and sliced up his--what's it called, Achilles heel or something like that--right there on that broken window glass! The idiot bled to death in a matter of minutes. They say he had drunk several bottles of Crown and God knows what else inside of him. If you ask me, it was that damn crazy Some Guy Upstairs. I always knew there was a reason why I never liked him right from the get go, sprawled out on the old Ship of Fools and floating in three feet of water underneath the disco ball. Knowing him, I bet that tape recorder was wrapped around his neck, recording who knows what. A bloody mess, I heard. At least he had the decency to zip himself up in a body bag. Don't ask my why he had one of them lying around, I didn't see it personally because they removed the body real quick-like, this being Uptown an all.*

A stranger stumbles into the barroom and sits down a few stools away. Mona takes his drink order. Without looking up from his own drink, Moose addresses the bar room. "Sure I'll take another. That's mighty white of you." The stranger nods, "You're welcome. It's hot as hell out there today."

"You know," Moose interrupts, not caring if the stranger is listening or not, "none of this would have ever happened if they had just listened to me from the get go. What did I keep saying over and over an--Excuse me!" He stares up at Mona, as she hands him a beer without his usual cup of ice. He glares at the stranger, then back at Mona again. "What's this? Are you tryin' to be funny? What do you mean you're out of ice? Come again? Are you working here or what, Ms Thinks Your So Hot in those tight-ass pants? Oh, you are, are you? Well let me tell you something. Do yourself a favor and get back on that damn phone of yours and find someone who has ice!"

Mona struts off as Moose tips his head back and gargles with the iceless beer. He swallows the warm liquid and eyes the stranger before grumbling like a slow and tedious fart. "Can you believe this mess? I swear. All I know is that Some Guy Upstairs had better not show his ugly mug around these parts no more, especially if you think I'm gonna start drinking my beer hot! I tell you what. You've got another thing coming!"

ZANE

Cocaine and blood taunt Zane's nerves as they mix with the passing landscape and create a host of visible ghosts that he can taste, running down the back of his throat. One minute he feels ecstatic, the next like a tumbling lunatic. *I want to wrap this coat around my bones, protect myself from the smells, sounds and tastes of a remembered past slipping closer. Someone pull these shades over my eyes until they hurt the bridge of my nose. Someone stop me from chasing the sun's outstretched shadows as they silently glide over the fields. Spare me from leaping from branch to branch and leaf to leaf, hoping nothing will snap as I slide off this car seat and scramble to complete this puzzle of what has gone where. Can't you see? My clenched fist resembles my father's voice, a reminder I can't let go of, an echo, spanning miles of outstretched string before bouncing back inside me. Are these murmurs of anger or fear I feel, churning up the past into the ever-present future? If I'm so wild and free, why am I shivering alone, snagging my Kiss This T- shirt on a barbed wire fence before resting at the edge of Morgan's Pond, discovering a mess of water moccasins basking in the summers stillness, fascinated by passing hours, watching the snakes reel and coil back over themselves, wanting to touch them as my reflection tangles in their play?*

Zane opens his eyes hoping to stop the swirling of images though his mind, but it don't matter now if his eyes are open are closed, his childhood memories continue to leak out of him. *Wanting to touch the impossible right then and there as I slowly lower my hand, feeling my fingertips pierce the water's skin. Then my knuckles. Then my hand recoils, jumping out of the water like a plastic bottle filled with trapped air. I trembled on the muddy bank guarded by a nonchalant heron, inspecting my unscathed fingers before taking an hour to run the mile home backwards, always running, past the nagging wound cut with a blunt knife into the stump of a lightning-struck oak tree: Zane + Ruth 4 Ever. This feels too close to home. I'm my father's fist, punching a hole into my own future, hoping old Mr. Broussard won't unleash his crazed Catahoula as I crawl back under the fence and into a harvest of falling pecans. Run, Zane, run. Run into your future.*

Sweat pours down his face. He isn't sure if he's tripping or dreaming or both as he studies his hand, clenched like a knot of water-logged pine. He glances out the window and starts. "We're here!" he shouts. "Turn left. Left!" His voice sounds frantic, unable to command. His words want to flee back inside his mouth.

"You're kiddin' me? In there?"

"Yes, that's right. No, left. Turn left, I said!"

The black limousine slows, uncertain, as if entering a cemetery. Instead of headstones, the car passes weathered signage tacked to peeling, painted posts. The old lettering has faded into "FO ALE." The car purrs deeper along the driveway, crawling past a row of rusted mailboxes filled with the remains of unanswered mail, and a field moose, industriously nesting in Past Due and Cut Off Notices. Next to the mailboxes, an abandoned office sags forlorn. Its broken windows and doorway have been boarded up with scraps of flaking plywood. Underneath its buckling roof, clouds of wasps swarm in and out of their paper nests.

"Where are we, exactly, boss man?"

"Plantation Mobile Park. Bunkie, Lou-easy-annaaa!"

"No shit?"

"See the sign?" Zane points to a pile of rusting farm machinery, propped against a collapsed fence. A torn piece of cardboard has been duct taped to one of the wheels, "4 ARLEN" written on it in black marker.

"This is my roots, Brah."

The driver laughs.

"What's so funny?" Zane asks.

"Boy, you ain't old enough to have no roots." He laughs again, "Always kiddin' ya-selves that you got roots. My ass! Shit, look around kiddo. This is nothing but a bunch of misguided pilgrims, drifting, anchorless and spat out by the American Dream."

Familiar street names crowd Zane's eyes as the limo drives past row upon row of empty trailer lots. The abandoned slabs are littered with sand boxes that are filled with ant nests, with turned over trashcans, and tricycles buried in weeds. Odd pairs of shoes lie rotting on concrete steps that lead to nowhere. Tattered clothing, bleached from the sun, hangs on sagging washing lines, completing a stage from which the cast and crew have fled in frenzy.

"Stop there, beside that LTD!"

"The one on bricks or the one without no doors?"

"The one on bricks."

"You sure you know where you're at?"

"Yeah, my folks, they live here, I think."

"I'll stay here. You go an' take as long as you need. Okay, the AC works just fine. I could use a break anyhowz. Don't worry I'll keep the engine running. Just in case."

Zane hesitates. "Thanks, man. See you in a few."

"No problem. I'll wait in the wilderness. Holler if anything rises from the dead, you hear?"

Zane steps out of the car and feels his body slam into an invisible wall of heat. A barrage of old songs sweeps through his mind. *"I'm back on dry land once again. Opportunity awaits me like a rat on a drain." Whatever Elton John.* He tries to hush the songs by focusing on a potted hibiscus plant wagging its phallic pink tongues at him. *"Crawfish pie, File gumbo" Cute, I never liked that song.*

In front of the trailer, an eight-foot banana tree shades an assortment of well-watered potted plants. *Ma finally got herself a garden,* one of the cluttered voices in his head says. To the right and several feet past the trailer, a shed has been slapped together. Corrugated sheets of lime-green plastic are nailed to the sides and roof. Sunlight, filtering through the green plastic, covers the contents in a neon-greenish glow as if they were submerged in a gigantic fish tank. Metal tubing, broken lawn furniture, legless barbecue pits and an assortment of bicycle parts rust inside the waterless tank. Entangled in cats claw, lawn mowers, leaf blowers and weed eaters pile on a dilapidated and engineless tractor chassis. In front of the shed, on the back of a flat bed trailer, coils of fence wire have been cut and twisted into figurative armatures of varying sizes and gestures. *Gone into the scrap metal business has he?*

Zane walks up to the chipped concrete steps, his right leg limping as if it was consumed with pins and needles. *How many years now? Weird to think about it.* He stops at the repaired screen door and notices above his head a hand-painted sign secured to the trailer by a pair of life size welded hands.

SNOW LEOPARD STUDIOS

What the heck? I always knew he was crazy. He grins, peering through a paisley curtain that decorates the tiny window in the front door. To his surprise, Miles Davis plays above the noise of the TV. *Maybe they have started smoking pot and became hippies.* He laughs, imagining his dad sporting a pony tail while his mom sits cross legged on a pillow caressing an organic water melon and sucking on a Hookah. Zane glances back at the limousine. The black roof shimmers like a knife blade suspended in sunlight. *Are you ready? After three now. One, two.* He takes a deep breath of hot humid air. *Three.*

Biting his tongue, he stares at his tattooed fist rapping on the aluminum door.

EMMA JANE

Poking her nose through the curtain at the kitchen window, Emma Jane sees a limousine with white-wall tires that are covered in a thick layer of crud pull up beside her trailer. "Good Lord," she says to a row of finger cacti neatly arranged on the windowsill. "The man from the papers is here already. I wasn't expecting him till the middle of next week, with all that mess from the storm an' all. I had no idea my Arlen was in such high demand, but you know that Arlen." She frowns into a heart-shaped mirror tacked onto a kitchen cabinet and lightly pats her new hairdo as if it was a misbehaving puppy. Peering through the curtain again, she watches a young man step out of the filthy car. "Heaven forbid!" she yaps. "What on earth is he wearing?"

The stranger is wearing, on earth, a full-length faux fur coat and a pair of mirrored sunglasses that rest on the tip of his nose, covering his eyes, cheeks, and most of his forehead. As he approaches the trailer, a curly afro wig bobs up and down on his head like an intoxicated poodle that has been slam-dunked in black ink. Decorating the young man's fingers, several hundred grand worth of assorted bling, bling, sparkle like stars falling from the sky. The weight of the diamond-encrusted rings make his arms droop at his sides so he resembles a toy robot on low batteries. To top it all off, a pair of paddle-shaped, six-inch platforms decorated with silver Mardi Gras beads, shimmer like puddles in the sun.

"He didn't sound colored to me on the phone," Emma Jane says to a spotted-cow-shaped biscuit tin, "but you never can tell these days!"

The loud knocking on the screen door sends her wobbling into a state of panic.

"Just a minute!" she shouts, scurrying to the rear of the trailer. "Arlen!" she yells, "Arlen, the newspaper man is here." She shuffles back to the front door and opens it, suspiciously eyeing the stranger from head to foot. "Err ... Come on in." She half curtsies in the same polite way of being formal and a little informal at the same time that her mother had always instructed her to do when meeting important guests. "Get your self out of that heat before you melt like a furry snowman. I wasn't expecting you quite so soon, but you're here now. Arlen is working outside. Rain or shine. You know that mad dog, Arlen." She titters and then remembers that her mother had always told her how impolite it was to laugh at oneself. "Please, have a seat on the sofa. You can throw them magazines on the coffee table. There you go. No, on second thought, stuff them under the couch for me, would ya? There's a doll. Excuse me a sec. I'll be right back." She disappears down the hallway, yelling for Arlen as if scolding a cat.

ZANE

"Hi Mom, it's me! I'm back home."

Stepping inside, Zane forces a smile and sits down as instructed. His mother does not seem to hear or recognize him above her own hollering and fluster. "Glad to see nothing much has changed," he mumbles, watching her disappear from of the room.

With the quickness of a magician's hand, he reaches into his coat pocket and pulls out a silver snuffbox. He snorts a large bump of cocaine. The case disappears and he leans against the vinyl couch. Adjusting his wig, he fidgets. "This is going to be rough," he says, letting out a long and exhausted sigh. "I knew it. I can feel it coming on."

ARLEN

Smack in the middle of his cluttered, industrial back yard, usually suspended above a twenty-foot ladder with a portable welding machine strapped to his back, Arlen works nonstop nowadays. The air and gas lines coil over his neck and shoulders like rubberized pythons, and across his face, golden flames arch and spark like mating fireflies. Consumed in the flames, he wields small strips of recycled metal onto a gigantic armature. In the blistering heat of sun and torch, he could fill a bucket with his own sweat in forty minutes without taking a break, and this suits him just fine, almost makes him comfortable in his own skin, especially now that he's knocked off the booze. In fact, thanks to the help of a few dedicated friends, he hasn't touched a drop since he lashed out at Zane more than six years ago. After that venomous night, he vowed to redirect his fiery energy into less destructive pursuits, and today he is working on a series of sculptures fabricated from scrap metal, scavenged and recycled throughout the parish. "Hands of peace," he likes to call his welded creations, his very own hand-made hands with outstretched fingers reaching for the stars.

As his thoughts sizzle and glow, Arlen grins underneath his flame-licked mask like a devil happy in hell. *I must be doing something right these days,* he muses. *Made dozens of these hands now for various organizations, public parks and fancy restaurants, all of them saying the same thing. Heck, about to have my first one-man exhibition at that Visionary Museum up north. Who would have thought? Oh no, what now?* In between the flashing dancing sparks, Arlen notices Emma Jane frantically waving and yelling at him to climb down the ladder. "What now?" he growls to his hissing torch. "I promised her I would stop to eat. It can't be that time already!"

MOOSE

"Come again? What you say? They're trying to close this place down again? For what reason? I don't believe it, no running water! ... What was I just saying about that a minute ago?" Moose gestures to Mona with his hands in the air. He's on the rampage like a bull who knows that his balls are about to be cut off. "You'd think there's enough water floating around outside if you really need some that bad. Hasn't anyone ever heard of buckets anymore? What about my ice, I say? And no electricity? How come we don't have none of that is what I want to know. Making me drink hot beer after all I gone and gone through! ... Y'all see, they'll have them parking meters eating your quarters every two minutes before there's any lights on around here, Uptown or no Uptown." He uncrosses his legs and examines the worn knees of his stained overalls. A moment later, he crosses his legs again so that his right foot wraps around his left leg's ankle, then raises his plastic cup to a photograph tacked behind the bar and belches, "Ain't that right, Jake, where ever you are? Bless your heart. See what you're missing down here? Here's some spit in ya eye." Moose looks over at the stranger, then back to Jake's photo. "Poor bugger, you never was the same after you gone and passed away. How's that rich missus of yours doing these days anyhow? I ain't seen her up in these parts much since the storm hit. I know she must be busy with her ghost touring, but still, I heard them tourists have been flocking right back into town as if nothing ever happened. You'd think they had better things to do than come back to this place just to get in everyone's business again."

The stranger lifts his head off the bar and orders another drink before lowering it again. Moose resumes his wheezing and grumbling. His slurred words exhale into the damp air until all that can be seen of him is a layer of thick smog swirling at the end of the bar. "There's bound to be a lot more ghosts running around now. Ha!" the smug blurts out. "And that baby of hers, what's its name? ... That's right, how could I forget? Getting old, I guess. Just think yourself lucky that you don't have to deal with none of that mess where you are, especially with the price of diapers these days. Don't know why they can't be sharing them like what we used to do growing up. None of that disposable stuff back then. In fact, my first memory was being pricked with one of them safety pins up mah butt. Not sure what was safe about them, come to think of it, especially when Ma got ... well ... you know... She did the best she could." He pauses to light a cigarette. "What with the twelve of us yapping at her heels all night long. Still, it don't make no sense to me them throwing them away like that these days, especially with no one collecting the garbage for weeks now. Damn health risk waiting to happen, in my books. They need to get some of them lazy niggers back here to start working again instead of them living in those fancy outta-state housing and collecting more free money. I don't see no one handing me any of it, like I don't have troubles enough."

Mona drags herself over to Moose with another beer in her hand. She bats through the fog, startling him. "What was that?" he shrieks, almost falling off his stool. "Oh, it's you! ... Did you ever find me some ice?"

"No!" Mona growls.

"What about getting that no-good, lazy punk Aaron to go get some."

"He's still cleaning up the rooms."

"Damn must be nice. How many weeks has he been goofing off on that one?"

"It's not just the rooms, there's a hole hacked in the roof and all that damn writing every place."

"Writing?"

"Yes, writing, if you can call a bunch of nonsensical scribbling all over the walls, ceilings and in the bathrooms that. Hell, I can see some right now on the mirrors of the disco ball. I found some just the other day inside the beer cooler."

"I wouldn't be surprised if there weren't none scribbled on your ass," Moose chuckles.

Ignoring Moose, Mona helps herself to one of his cigarettes. "You know his van's gone," she says indifferently.

"Yeah, they finally towed away that piece of junk. I saw the Popeye's security guard the other morning. Says he was the one that found it all smashed up against the back of the dumpsters. Seems that idiot was so wasted he left the keys in the ignition with the engine running. Like I said before, I never liked the guy to begin with. You know them damned Yankees."

"Yankees? I thought he was from Bunkie, or someplace like that."

"What? ... Naw, he just always pretended to be from around these parts. Easton P.A., I think he told me once."

"I thought Aaron--"

"Aaron don't know fiddly squat!" Moose blurts back, "I told you he was a crazy lunatic!'

"Who?"

"Some Guy Upstairs, that's who! Remember that time his father came to town looking for him?...And Some Guy, so damn wasted, ranting all rude at his own kin like that with his tape recorder repeating everything. Yeah, don't look so surprised. That was his dad, for real! A preacher I think he said. Seemed like a nice enough fellah. You don't remember how the Chemical Sisters had to drag his sorry ass back up to his room and keep it locked for a week, leaving his dad all embarrassed, twiddling his thumbs?

"The preacher?"

"No, you idiot, Some Guy Upstairs."

"How are they doing?"

"Who, the Chemical Sisters? You know those two, up to their usual, twisted nonsense, I'm sure. I heard they have been working with them Mardi Gras Indians and the Mothers of the Saints, if you can call them that, busy sewing and stitching them FEMA blue roofs tarps up. Their plan is to cover the entire damn city with them and then throw a party in the Superdome. Working round the clock like it was Mardi Gras or something. They said they're going to hot wire the entire airwaves and broadcast it across America."

"How they plan on doing that? Sounds like fun."

"Don't ask me. Probably got some geek boyfriend from Tulane helping them out."

"The blonde-haired guy with the cute butt?"

"No. I think they said his name was ... Hell it slips mah mind ... Fill her up, will ya? ... You want one yerself?"

"Why not? So the girls are back in town, huh?"

"I saw them the other night as a matter of fact. Said they've had enough with everybody forgetting this whole hurricane thing ever happened. I tried telling 'em, I did. "Everything takes time", I said. "Just look at New York after all that 9/11 mess. How many years was that, now? And that was only one city block and still it's just a hole in the ground with a few tractors driving around for the tourists."

"It seems like it's one disaster after another these days."

"Of course it is! It's always been like that, but no one won't listen. Just like them girls. I say to them, you try time-sing that hole in New York by two-thirds of a city and then add the whole Gulf Coast. "Well", they say, "that's what's wrong with America today." "What's that?" I say. "Our elected leaders just sit around on their fat asses doing absolutely nothing except get fatter on everyone else's sweat, making up the rules as they go along. Then come election time they conveniently lower the price of gas, saying how they help the people and then a month later, after they have been reelected, you'd better get praying again and check under your bed for a terrorist." So I say, "I know exactly what you mean, my girls." And they say, "We're not your girls and would I kindly remove my hand from their thighs." Don't ask me why, not into real men, I guess. And then they say they're going to blast their concert all across America during the next presidential debate. "Sure," I say. "Suit yourself. It's not like anyone ever watches that show now. Damn waste of time, if you ask me." So off they stomp out of the bar and I haven't seen no hide or hare of them since."

"I'm just glad they're all right, that's all," Mona says as she fades into the bathroom, licking the salt off the edge of her plastic cup like a child eating an ice cream cone.

"Whatever." Moose replies just as the barroom door opens.

"Well, well, well. Look what the cat dragged in," he says. "Just kidding Sophia. . Got anything for me today?" He pats the stool next to him. "Bless your heart, you look like shit. Nothing except more of them water bills, I bet. What a joke. We ain't had no running water for weeks and somehow someone manages to keep sending the bills out, trying to bleed us dry, I tell you what. Someone's going to pay big time if my social's late again."

Sophia stands on the other side of the vacant stool, trying to ignore Moose.

"Oh come on, Sophia!" he continues, "Where's that pretty sexy smile of yours these days? I know, I know, the stress of it all. Same in here, you know. Don't think you're all alone. We don't have any more ice. Getting everybody down, it is. What? They're planning on cutting y'alls hours at the post office? Did you hear that, Mona? Seems to me after all this mess they'd be needing more postmen,—I mean post mistresses—not less. You've been working with them for how long now? Ever since Treme."

"Six years!"

"Well anyways, I heard about your house. At least you're not alone. I mean half the city is like that! They say it happened before, you know, when they blew up the levee back in—when was that?—Nothing surprises me anymore these days, not with them bureaucratic types running everything on self interest. Can't trust no one, ain't that right, Mona? Where'd she go now? Hey, calm yourself down, Sophia! Crying won't help nothing. Have a drink or something. Hey, Mona, where ever you are. Same again. And while you're at it, buy Sophia here a root beer for me. there's a good girl."

"I can buy my own, thank you, Moose!"

"Suit yourself. No need to get hostile about it. Can you believe this weather? We gone an' had all that rain for a lifetime and look at it now, dry as a bone out there. Good for mah arthritis though."

Sophia looks around the deserted bar room. "Whatever happened to dat fine old red couch dat used to be up in here?" she asks.

"You mean the Ship of Fools?"

"Yeah, that one."

"You haven't heard what that crazy idiot gone an' done this time."

"Which one?"

"Some Guy Upstairs. You remember, always wasted at the bar fantasying about becoming a hot shot DJ. Trying to impress what's his name's sister."

"The nurse?"

"That's him. Ruth. Real cutie with the big tits, works down at Charity Hospital. – Well, used to, until they gone and shut the place down. I mean, it's not like we all haven't got enough troubles without them adding one more. Just look at me. I'm due for my annual checkup for my benefits and I can't get no one to answer their damn phone. No one around to schedule my appointment for me. No one to come and pick me up or nothing. I don't know what's the problem with people these days. It's not like we're talking about them driving me more than a couple of blocks, now is it."

"Anything serious?" Mona shouts rather hopefully as she stumbles toward them.

"Don't you worry your fat ass! Nothing's the matter with me. Thanks for the concern though. Fit as a fiddle. Wanna feel? Still, you can't be too careful these days, especially with all the stress that's going around. And anyways, a check up is a check up!"

"How's Ruth doing?" Sophia asks, trying to change the subject. "Everybody's so scattered now."

"Oh, she's just fine," Moose replies, "Her apartment was in the Garden District. Just lost most of her roof in them 130 mile an hour winds, that's all. I heard she's volunteering at one of those free crisis centers down in New Orleans East. Like we need more of them kinda places in this city, especially now we got a bunch of Mexicans swarming the place. We get rid of one lazy lot and another shows up just like that. Breed like weeds, they do. No offence, Sophia. You're different!"

"And how am I different, Moose?"

Moose shuffles uncomfortably on his seat, fumbling with an unlit cigarette. "What kinda question is that? After I go an offer to buy you a root beer an' all! You're from here and play by the rules. That's how. Oh, come on. Just kiddin ya, Sophia. You know I totally agree with anything you say, wink, wink."

"You should be in the hospital. Permanently, I might add." Sophia picks up her postbag and storms out of the bar, slamming the door.

"Well fuck you, too!" Moose blurts back before lighting a new cigarette with the end of his old one. He squints suspiciously at Mona. "How come everybody is so uptight these days? Hello! Bar girl, anyone home? You ever find me mah ice or what?"

MARTHA

Carnivorous butterflies haunting me on my birthday, of all times. Why are you back here robbing me of all my inner charms, you fluttering furies, you nibbling nasties? How dare you try and tear me apart with wasted reminders of servitude to a past I've been dissecting with a scalpel and microscope in the bowels of hospitals and sterile clinics, oh you flapping, flower-powder sniffers. Underneath this fragile veneer, this priceless and spotless leopard's skin, there's a lifetime of exploring withered futility. Haven't I told you already? Haven't you seen enough? Wasn't it you who sent me the sign in the first place, convincing me I was the special one back when I walked hand in hand with youth? Oh, those early years, I can sigh about them now, before my hollow attempts to find a cure for why I am who I'm not, were graced with such fragrant smells of memory, thanks in part to my parents' flourishing flower shop and their entwined heritage of exquisite French taste and sound Germanic mind. Back then I was endowed with Rimbuad's cock and Rilke's equally dexterous tongue, two Herculean attributes that bestowed upon me a sensibility to explore the darkest bed chambers and deepest haunts of my very inner being. Yes, my sweet-scented youth was filled with all the softness and caressing expectations of endless foreplay, happy lost hours sneaking into mother's wardrobe and kissing my innocence in the full-length gold-leafed cupid-clad mirror, a time of preparation, with endless dress rehearsals wearing only the finest silk shoes with the excuse that my feet were far too sensitive in anything less perfect, delicately pampering myself for the admiring audiences who were sure to be waiting with baited breath for my grand entrance of operatic proportions. And they did. In fact, to this very day, I much prefer slippers to heels! Yet my fondest, most venerable moment was not experimenting with lipstick or curtsying to the mail man, who so many years later somehow choose to forget rudely fondling me in broad daylight on my parent's wraparound porch in the middle of that hot, hot, summer day while our gardener pretended not to notice his explicit antics. Oh no, when I found him again, abandoned in my favorite wayward brothel, all pant-less, stiff and ejecting a sack full of returned mail, I assured him how he had helped me accept that I'd been sent from the gods to expel the myth that cheap, raw love is dead. Don't you remember? The gods gave me the sign via you, who now tear off strips of my flesh with your vampirish tie-dyed wings! You, who have come back to remind me of that Easter-Sunday Mass down in the French Quarter when the tips of the budding tress look so edible and the live oaks shade fresh lovers abandoning their socks, believing they're the first to discover the eroticism of spring. A time when, if you're patient as only a secretive child filled with wonder can be, you can crouch or kneel in the virgin-cut grass open mouthed or sucking a lollipop, staring in awe at the butchered stumps of banana trees, watching spell bound as the tender young stems, the size of fresh asparagus, rise up from the dead. Rising up! Not one, not two, but often three inches in an afternoon, pushing themselves out of rotting innards of their hacked, dry stumps before my very eyes as if expelled from the grave into the resurrection of Life.

The bathtub erupts and Martha emerges spitting and snorting like an anorexic hippo. She wipes the soapy bubbles out of her eyes and inspects her prune like skin. "It worked," she shouts, splashing the water with glee. "I drowned those ghastly flapping insect shits!" She splashes again before nervously looking around the bathroom. Satisfied her world is once again insect free she slouches back into the tub and exhales a weary sigh of relief. Her eyes close as she searches for the rubber ducky hiding between her legs. *It was the Holy Day of Resurrection, and I saw an old woman sitting on the Cathedral steps with a basket of flowers in her lap. I remember her dressed in an array of colored fabrics like a medieval gypsy, perhaps of Eastern descent, with delicate flower petals reflecting her shimmering skin. In her hair was a garland of poises innocently braided in the incoherence of Christ's thorns. I can still see her thin, outstretched hands asking for change as I walked up those cold, immobile cathedral steps, badgered by my parents. I was awestruck by her, unable to move, mesmerized by her beauty. "Look at the butterflies flying above that lady's head," I said. "Look at all those gorgeous butterflies!" But my parents couldn't or wouldn't see the old woman's wonder, both of them unaffected and stuffed with sanctimonious purpose. "Move along," they said. "Move along now, Martha. We cannot be late for mass." Then they shoved me forward and pushed my face to kiss the priest's hand. I stumbled, staring at the ringed fingers, blinding me; the same fingers that I knew wanted to explore every orifice of my twelve-year-old body. It was too much. Too much contrast for a child's innocent mind to fathom. One image filled with infinite beauty, the other oozing with betrayal and piety. I wanted to scream at God to blind me, but instead I bit down on the priest's finger before kicking his shin. Then I turned and ran, out of the cathedral and down the stairs, three steps at a time, running past the gypsy with her miracle of butterflies, past the ever- present shadows of the cathedral and out into the quagmire of the rising heat. I didn't look back. How could I? I couldn't stop until I had reached the park where the dirty pigeons bathed in a dirty fountain and the Krispy Kreme tourists snap photos of their Krispy Kreme lives. I was out of breath and collapsed under a bench beside a bed of flowering tulips, shivering in dread, afraid of the ramifications of my actions both from my parents and the priest and, I guess, from God. I sat with my knees under my chin, concentrating on the memory of the flower lady's smile and her butterflies. It was then that I became filled with the courage to believe I had seen a real, live miracle and as if to confirm it, another butterfly landed in front of my very feet. I can't remember how long I watched her fan her wings in the fresh, spring sunlight. A child filled with wonder has no sense for time.*

Martha opens her eyes and scans the steamy bathroom in search of a drink. She pulls the bath plug out with her big toe and feels the water suck down the drain. Stepping out of the tub she rummages through a waist high pile of disheveled clothing in search of a dry towel. Exasperated, she yanks off a bed sheet and wraps herself up like a delicate Christmas ornament about to be boxed and stuffed in the attic for another year. She finds her pill box and swallows handfuls of Something or Other as her thoughts continue to float like a plucked chicken feather caught in a summer breeze. *Tell me Martha, what was all that really about? You're a sensible sort. Do you know? Surely nothing other than a sign trying to show me how I see things differently from the rest of this stale and drab, cruel, cruel world. And if my eyes are different, so too must be my soul, however riddled in melancholy it might be. After all, both are related. Both are keys opening the doors to the universe. And if my soul is different, then surely the vessel that houses the soul is, too. Of course I prayed about all that. Of course I kept asking for some kind of divine explanation, but nothing happened. And after several years of patiently waiting, I decided I'd decipher for myself the whys and the hows of who I really am. I became industrious like a busy queen bee and before long waltzed into medical school...Of course I was brilliant. No amount of studying really helps the gifted, so I forced myself to delve in deeper and found myself breaking free from the priests and teachers and rough pawing of drunk tourists on Bourbon Street. Soon I'd closed the door to the desires of the flesh and found myself clinical and unaffected, merrily dissecting cadavers on Saturday nights. I became plain, part of the pastel hospital décor, determined to conquer and find a cure for who I am, resolute to seek the solution to what separated me from a world riddled and infected by the undone and obvious. As my research consumed me, it became a monster unto itself, drying me out, wilting me like a flower in a waterless vase. I realized I'd started to digress until I became painfully aware that even in the finest hospitals, in the innermost sanctuaries of medical science, my studying led me along one single path, the same path that every doctor and scientist past and present has traveled. I found myself devoid of originality as my mind morphed into the minds of all the other great minds driven by that one, single, menial thought of how to live forever, how to break free from the shackles of the only thing that is freely given to us at birth. This realization snapped my world like a brittle twig because death, still to this day, does not interest me in the least because I am already immortal with every second I breathe. Because every time I wake up is all the proof I need. However, this epiphany like every self-realization filled me with bitterness. I had transgressed for too long and felt my uniqueness slipping into the inevitable conformity of clinical boredom. I felt sour and became indifferent toward the medical world, knowing that I must break away. I had to, to save myself and preserve my uniqueness. I had to flee back into the deepest and darkest corners of confusion and accept that I'd never be able to decipher the complexities of my own existence. I had to be me again and be reborn. I had to live every second of my immortality exploding in a bubble of chaos.*

ZANE

On the center of the stage is a large beige vinyl couch. Nestled beside each of its arms is a pair of brightly striped red and white cushions. On either side of the couch stands an imitation banana tree potted in a five gallon sheetrock buckets. The plastic plants are spray painted to look scorched and blistered by the sun. Behind the couch is a brightly wallpapered wall with a cut-out door and window.

Zane sits in the middle of the couch. He is obviously nervous and keeps rummaging through his coat as if searching for some loose change or an old receipt. The stage is lit with three 60-watt light bulbs attached to a ceiling fan.

Emma Jane and Arlen enter the stage via the cut-out door and sit on either side of him. As the couch sags they constantly slide toward their son. At random intervals, all three notice their proximately and, after an uncomfortable silence, Arlen and Emma Jane shift away from Zane.

SCENE ONE

Emma Jane: Here is the famous Arlen, the artist.

Arlen: (Chuckling, obviously proud of himself) Emma let the man alone. We all know it's not the fame that I'm about.

Zane: What's it about then, Arlen?

Emma Jane: He's about making the world a better place, trying to give back a little beauty to this tired and dreary world.

Arlen: (Smiling smugly with his arms folded against his chest) Emma is a very passionate woman.

Zane: I was addressing you, Arlen. What are you about?

Arlen: Well, they say I'm an Outsider, which suits me just fine because I do all my work outside. (he gestures to the back door.)

Zane: And what work would that be? ... May I smoke in here?

Emma Jane: We don't normally, but seeing you're from the press an' all, let me get you an ashtray.

Arlen: Thanks Emma.

Zane: Thanks Emma.

Emma Jane: (Gets up and gives Zane a puzzled look, as if she's heard a voice from her past but can't figure it out.) Ice, anyone?

Arlen Sure.

Zane: Sure. So you're an outsider because you work outside?

Emma Jane: He's a visionary too! Everything he does comes from a dream.

Arlen: Well, it did kinda all start from a dream, I guess. That and ...

Zane: Please, go on.

Arlen: Several years ago, I made the mistake of hitting my son and—

Emma Jane: Arlen! This gentleman didn't drive all the way up here to hear your personal life story. Tell him about the Snow Leopard.

Zane: Snow Leopard?

Arlen: I was in Afghanistan and, that's when I saw it and started drinking real heavy-like and got home confused and .... Hit my son.

Emma Jane: Arlen, he doesn't want to hear all that.

Arlen: Hush, woman! I have to tell someone what really happened. It's been too long now pretending I never...

Zane: Go on, Arlen. Take your time .... Please.

Arlen: We all do a lot of stupid things in our life, don't we? Some more than others. I've done my fair share, a lot you know. Acted out, got mean, that kinda stuff. Anyway, I lashed out at my son and never seen him since, and to be honest, that's what got me doing all this artwork.

Emma Jane: And the dream. Tell him about the dream.

Arlen: The dream happened the same night I hit my son. It was just part of it all, I guess. Maybe a punishment. I don't really know, but it sure added another match to the fire burning inside me.

Zane: So you're telling me because you hit your son, you became an artist? How strange! Do you have any other children?

Emma Jane: What's his children got to do with anything? Don't you want to take some pictures of his work with him standing next to it? What's with all this personal stuff? It's weird, but I feel like I've seen you some place before, although it sure is hard to tell under all them sun glasses. Have you been on the TV lately? (She hands them their Diet Coke.)

Arlen: Thanks Emma. I was getting mighty thirsty outside. It's a scorcher today. Funny thing, all that rain seems to have made it worse.

Zane: Yes, it is.

Emma Jane: Why don't you take that coat off then, and while you're at it, them silly shades. In case you haven't noticed, it's not sunny in here.

Zane: Maybe in a little while, thanks. I'm feeling rather cold at the moment.

Emma Jane: As you wish, Mr ... What did you say your name was?...I'm sure I've seen you some place else.

Arlen: Please, Emma Jane, let the man be. He came all the way from the city to be here.

Zane: Where were we again? Your children?

Arlen: We had two of them. One's a nurse now in New Orleans. We hear from her every now and then. The other, my son that is—Do we have any photos of them Emma?--Is somewhere—I think there's one in the bedroom. I've kept all his things in his room, like how they were before he left home.

Zane: When was the last time you saw them?

Emma Jane: If you must know, we saw Ruth a couple of Christmases ago when she came up here to help her friend Irene pack up her things and move down there. They live together. I don't mean like that. She's a diabetic. That's what I meant.

Zane: And Zane?

Emma Jane: How did you know his name? Who are you? There's something not right here. You're not like those other reporters that come up in here.

Arlen: Honestly, we don't rightly know. Emma sends him letters when she can to an address in New York City. I think he must be doing okay if he can afford to live up north. It costs you 20 bucks just to fart up there.

Emma Jane: Arlen!

(All three laugh nervously and readjust themselves on the couch.)

Arlen: I thought I'd break the ice a little. I find these `interviews awkward, but you're probably used to meeting strangers in your line of work, all the time I guess. Myself, I like being by myself. Well with Emma, too. It's all I can do. Helps with the voices in my head. I'm always envious of those people who can be real social-like. They seem so happy and can laugh at anything, even if it's not funny. I always wondered what kind of secret ingredient they fix in their morning coffee to make them that way…I'm getting better though. aren't I Emma? Thankfully making art helps.

Zane: Helps what?

Arlen: Calm the voices always bickering in my head. Helps with the pain, too.

Zane: The pain?

Arlen: The pain of not knowing how to fix my mistakes. The daily pain of second guessing at everything. I guess, if I'm honest, I'm scared I'm going to get it all wrong again, and I'm not sure I can keep starting over, but as I said before, creating stuff helps. Do you know what I mean?

Zane: I think so.

Emma Jane: More Diet Coke?

Arlen: No thanks.

Zane: I'm okay. Thanks moth—(Zane bites his lip)

Arlen: After you realize you've made a mistake, you're kinda stuck as to what to do next. I guess that's why so many of us just hide away and do as we're told, even though we feel sometimes it isn't the right thing in our hearts to do. I don't blame anyone. Who wants to live their life running around second guessing all the time? Shit, look at me. I guess everything wrong.

Emma Jane: Not everything, Arlen. Not all the time.

Arlen: (Smiling weakly.) You're right. I guessed Emma Jane right from the moment I laid mah eyes on her. I knew from the get-go she was ma gurl!

Zane: That's rather sweet.

Arlen: Not sure where I'm going with all this, but I do hope my son is all right. That's all really. Getting a second chance ain't all it's cracked up to be sometimes. It just gives you a whole lot longer to look at your mistakes, that's all. Regrets can take a man back down the hole he spent all that time trying to dig himself out of. Get you all twisted up inside like there's bombs going off in your soul. Hell, I should know. I've been around enough bombs in mah lifetime. That's why I'm so grateful to be doing my art stuff, helps gets those bombs out of my mind and into the world. Helps create a little explosive calmness, if that makes sense. You know, this might surprise you, but I've taken to reading some lately, and I think I'm one of those types who isn't naturally happy. I mean born with a smile all over mah face. Sure I know I'm moody, who isn't? But I think I have a melancholy like disposition. Sure, Emma tries to soothe me with her simple ways, but even when it seems that I should be happy like everybody else, like at Christmas time, I'm still not someone you're going to pick up the phone and say, "Hey, Arlen, let's go party." Even when I was drinking, no one really thought me much fun.

Zane: Is that so?

Arlen: It seems to me, if you watch TV and read them magazines that Emma hides under her couch, if you're not perfectly happy, then there's something's wrong with you and that makes the likes of me even more unhappy. Seeking happiness is not what I'm about anymore. I tried that, and it got me into a lot of trouble. I'd rather call myself dull. Not happy or unhappy, just plain dull, because when I accept that, I can feel a little more content. Does any of this make sense?

Emma Jane: Oh, Arlen, just listen to him, would you? You're *always* making jokes and saying such silly, funny things. Should I get the album for this gentleman to see your artwork and news clippings? It might give him some ideas for his newspaper. What did you say the name of it was again? (She reaches under the coffee table and pulls out an album.)

Zane: Err, *Picayune … Daily … Herald*. Continue about your art.

Arlen: There's not much else to say, really. I don't think too much about my work. What's funny is that I'm able to see the finished piece before I even start making it.

Emma Jane: (Pointing at a picture in the album) This is us at the museum. That's Arlen, and that's me with my new dress Arlen brought me special for the occasion. That's the fountain, there, and there's the glass building that has his work inside it. I don't know who that is standing next to him. In this one you can see my dress a little better. Real fine, ain't it? Oh my Lord, what's that red stuff running down your nose?

Zane: Excuse me?

Emma Jane: Look! There's blood pouring out your nose! Let me go get you a Kleenex.

Arlen: Damn, you're really bleeding. The bathroom's over there.

Zane: I'll be right back. (He stumbles up off the couch, wiping blood from his face with his hand. He exits through the cut-out door. Arlen and Emma Jane stare at each other confused.)

Lights dim.

SCENE TWO

Emma and Arlen relax on the couch, going through their album when they hear a loud knocking. A moment later, Zane's chauffer enters.

Chauffer: You got any cold compresses in here?
Emma Jane: (Startled and uncomfortable that a black man has entered her home) Any what? Arlen, do something. Yes, can I help you?
Chauffer: First Aid. Cold compresses. Ice? How about some ice? Good God, is that you Arlen?
Arlen: (Making his way to the kitchen, he turns and stares at the man) Sarge?
Chauffer: What you doing here?
Arlen: I live here. What are you doing, more like?
Chauffer: I drove Zane down here. He's on his way to New Orleans to promote a benefit concert for the hurricane victims. He's in the back seat right now with blood pouring out of his nose. Too much damn cocaine if you ask me.
Emma Jane: Excuse me. What are you talking about? Whoever you are, you'd better get out of my house this instant or I'll phone the police and—
Arlen: Emma, Emma! Everything is okay. It's Sarge, you remember? Crazy George? From the good ol days!
Emma Jane: (Walks up to Sarge and stares at him suspiciously) Are you sure?
Chauffer: Yes! It's me al right. I need some ice, your son is making one hell of a mess in my car! Thank you, Arlen. Glad you're alive! I'll be right back.
(He exits carrying a cup of ice. Emma Jane and Arlen stand in front of the couch, bewildered.)

Lights dim.

SCENE THREE

Arlen and Emma Jane are embracing each other in front of the couch. Arlen is to consoling Emma, who is crying violently.

Emma Jane:	I thought I recognized that voice. That's so mean, to show up unannounced and not say anything like that to us. What does he think we are?
Arlen:	It's all right, Emma, can't you see? It's a good thing.
Emma Jane:	He could have at least given me a hug and asked how we were doing. What's he dressed like that for, any ways? If Mrs. Granger next door sees him, we'll never hear the last of it.
Arlen:	Hush now, Emma. Hush. Sit yourself down. That's it. Look, here comes Zane. (Zane enters holding a bloody handkerchief over his nose. He has taken off his wig and sunglasses. He sits down in the middle of the couch and tilts his head back.)
Arlen:	Welcome home, son.
Emma Jane:	(Nervously) It's so good to see you again … Thanks for … just dropping in all informal like this. Your father and I were just thinking about you, weren't we Arlen!
Arlen:	All the time, Emma. I think about you all the time. Look at you! You're all grown up. And a good six inches taller than me.
Zane:	It's my heels, see! (He raises his shoes. Emma Jane and Arlen look at the shoes then back at their son)
Emma Jane:	Really, Zane. Why are you dressed like a … One of those—
Arlen:	Emma Jane, for once in your life, just shut up.
Zane:	Still worried about me being queer, Mom? Glad to see nothing's changed in the past six years.
Arlen:	No, son, it's not that. I ain't worried about what you are, no more.

Zane: Sure you ain't. It's written all over yall's faces. You got something to drink beside Diet Coke? I know you must have some booze some where.

Emma Jane: I'll have you know your father hasn't drunk since—

Arlen: Emma, for the last time, I said hush!

Zane: No shit? Good for him. What made you stop?

Arlen: You helped me son.

Zane: My driver says he knows you from when you where in the army. Is that true? You were actually a real soldier going to war, and stuff? I thought you just made that all up as an excuse to act stupid.

Emma Jane: Zane! I don't know who you think you are talkin' to your father like that.

Arlen: Emma, it's okay. He has a right to be angry with me. Yes, that's Crazy George.

Zane: Damn small world. Something to drink? Yes? No? Then another Diet Coke will work.

Arlen: We kept your room the way you left it. We thought … I hoped you would be back sooner. You gave your mother quite the surprise, like a ghost or something.

Emma Jane: See? Arlen is all changed now Zane. He's gone and done a lot of work on himself, and now he's a famous artist and we're thinking about getting another trailer added on to this one, and make a beautiful sculpture park out here.

Zane: Glad y'all are doing so well. Need any money? (Zane lifts his head off the back of the couch and pulls out a thick wad of $100 bills. He hands the money to Arlen) Here, buy yourself some art supplies and another potted plant for Ma's garden.

Arlen: That's very generous of you Zane, but I can't go taking your money.

Emma Jane: How much is there? Heavens where did you get all that? Are you one of them drug dealers? Did I give up the best years of my life to watch my son turn into a drug dealer?

Zane: Don't worry your busy little self. It ain't no drug money. Thanks for the hospitality and vote of confidence, but I gotta go! This was one big mistake coming back here again. (He stands up and begins to exit)

Arlen: Wait, Zane!

Zane: What now?

Arlen: I am sorry.

Zane: For what? ... Me coming back here?

Lights dim

SCENE FOUR

Emma and Arlen are sitting on the couch. Emma Jane is counting the money. Arlen stares at his hands, occasionally balling them into a fist.

Emma Jane: There's over $8000 here! Do you hear me, Arlen?...Eight thousand U.S. dollars!

Arlen: And?

Emma Jane: And? Are you crazy? And! Think what this can buy! And indeed.

Arlen: What Emma Jane? A place in paradise? A brand-new second skin. Why do you think he came back here?

Emma Jane: Who, Zane? To give us this money, of course, silly! (They hear a loud knock. Instinctively, Emma hides the money under the couch. Arlen grabs her hand and grabs the cash as Sarge enters)

Sarge: Hey, Arlen, can I use your wash room?

Arlen: Of course. Is he going to be all right?

Sarge: Your son?

Arlen: Yes, Zane. Is he going to be all right?

Sarge: I think so. The bleeding has stopped. He just needs to relax a little. Shame yall got into it after he came all this way to—

Emma Jane: That's none of your business! You're probably the one giving him—What was it called?—That cocaine thing in the first place.

Sarge: Excuse me?

Arlen: Emma Jane, I'm not going to say this again, but you need to CALM THE FUCK DOWN. Now go fix this gentleman a Diet Coke while he washes his hands. Please, have a seat, Sarge.

Sarge: No diet coke for me thanks. Water will do just fine.

Arlen: Water then. Did you hear me, Emma Jane? And I'll have the same damn thing. It feels like a bomb is goin' off in my stomach again.

Sarge: You trying to be funny, Arlen?

Arlen: Not at all. It's my ulcers, I think the doctors calls them. Always happens when I get stressed out. Personally, I think I'm getting the same disease as my daughter.

Sarge: And what's that?

Emma Jane: Diabetes. It's a sign from God that's been cursing our family for generations.

Sarge: What are you talking about, a curse? Shit, sister, I got diabetes. I know lots of folks with it, as well. Are you trying to tell me we are all cursed?

Emma Jane: All I can say is we're all entitled to our own opinion. I just think if Arlen ever went to church, he wouldn't be having half of all these problems. The Lord gives us all what we deserve, is what the book says, nothing more and not a thing less.

Sarge: Shit! Excuse mah language, but now you're trippin on me. I go to church every fucking Sunday. Since when did you become so high and almighty? You are the same Emma I knows back in the army aren't you?

Arlen: Please, will the pair of you, cut it out? Tell me, Sarge, what I want to know is how come you know my son so well?

Sarge: That's the Fly out there! That's Zane Da Main Man!

Arlen: I don't understand.

Sarge: Obviously. It just so happens, your son is one of the hottest DJs in the country.

Emma Jane: What do mean Dee Jay? Someone who plays records at church weddings?

Sarge: No Sister! I mean DJ. Making thousands of kids party and dance and have a good time, like what healthy kids are supposed to do.

Ariss: I never knew.

Emma Jane: Me neither. So this money he gave us, isn't drug money?

Sarge: Did you even think to ask him? You two make me laugh. That boy of yours makes more money an hour than the president of the United States. Shit, he gave me a grand just to drive him down here, and that's before the tip. I thought you were bigger than that. That's your only son out there! It's not my business, but you folks got some problems communicating with your own kin. I know you ain't had no breaks in this world, Arlen, but look around. How many folks really do? Zane told me you accused him right off the bat of being a drug dealer, and now he's out there crying and cursing the pair of you. I feel more sorry for you than I do him. At least he has got a life. I got to wash mah hands and get going. Your right Emma, it's none of my business how you treat your children. I'm sure you're both good people that mean well. I just hate to see it when parents don't communicate none with their kids, that's all. It's like you never know when your time is up and it'll never come back. Shit, Arlen, didn't the army teach you nothing?

Arlen: You should know! It taught me plenty, thank you very much.

Sarge: Well, stop worrying about make-believe curses and go talk to your son some. There's something between y'all that has the chance to be worked out right now, and driving him to New Orleans without fixing the problem sure ain't one of them.

Emma Jane: Are you trying to tell me my son is now a famous person? Kinda like my Arlen, here?

Sarge: You just don't get it, do you? Your son ain't no famous person like your Arlen here. Try Gold Dust or Snoop Daddy.

Emma Jane: Who?

Sarge: Never mind.

Emma Jane: Well, excuse me. If my son is famous, he needs his mother. I'll be right back. (She exit's, leaving the two men awkwardly facing each other in front of the couch.)

Arlen: You're looking good these days.

Sarge: You too, Arlen. It's a Hell of a trip seeing you again.

Arlen: I didn't ever think I would see anyone after what happened over there an' all.

Sarge: Yeah, me neither. I'm sorry man. That was a heavy deck of cards you were dealt.

Arlen: I'm sorry too. Everyday I live with the big what if.

Sarge: What do ya mean, Arlen? It was our job, and you were real good at it.

Arlen: The what-if-I-had-done-things-differently what if. I loved the army, you know that, it gave me a sense of purpose, but the shit that went down.

Sarge: Shit, that weren't your fault.

Arlen: What are you talking about? I was dishonorably discharged. Remember?

Sarge: Dishonorable my ass. You never heard? No one ever told you?

Arlen: Heard what?

Sarge: The final official report.
Arlen: I haven't heard nothing about no report.
Sarge: Brass orders an independent investigation after all that went down. Several months later, they always like to find out everything. No one wants no diplomatic scandal to drop on their door step without Brass knowing about it first.
Arlen: So what?
Sarge: You really don't know do you? Well, you were right.
Arlen: Right about what? What are you talkin' about?
Sarge: The friggin' snow leopard. Had her lair right there in the middle of the mine field, just like you said. When she jumped, she set every one of them mines off. Don't ask me how or why it happened then, but they found her head five hundred yards from her tail.
Arlen: Really? Then why was I? … How come I never? ... Does that mean I can get my charges reversed?
Sarge: I don't know about all that. You should know by now. There will always be two kinds of people in this world. There are those who fuck up and those who get fucked.
Arlen: I don't understand.
Sarge: Well that's because you're one of the ones who gets fucked.
(They start laughing.)
Arlen: You're just trying to make me feel better, is that it?
Sarge: I wish I was.
Arlen: Well what about Peterson's hand? Was that real? I swear sometimes I feel like I dreamed the whole damn nightmare.
Sarge: Arlen, in all my years in the service, I never had me no injury. No bullet up my ass, no grenade down mah pants. I only got one wound, and that was from crossing the line. (He lifts up his shirt and reveals a twelve-inch scar running down the side of his rib cage)

Arlen: Damn, Sarge! How did that happen?
Sarge: (Laughing) You're still a trip man. From your knife is how it happened. You don't remember when I tried to yank that bloody hand away from yours?
Arlen: You are kidding me, right?
Sarge: Does this scar look like I'm joking? Laid up in the hospital for more than twelve weeks. That knife of yours missed my lung by a whole pubic hair. Gone any farther in and I wouldn't be standing here right now. They discharged me after that, if that makes you feel any better.
Arlen; I don't know what to say.
Sarge: You and everybody else. Shit. When those mines started going off like it was the fourth of July, there wasn't one man left who wasn't in some kind of shock. We all went a bit crazy. They only found us because one of them natives was able to use his cell phone. ... Go figure!
Arlen: I'm so sorry.
Sarge: For what? Being a human being? There's nothing nice about any kinda conflict. You should know that by now. If you really feel that you want to make something up to me, go talk to that wounded son of yours.
Arlen: Right now?
Sarge: No, sixty years from now! But, before you go.
Arlen: Yes sarge
Sarge: Wake up!

Lights dim.

MOOSE

"What do you mean you're going to get a job at Popeye's?"
"They're paying ten bucks an hour!" Mona replies, "and I've been missing my mashed potatoes and gravy."

"You're kidding me. How much an hour? What's this world coming to? They'll be forming a union next! Who do they think they are? Anyway, you can't quit here."

"Why not?"

"Who's going to get mah lunch everyday? I can't be looking after everything. Look out, here comes Martha and boy does she look rough." Moose smirks as Martha slumps down at the bar wearing a white doctor's smock and leopard-skin slippers. Ignoring Moose, she lights a cigarette and orders a drink.

"Where you been? I haven't seen you lately," Moose asks.

"Researching. Something you wouldn't know nothing about."

"Doing what? Helping out those young army fellahs in the bathrooms downtown?"

"Actually, it's something like that. Thanks Mona. Did you hear Zane's coming back into town? I saw Ruth last night on her way to work again."

"That skinny red neck fellah, the one that got all fancy after he went to New York? I hear he's a real hot shot up there."

"No one's talking to you, Moose!" Mona interrupts, fixing herself a cocktail.

"Oh yeah, well, just remember the next time you go and get my lunch who's the one buying you your French fries. You're not eating no fancy Popeye's chicken yet."

"Will you guys just quit it?" Martha snaps, slugging down a vodka with warm milk.

Mona starts to make Martha another. "Thirsty, huh. Bad trip? ... What's he coming back here for anyways?"

"They're about to put on that concert at the Superdome, the Spirit of Jelly Roll, I think it's called. It's going to be larger than life, knowing the Chemical Sisters. They say they're trying to get the whole city to turn out. And some."

"No shit? Good for them. Moose told me about it, but I don't believe a word that dribbles out of his mouth."

"Coming back here, huh? What was that, Mona?" Moose looks around the bar room, then back to Martha, "I say we need all the help we can get in these parts. Right now wouldn't be soon enough!"

"Speak for yourself, Moose."

"What?" He wags his finger at Mona. "Did you hear she's trying to get a job at Popeye's? She says it's paying twenty bucks an hour and a union. What I want to know is how come they got power and we don't. Hello, who's this coming in here?"

A man enters the bar, wearing a set of oil-stained overalls and thick-rimmed glasses. He stares blindly around the smoke-filled room, blinking wildly as his eyes adjust to the dismal light. He stumbles into Martha and whispers, "Excuse me, sir, are you the proprietor of this establishment?"

Moose stands up and starts shouting."What's it to you? Yes, I do seem to run things around here. Who's asking anyway?"

The man seems confused. His eyes squint as he focuses on Moose. "I'm looking for two girls, R&R, the Chemical Sisters," he says, rubbing his ears with his oily hands.

"Sorry, never herd of 'em! .... Shut up, Mona!" Moose snaps like a rotten twig.

"They said I could find them at this here Hurricane Hotel," the man continues, "or at least someone who would knows hows to reach 'em. Their phones don't seem to be working none too well."

"What you want them for?" Martha ask suspiciously.

"I drove all the way down here to fix their car. They said I was the only one they trust with it. Apparently it got flooded real good-like."

"Oh yeah? And who are you again?"

The man reaches into his back pocket and pulls out a well-worn leather wallet. He opens the wallet, licks his fingers and produces an oil-stained business card. He sheepishly hands the card to Martha as if it were a hand grenade missing its pin. "Here I am, sir." Martha reluctantly takes the card and reads aloud, "Morgan Towing and Garage Services. Established 1962. Bunkie, Louisiana. That's you?"

Morgan nods proudly. "Yep, that's me. Since 1962."

Martha hands the card back and, pointing to Moose, says to Morgan, "Ignore him. I see them sometimes, quite a lot actually. I'll tell them your looking for them."

"Thanks kindly ... Mr. ..."

"Martha."

"I'll be off, then, Mr. Martian." He exits the bar.

Moose sits back down, takes a long sip of his hot beer, and starts nodding his head. "Towing, huh? Making a small fortune in this city right about now, I bet. Would have said something if he had offered me a drink. Here we go, it's a full deck of jokers now. Here comes that lazy punk Aaron."

Aaron slumps onto a stool between Moose and Martha. He doesn't look at either of them as he lights a cigarette and orders a beer. "What's up y'all?" he asks, looking at the over flowing ash tray and row of empty plastic cups.

"Nothin'" Mona replies.

"Nothin'" Martha repeats.

"Shit Boy!" Moose squeaks like a fingernail running down a chalk board. "You look as bad as I feel. You been trippin' on that happy backie again? When you goin' to get all that writing scrubbed off them walls so we can start to forget about all this mess ever happening is what I want to know. Just because you don't have any running water don't mean diddly squat around here. Haven't you ever heard of a fellow called Mr. Elbow Grease?"

"Its everywhere," Aaron sighs. "And about 150 degrees up in that attic."

"I know its everywhere, son. What you been doing the past month any how? Go get yourself a bottle of pneumonia, I say, and don't go drinking it all at once."

"What I want to know is who wrote all that in the first place?" Mona asks, weaving beside the open cash register.

"That idiot Some Guy Upstairs," Moose blurts. "That's who!"

"Oh yeah, well it would take a year to write that much down. And any way, I thought you said he was found dead or something, zipped up in a body bag."

"Well, that's what I heard."

"From who?" Mona asks. Aaron and Martha look up from their drinks and glare at Moose. "From who?" they repeat in unison.

Moose uncomfortably shuffles his bony rump on his stool like someone trying to fart between a nest of hemorrhoids. He ignores his audience's questioning as an ambulance wails down the avenue.

"You know," Aaron says, "It doesn't really matter who wrote all that stuff anyway. Who or what it was sure got the last laugh."

"What you mean?" Mona asks.

"Every time I go and paint over all them words, as soon as the paint goes an' dries, the words just seep back up through the walls again. You can read everything as bright as day."

"No shit?" Mona says.

"No Shit." Aaron repeats.

"That's because whoever it or they were used permanent markers," Martha replies. She slugs down her drink and wobbles to her feet. "Try calling me a cab, would you, Mona? I got to step outside for a while."

"Where you going?" Aaron asks, staring at his empty beer bottle.

"Nowhere fast," chuckles Mona.

"How about another round of drinks, before you leave?" Moose asks, ever hopefully, "On the house, I say. What's that you said again, about all that writing on the walls? ... Peppermint markers? ... I never heard of 'em."

MARTHA

Blinded by the afternoon blaze of a shell-shocked city, Martha wobbles out of the Hurricane Hotel. Under her arm she carries a well-worn copy of Grant's *Atlas of Anatomy*. In the aftermath of the flood, since Mona had started volunteering at the makeshift children's preschool and Ruth continued nursing without pay, Martha took up riding taxis using her parents' expense account. Daily she travels through the dilapidated and crater-infested city streets, staring vacantly at the passing discarded wreckage. Occasionally as she rides through the decapitated neighborhoods, she flips through her atlas, brushing up on familiar terminology. Every day she asks the driver to take her on a different route, and everyday she finds herself in the same dilemma; should she leave town or stay and offer her medical expertise.

Today's driver knows her routine. They've traveled together at least a dozen times now. Journeying past the endless piles of abandoned refrigerators and forgotten rat-infested trash, Martha talks to her own reflection in the vehicle's smeared window, pausing to turn a page or take a swig from her bottle of Southern Comfort. *Dr Martha,* She muses. *Oh spare me that one. Hospitals make me sick enough. Been there, done that, and some.*

The cab passes an elderly couple dressed from head to foot in disposable, protective clothing. The man has his hands on his hips as he stares down at a chunk of sheet rock wall that has fallen off his borrowed wheel barrow. He kicks the soggy plaster, coughing uncontrollably as it disintegrates into a thick, grayish blanket that covers his dead lawn like some kind of toxic, unmeltable snow. Silently, hypnotized with grief, his wife walks past him as if he weren't there. In her cupped hands is a rotting red tap shoe. She stops at the discarded remains of her lifetime, reduced now to a fourteen-foot high pile of rubble that runs the entire length of their modest yard and leans forward to carefully place the shoe on what looks like or might once have been an upright piano. Hesitating, she picks the shoe up again and holds it to her breast. Martha randomly flips atlas to Section Three; The Perineum. Glancing at the illustrations, she thinks, *That's a nice corona glandis. I haven't heard that delicious word in a while. How long has it been? Sweet spongy urethra, I always did like the sound of you. And to think I once contemplated removing mine. My, my, the sphincter ani. His and hers. What is it that separates my bulb from yours? Can anyone answer me that?*

The cab journeys on deeper and deeper into the broken crumbs of a ravaged world that looks more like the front page of the *Daily Iraq Times* than an American city. They pass a thirty-foot, two hundred ton, metal barge marooned and rusting in the middle of a public park. No one is quite sure how it got there or how it'll be removed. On the side of the boat's rusting carcass some one has spray painted;

DO NOT REMOVE
GOVERNMENT PROPERTY
THANK YOU

Martha lets her cigarette burn down to the filter. She rubs the butt with her fingertips and then places it into her coat pocket. *Once the superficial fascia is pulled back, once the colles fascia has been peeled away, you tell me what do we have? Mine you call a dick, and yours a clit ... Ever examined them? I have plenty of times. Yours is simply an inverted version of mine, and that's about all, comprising of two corpora cavernous bent and suspended by a ligament and then capped by a glans –Yes, my bulb is the same as yours, his and hers. Hers and his. Both offering the same damn thing, except, perhaps, that mine needs to be watered and fed a little more regularly.*

The cab stops. The driver leaves the engine running and steps out into the blistering air. He ambles over to a pile of trash and removes a sixty-four-inch flat screen TV that was partially covered with carpeting, broken furniture and asbestos shingling. He wipes the fractured screen with his sleeve, then carefully examines the back of the set before placing it in the trunk, which he ties with a couple of shredded bungee chords. He shuffles back into the cab. Martha offers him a swig of her booze. He reluctantly declines and continues along the heaped and congested corridors of mass devastation.

The male bulb and the body of the corpus spongiosum are represented in the female by the bulbs of the vestibule and the commissure. So many bulbs all doing the same thing. So many wanting to be loved and nurtured watered and fed. All of them hoping to find the right gardener to tend to their specific needs and take care of them after they've bloomed.

The taxi parks beside a small, decimated church in New Orleans East. Nothing suggests there was ever a roof. Protruding from one of the crumbling walls is the remains a four-door car. A thick layer of mud and silt has dried over the vehicle. Children take pieces of the church's broken stained-glass windows and decorate the car's doors and chassis. The driver bursts into tears as both he and Martha watch them embedding the glass into the encrusted mud. Innocent laughter can be heard amongst the diligent artists as they construct a mosaic of beautiful, blooming flowers. Martha taps on the driver's shoulder and once again offers him her Southern Comfort. This time he accepts the bottle, and for the next hour, with the meter still running, they drink in silence, consumed by the children's play.

His and hers. … Mine and yours. … Both the same, and yet how easy we forget. How busy we become in our own little worlds to forget to water.

"You say something?" The driver asks as he polishes off the bottle.

"Not really," Martha replies, firing up a joint. "Turn on WWOZ. They're about to play that live broadcast from the Superdome. And when you're ready, take me over to the emergency hospital shelter."

"Which one?"

"The one down at the Convention Center … I got some work to do."

"Sure thing, boss."

"Hang on a sec."

Martha ceremonially closes her atlas and rolls down the window. She calls one of the children over to the cab and hands the shy child the heavy book. "You are the reason why I cannot leave," she whispers, watching the happy child run off to show his friends the gift. "After all, isn't the poet condemned as soon as she breathes? … How can I desert a wounded set of wings that offers me the vigor to fly above the flames of apathy?"

Several minutes later, the cab weaves along the interstate. Leaning her head out the window, Martha gulps in mouthfuls of dry, dusty air. Pursuing the cab, two policemen in a beat-up squad car are doing the same thing. Martha waves at the approaching flashing lights. Above the noise of the sirens she screams from a war-ravaged heart; "My city, my home, like Lazarus shall RISE!"

JESSE

Curfew settles over the war-torn French Quarter like a layer of sheet rock dust as Jesse "Preacher" Johnson shuffles along Chartres Street, making his way to his favorite watering hole, hoping to grab a last-minute drink. The streets are deserted except for a few army vehicles on patrol. The sound of the armored wheels as they rumble past the boarded-up shop fronts and vacant parking lots makes the streetlamps tinkle. In the fading light, he approaches Preservation Hall and notices a large, black bag slumped on the stoop. He turns to see if he is being followed, then walks up and kicks it. He looks up and down the street again and kicks the heavy black bag again. "Damn," he says to himself, "It sure don't feel like no body inside dat ting."

Half hidden in the shadows he sits and waits to see if whatever is in the bag will move. When it doesn't, he pulls it onto his lap. Another patrol car rumbles past the end of the street just as Jesse starts to wrestle with the rusting zipper. A bare bulb above the doorway of Preservation Hall flickers on, then off, then back on again. Jesse squeezes his hand inside the bag and carefully removes a wad of crumbled sheets of soggy paper. He carefully unfolds the sheets and one by one irons them out on his thighs. Later on, he would say that he wasn't no religious man, but as he deciphered what had been written, he realized that as he randomly pulled out sheets of paper, they came out in a coherent order, word for word, line by line, and page by page, so that by the time the bag was empty, he had an entire book, ready to read sitting on his lap.

The French Quarter was sinking into a well-deserved sleep, exhausted from another day of offering sanctuary to the workers and loyal residents who were trying to rebuild. The bells of St. Louis Cathedral rang midnight, and all the lights went out save for the bare bulb flickering above Jesse's head. He sat, quiet and still, hidden in the doorway, immersed in the book. Using his finger to underline each word, he read out loud what had been scratched into the flood-stained paper.

The Revelation of Jelly Roll *descended upon his humble servant as I was drowning in the quagmire of a displaced world and loosing my mind in the rented wombs of the Hurricane Hotel.*

Blessed are they that readeth *these words that appeared before me on the peeling walls and ceilings of the hotel rooms, for they that hear the divine music of this prophecy shall sleep well tonight and* *wake refreshed tomorrow. Listen then, all of y'all, for the time is at hand that these things shall surely come to pass.*

Behold, the Great Spirit of Jelly Roll cometh, *rising from the sewers and broken sidewalks of the drowned streets of New Orleans. Like a warm breeze blown in from Africa, it can be felt caressing your cheeks, flickering through the leaves of the magnolia trees and seeping up through the carved stones of raised tombs on a Super-Sunday afternoon. Feel the Spirit now as it lifts itself above the battered rooftops and splintered spires, forming a cloud hovering above the Superdome, slowly vibrating as bus loads and bus loads of displaced souls return from their long forsaken exodus.*

And the Great Spirit of Jelly Roll lifted me *up into the cloud where I looked down and saw on a U-shaped stage a lone figure standing in the shadows of the Great Spirit's wings. No microphone was to be seen as a harmonica murmured and drum begun to beat. The curtains drew back and an angel issued the words of the Great Spirit's faithful prophet, Bob Dylan.*

Listen now as he starts to sing with a voice ringing like a distant bell on an ancient sea-faring vessel ushering in a new land.

When you're sad and when you're lonely
And you haven't got a friend,
Just remember that death is not the end.

FEMA plastic tarps *stitched together, covering the Superdome's roof, gently rustle and bellow like gigantic blue sails making ready to sail. And as the air fills with the Great Spirit's music, piano keys appear shimmering as if they were stars falling from the heavens onto the stage. Hands with diamond-ringed fingers chase after the keys, rising and lowering, twisting and turning before rising some more, dancing like a feather caught in the draft of a revolving door.*

And all that you've held sacred falls down
And does not mend
Just remember that death is not the end.

***Golden trumpets** and diamond saxophones, mother-of-pearl key-boards and guitars made from the moon's shadow follow the piano keys onto the stage. Double basses and drums usher in a flock of home-less school children, shy and excited. They skip and hold each other's hands as they assemble in front of our great city's church choirs and gospel singers, who, as if sharing a forgotten secret, sway, whispering in the chorus, echoing in the anthem.*

Not the end, not the end
Just remember that death is not the end.

***The Great Spirit of Jelly Roll breathes** from the cloud, and a multitude of musicians who have been blessed by its Grace appear on the stage. Professor Longhair and Dr. John, Ernie K. Doe and Fats Domino, play alongside Henry Butler, James Booker, Theresa Anderson, Grayson Capps and Trombone Shorty. Beside them the Mardi Gras Indians, Jon Boutte and Kermit Ruffins are second lining with Coco Robicheaux, Boozoo Chavis, Rosie Ledat, and Washboard Lisa. Galactic, Mike West, John Sinclair and Myshkin join in the harmony with The Funky Meters and The Meters waving white handkerchiefs.*

When you're standing at the crossroads
That you cannot comprehend,
Just remember that death is not the end

***Three-Winged Messengers appear** in the form of Satchmo, Sydney Bechet and Cosmos Matassa. Their winged backs are cov-ered by the Rebirth and New Birth, The Olympia, The Treme and the Algiers Brass Bands, to name but a few. Countless more generations of musicians, past, present, and future now descend to the stage, filter-ing into the sound waves and morphing into space, transcending the universe before absorbing through your radios and juke boxes, your sound tracks and i-pods, your commercials and weddings, your funer-als and festivals, your dancing while doing the dishes, your humming and whistling, your merriment of sing-a-longs, your clicking fingers and toe tapping.*

When storm clouds gather round you,
And heavy rains descend,
Just remember that death is not the end...'

And the Brave Multitude of People, *who held New Orleans together, during the storm and after the flood waters receded, begin filing in through the gates of the Superdome. They hug each other in brotherly and sisterly love as they join in with the chorus. I can see them all before me now! The tall and the shorts, the narrows and the wides, the mayor and the street cleaners, the cops and the school bus drivers, the bakers and the bar owners, the students and the house maids, the firemen and the journalists, the doctors and the nurses, the wise guys and the street performers, the priests and the rabbis, the black panthers and the greens, the some bodies and the no bodies, the sinners and the saved, the waiters and the chiefs, the beer delivery truck drivers and the carnival float makers!*

And there's no one there to comfort you,
With a helpin' hand to lend,
Just remember that death is not the end.

Healing Music Resounds*, getting louder and louder, ricocheting off the Superdome walls and rising up into the Great Spirit of Jelly Roll, shaping the cloud into a winged prayer and sending it over the Mississippi River.*

Up, up and away, the winged prayer journeys into the deep, medium and higher South, passing over deltas, farmlands, streams and mountains ranges until it reaches its neighbor, the living voice of New York. The prayer kisses the Empire State Building and with gratitude the Empire's lights change to purple, green and gold. The prayer then hovers above Ground Zero and silently meditates before sprinkling rain-like-tears shaped as musical notes onto the tortured and bloody earth. Out of the ground, a majestic park appears, filled with organic apples and oranges, grapes and figs, watermelons and strawberries, a meditative sanctuary without any fences or hidden fees, without any tolls or past-dues, for every citizen of the world, for every generation to come to picnic and play in.

Oh, the tree of life is growing,
Where the spirit never dies,
And the bright light of salvation shines
In dark and empty sky

The Winged Prayer of Jelly Roll *continues its journey, sailing across the great skies before settling and praying above the corporate white houses of Washington, D.C. All the pristine buildings' occupants, from CEOs to armed officials, from judges to presidents, spill out onto their manicured lawns. They laugh and giggle, hug and kiss, wearing pantomime costumes with blinking plastic beads, manufactured in China. None are quite sure what they should do next, so they party like it's Mardi Gras in the middle of the summer. Some exchange frilly underwear that they then stash in their cabinets. Others wobble like Weebles, and write out more hot checks.*

And you search in vain to find,
Just one law abiding citizen,
Just remember that death is not the end.

Journeying On, *across the entire majestic land of America, the Great Spirit of Jelly Roll visits many grand cities and national monuments, many more coffee shops and Laundromats, spreading the Soul of New Orleans to everyone that cares to listen before making the long trip home. Back to where we all first come from.*

Not the end, not the end,
Just remember that death is not the end.

And It Came To Pass *as I opened my eyes, behold, the Superdome is once again hopping and wailing and shaking its tail feathers with handkerchiefs waving and bandanas sailing. The* Joie de Vivre *has been resurrected and healing music is rising from the stage to the rafters, filling the stitched FEMA tarps like one giant a hot-air balloon.*

And I can see with my eyes shut all the battered and undone finally making the long journey home. They are clapping and singing, dancing and jumping onto the U-shaped stage as it floats upward, leaving the ground.

I can see Martha and Ruth helping Molly give birth to a healthy strapping boy who is the spitting image of Jake. Mah brother Treme is beside them, firing up a spliff and sharing it with multitudes as Mona and Sophia slash at the ropes and let the safety harness fly. Zane is there alongside Arlen and Emma Jane, dancing with Crazy George and the ghost of Private Paterson. The Chemical Sisters debate politics with a delighted Mr. Morgan, who rescued Karma Queen and drove her safely backstage before casting off the anchor. Even grumpy old Moose made it without any ice. The two Swiss tourists finally surfaced from the swamps of the Enchanted Spanish Lake and are helping the sisters from the Audubon Natural Institute of Preservation check in their botanical equipment before climbing on board the U- shaped stage, rising like the arms of a protective mother lifting her new born into the future.

Yes, I can feel this all now, as the Great Spirit of Jelly Roll and the Heart of New Orleans soar into the sky with a primal rhythm, forged from the blood and fury, found in the infinity of every second of every day, beating across the universe, on the tips of every displaced tongue, with two thousand and five ... BIG BASS DRUMS!

ISBN 142513096-8

9 781425 130961